PRAISE FOR CHRISTOPHER LENTZ

"AN ENTERTAINING FANTASY.
Lentz offers a well-judged blend of romance, wish
fulfillment, glamor, suspense, and the paranormal. It's fun…"
—*Kirkus Reviews*

"AN INCREDIBLE STORY AND A BRILLIANT PLOT.
His ability to paint scenes and events with words made me
feel like I was watching a movie. It deserves a perfect score."
—*OnlineBookClub*

"GO ON WITH BLOSSOM BOOKS!"
—Debbie Macomber,
#1 *New York Times* and *USA Today* bestselling author

"FAST-PACED, PACKED WITH EMOTIONS…
Blossom on the Road of Dreams will grip you from the start and
keep you enthralled throughout. Talented author Christopher
Lentz takes readers on an unforgettable journey featuring
layered, multicultural characters, well-drawn authentic settings,
and a powerful, extraordinary romance worth savoring.
AN ELECTRIFYING READ."
—*NY Literary Magazine*

"Lentz describes the novel as '*Titanic* on land.' It, too, features
STAR-CROSSED LOVERS FROM DIFFERENT SOCIAL
CLASSES, as a humble fortune-cookie maker meets the heir to a
silver fortune. And it also builds suspense by letting readers
know of an impending disaster the characters don't expect."
—*The Orange County Register*

"BETWEEN ROMANTIC TENSION AND HISTORICAL
EVENTS, it's impossible to not be immersed in this story of
passion and tragedy!"
—Midwest Book Review

D1607667

ALSO BY CHRISTOPHER LENTZ

THE BLOSSOM TRILOGY

The Blossom Trilogy has everything: the juxtaposition of rich and poor; the constraints and rules of a bygone era; the timeless clash of generations and traditions; the arrogance of man and the wrath of Mother Nature.

The lessons to be learned are clear. Life is uncertain. Love can be unshakable. The future is unknowable. The unthinkable is always possible.

The Blossom Trilogy brings together a variety of people who call California home. From the gold fields of Northern California to the whorehouses of San Francisco, and from the mansions of Pasadena to the new-born movie studios of Hollywood, the series embraces three vibrant generations of Americans.

BLOSSOM
Book 1 of The Blossom Trilogy

BLOSSOM ON THE ROAD OF DREAMS
A Blossom Trilogy Novella

ABOUT THE
GREAT AMERICAN DESTINATION
SERIES

The Great American Destination Series offers stories of hope, history, romance and self-discovery set at locations you can visit.

At the center of these books, you'll find grand hotels, impressive mansions and inspiring one-of-a-kind sites that have as much warmth and life as each story's characters. In fact, the locations play pivotal roles.

And when the time is right, you can walk in the fictional characters' footsteps and create memories of your own.

My Friend Marilyn takes place near San Diego at the famed Hotel del Coronado.

Permission has been secured from the owners and operators of the following locations for upcoming books in this series:

- Grand Hotel, Mackinac Island, Michigan, www.grandhotel.com
- Glensheen Mansion, Duluth, Minnesota, www.glensheen.org
- Fairlawn Mansion, Superior, Wisconsin, www.superiorpublicmuseums.org

ABOUT HOTEL DEL CORONADO

Hotel del Coronado is an iconic destination at the Pacific's edge just minutes from downtown San Diego.

Opened in 1888, "The Del" debuted as an architectural masterpiece, acclaimed for its seaside setting and its world-famous weather. Outfitted with electricity and every modern amenity, The Del was a destination resort before the term existed, attracting a wealthy clientele from the Midwest, East Coast and Europe. These guests—who arrived with their own servants in tow—generally stayed for months at a time.

Although seaside resorts were commonplace along both American coasts during the late 19th century, few were as large as The Del or as distinctive. With its one-of-a-kind sweeping silhouette—once likened to a cross between an ornate wedding cake and well-trimmed ship—the resort was recognizable throughout the country and around the world.

Coronado's island-like allure and year-round sunshine further ensured The Del's reputation as a standout resort, described as the unrivaled queen of seaside resorts. And where else can you frolic on the same beach as Marilyn Monroe in the acclaimed 1950s romantic comedy, *Some Like It Hot*?

To learn more, visit www.hoteldel.com.

Hotel del Coronado®

MY FRIEND
Marilyn

THE GREAT AMERICAN
DESTINATION SERIES

Hotel del Coronado

CHRISTOPHER LENTZ

DEDICATION

I dedicate this book to my mother, Betty Jane Kollmorgen Lentz, for taking me to dime stores in the suburbs of Detroit as a kid. I'm the youngest of four children, so our time together at Woolworth's, Kresge's and Grant's was one-on-one time. Cherished one-on-one time. Except for when I wandered off. Yes, I was *that* kid.

Thanks, Mom. I hope you're still experiencing the satisfaction of acquiring "things," along with your sister, Eileen. You knew what it was like to "go without" during the Great Depression on a self-sustaining farm on 15 Mile Road. Now you two get to shop in heaven. I hope you've traded up to Hudson's and Crowley's department stores. The next time we meet will be forever.

I also dedicate this book to the incomparable Melissa McCarthy. Her performances inspired this story's heroine, Penny Parker. In fact, I had a photo of her in the corner of my laptop screen as I developed Penny's tale.

And lastly, I dedicate this book to people of all shapes and sizes, but especially women. The added pressure women often put on themselves—and that society, Hollywood and the media heap on—is unfair and unhealthy. Fat shaming or skinny shaming are simply shameful.

Happiness is what life's all about. And acceptance. And friendship. And most of all, love. Because, as you'll find in all my books, love changes *everything*.

TRAVEL BACK TO 1958

Dear Friends:

As you settle in to spend some time with *My Friend Marilyn,* allow me to set the stage. Dwight D. Eisenhower is President of the United States. A gallon of gas costs 25 cents. Postage stamps are four cents each. The average annual salary is $5,500. The Hula Hoop is the must-have toy. Elvis Presley, Ricky Nelson and Chuck Berry are burning up the charts.

At the movies, *The Bridge on the River Kwai, South Pacific* and *Gigi* are entertaining the masses in the magical darkness of cinemas. And Marilyn Monroe, Tony Curtis and Jack Lemmon are filming a nostalgic, 1920s comedy confection called *Some Like It Hot* near Los Angeles. On September 8, eight days of on-location shooting is expected to begin at the Hotel del Coronado across the bay from San Diego.

And a plus-size, wise-cracking dime-store cashier's life is about to be turned upside down.

Welcome to Penny Parker's world!

Chris

Christopher Lentz

PS: If you want help visualizing the setting and characters, visit my Pinterest boards. They're packed with images I used as inspiration as I wrote this fictional story.

MY FRIEND
Marilyn

Julie—

Always make
new friends!!!

Chris 2024

CHAPTER 1

As unlikely and unbelievable as it may sound, Marilyn Monroe invited me into her bedroom.

Few people can say that.

But I can.

In an instant, the script of my life went into "rewrites." My black-and-white world turned Technicolor with a dizzying sequence of fade ins and fade outs.

And it went something like this.

FADE IN:

- SEPTEMBER 8, 1958
- FIRST DAY OF ON-LOCATION SHOOTING IN CORONADO, CALIFORNIA
- INTERIOR, MARILYN MONROE'S COTTAGE (DAYTIME)

I was guided into the star's room.

I saw nothing but Marilyn Monroe's face.

Everything else faded away.

"I'd like to introduce Miss Penny Parker." My escort backed away, leaving me front and center. "She's going to be with us during our time here at The Del."

"You're the contest gal...the *winner*." Marilyn blinked in slow motion, just like in her movies.

"Yes. Yes, I am. But I've never thought of myself as much of a win—" I stopped speaking and wished I could eat those last words.

Marilyn hummed as her eyes took a walk all over me. "They told me I'd have an extra pair of hands during this shoot. How lovely."

I glanced down at my hands.

"Not your hands, honey. I meant how lovely to have *you* with us." Marilyn scooped some of her platinum bangs to the side and took a step forward.

I repeated the same words in my head. *Don't blow it. Don't jinx it. Don't blow it. Don't jinx it—*

"The pleasure's all mine, Miss Monroe. Truly."

I was so determined to not come across as some silly star-struck spectator and I was successful for all of about ten seconds.

My eyes stretched wide open to the size of hub caps as I added, "God Almighty. You're so much more beautiful than your photographs and movies." My words exploded like popcorn tap dancing in hot oil. Her stunning beauty, however, made me instantly feel the opposite of beautiful. "Did that just come out of my mouth? I'm so sorry. I think and speak at the same time…and usually I speak more than I think."

I'd blown it.

I'd jinxed it.

After a few awkward moments of silence while my heart rat-a-tat-tatted in my eardrums, Marilyn flashed a wedding-dress white grin. "I can see we don't need to coax you out of your shell." She added, "We're going to get along famously. I'm certain of it."

Marilyn turned on the ball of her bare foot. The glamourous, camera-ready waves of her hair followed her with a momentary delay and a slight ricochet effect. Marilyn studied her reflection in the sliding-glass door and then in a floor-length mirror. She peeled open her white terry-cloth beach wrap and dropped it to the ground.

"Penny, give me your first impression. What do you think of this swimming suit?"

A not-so-subtle wave of Chanel No. 5 passed over me, along with an undercurrent of sweet vanilla.

I took a few steps forward and my right foot collided with a coffee table leg that I didn't see because I couldn't stop looking at her. When I did gaze down to see what caused the clinking sound, I spotted three nearly empty white-ceramic custard cups settling back into their places. Oddly, there were no spoons.

"I'm such a klutz. And that just scared the bejeezus out of me." I put some fingers over my lips. "I sure hope The Del doesn't have a you-break-it-you-bought-it policy or I'll be broke before I leave this room!"

I shrugged and squinted like a child who just spilled a glass of milk.

Marilyn licked the spoon in her hand—which I hadn't noticed until that moment—and winked at me. We exchanged a knowing-sort-of look. It was clear who'd emptied those custard cups.

"You'll have to excuse my lack of manners today." Marilyn shifted the spoon to her left hand and reached out her right one. "It's a pleasure to meet you, Penny." Her skin was as soft as a grandmother's kiss.

"Well, what do you think…about this getup?"

I inspected Marilyn's front side, then glanced at her backside. Was she expecting me to say *va-va-voom* or something like that? I just couldn't. "It's just awful. Doesn't do a thing for you." I shook my head.

"I agree, but I'm going to do my best to sell it out on the beach…and for the cameras. Even for me, though, it's going to be a tough sell." She giggled a bit. "At least I'll look better in it than Jack. He's wearing the same one, with a wig and ghastly makeup." She leaned over and set the spoon down on the coffee table, next to the three custard cups.

A recent newspaper headline flashed in my mind: Blonde Bombshell: Part Little Bo Peep, Part Mae West. Without editing in my head, I said, "More Peep than West, except that arm hole. That's *all* Mae West."

Marilyn was either confused or had smelled something bad. She must not have followed the Peep/West comment.

"Sorry. Just me speaking and thinking out of order again. I was remembering a headline that described you as part Little Bo Peep and part Mae West."

"I kinda like that." She rested her open palm over her heart. The tips of her elegantly extended fingers touched her chest one at a time. She worked her eyelids like a skilled geisha with two painted-paper fans.

The dark navy-blue wool swimming outfit did showcase Marilyn's legs. As for the middle of her, the swimsuit was a barrier to her beauty and her curves, except for the arm holes which were loose enough to show some breast if she turned just right.

"I've always admired Mae West." While gazing at herself in the mirror, she scrunched her nose, making it clear she didn't admire what she was wearing. "Beats being called 'the tart with a heart,' I guess. Hmmmm, girls back in the '20s didn't have it easy." Marilyn pulled at the top's white band of piping. "I don't even want to know what this thing smells like—or looks like—wet."

"You will. We *all* will." I couldn't believe I'd just said that.

"I know, I know. The script calls for me and the orchestra girls to be in the surf this afternoon. Splashing and playing around. Jack too."

A stout woman in a simple black dress came through the doorway. "This is true. You will be in the water. And the wool *will not* smell of violets and roses. But you *will* give Mr. Wilder a performance that will awe him."

"This is Paula Strasberg, my acting coach. Without her, I'd struggle even more than I do. She brings out my best. Don't you, Paula?"

"The talent is all yours...a true gift. I am delighted I can assist you in honing your craft." She turned to face me. We shook hands. It was a limp one. "You work in a dime store. Is that correct?"

"Yes ma'am. I do. But I believe I've been lingering around there far too long. Treading water, you might say. And you know what happens to someone who treads water too long, don't you?"

"No. Tell me, please." Annoyance dripped from her words. I must've been talking too much, at least in her opinion.

"You drown, that's what. Working with you fine folks is just the lifeline I didn't know I was looking for!"

I caught Marilyn as she shrugged and smirked.

Paula continued, "I assume you have been briefed on your role and, more importantly, what your role is *not*." This time she pounded her words like a secretary on a typewriter. Precise. Paced. Punctuated.

"Yes, ma'am. I've been briefed. And I'm a quick study. I promise, you've only seen the tip of this iceberg."

"Iceberg or not," Paula said, "you'll do as you're told."

"I'll do whatever I can to be an asset—and not an ass."

Marilyn giggled. "Now that's refreshing. You keep that up. I need more straight-talking people in my life."

I looked at the floor while my cheeks flamed. I rarely blushed.

"People are much too controlled around me. It's not like I'm in control of myself...or much of anything! Besides, I've been getting more selective lately about who I spend time with. You know, I can only give so much of myself. Honestly, I try to give to everyone, but I only have so much affection. I'm not going to waste mine on anyone who's against me."

She blinked in slow motion again, which drew me in more. I couldn't stop staring at her. She was impossibly beautiful, even in that horrible wool swimming suit.

"From now on," Marilyn confided in a girlish whisper with words spoken as if they were floating on pillows, "I'm saving my friendship for people who matter most."

That's what meeting Marilyn Monroe was like for me.

How destiny brought us together—well, that happened a week earlier while I was working at the Cornet Five & Dime. And it was just as unlikely and unbelievable as Marilyn Monroe inviting me into her bedroom.

FADE OUT

CHAPTER 2

FADE IN:
- FIVE DAYS EARLIER
- SEPTEMBER 3, 1958, FIVE DAYS UNTIL ON-LOCATION SHOOTING BEGINS
- INTERIOR, CORNET FIVE & DIME STORE (DAYTIME)

"You're a winner!" His words hit like a Frisbee to the forehead. Girls like me didn't hear the word *winner* often. "Out of all the gals in town, you've been randomly selected to be Marilyn Monroe's go-to girl." The man's words stirred up a swarm of pointy-nosed hummingbirds in my belly. If my life had a soundtrack, I would've been bouncing around to *The Bunny Hop*.

Me and Marilyn Monroe.

Me, Penny Parker.

My fingertips slid down the cash register's chunky keys. My eyelids and eyebrows rose like runaway elevators. I shot back, "This girl—from the Cornet Five & Dime—and Marilyn. HOE-LEE-SHIT!"

"Yes. Well, that's one way of putting it." He cleared his throat, and gave me a sideways second take. Perhaps I shouldn't have been quite so enthusiastic and used the word *shit*. Much less *holy shit*. In a public place. In my workplace.

He continued, "On behalf of the *Coronado Eagle & Journal*, I'm here to let you know you've won. And to hand you this packet." He jabbed me with the corner of a manila envelope, and held it up for all to see. His not-so-intoxicating scent of Old Spice and onions slithered around me.

"By the way, I'm Stan Drake, the paper's newest reporter."

I closed my eyes and shook my head. When I stopped moving it, my eyes popped open. My pupils must have looked like the spinning numbers in a Las Vegas slot machine. And I'd just hit the jackpot. The jingle-jangle of my swaying mismatched earrings—a dangly pink flamingo on the left ear and a canary-yellow pineapple on the right—distracted me as they stayed in motion. I blinked a couple of times to be certain it wasn't one of my daydreams.

"Wait a minute." His words were sinking in, but not making sense. "Must've been more than a random process. My name couldn't have even been in the barrel...or drum...or hat...or whatever you used."

"Are you saying you didn't enter?" Stan whipped out his pocket-sized notepad and reached for the pencil tucked behind his ear to take notes. An ear that was so hairy it could've been mistaken for an arm pit on the side of his head. He must have sensed a breaking news story unfolding right there in the dime store.

"I have to admit I *thought* of entering. I thought about it a lot. And I almost did. But I didn't." That's because I was leery about being part of Hollywood's magic instead of just witnessing it safely in my favorite seat at my favorite theater. I was even more leery about discovering there may not be any magic at all.

And then there was me. Not even in my most fantastic daydreams did I think I'd have anything in common with her.

I spoke directly to Stan. "Just think about it: the most beautiful woman in the universe is coming to town—that would be THE most beautiful woman in the universe. Now look at me. What would you expect us to talk about?"

"I believe she'll be talking *at* you, not *with* you. You aren't going to be there to become her bosom-buddy friend." Stan made a tongue-sucking sound, perhaps to dislodge some of that stinky chopped onion from his teeth.

Our conversation screeched to a halt when we heard, "Did someone say Marilyn Monroe?" Nearby, a woman's deep voice released a mocking-manly *hey-hey-hey* laugh. "Most women have sex. She *is* sex!"

"Ohhhhh geeeeez, Madge! Just because you used work here, you don't have permission to be so loose-lipped. Store's open and shoppers are around." Trudy, the uniformed woman under the nearby Luncheonette sign, scolded Madge with a buttermilk-thick Mid-Western accent, filled with never-ending vowels. "Do I need to skedaddle over there, take you by the shoulders and shake you like an Etch A Sketch? Like I used to? Because I will." Trudy raised her index finger to her shushing lips, then swiped her hand across them as if she was pulling a zipper. She turned an imaginary key and threw it over her shoulder.

Madge raised a magazine from the store's newsstand that had Marilyn Monroe on the cover. "It's not *me*. That's what it says, right here."

"I see. Just the same, get back to your shopping, Madge."

I scanned the store. Stan was swaying like he was on a boat deck. Impatient with me. That was certain. The Teddy Bears were singing *To Know Him Is To Love Him* over the public address system. They'd joined the chorus of the store's squeaky, in-need-of-an-oil-can shopping carts.

"Alright, what's going on? It's not April Fool's Day." I yelled, my words sounding like a mother calling in kids for dinner from the front porch. The flock of buzzing pointy-beaked hummingbirds in my stomach was heading up my throat. I swallowed hard to keep them down.

Frankie strolled by with a dolly of boxes led by one hand and a pricing stamper in the other. He shrugged, but didn't stop to comment. The smirk on his face was one I recognized since we were kids. For the life of me, I couldn't understand why some cute little thing hadn't scooped up Frankie and married him.

"Franklin Holland. Do you know something I don't? Cough it up."

"I got nothing." His smirk had turned to a grin and glided out of sight.

"Miss Parker, I assure you, this is legitimate." Stan's left brow and eye scrunched up. He jingled some coins in his pocket to send a not-so-subtle message about his annoyance.

I ignored how my lower back ached. I ignored how tight my shoes were. And when Madge rolled up to my station with her cart, I ignored her too. For a long moment, anyway.

"So what can I ring up for you?" I snapped my chewing gum as I positioned my right hand to battle the register's obstinate keys. "Someday, cash registers aren't going to have keys. There'll be a wand or some other magic tool that reads the prices. Mark my words—"

"Yeah, then you won't have a job."

"Don't worry about me. I'll find another one. Besides, didn't you hear? I just got a new job. Stan the Man here told me I won a contest to be Marilyn Monroe's assistant. And some mystery person entered me."

"You don't say." Madge had that all-agog look on her face.

"I did it. I did it *for* you."

My eyes followed Trudy's voice. She was still just an aisle away behind the lunch counter, flipping a grilled-cheese sandwich onto a teal-toned Melamine plate. "What's the matter with you? Have you lost your mind?"

"That's entirely possible, but I'll discuss that with you later. Now listen to this gentleman. You're perfect to be Miss Monroe's Girl Friday. For so many reasons."

"Trudy Vanderhooven, I'll—"

The sound of merchandise being placed on my counter forced me to focus back on Madge. "This city's swarmed with sailors and the one and only Marilyn Monroe is going to put all us ladies to shame." Madge and I nodded in agreement. "Her hourglass figure will make mine look as shapely as…this can of baked beans." It was true. I was shaped like a can. Always had been. Making fun of it made it easier for everyone—including me—or so I thought. I should've been kinder to myself.

"Miss Parker, may I continue?" Stan's impatience was on full display. The coins jingling in his pocket were getting on my nerves. "As Miss Monroe's go-to girl, you'll be her personal assistant during her time at our very own, world-famous Hotel del Coronado. As you may already know from reading my newspaper—which I'm certain you do—she's starring in a Hollywood blockbuster. Or so Hollywood hopes. You'll be staying at the hotel so you're available when she needs a towel, a glass of lemonade…*whatever* she needs."

"Sounds swell. Just swell." Thankfully, Madge and her merchandise selections were time-consuming distractions that allowed me to process everything Stan said to me.

I took a deep, long, slow breath, adjusted my pink smock and continued ringing up Madge's order. A cellophane-wrapped package of prickly bottle-brush hair curlers. Twenty-nine cents.

An oblong box containing a blonde ponytailed Barbie doll. "These things will never catch on. There isn't a woman on the planet shaped like this. And three dollars. Sheesh!" I punched the keys on the register.

"I *completely* know what you mean. Girls should only want to play with baby dolls. Not dress-shop mannequins. But there's lots of talk about this Barbie girl. She'll make a nice little gift—more like a bribe—for my daughter out in the car. She's watching the baby." Madge fluffed her hair in the back and shifted her weight to one hip.

"How old's your daughter now?"

"Her birthday's coming next Tuesday. She's going to be six."

"What a great little helper you have. Babysitting in a hot car, in a parking lot out back. At just five years old. Gosh. She's a *real* keeper."

I let my words hang, hoping Madge might realize the absurdity of what she had going on in her car. No such luck.

"Miss Parker," Stan interrupted, "would you kindly pay attention to me?"

"Yes, sir. I'm listening. I'm capable of doing two things at once, which might come in handy for a go-to girl. I'm not saying I'll do it. But I am saying it would come in handy. Besides, I'm on the company clock right now. Ringing and bagging is what old man Hamilton pays me for, not talking to people who aren't shopping."

"Penny, your mother raised you with better manners. Lord knows your father did." Trudy made a tsk-tsk sound. "You hush up right this instant and listen to the man."

Not waiting for an invitation to begin again, Stan went on. "This is quite an honor. You're going to be the next *big* thing around here."

"I beg your pardon." I put my fists on my hips.

"For goodness sake, I didn't mean *big* in that sense. I meant big in a wow-she's-a-new-sensation way. Besides, how many girls wouldn't beg for this chance?"

"I'm sure plenty would," I replied. "So why didn't someone just ask that new Miss Coronado beauty queen to do the job. She shops here and she'd be perfect. So pretty and perky."

"You go to the movies more than anyone in Coronado. More than anyone I've ever known," Trudy said. "Who could be a better choice than you for this job? You practically pay the stars' salaries with all the tickets you buy."

"I do go to the movies a lot. There's no denying that." I turned my head a bit and squinted. I wondered if they thought I was running away from something or hiding there. For me, it had always been more like running *to* something. Something more adventurous. More colorful. More glamourous. More exciting.

I hit the cash register's total bar. The numbers in the window at the top of the machine prompted me to say, "That'll be eight dollars and forty-seven cents, please. By the way, we're running a special on ice-cream sandwiches today. Got a hankering for one? Only eight cents each. Do you think your daughter would like one?"

"No, but thank you."

Madge handed me eight paper bills and some coins.

"Thanks. Come again."

She didn't leave with her package. Madge stood there. She didn't budge. "Did you need something else? I know our selection is limited. You'll have to take the ferry to Woolworth's or Newberry's in San Diego if you didn't get something." Madge didn't respond.

I stared at her until I realized I'd forgotten something. "I am so, so very sorry." I opened a drawer below the cash register and foraged around in it. I handed Madge an assortment of S&H Green Stamps. "Did you need a new Saver Book to put these in?"

"No, I just started a new one. I redeemed the last one for the cutest ceramic three-tier tidbit tray. Mother of pearl finish, no less. Perfect for serving the card-club gals. Got my eye on a hi-ball caddy set with the next book. Eight glasses and a brass serving rack. Gotta love these Green Stamps."

"I *know*. Buh-bye for now."

Madge clicked the latch on her purse and reached out for me. Before I knew it, she held my left wrist with both hands.

"There are times in life to say *no*. This is not one of them. My dear Penny, stop watching people pretending to live their lives on the screen and live your own—right here in the *real* world."

Madge released my wrist. I watched her back as she walked away.

The absence of customers in line allowed Stan to have my full attention. "So, are you in or are you out?"

"You betcha she's in. She'll be there. I'll see to it. Dern tootin' she'll be there," Trudy said with a lingering Minnesotan accent that held onto her o's, as in *a rootin'-tootin' good time.*

Stan pointed to the envelope he was in the process of handing to me. The word "WINNER" was handwritten on it. Trudy wiped her hands on the white apron that shielded her stiff pink uniform and took it. "I suppose that makes me a winner, too."

He didn't acknowledge her last remark as he began to walk away. "Just see that she reads through what's inside. And that she shows up."

"I haven't left the building. I'm still part of this conversation, right?" I wildly waved my hands in the air.

"Good day to you then. Congratulations." Stan left the store's front door out to Orange Avenue.

I stood there, silent as a tombstone. However, my thoughts were anything but silent. They tumbled around like alphabet-shaped noodles in a boiling pot of soup. Nothing made sense and yet there were so many possibilities in the mix. *Everything* seemed possible.

"Sweetie, can I get you anything?" Trudy was always looking after me. She smoothed her hair-netted hairdo. "A cup of water?"

"How about a husband, a home and a family of my own making? In that order, if possible." As much as I not-so-secretly wanted to escape the cash register, I'd been coming to realize that what I truly wanted was a normal life. Or something closer to *normal* than what I had.

"Sorry," Trudy chirped. "That's not on the Luncheonette's menu today."

"I'd settle for a best, best, best girlfriend."

"Penny, how about that cup of water?"

"Sure thing. That's just what I need, something to wet my whistle."

"How about a slice of Princess or Pioneer Toast to go with it? Won't take but a second."

"No, thank you." Trudy came up with the idea of those snacks for unruly kids while they were acting up in the store. Princess Toast had bubble-gum pink frosting and a red jelly bean. Pioneer Toast had melted butter, cinnamon and sugar, plus a root-beer barrel. Trudy always had good ideas, though I still wasn't convinced about the goodness of her idea to sign me up for the job with Marilyn.

Frankie came around the corner of the aisle pushing an empty dolly.

"Don't that beat all?" Trudy raised a hand to make sure her white cloth tiara was still secure.

"What's that?" Frankie stopped.

"After all those movies she's watched, our lucky Penny is going to be part of making one." Trudy turned and gave me a breath-stealing hug.

"Hip-hip-hoorah!" I had to squeeze and wheeze my words out.

"You're going to be in Miss Marilyn Monroe's presence." Trudy released her grip. "No, in her *inner* circle. Do you think she's anything like they say she is in the magazines? I wonder what she looks like when she rolls out of the sack in the morning." Trudy put her hands together in a frozen-in-time applause position. "My sister, Judy, will toss her tapioca when I write to her about this."

"You. And Marilyn Monroe?" Frankie wiped his forehead with a handkerchief from his back pocket. "That I gotta see."

"She won a contest to be her Girl Friday while they film a movie at the hotel." Trudy's face glowed.

Frankie leaned on the edge of a shelf. "Sounds like it's right up your alley. And if I know you, you won't miss out."

I gave him a sideways glance and bat my eyelids. "You know me better than most, Mr. Goody-Two-Shoes Eagle Scout. Seen me at my worst and seen me—"

Trudy pointed her index finger in my direction and waved it. "One thing that must change is you watching your mouth, little missy. None of your smart-alecky remarks of yours will do. And you mustn't take *that* tone of voice to The Del." Her warning sounded heartfelt. "You've just *got* to do this. I've watched my ships come and go in life. This is one you can't let pass you by, Penny. You just can't."

"Fine, fine, fine. Deal me in. I'll do it, but only if old-man Hamilton gives me the time off. He'll have to unlock my handcuff to this register."

"Wait until everyone hears the news. You're going to be every high-school boy's best friend," Frankie said.

"And every sailor's *new* best friend," Trudy added.

"This is sounding better all the time." I didn't want to show it, but my head was spinning like a 45 on a jukebox turntable.

"But what about The Commander?" Trudy went on, "What's he going to think?"

I narrowed my eyes and gazed at the ceiling. "Daddy will hate it. He'll be furious. Like I said, this is sounding better all the time!"

FADE OUT

CHAPTER 3

FADE IN:
- SEPTEMBER 3, 1958, FIVE DAYS UNTIL ON-LOCATION SHOOTING BEGINS
- EXTERIOR, THE VILLAGE THEATRE (NIGHTTIME)

The pink and turquoise neon marquee of The Village Theatre drew me in like a moth. There was something reassuring about witnessing people beating the odds in ninety minutes or less.

It was Wednesday night, the best night of the week. That's when new movies were first shown. I walked up to the glass case that displayed promotional lobby cards and instantly grinned.

Cat on a Hot Tin Roof. Paul Newman and Liz Taylor. This is going to be a good night. The thoughts waltzed in my head.

"One, please." I put two quarters, a dime and a nickel on the silvery counter and slid it through the hole in the window. "Hey Tilly, that Tennessee Williams can sure tell a tale about screwed-up families. The words he chooses, well, they're pure magic."

"Penny, when I was on the silver screen, we didn't need words. Our eyes and our hands told fantastic stories." She raised her spotted, knobby hands to each side of her face and wiggled her beautifully manicured, hell-fire red fingernails. "When *Sunset Boulevard* comes back to my screen, we'll watch it together. You'll learn about faces and eyes and hands. There's still a little grace and beauty left in this old gal."

"I'd love that. You know you've always been my Hollywood connection. But that's going to change, though."

"Yes, I heard. You and Marilyn Monroe. That should be

something…precious." Tilly added a flourish to the word *precious*.

"You should come down to the beach one afternoon, to give her some pointers."

Tilly nodded and then rotated her head side to side. Her lipstick-heavy lips tightened to the tiniest of grins. "Perhaps, but probably not."

I turned to see if a line had formed behind me. "Since no one's here, I have a question for you. Did you know that the title is about Liz Taylor's character?"

Not waiting for a response, I leaned in as if I was sharing a secret and whispered, "Liz is a frustrated wife, which is probably not too hard a part for her to play. Anyway, Maggie's her name, and she's called 'Maggie the Cat.' I read it in a magazine. Truth be told, I have the play's script too. She's not sure how long she can hang on to her messed up life, like a cat trying to stay up on a hot tin roof, afraid to jump because she's not sure where she's going to land."

I winked at Tilly, who gave an agreeing nod. "Now *that's* something I can relate to." I pulled away, moving toward the ticket taker's doorway. The routine was about to be set in motion.

Popcorn, buttered and salted. Check.

Coca-Cola poured over a cup full of ice cubes. Check.

Enough ice cubes to chew on after the popcorn and Coca-Cola were gone. Check.

I headed into the theater and took my seat. It was always the same seat. *My seat.* I glanced over at the empty seat to my left and released the air from my lungs.

The lights dimmed, allowing the darkness to swallow the light. The screen came to life. My escape began.

Later, when the theater's lights got their turn to devour the darkness, the real world returned, like dusk to dawn.

I sighed, more heavily this time. A woman sitting alone down the row commented, "I just love the movies, don't you?"

"It's kind of an addiction, I guess."

"I know what you mean. It's a cheap ticket to freedom."

"Don't think I've seen you here before?" I brushed off a few stubborn popcorn husks that were clinging to my sweater.

"Just visiting my sister. I'm Doris. From Garden Grove, up near Anaheim."

I looked at the screen and turned back to the woman. "I'm Penny. When I was growing up, I *ate* movies. Simply devoured them."

She looked stunned. Maybe *ate* wasn't the best word choice.

I went on, "It seemed like anything was possible in the movies for my Grandma Jenny and me here in the dark." I looked over at the empty seat next to me.

"That was her seat. She brought me here to get away from my brothers. And she came here right after she married my grandfather and he shipped out with the Navy. It's like she's here—right here—with me sometimes." Like all the other wartime brides, she wanted to see herself reflected back from the silver screen in a happily ever after story.

"That's sweet," Doris said.

"You know, when I was here as a kid I could be whatever I wanted to be…a princess, a ballerina, a mermaid. All from this chair. Right here. The good guys won. The bad guys didn't."

Before Doris could respond, I added, "I even played movie star in the backyard and out on the beach. You could say I had— have—a rich fantasy life."

"I did the same thing. I suppose lots of little girls did…and do."

"Except when those girls grew up to learn French or Latin, I became fluent in film!"

She gazed at me in a knowing way.

"It's always beautiful. Isn't it, Doris? It's always paradise at the movies. Listen to me. Going on and on."

"I am. But you're saying things that I *completely* understand."

"Doris, you know, the lady selling the tickets out there, her name's Tilly. She was a real dish in her day. In Hollywood. In the movies. Her given name is Tallulah Carlisle. As they say, she chewed up the scenery. But it all ended, sort of. She stayed in the business, but off the screen. She owns this theater." I lowered my voice. "She sells the tickets, decked out like a Christmas tree with all of her costume jewelry on. And always a turban that's so tight it pulls her face back and up. We've been friends, well, forever."

"You're lucky to have a friend like her." Doris stood up and side-stepped to the aisle. "Penny, it was nice to meet you."

I stayed seated.

I wasn't ready to rejoin the outside world.

Not just yet.

FADE OUT

CHAPTER 4

FADE IN:

- SEPTEMBER 4, 1958, FOUR DAYS UNTIL ON-LOCATION SHOOTING BEGINS
- INTERIOR, CORNET FIVE & DIME STORE (DAYTIME)

"Liz Taylor, she's one hell of an actress." I couldn't tell if Trudy heard me. She was getting the lunch counter ready for the new day's ebb and flow of diners. Her hand and a wet bleached-white cloth moved in circles from one teal Naugahyde-covered stool to the next. I spoke up this time. "She delivered her lines with a Southern accent. She shimmied and sashayed around Paul Newman—who would have nothing to do with her. He was gorgeous. His blue eyes were gorgeous. She was gorgeous too."

I put my right palm on my hip and the left one behind my head. I shifted my weight back and forth as I strolled. "Sugar child. I look just like her, don't I? Like Maggie the Cat?"

Trudy waved her towel at me. "What the heck! You stop going on about Elizabeth Taylor and focus yourself on Marilyn Monroe." She paused. "I can't believe I just said that. You're going to be focusing on Marilyn Monroe, right here in town. Just down the street. You!"

"I know, I know. It's every girl's dream. It's like a Hollywood fantasy. I can see the headline: FAT GIRL CHOSEN TO PICK UP AFTER BLONDE BOMBSHELL." I tugged at my blouse's bottom hem. In my head, I asked myself why I always said I was fat? I knew thin people were insecure too. I made a mental note to myself: try to stop beating myself up, or at least not beating myself up out loud.

I pulled a small blue paperback book from my purse. I flipped through it and stopped abruptly, opening the pages widely.

"See, here's the script. I read it last night after I got home."

"By the way, what time did you get home? I waited up as long as I could. But I was bushed and had to go to bed," Trudy said.

"You're my landlady, not my mother. But I *love* that you care about me."

I cleared my throat. "I was doing some thinking and walking along the beach if you have to know. Yes. In the dark. Alone. And I was just fine." I waved my hand dismissively.

"Just listen to this. These words *spoke* to me. You know how I don't tolerate the shenanigans of brats, especially at the store. Sticky fingers. Touching things. Getting lost. Anyway, here's what Mr. Williams has Maggie say about her horrible nieces and nephews. I'll read it with my best Southern accent. Which isn't *the* best."

I sucked in an enormous breath and started.

"One of th' no-neck monsters messed up my lovely lace dress so I got to cha-a-ange! I swear they've got no necks. None visible. Their fat little heads are stuck on their fat little bodies without a bit of connection. An' it's too bad, 'cause you can't wring their necks if they've got no necks to wring! Yep, they're monsters, all right. All no-neck people are monsters. Hear them? Hear them screaming? I don't know where their voice boxes are located since they don't have necks. I tell you I got so nervous at that table tonight I thought I would throw back my head and utter a scream you could hear clear across the Arkansas border and parts of Louisiana and Tennessee."

I lowered the book and I replenished my lungs. "Now don't get me wrong. I don't hate kids. Hate's an awfully strong word. Dislike might be a better one."

Trudy straightened the napkin dispenser and salt and pepper shakers in front of her with one hand, and wiped the counter with the other. "I agree with you."

"The whole time I was watching that movie, I couldn't stop thinking about what I read during my break the other day. Did you know Liz was still in shock during the filming? Mourning Mike Todd—her *third* husband—after his plane crashed. She'd burst into tears on the set. There were rumors she almost committed suicide."

"Now how in heaven above is a woman to *almost* commit suicide. Geez. Either you do or you do not." Trudy's shoulders raised in unison.

"On top of all that, she had an affair with Eddie Fisher. Mike Todd's best friend. And he was still married to Debbie Reynolds. Can you believe that?"

"Dern tootin' I can. It's Hollywood." Trudy kept wiping the counter. "Anything else you need to share with me at this very moment?"

"Oh, and when she shrilled 'Maggie the Cat is ALIVE,' it was like a wrecking ball bashing into my brain. I'm alive too. And I'm going to figure out how to start living again and not just existing. Best of all, Marilyn Monroe's going to help me."

I glanced down and fiddled with the sterling-silver French poodle dangling from my charm bracelet.

"She just doesn't know it yet."

FADE OUT

CHAPTER 5

FADE IN:
- SEPTEMBER 4, 1958, FOUR DAYS UNTIL SHOOTING BEGINS
- INTERIOR, TRUDY VANDERHOOVEN'S BOARDING HOUSE (NIGHTTIME)

"So what do you gals think?" I closed Trudy's front door behind me. "I paid a call on the Emerald City girls from the Wash & Brush Up Company for a clip-clip here and a clip-clip there. I fought the urge to sing *The Merry Old Land of Oz*. "I think I shined up right fine, don't you?" I twirled around, chirping "Ha-ha-ha, ho-ho-ho and a couple of tra-la-las." The twirling gave everyone a full view of my new hairstyle. Pulled back, swept up and secured in a smooth-as-a-baby's-bottom bun.

"Well you look like a shiny new penny." As my landlady, co-worker and second mother, Trudy didn't let a day go by without making some remark that played off my name. On bad days, I might hear Penny Dreadful or Bad Penny. Other days, I was sure to hear Penny Arcade, Penny wise and pound foolish, or Penny's worth. My favorite was Pennies from Heaven, though it should be spelled Penny's from Heaven.

The two girls who also rented rooms from Trudy—Gina Lombardi and Bootsie Waldon—could be counted on to call me Bad Penny, even when I was good.

"Actually, I went to see Elma at the beauty parlor. I could've used a spell from the grand Wizard of Oz himself, but I settled for Elma's magic touch."

Trudy rested her needlework on her lap and took a closer look. "The reddish rinse she put on really sets off those emerald eyes of yours. What I wouldn't give for your eye color, instead of my dirt brown ones…like mud in a wet corn field."

She turned down the volume on the radio that was playing Bobby Darin's *Splish Splash*. "I just love that tune. Bobby's not so bad either." As she said it, the song transitioned to *Sugartime* by the McGuire Sisters. She picked up her cup of heavily creamed coffee. "First off, you missed supper. There's a plate for you in the oven. Kept it nice and warm. We had tuna casserole, with peas and potato chips. Just the way you like it. And, I whipped up your favorite lime-Jello salad, with grated carrots, pineapple and celery in it." Trudy smiled and leaned in as if hoping to get a positive reaction.

"Second, there are clean linens sitting on top of your bed. Please take a second, and trade the old ones out." She took a sip of her coffee. "And third, you look deeeee-vine!"

"Thank you for saving me dinner, the clean sheets and the compliment. I hope I didn't interrupt anything."

"Oh no, we were just debating the merits of Elvis Presley, Marlon Brando and Ricky Nelson."

I sat on the couch and pulled out the contents of the envelope that outlined what was in store for me at The Del. Without a spoken word, I had everyone's attention.

"Read it…out loud." Bootsie was nosey and always wanted to know everything about everyone. I always assumed it was because she cared. "Maybe it'll bring you good luck."

"Oh, don't be so superstitious. Just admit you're curious," Gina said.

"No more curious than the rest of you hens." Bootsie play-slapped Gina's upper arm.

I started with the cover letter. It welcomed me as a guest of Hotel del Coronado. "I've never spent the night. Never needed to. Never could afford it. Only hung out on the beach and had dinner, once each year to celebrate my parents' anniversary. Which is in a few days. Imagine that, I'll get to come down to the dining room from my guest room to have dinner with my folks."

"What makes you think you'll be free to have dinner with them. Read some more. Let's see what you got yourself into," Bootsie said.

I scanned down and mouthed words in relative silence. I turned the page. "Ah, here it is. I'll need to squeeze my fat ass into a 1920s-wool bathing suit and make the actresses look fit and shapely on camera."

"Be serious." Gina asked, "What does it say?"

"It talks about the movie they're filming. It's a comedy set around the time of the St. Valentine's Massacre."

"That doesn't sound like a comedy to me," Trudy said. "Besides, that was in Chicago."

"Hold on. Let me keep going." I read more words silently. "Okay, here's the summary. It's a love triangle. Two buddies who are down-on-their-luck musicians. Tony Curtis and Jack Lemmon are the buddies. They witness a shooting and escape the gangsters by dressing up like women and joining an all-girl orchestra."

"So where's the triangle?" Trudy added, "You need three for a triangle."

"Says here...um...there's a singer. In their own ways, they both fall for her." I read further. "Oh, that's not supposed to be public information. I'm supposed to know it so I understand what's being filmed at the hotel and how it fits into the overall picture."

"Mum's the word," Gina said.

Bootsie saluted me and nodded for good measure.

"Got it, kiddo." Trudy winked with both eyes.

I leafed through the pages in a clown's handkerchief sort of way. "Blah, blah, blah." Then, "not important, filler, filler, filler, not important."

"What about the hotel's ghosts?" Gina also asked, "Do they have parts to play?"

"Geez, I didn't think of that. It's one thing to eat there and go home. It's another thing to put your head down on a pillow and have the tortured, bullet-riddled spirit of Kate Morgan haunt my dreams. And room."

"Now who's being superstitious?" Bootsie said, "But people who work there claim the place is full of ghosts. I guess that's true of most hotels, though. Sad people commit suicide at hotels all the time and no one hears about it. Now, a murder, that's another thing entirely."

"Penny, you've seen Kate, haven't you?" asked Gina.

"Sure. Lots of times, especially when I was a kid. With her big black hat, flowing black-lace dress and a black parasol. She's always walking along the shore, right in the daylight."

We stopped talking and looked at each other. Silence filled the space between us.

"Well then, let's get back to this packet of information. I need to report to The Del this Sunday as the crew gets everything in order. The filming is scheduled to start the next day. I'm to be available for two weeks, but it looks like only a small part of the movie will be filmed here. Eight days of shooting." I looked up from the paper. "That means I have eight days to get to know her and become her best girlfriend. Piece of cake."

"It's a piece of something, but not cake." Bootsie's sarcasm was not appreciated.

I made slits out of my eyes and tried to burn her with my super-amazing x-ray vision. I failed and read some more. "The rest of the filming is being done up at MGM Studios. Just exterior scenes will be shot here. And it's supposed to be Florida, not California. That's the answer to your question, Trudy. The story must move from Chicago to Florida."

"We'll know the difference, won't we girls?" Trudy asked.

"And so will anyone who's been to Coronado or The Del. Is there anything else on those pages we should know?" Gina scooted to the edge of her seat cushion.

"Yes, it says right here…billions of broads have sex. But Marilyn Monroe *is* sex."

"Don't be crude, dear. You sound like Madge in the store today."

I gazed down and leafed through a few more pages. "Alright, my job will be to do whatever *Miss Monroe*—that's what they call her—requests." I held up the page, and turned it around as I pointed to the words *Miss Monroe*.

"I'm to be gracious, kind and prompt. I'm to be an ambassador for all of the fine people who call Coronado home." I looked up from the page, "In other words, I'm to be the welcoming committee and red carpet all rolled into one."

"More like a door mat." Gina guffawed. I wondered if she was getting jealous.

"Or a beck-and-call girl." Bootsie added, "A call girl, for short." At that point, I could tell that even though they were being playful, they were both jealous, which made no sense since we were such good friends. But it was, after all, Marilyn Monroe. "Nothing like being passive aggressive. Besides, if that's what you think, don't ask me to get you an autograph or any teensy-weensy thing." I squinted my eyes when I squeaked out *weensy*.

"Hey, I didn't mean it," Gina said. "Of course, I want an autographed photo and something personal of hers. A wine glass with her lipstick print on it. Or how about one of her extra admirers from the long line of men outside her door?"

"Are you kidding me?"

"A girl can dream, can't she?" Gina fired back, "Just think Penny, you'll have a chance at her castoffs."

"Her castoffs are so out of my league that—" I hadn't thought about that before, but it was possible.

Trudy chimed in, "Do I need to pinch you and bring you back to reality? It's fine to dream, but I don't believe in counting my chickens until they're all hatched...and boiled and served with dumplings!"

Trudy crossed her arms for emphasis. "And let's not forget, Penny, you're going to need something to wear. We can all help. Let's pool our resources girls, and see what we come up with and what she'll need to buy for herself."

"*Your* clothes. I think not. None of you are barrel-chested like me." I put my palms where my waist should be. "Hell, none of you are shaped like this barrel."

Trudy responded, "Those are your words, not ours. Our clothes may not meet your...um...unique needs, but our accessories might. Maybe you should go to Kippy's tomorrow during your lunch break and see if they have something that's not too fussy or loud. Something you can wear a couple of times, with different scarves and jewelry. We must stretch our money to make the best possible impression."

"We? Are *we* all going to wear that plain navy-blue dress? Or forest green one? Are *we* going to wear a black pencil skirt?" I ran my fingers through the dangly charm bracelet that accompanied the chunky red-plastic bracelet I was wearing. "See. Look here. Most girls wear one bracelet. If one is good, two must be better. Besides, it's distracting."

"Why the heck do you think you need things that are distracting?" Trudy's voice had a softness to it that was missing before.

"I learned long ago that a girl like me was not ever going to blend in. Ever. So, I took that and ran with it." I shrugged.

Trudy asked, "You did?"

"Yeah. If I wasn't going to blend in, I might as well stick out. And do it for reasons I choose. Voice. Hair. Clothes. Jewelry. Whatever I choose. The wallflower approach was never going to work for me. Besides, I was told that big girls should wear big prints, choose big jewelry and carry big handbags. To make us look smaller."

"But that has nothing to do with looking trashy and cheap, like Tilly the ticket seller. It's not enough that oh-so-famous star walked away from Hollywood. But she's still doing it...every single day...in grand, glittering style!" Bootsie's words stung me.

I shot my challenge to Bootsie. "You take that back. If you think Tilly and I look trashy and cheap, why do you borrow my things?"

"I don't think you look trashy and cheap. Some of your homemade jewelry does. And, if you must know, I borrow it to save money."

I clucked my tongue. "And that's my point. It takes a lot of money to look this trashy. Oh, that didn't come out right. What I mean is, I have to work extra hard to look my best."

Trudy jumped into the conversation. "And no one is disagreeing with you. Are we girls? What you might want to do is tone it down a tad when you're at The Del. You'll want to stand out for the right reasons. Not for your bowling-ball or totem-pole earrings."

"My mismatched earrings are tons of fun. Mismatched—and fun—like me. Face it, how many girls do you know who can craft spectacular jewelry—like these earrings, for instance—with nothing more than a few charm-bracelet charms or Cracker Jack prizes?"

No one responded.

"None." I answered the question myself. "There's only me."

"Penny, do you know what your problem is, besides your kitschy, tchotchke ear ornaments?" Bootsie crossed her arms in front of her chest, perhaps pleased by her impressive word choice.

"I have a strong feeling I'm going to find out." I stood and smoothed out my blouse. "Well, come on. Tell me."

"You're not like the other girls. No one is. We're all different

and that's a good thing. I'm a bag of bones. Not a curve or comfy cushion to be had. You're voluptuous. And your personality—"
I interrupted, "Oh, not the personality thing."
"Yes. In your case, it's not just something that's polite to say. Your personality is wonderful, most of the time. You laugh louder than anyone. You smile bigger than anyone. Your dimple is cuter than anyone's, even if you only have one."
I readied my comeback. I tugged at the hem of my untucked blouse, took a few steps and placed my right index finger on my lips. "Thank you for that, Bootsie. I've considered what you said. And I agree. I'm comfortable with the way I look. Hell, I love it. With the three of you, I can hold my own. At the dime store, I'm large and I'm in charge. With Marilyn Monroe, I don't think so."
"Who said you had to compete with Marilyn Monroe?" Bootsie shrugged. "She's going to be here to do a job. And will you too. That's it."
"I know," Gina added, "why don't you ask her what she thinks about beauty. She must have some thoughts about that."
Trudy weighed in, "Why is it that we gals—probably from the first time two cavewomen met—have an unavoidable and instant need to compare ourselves to each other? Whose eyes are brighter? Who looks best in a little black dress? Whose bust and backside are the shapeliest?"
Their heads bobbed.
"I know you can't see it now, but I was quite a hot dish in my day." Trudy adjusted her skirt's hemline. "Whether I was or not, my husband thought so. I could see it every time he looked at me. I was his Cinderella at the ball. No matter what I was wearing or what I was doing. He saw me that way. I did my best to see myself that way too. But he's gone now, may he rest in peace. And I haven't found a mirror yet that reflects what my Vernon saw in me." Trudy stopped. She released the handkerchief that was tucked under her wristwatch and rolled it between her fingers.
I stepped over to Trudy and put my hand on her shoulder.
"I tell you this because you need to find a way to help people see you the way you'd like to be seen," Trudy said. "Don't you worry about that movie star or the caravan of fans she's bringing with her. I'm sure she has problems all her own. You're there to help make her time in Coronado as pleasant as possible. Of course, it won't hurt for you to see how they do her makeup, and share

any tips you pick up with us."

I rolled my eyes and patted Trudy's shoulder again.

"You can count on me."

If I'd known at that point what it took to look like—and be—a big-screen bombshell, I would've run for the hills. And it wouldn't have been the Hollywood Hills.

FADE OUT

CHAPTER 6

FADE IN:
- SEPTEMBER 4, 1958, FOUR DAYS UNTIL SHOOTING BEGINS
- INTERIOR, TRUDY'S HOUSE (NIGHTTIME)

Just as we started to settle down and settle in, an announcement stirred things up again.

"Get your war paint and tight sweaters on girls. Penny, your dinner has to wait." Gina kept her hands up by her mouth in the shape of a megaphone directed up the stairs to the bedrooms. "We three amigos are heading to Fiesta Village. Five minutes. Front door. Ready. Set. Go."

"Are you sure that's such a good idea?" Trudy's voice traveled through the house from the kitchen. "Fiesta Village is so scandalous. You may not live to see the dawn."

"Oh for goodness sake." Gina directed her voice toward the kitchen. "We'll be fine. We have each other. Want to come with us?"

"It's chilly and people-y out there. Lots of strangers. *Strange* strangers at that," Trudy said. "I get enough of them at the lunch counter. Besides, there's nothing for this old gal at Fiesta Village."

Tequila was playing on the radio. "Well that's appropriate," Gina muttered to herself, "considering where we're off to."

I followed her into the kitchen and we found Trudy at the sink. One hand in soapy water. The other wiping her forehead. She acknowledged that Fiesta Village was notorious in Coronado. In all of San Diego, for that matter. Just a few miles from the border with Mexico itself, the faux Mexican-village setting was a cluster of shacks and courtyards. The sole purpose of the place was guzzling booze and picking up broads. Sailors loved it. Women loved it too.

"You know what they say. If you don't get picked up at Fiesta Village, there's no fiesta in your future," Gina said. "And Penny needs a pick-me-up...and to be picked up."

"I'm not so sure about that." Trudy wiped her hands on her apron.

"Sure I do. A little attention from a man would do us all good." I put an arm around Gina and Trudy and pulled them in.

"It'll give her the confidence she needs to be around Marilyn Monroe." Gina shook her head side to side. "God knows I would."

I rarely had a shortage of confidence. But for the first time in a long time, my palms were wet and my mouth was dry as sand paper. I considered how a jaunt to Fiesta Village with the girls might be just what the doctor ordered.

"You have a point there, Gina. What time will you be home? I'll wait up."

"No you won't. We're not teenagers. You go to bed and dream sweet dreams about—"

"Sweet dreams?" I added as I released them from the three-way hug. "I want some."

"And I want you to have some too, dear." Trudy patted my shoulder. She made her way to the front door and opened it. Bootsie arrived just in time to step out first. "The least I can do is stand here and see you three chickadees off. I'll go to bed and pray you all make it back to our little henhouse."

"That's sweet of you." I shook out a colorful satin scarf and wrapped it over my newly set hairdo. "Paid good money for this do. Not going to let the moist night air have its way with it."

"I wouldn't worry so much about the air having its way with your hair. It's those sailors—and their hands—you'll need to look out for. All they want is *their* way."

"They won't get it from me."

"Me either. I have something else planned for us," Gina said.

"I don't like the sound of *that*." I looked back at Trudy.

We turned to wave to Trudy as we got to the edge of the sidewalk.

Trudy stood there with her hands in her apron pockets.

"Guardian angels. If you're listening, stay with them. Bring them home to me safe and sound."

"Heard that," Gina said. "We don't need guardian angels."

I barely heard Trudy say, "*Everyone* needs guardian angels. And this may be the night you find out why."

FADE OUT

CHAPTER 7

FADE IN:

- SEPTEMBER 4, 1958, FOUR DAYS UNTIL SHOOTING BEGINS
- EXTERIOR, FIESTA VILLAGE (NIGHTTIME)

Gina grasped my hand as we entered Fiesta Village's colorful arch. Even at night, the garish mix of painted flowers on the walls and sombreros hanging from the rafters looked tacky. As if the colorful riot in our eyes wasn't enough, the brassy blats of the mariachi band's trumpeter assaulted our ears.

"We're on a mission." Gina yanked my arm.

"We are?"

"Yes. We are."

Gina pushed me up against a sailor. I knocked the white-canvas Dixie Cup hat right off his head. He turned and scanned me up and down. He burped and, like my brothers learned to do, he spoke through his belch's rumblings, "Bitch."

"Why thank you." My words of gratitude merged with the beer-scented cloud he'd created.

"For what?" He bent down to get his hat.

"For not calling me a *fat* bitch."

We walked away. So much for getting hit on right off the bat. I told myself that the night was young and so were we, sort of.

A few steps later, Gina halted. She stared at the fortuneteller's booth. The curtain was drawn. Gina scanned the area and started to move again. This time, toward an elaborate birdcage with a man wearing a sombrero behind it. We passed a woman making tortillas by hand. The heat of her cooktop warmed the air and made me long for a melty-cheesy quesadilla. But it became clear that eating was not part of Gina's plans.

"It's a birdcage for a fortune-telling bird. It's the newest attraction here," Gina assured.

"Honestly? A bird?" My feet stopped moving, which yanked Gina back and caused Bootsie to bump me from behind. "I don't know what you're cooking up, but count me out."

"Not a chance. We're going to find out what's in your future from that bird and the lady behind the curtain. The man of your dreams? A deadly car crash? Who knows? Tonight, it all becomes clear. Now step up to the bird." Gina gave me a strong shove.

The small sign read, "Destiny, The Mystical Canary."

"I did this on a dare last weekend." Gina moved me directly in front of the cage. An ivory canary hopped around inside the cathedral-shaped structure, with spires painted coral and sky blue.

"Buenos noches, senoritas. I am Miguel. This is Destiny. She has powers beyond our understanding. Just two quarters can change your life. Just fifty cents is all it takes for Destiny to speak to you."

He pointed to a row of small pieces of paper in front of the cage.

"Your future is here. Right here. Destiny is waiting for you."

"Fine." I reached into my coin purse and handed him two quarters.

He nodded. "Gracias. What is your name?"

"Penelope."

He waved his hand over the cage, then over the papers. With the grace of a magician on stage, Miguel danced his hands around until his right one rested on the cage's latch. He opened the door and caressed Destiny with his index finger. He stroked her back while chanting something in Spanish.

"She is ready now." Destiny hopped out onto the bottom of the doorway and then onto the small tabletop. She hopped over to the row of papers.

"Destiny, what must you tell Penelope? What do the stars and spirits need her to know?"

The bird's beak touched one slip of paper. But she released it. She hopped over to another. And then another. She chirped three times and pecked at the third slip of paper, the one that she'd most recently touched. Miguel picked it up and handed it to me.

"Here is your future. Gaze upon it."

I took the paper and read it to myself, my lips shaping each word.

"On your way to a dream you will get lost and find a better one." I looked up, chewing on my lower lip as I thought. "I can live with that. I guess."

"What's it say?" Bootsie reached for the slip of paper.

"Not so fast," Gina warned. "That's for Penny to know. Only Penny. Wouldn't want to spoil her future, would you?"

I turned to Gina but was intercepted by a sailor. A drunken sailor, I suspected by the stench of him and his sloppy posture. "Say, are you a parking ticket? Because you have FINE written all over you."

I couldn't think of a quick comeback, so I just made eye contact with Gina and started to speak. "Are we done here?"

"Not in the least. We've only just begun." Gina grabbed my and Bootsie's elbows and headed back to where the closed curtain was. "Now you visit Madam Esmeralda."

"Madam?"

"What else would you expect to call a gypsy fortuneteller?"

Gina waved to the woman standing next to the curtain, which was open. She winked back and ran her fingertips through the beaded trimming before she outstretched her open palm. Her long red nails sliced the air as she made a come-in gesture.

"Buh-bye now." Gina handed the woman some money and pushed me in. The curtain closed behind me. The flickering light from a couple of hammered and pierced tin lanterns skipped around me like fireflies, as the scent of wax and taco meat perfumed the air. My desire for a quesadilla was replaced by a hankering for a crunchy-beefy taco.

"What is your name, my child?"

"Penelope." My voice wavered. Any annoyance I was feeling from being pushed around passed as I pondered what she might tell me.

"And what is it you need to know from Esmeralda tonight? I am here for you. Only you. Please sit."

"Thank you. I have to confess that it wasn't my idea to come here."

Esmeralda's fingertips slid over several playing cards on her table and then across the tablecloth to my hand. I started to pull away, but stopped.

"Let me get a better sense of you and what your future holds. Place your hand on mine."

Esmeralda closed her eyes and inhaled. "Such power you have. Your energy buzzes like the bees. Excited bees. Very excited bees. You see things, don't you? Things other people do not? And feel them too?"

"I suppose so."

"That is a gift. A *rare* gift. Most children have it, but they lose it…some so much quicker than others. But you kept it. Your childhood was not easy. Not loving. Not warm. For that I am sorry."

"Thank you?" Was I supposed to thank someone for saying that? It seemed like a polite thing to do.

"However, that has allowed you to keep your mind's doors and windows open—"

Esmeralda's words stopped flowing. I wasn't sure what to do. My eyes shifted from side to side, spotting half-burned candles and strings of beads. When I wove my fingers together, I discovered my palms were clammy.

"Doors and windows—" she said in elongated whispers, as if she was drifting away.

"Are we going to talk about doors and windows?" I was growing skeptical. "Did you know that Coco Chanel said something like, 'Don't spend time beating on a wall, hoping to transform it into a door.' Does that have anything to do with what we're talking about or are going to talk about?"

Esmeralda opened her eyes. "I could wave my hands over a crystal ball and say something like: 'Serpents and spiders, tail of a rat…call in the spirits, wherever they're at,' or 'Rap on a table, it's time to respond… send us a message from somewhere beyond.' That's a bunch of hocus pocus and mumbo jumbo for tourists and smashed sailors. You're beyond that. I know it. You know it too. Let's talk…*really* talk."

"I was sort of hoping for some Professor Marvel stuff. You know, visions of Auntie Em putting her hand on her heart, dropping on the bed and the crystal going dark. Dorothy was moved by it."

"Something…someone…is about to enter your life and change

everything. *Everything.*"

"You don't say. Do you read the newspaper?"

"No, I do not. I see things. I know things. Now focus on what I am telling you."

"I am. I already know that Marilyn Monroe is coming to Coronado and I'm going to work for her."

Esmeralda held my hand and closed her eyes again. "That is all fine and well. But that is not the someone I am seeing. He, yes he, will be a dream come true. To your heart, he will be Mr. Right. But there is a shadow that follows him."

"We all have shadows in the sunlight."

"But his shows in the dark." She slammed her palm on the table and swiveled to reach a deck of cards. She shuffled and fanned them out on the tabletop.

"Poker or gin?" I couldn't resist being a smart aleck.

"Not funny. Each card has a purpose and a meaning. These were my grandmother's." She opened an intricately carved box, scooped up the cards and placed them inside. "Her energy is still with the cards. In them. In this box. We will need to connect with that energy."

"We will?"

Esmeralda pulled an extra chair over by her place at the table, but turned it to be facing out the tent's opening. An ashtray, a burnt cigar and a box of matches rested on the seat. She struck a match and lit the cigar.

"I don't smoke." I scrunched up my nose.

"Neither do I. This is for my grandmother. Our words and wishes will ride the cigar's smoke to reach her in the spirit world. When she comes to us, she can smoke the cigar if she likes."

She removed the cards from the box and laid them out in piles of six across and eight down. "We usually read all the cards, but tonight we jump ahead. Close your eyes. Stretch out your right arm and point one of your fingers down."

I did as I was told.

"You still alive in there, Penny?" Gina's voice penetrated the curtained doorway.

"Do not respond. We must continue," Esmeralda said.

I closed my eyes and pointed a finger. I was peeking, though. I didn't want to miss a thing. Besides, even though the girls were just on the other side of the curtain, I wasn't completely comfortable with what was happening, much less what *could* happen.

"Now, as I speak these words, move your hand in a circle. Like hands on a clock. Above the table. Doesn't matter which direction. Just move in a circle."

I began to move my hand.

"Grandmother, help my new friend to see and understand what is coming to her. Help her to have an open heart and open mind as she lowers her hand to touch one—just one—card. Yes, one card that I can tell her about."

"Lower your hand. Round and round until you feel your hand is too heavy to hold up. That's it. Open your eyes."

I looked down to find my finger on the edge of a card. I didn't peek when I lowered my hand.

"The Knight of Wands. This aligns with what I saw. A man. A beautiful man. Strong and proud. Determined."

"Sounds like a dream come true to me."

"Ah, yes, however once he has your attention, he will not leave you. He will possess you."

"PENNY! Are you still in there? We're getting worried. Did she hypnotize you or—"

"Bootsie, you ding-dong." Gina's voice traveled through the curtain. "If she was hypnotized how could she answer you."

"Friends of Penny, she is fine. She will be with you in a moment. Patience, please." Esmeralda refocused on me. "This man is charming. No, he is a *charmer*."

Her fingertips worked through the trinkets and treasures in her grandmother's box. "Hold out your hand. Palm up." At that point I trusted her. Nothing about this seemed fake or trumped up.

I extended my right palm. Esmeralda placed...ever so slowly...a small card on it. "My grandmother wants you to have this."

I was amazed—but also touched—that an old dead woman wanted me to have *that* card.

I looked down at the bright-colored card. Smaller than a playing card, it had blue water, blue sky and a bare-chested, dark-haired mermaid with a shocking-red tail. The words "LA SERINA" appeared at the bottom. "This is a loteria card. Kind of like the Mexican version of your bingo game. My abuela says this will mean something to you...soon. Listen for the siren's call, but do not become dizzy by it."

"I'm going to meet a singing mermaid?"

"My abuela says to keep your head clear. Do not get carried away."

"That's better. I got it." What a relief that was. I closed and tightened my lips. My eyes squinted. "I'm not sure what to say. *Thank you* doesn't seem quite enough."

"Your thanks to me will be to consider what we uncovered tonight. To take it to heart. To be ready when this charmer crosses your path."

FADE OUT

CHAPTER 8

FADE IN:

- SEPTEMBER 4, 1958, FOUR DAYS UNTIL SHOOTING BEGINS
- INTERIOR, TRUDY'S HOUSE (NIGHTTIME)

Standing in front of the refrigerator in my nightgown with a spoon of chilled chocolate-chip cookie dough in my mouth, I jerked when Trudy came into the room.

"A little snack?" Her voice raised on the word *snack*.

"Yes." The word came out with a slushiness to it.

"I mean, no." I shook my head.

"Maybe." I was caught. Might as well fess up.

"Yes. I'm sorry to get into the cookie dough."

"Penny, that's fine. I'm just glad you girls are home safe and sound. Did you have a good time?"

"Uh-huh."

"Now scoop up another spoonful of dough and head back upstairs to your bed. Go on. Take it with you." She shooed me like she would a pesky cat. "You have some *big* days ahead. You'll need your rest. Who knows what kinds of surprises you'll have?"

"Esmeralda does."

"Who?????" I could almost see the question marks coming out of Trudy's mouth.

"Oh, never mind. Nighty-night."

"I'm so happy you're doing this. When we were in the dime store with that newspaper man, I was about to bring you to your senses by jiggling you like a kid jiggles a piggy bank when the

Good Humor ice-cream truck's bells are ringing down the block. I'm glad I didn't have to, this time."

I took a few steps forward and stopped. "Thank you."

"For what, sweet-ums?"

"For being you."

"Well, I wouldn't know who else to be. But that new actress friend of yours will know a thing or two about pretending to be someone else. I hope you learn about it. But not *how* to do it yourself."

Trudy went on, "I know you're getting impatient with life."

I cleared my throat. "It's more like frustrated than impatient. I'm in my twenties and I feel like I'm too old to be young and too young to be old."

"Pish-posh." She made a dismissive smashed face at me. "But just know, it's okay to take a leap of faith. But look *first*...before you leap. Will you do that for me?"

"Sure."

That's what she wanted to hear. But that was not what I was going to do.

FADE OUT

CHAPTER 9

FADE IN:
- SEPTEMBER 5, 1958, THREE DAYS UNTIL SHOOTING BEGINS
- INTERIOR, TRUDY'S HOUSE (DAYTIME)

I jerked the morning paper to make it behave. I hated how damp coastal air always made newspapers limp. A headline grabbed my attention: MIAMI MAYOR SPEAKS OUT ABOUT FILMING AT THE DEL." I wondered why he would care. I read on.

Miami Mayor Robert King High reportedly "thundered off a wire to the actress (Marilyn Monroe) saying Florida sunshine could not be duplicated anywhere and that it was sacrilege for California to double for the so-called sunshine state."

The mayor of Coronado, Admiral Beverly Harrison, wired back, "Some like it hot, but not as hot as Miami in September. You forgot to mention gnats, mosquitoes and hurricanes. Give them my best."

I smiled and folded the paper in half and tucked it inside my binder to share with Marilyn in a few days, if she hadn't already seen it.

That day, however, was all about time off from the dime store. Frankie asked me to go to the beach and relax. With Frankie, I could relax. Especially at the beach. So, we both asked for the day off.

Nothing sounded better knowing—and not knowing—what I faced in the coming days.

FADE OUT

CHAPTER 10

FADE IN:
- SEPTEMBER 5, 1958, THREE DAYS UNTIL SHOOTING BEGINS
- EXTERIOR, CORONADO BEACH (DAYTIME)

An overweight girl. A bathing suit. A public beach. Staring eyes. Judging eyes. Squinting eyes. Let them look. There's more than plenty to see. Should be a nightmare in daylight. But not for me. I always tried my best to not care what other people thought. Truth be told, a small part of me did. How could I not?

I opened and slipped out of my white-terrycloth beach wrap.

"Nice bathing suit. New?" Frankie never judged me. For my looks. For my thoughts. For my fears. He didn't know I tried on six before settling on this one. "What do you think of mine?" He posed like a body builder.

"Better than your *birthday* suit." I bugged my eyes and pushed out my lips. "Men's swim trunks are pretty much the same. Like boxer shorts, but tighter. Not too tight, though." I looked again. "Say, that's not a swimsuit."

"Nope. Just a pair of track shorts. Nothing else was clean. Just these shorts."

I folded my beach wrap and dropped it on our blanket. "Well, it doesn't make any difference to me. Come on. Let's walk."

"Doesn't make me look too thin, uh? The guys still call me Lanky Frankie and Franken Furter. At least I don't get called Knobby Knees anymore." Frankie's shorts didn't appear to restrain anything contained in them. He caught me looking at his butt. At least he didn't catch me glancing at his crotch. I hoped so, anyway. "I can't help it if all the running does this to me."

"Not to mention that you hardly eat anything."

"Wha—whaddya mean? I do too."

I stared into his sky-blue eyes. "Do not. You eat like a parakeet. A *sick* parakeet. Always have. Your mom packed you everything I wanted my mom to pack."

I held up my fist. With each of the next words, I extended a finger like an umpire behind the plate. "Bologna. Egg salad. Chips. Brownies. Leftover popcorn. How many times didn't I finish your lunch at school so the lunch lady wouldn't nag at you?"

Frankie ran his fingertips through his sun-bleached hair. "And who made you slow down when you ate so those same lunch ladies wouldn't nag at you for gobbling?"

"Touché."

The beach was sun-drenched. Not a cloud to be found. We walked as the cool ocean water swirled around us. He took the spot closest to the water. I was on the sandy side as we made our way up the beach toward The Del.

My chub rocked and rolled with each step, a delayed jiggle followed like a shadow, but attached and squishy.

"I'm glad we still hang out together. Other than you, most of my school friends were hefty girls who snuck Scooter Pies, dreaded rejection and ached to feel pretty."

"I'm glad too."

"So you like my new swimsuit, do you?" I tugged at the shoulder strap.

"Sure. Green's a nice color."

I should've been mortified to walk along the shore next to his fit-and-trim body. But I wasn't. Any notion of being a beach bunny had been sandblasted away years ago. My goal was not beauty, but how to be the best person possible in an impossible world.

We talked about work and the bowling team and the weather and Marilyn Monroe and the surf. We walked in silence too.

"Wanna exercise?" Frankie started to trot.

"No. Oh, excuse me. I mean yes. Wait a minute, did you ask if I wanted *extra fries*."

"EX-ER-CISE?"

"I don't need to get all sweaty. I'm in shape, you know.

Unfortunately, it's the wrong one."

Frankie turned and made his face screw up. "But you know how hard it is for me not to run out here. Anywhere for that matter."

"Just walk with me. Talk with me. You can do that, can't you?"

"Sure."

I bent over to pick up a piece of green sea glass.

"Why do you always do that...pick up glass?"

"I like broken things. I collect them, I guess." I studied the piece of glass. "Think about it. This was a 7 Up bottle once...or part of one. It broke into a bunch of sharp pieces and now it's all smooth and frosty. Still broken, but not at all the same."

A piece of time-worn blue glass caught my eye just a few inches away. I reached for it and as I stood, I glanced at the front of Frankie's shorts. It was impossible not to. It was right there in front of me. Funny thing, though, I caught him looking at my chest. I asked myself what was going on. What was making us curious, maybe even frisky? It seemed to come out of nowhere.

I strained to look out over the water as if I could see China as we were stepping in its ever-changing fringe. "I know this is the Pacific Ocean. And there's only one. But it's amazing how we aren't stepping in the same water twice. It comes and goes and mixes. Always flowing. Always moving, kind of like you."

Frankie grinned.

"I wish we could live like that."

"Yeah, it's like when I run. The sand is never the same sand either."

"I can see that. Nothing's permanent."

"Nope."

"Not even the breakwater's rocks. They change too. Slower. But they do."

We headed toward our blanket. Heat rose from the sand with the intensity of a kid's fever, making us prance like we were walking on hot coals. The blanket hadn't gotten sanded yet by wind or too much foot traffic. We laid back and looked at the sky.

"I had the weirdest dream last night. Actually, I've been having lots of weird dreams and I can remember each one like it really happened."

"Was I in one? Did I have clothes on?" Frankie poked my shoulder with his finger.

"Yes, you were in some of them. And, yes, you had clothes on. Anyway, about this dream, we were at the zoo. By the elephants. My *favorite* spot."

"Yeah, I know that. The last time we went I could've seen the whole zoo by the time you'd had your fill of the elephants."

"So, in this dream I can hear The Commander calling me Penelope the Pachyderm. He didn't choose to call me Princess or Precious. Me, I was an elephant in his eyes."

"It's better than being a buffalo or an anteater."

"Watch it, Mister Wisenheimer. So, there we were. The Commander shouting. My mother, all sloshy-mouthed and slurring her words and holding onto any fence or handrail she can find to keep from falling over. My two brothers yanking on plants to make swords or machine guns to kill each other or the animals with. I'm eating out of a box of animal crackers and looking at the elephants. Just looking. The elephants stood there. Swaying. Taking it all in, but not flinching at our family freak show. They probably thought the Parkers should be in the enclosure and the animals run free."

"Fascinating. What's your point?"

"My dream was telling me I grew up in a freak show, even though I prayed to Jesus, Mary and Joseph that nobody noticed. It was like I was keeping a secret. The biggest secret ever. No child should have to learn to keep secrets before she learns to ride a bike. No child should have to learn to tuck booze-less bottles into empty Corn Flake boxes in the trash can to cover her mother's bad habits. No child should have to learn it's better to organize shoes and socks inside her bedroom closet than to deal with the screaming or, worse yet, the scarier silences."

"Sheesh, I'm not quite sure how to respond to that."

"I don't expect you to. And I'm sorry to spew all of that, here on the beach, on such a beautiful day."

"So tell me again why you moved out and don't live with your parents anymore?" Frankie's voice had a mocking tone.

"Ever hear of Lizzie Borden?" I held back a laugh.

"Got it."

"No matter how old you are, you're always a kid in your parents' house. I had to leave. And I still find it hard to go back there."

"Strange, isn't it?"

We both kept looking up at the sky.

"What?"

"Parents are supposed to teach kids everything. In our cases, they taught us everything *not* to do. How *not* to be. How *not* to behave. What *not* to do."

"If it makes you feel any better—and not that this is a who-had-the-shittiest-childhood competition—but I'm a casualty of past wars too. My dad left a bread-crumb trail of beer bottles wherever he went. He'd blow all the money he had, but never follow the trail back to our apartment. He'd drink the food money. He'd drink the rent money."

"That must've been awful." I didn't make eye contact with him.

"My mom would take me to the bar or the pool hall and beg the guys to help her. They didn't. She told me I spent more nights sleeping on a pool table than in my crib."

A seagull flew overhead. "Close your mouth or you might get a gift from the bird." I put one palm over my eyes and the other over my mouth.

"Speaking of gifts, did I ever tell you about what my dad did a few days before Christmas when I was little?"

"Don't think so." I couldn't believe there was a story about his childhood that I hadn't heard.

"It's not one we tell. Kind of a sore subject, if you know what I mean. When I was around six, my sister and I were with him. Mother was out shopping. Dad was in charge. But he was smashed. There were wrapped presents already under the tree. Dad spilled the beans about the whole Santa thing."

"Geez, that stinks."

"Yeah. My sister asked him if we could open the presents. Right then. Not wait until Christmas morning. He said, 'Sure. Why not?' So, we did."

"You didn't."

"We did. We opened them all. It should have been more fun than it was. And, let me tell you, it was no fun when Mother got home. She walked into the end of our version of Christmas morning with an armload of shopping bags. My sister and I ran out back before she even said a word. They fought, long and hard and loud. He could be a fun drunk. Sometimes. That day, he was an *ugly drunk*."

I elbowed Frankie. "Well, what did you do?"

"We stayed out in the backyard in the dark. I don't remember this part of it too well. We may have come over to your house. But, once Mother found us and got us home, there were still no words. No dinner. And you know how much my big fat family likes to eat."

I nodded.

"There weren't any parties. The Christmas tree vanished. And, to tell you the truth, there's never really been a Christmas since."

"I'm so sorry. If anything, kids should have Santa and the Easter Bunny and the Tooth Fairy." I kept my eyes on the sky.

"And what about the time I started laughing at the dinner table, even after I was warned not to? I'm sure I told you that one."

"About the spaghetti?"

"That's the one. I had a mouth full of spaghetti and I laughed so hard it came out of my nose and back onto my plate."

"And your mother made you eat it a second time, right? That you shouldn't waste good food." I shook my head. "That's just awful. No wonder you hardly eat."

"And it's no wonder we're as messed up as we are, even though—"

I broke in. "I beg your pardon. It's a wonder we turned out as *well* as we did."

"Looking back on it, we grew up fast. Maybe that's better. But I gotta say this: Adulthood...who needs it? They can have it. ALL of it."

"Yeah, they can have it." Frankie rubbed his palms together and then flung them apart as if to wash it all away.

"Tell ya what. Starting this second, we'll settle all fights by the fairest of all fair methods: our choice of Rock-Paper-Scissor or Eenie-Meenie-Minee-Moe. And, while we're at it, it's okay to hit back when you've been hit."

Frankie bugged his eyes. "And we'll make totem poles out of fruit cans and Mickey Mouse watches from toilet paper rolls. Remember that?"

I laughed and held my stomach. "And we'll get recess four times a day. Beat you to the swings!"

The sun was getting to me. It was time to get in the water and cool off.

"Come on. Let's swim." I knew he wasn't comfortable in the

water. He never had been. "I double-dog dare you. We won't go where it's deep. I promise."

"That's okay. You go. I'll watch from here."

"Sometime in your life you're going to have to get used to being *in* the ocean, not just running next to it. One day you might need to save someone. You'd do whatever you could to help, wouldn't you?"

"Sure." A hearty serving of reluctance came with that answer.

I stood up and put my fists on my hips. "There's hardly anyone out here today. I'll help you."

"Are you serious?"

"As the plague."

"Well, I wish you wouldn't be so bossy."

"I'm not bossy. Not much anyway." I took a moment to reconsider my words. "Alright, I'll admit it. I *am* bossy. I learned right away as The Commander's kid that I'd always be outranked under his roof…and, as you know, it's better to be in charge. So, that's it, I'm in charge, but not bossy."

Frankie scanned the beach. "Alright, I'll swim with you. But if you do something that—"

"You can trust me. Really. I've been teaching little kids how to swim forever."

We watched the pattern of the waves as we waded in. I taught him what to look for and what to avoid. When we got behind where the waves were breaking, the water was about four feet deep. Frankie stopped. "Now what?"

"Tread water." I held his hands and led him a bit farther from the shore until my toes couldn't touch the sand. "Run in the water. Point your toes, and don't bend at your knees too much. Kick your legs like scissors cutting paper." I knew that making the connection with running would help him with his fear of water, much less deep water. "Good. Now let go." He needed to let go of me. If I let go first, he'd panic. I'd seen that happen with kids far too many times. It took a while, but he did it.

"Now let's go a little closer to shore, where we can stand. Well, where *I* can stand."

When I could plant my feet solidly, I casually urged him, "Now float. Just float."

"With my face in the water? On my back? How?"

"On your back. That way, no matter what happens to you out

here you'll be able to keep your head up and breathe. Here, let me—"

I put a straightened arm behind his back and bent over to put my other behind his legs.

"Are you sure about this? It feels—"

"Do you want me to help you or not?"

Frankie laid back and, with my support, his lanky body buoyed to the surface. I looked him over. "Put your head back so you're looking up. Now breathe. In and out. Think about how you're floating in the ocean and swimming in the sky."

I kept my eyes on him and not the sky. I'd never touched him that way in all the years we'd known each other. Friends don't touch like that.

My left palm supported his ribs. Bones ridged between my fingers. I couldn't remember feeling my own ribs without probing and pushing into them with pokey fingertips.

My other palm was behind his knees. There, my fingers were in contact with solidness. Not as solid as Frankie's rib cage. His leg muscles were tight under a layer of soft, bronzed skin.

I looked down and studied him. Closely. His nipples showed that the water was chilly. His stomach was flat. You could bounce a dime off it. No, you could iron a prom dress on it. Not that I ever had a prom dress or even went to prom.

"Did you know that fat floats better than muscle?" I said the words loudly since his ears were below the water's surface.

"That must explain a lot, uh?"

"Watch it, you jerk. Now slowly kick your feet and wave your hands and arms. See, you're floating." I began to pull my arms away just as his middle started to sink. "Tighten your butt and push up. You're sagging."

"You sure about that?"

"Yes, just do as you're told, young man."

He did and grinned.

"Why are you smiling?"

I looked down the length of his body and flinched. Above the surface, Frankie's wet running shorts were clinging. Tightly.

"Hey, buckaroo. Put that pistol of yours away." I shook my head. "I can't believe you made me look there. I'll never be able to *un-see* that."

I was confused. Was he flirting with me? Was he showing me

he liked me, *that* way? And did I want him to?

My response was to punch him in the stomach, after which he folded under the water.

"Are you talking about my *erector set*? That's just what you get when you don't have a swimsuit or anything to wear under a pair of running shorts."

"Yeah, I got it alright."

"So just why are you uncomfortable in the water?"

"It's my parents. I know we both blame our parents for everything, but this time it's true. When they were in high school, they used to go off to an abandoned—but flooded—quarry with friends. No one knew how to swim. They just laid in the sun and splashed around in the water. Shallow water."

"So?"

"So, one time a guy who was a friend of theirs decided to dive into the water in an area they didn't usually hang out in. He smashed his head on some rocks. He floated up and away from the shore. Since nobody could swim, nobody could go out and get him. They didn't have life preservers or air mattresses. They all watched him die."

"How awful."

"Yep, and so their fear became mine. Funny how that works."

That explained a lot. Thank goodness he'd become more comfortable in the water…especially since someone's life would soon depend on it.

FADE OUT

CHAPTER 11

FADE IN:
- SEPTEMBER 5, 1958, THREE DAYS UNTIL SHOOTING BEGINS
- EXTERIOR, CORONADO BEACH (DAYTIME)

"This is what a piece of toast must feel like." The sun warmed our bodies, along with the brown-sugar colored sand and blanket that snuggled us. We were still separated and looking at the sky.

"Did you know the sun loves the moon so much that she dies every…single…solitary night to let him breathe? I just think that's a wonderful way to look at dawn and dusk." I sighed.

"Yeah. Sure."

"Here's another way of saying it. See if this moves you. Listen carefully." I cleared my throat to give my words a poetic delivery. "Since the beginning of time, the ocean refuses to stop kissing the shoreline, no matter how many times she sends him away."

"Better." Frankie's response was clipped and less than sentimental.

I sat up. "How about this? The sun loved the moon so much…so much that he chewed tin foil and light bulbs for her."

"That's love alright." He snickered as he sat up too.

I grinned and caught him staring at my chest again. "Hey, talk to my eyes, not my cleavage." Truth be told, I'd decided it was alright if he talked to my chest. It was an odd twist to our relationship. I wondered what had gotten into him? Was he jealous about my new job and being around those Hollywood types?

I reached into my beach bag and pulled out a stack of

chocolate-chip cookies wrapped in wax paper. The sun's heat made the paper go limp and the chocolate chips melty.

"Want one?" I barely had those two words out before he was grabbing at the air in the direction of the cookies.

"Aren't they the *best* when the sun bakes them a second time?" He'd said that for as long as I could remember. Right there on that same beach. Every time I'd unearthed a stack of wax-paper wrapped cookies from my beach bag. I hoped I'd never forget it until I was senile and I forgot everything else along with it.

"Yes. They're good in the kitchen, right off the hot cookie sheet. But they're the *best* here on the beach when they're gooey and droopy." I thought about how good the chilled cookie dough was that I ate with Trudy the night before, but didn't mention it.

I savored the cookies and the moment we were sharing. He savored the cookies most, I suspected.

"I need to visit Great Auntie Edna when we're done here. Wanna come with me?"

"Great Auntie Edna…sure. I've always liked her. We could always count on her to play with us out here on the beach when we were little. Remember, she even gave us a wedding present?"

"How could I forget?" Frankie scooped up a handful of sand and let it pour like it does in an hourglass. "It's not every day you get a five-pound bag of flour with a ribbon on it."

"It was sweet of her, I guess. She told us to carry it around for one week. Never let it out of our sights. She warned that's what it's like to have a baby. And just because we got pretend married, it didn't mean babies were all fun and games."

"How would she know?" Frankie brushed his hands against each other to clean off the remaining sand. "She was never married and didn't have any kids."

"I'm sure she babysat."

Frankie looked away from me, like he needed to think. "Makes sense. You women know stuff and feel stuff that us guys just don't."

"Yeah, we're *gifted* that way." I accented the word *gifted* by opening my eyes as if I'd been goosed.

"Maybe she'll tell us something about the *Wizard of Oz* we haven't heard before. Or Mr. Baum. Maybe she'll finally confess to having a *fling* with him." Frankie lingered on the word *fling*.

"Do you think she did?"

"Nah. She's always been a spinster. Not a man in sight. But what she's got lots of is Oz books." He nodded. "They're hand signed. There are even some pencil sketches."

"Everyone knows he wrote some of the books while he was here in Coronado, but I didn't know he was an artist too."

"Maybe he wasn't," he said with a hint of a shrug. "We can ask her. She'll tell us."

We got up, shook out the blanket and brushed off everything we brought with us.

It was a short walk to Green Gables, Great Auntie Edna's house. It was just across the street from the beach. "Can't miss it, can we?"

"Nope! I always thought dolls lived in it. I never had a doll house, but Betsy next door had one that looked like Green Gables. She never played with it, and I always wanted to. Isn't that typical? You want other people's stuff and they want yours. Never satisfied. Never content."

We walked up the pathway. I stopped to gaze at the dark-emerald tarpaper shingles on the house's main turret. I studied the sea-green wood siding and the white front door.

"You want to ring the bell? Or should I?" Before I could answer, Frankie playfully pushed me toward the front steps with his shoulder behind mine.

"She's your aunt. Not mine."

"That's right. And you can't have her." Frankie climbed the stairs and put his thumb on the doorbell's button. No response. I looked at the house more closely as we waited. Warped boards. Dust-crusted spider webs. Blistered paint. Scrawny red geraniums in the final stretch of a life sentence in a too-small terracotta pot.

The lace curtain on the door's window was pulled back with a single finger, followed by the one-eyed peek of someone inside. The patinaed brass knob turned and the door opened.

"Franklin, my favorite nephew. And Penelope. My favorite friend of my favorite nephew." The door opened with its familiar—yet welcoming—creaks from hinges in need of oil. "Come in you two. I haven't had visitors in quite a spell...or at least I can't remember if I've had any visitors lately."

"Well, here we are."

I inhaled as we entered the house. I could count on a wave of rose-water perfume to greet me. I wasn't disappointed.

"Let's sit and chat. Shall we?" The elderly woman made her way through the parlor's archway and kept walking. "I'll join you two in a moment. I just want to get us a quick snack. Cookies, perhaps? Looks like you two have been down on the beach. Did she get you into the water, Franklin? You look salty. Am I right?"

"Yes ma'am. She gave me a floating lesson. Worked up a real appetite too. You know me, I never met a cookie I didn't like. Neither has Penny."

I drilled Frankie with my eyes. We shared an eye-to-eye shorthand. We always had. I whispered, "Was that a wisecrack about my weight? I like cookies as much as the next—"

"Then cookies it is," Great Auntie Edna said from the kitchen. "You know, Frankie. One day, all of this will be yours."

I rolled my eyes and pointed at Frankie. I mouthed the word, "Yours?"

Frankie raised both of his shoulders up to his ear lobes and turned his head to the side while keeping his eyes on me. Both of his feet were in motion, jiggling like he was running a fifty-yard dash. I put my hand on his right knee. "Sit still, would ya?"

Green Gables was the place where old doilies went to die…and new ones were born and never escaped. Great Auntie Edna's handiwork-in-progress rested on the chair next to the front window. It was like a blizzard of lacey snowflakes had settled everywhere. On tables. On each chair's arms and head rests. On tea trays. Under lamps.

Green Gables was also the place where time passed for all to see and hear. Each second was tic-tocked by a grandfather clock and several Bavarian cuckoo clocks. Life slipped away there, one little piece at a time.

"I've worked it all out with my lawyer." Great Auntie Edna rounded the corner with a package of Oreos under her arm and a small tray with three glasses of milk on it. "Nothing fancy. If you'd given me some warning, I could've put something more elaborate together for us."

She set the tray down on the oval coffee table as I got up to take the Oreos before they escaped the old lady's armpit.

"Sit down, my dear. Sit down." The Oreo package didn't fall to the ground. She handed us each a glass.

"So, as I was saying, I'm leaving you Green Gables and everything in it. Frankie, you've always been special to me. The *most* special."

"But what about my parents?"

"Oh, they have all they need. And your father will just drink it all away. Or eat it all away. Pigs to the trough. That's how they've lived and I suspect always will be. I'd rather give you a strong start in life. Green Gables can do that. And Frank's things. But you must promise not to flaunt them or, God forbid, sell them."

"Not a chance." Frankie extracted a handful of Oreos and passed the package to me. "They'll be safe with me."

"Safer than the rest of the cookies in this package." I took out two, even though I was starving and could have gobbled a dozen of them.

"My dears, I'm pert-near eighty years old now. But I was once a young lady. In fact, I was just about your age—in my early twenties—when I met Frank down on the beach."

She gazed out the window.

"I know I've told you this before, but I introduced myself to him while he was sketching The Del. We chatted for a while. He told me he was an author and that the shape of the hotel looked just like a place he was writing about: *The Emerald City.* He wasn't a healthy man, but he loved to sit on the beach and tell stories to the children. Gosh, he was around here quite a bit. In all, I believe he wrote three of his Oz books in Coronado."

"What kid hasn't read the books and seen the movie? Pretty amazing that he left that all behind for us."

"Yes, Penny, it is amazing. *He* was amazing. Everything and anything inspired him. Did you know that Oz almost didn't happen?"

"Really?" The pitch of my voice rose as the word passed my lips. I'd heard the story before—more than once—during previous visits to Green Gables, but I didn't let on.

"He told me that story had been banging around in his head for years. But no publishers were interested in it. They told him it was too different. They only wanted Mother Goose rhymes and such. They thought no one would buy a novel for children. He waited long and hard, but it paid off."

Great Auntie Edna got up and pulled a book from the floor-to-ceiling bookshelf. She caught a glimpse of Frankie's legs and feet. "Still jiggling I see. You never were one to sit still. Not that you were wild and broke things. You just never sat still for long." She winked at him as she opened the hard cover and ran her finger along the side as the pages slipped by.

The page flipping stopped. "Ah, here it is." She pulled out a folded piece of yellowed paper. "It's a poem he wrote about Coronado."

She looked up at the ceiling, as if to collect her thoughts. "You know, Frank's characters were real. Real to him, anyway. He told me how things that happened to him landed on the pages of his stories. Like when he was a boy. He loved to run wild in the fields. One time, a scarecrow scared the tar out of him. Ironic, uh?"

I nodded.

"That fear stuck with him and he turned it into a character who has feelings, but can't think. Or at least he thinks he can't. Oh, you know what I mean."

I nodded again.

"Another character came from his days as a traveling salesmen. He'd stop to sell his pots and dishes or whatever he was offering at the time, and he'd be amazed at how the shopkeepers just had paper boxes and junk in their front windows. Frank taught them to design window displays to attract shoppers. To make them curious. One time, he took a pie pan, a funnel and some other kitchen items and created a man made of metal. Guess who that became?"

Frankie and I responded in unison, "The Tin Man."

Frankie's legs were jiggling and I caught Great Auntie Edna staring at them. Her eyes darted away and then shot down as she leafed through the book some more and retrieved another piece of paper. "There's Frank's Emerald City. He gave it to me. It was a special gift on a special day. There was nothing unsavory or inappropriate about our relationship, even though the gossips in our family love to paint a different picture. He was a gentleman, a genius, a married man with children. I was an admirer. Nothing more. Especially no hanky-panky."

"Sheesh." Frankie waved the air with an open palm. "You're embarrassing me."

"Let me see your ears, my dear."

He leaned in closer to the old woman.

"By Jove, you're not teasing this old lady. Your ears *are* rosy red." She turned to me. "They've done that since he was a little sprout." I knew that, but didn't let on. "And he's been jiggling since then. Penny, did you know I used to call him Mr. Fidgety Feet?"

"No ma'am, I didn't."

"Well, I did. And I can see that I can still call him that and it would be an accurate description." She patted his hair and slid her palm down his temple, to his cheekbone and rested on his jaw. "You see? You've always been special to me. That's why I want you to live here someday. Not today. Not tomorrow. But someday."

He didn't say anything. Neither did I. Great Auntie Edna didn't say anything more. The ticking of the mantle clock marked off time as it slipped by.

"Well, what do you think of living here, Frankie?"

"I'd be honored. No, that's not saying it right. It would feel right—no, it would feel more than right—to live here. Thanks for thinking of me."

"What about your wife?"

I turned to Frankie.

"You heard me correctly. Your wife. You two are still married, aren't you? None of that runaway bride business this time?"

We started laughing. Awkwardly.

"This is no laughing matter. In the eyes of the law, you two are still married. You know, that whole until-death-do-us-part promise?"

"That was pretend. We were kids."

"I'm not so sure. I've always sensed a spark between you two. Penny, could you live happily ever after here in the house?"

"I hope I get a happily ever after…period. If that happens here, it would be icing on the cake. And speaking of icing—"

I unscrewed an Oreo and scraped off the white cream with the back of my front teeth. "I wouldn't do this out in public," I said as the icing sloshed around my mouth. "But since I'm feeling more at home here now, I'll act that way. If that's alright?"

"My dear, that's fine with me. Say, Frankie told me you're going to be working at The Del, with Marilyn Monroe no less. You poor thing. Having to deal with that floozy. She's no actress. Just pouty lips and too much eye makeup. Cheap. That's what she is, cheap."

"Well, I'll find out soon enough. And I'm sure it'll be something I'll never forget. Like your time with Mr. Baum."

Great Auntie Edna didn't respond at first. She gazed at me. Then at Frankie. "Yes, I'm certain it will be something you'll *never* forget."

We munched on Oreos and continued to chat.

Frankie stood as he drained his glass. "Time to get going. Thanks for the snack. It hit the spot."

"Yes, ma'am. We should be on our way. Our team bowls tonight. Have to get ready, you know." I hoisted and drained my glass of milk.

"Well, you give that other team a good run for their money." Great Auntie Edna put her glass on the tray.

"We'll do our best." I stood. "Our *very* best and no less."

"We sure will." Frankie turned to face me. "I wonder who we're playing?"

"I have a feeling...not a good feeling. There's one team we haven't bowled against all season."

Frankie took a few steps toward the front door and stopped in his tracks. "You don't mean—"

"Yep. Them."

FADE OUT

CHAPTER 12

FADE IN:
- SEPTEMBER 5, 1958, THREE DAYS UNTIL SHOOTING BEGINS
- INTERIOR, CROWN LANES (NIGHTTIME)

The crisp cracking explosion of a sixteen-pound ball obliterating a cluster of bowling pins had long been a Thursday night occurrence for me. I heard the crash all the way out in the parking lot. The early evening fog glowed around the neon light for the Crown Lanes, softening the outline of a bowling ball with a flashing crown on a make-shift face formed by the eye-shaped finger holes. I saluted the sign on my way toward the alley's open front doors.

The smoke-heavy air pushed back as I walked in.

I spiced up my stride with some swagger, and I swung my bowling bag like a playground swing at recess. I had an arm made for bowling.

Light-catching cocktail glasses and beer bottles dotted the place and made it shimmer. And the usual suspects were lined up at the bar, ass-cracks displayed on just about every barstool. Good old Mimi kept the beer flowing and the wieners turning on a series of hot-metal rollers under a red-hot warming light. The scent of simmering bologna-like meat hung in the air and mingled with whiffs of cheap cologne, cigarette butts, over-used hairspray and sweaty armpits.

The alley was filled with teams representing local businesses and churches. It was no surprise that some sailors were reveling at the far end of the building. The owners always reserved those lanes for servicemen. They could be counted on to drink and draw in women.

An arcade of flashing pinball machines lined the back wall. What a sight. Players were involved in obscene herky-jerky mating dances with flashing contraptions in hopes of scoring more points or a free game, without getting caught tilting the machine. With fingers to flipper buttons, they took the games of chance far too seriously. Signs and artwork of big-bosomed babes enticed them to play "Balls-A-Poppin," "Hawaiian Beauty" and "Grand Slam." As I passed by, bells rang in machine-gun repetition, while players either praised or goddamned their mechanical dates for the night.

I tore myself away from the pinball spectacle to watch the action on the alleys. A couple clever team names on a virtual rainbow of shirts made me laugh. One even made me blow an embarrassing snot bubble. There were the Bowl Movements, the Turkey Baggers, the Pin Pushers, the Gutter Gang, the Dolls With Balls, the Alley Gators, the Thunder Balls, the Gutter Girls and the Wrecking Balls. There was even a team of nuns in black habits. I said softly to myself, "Hope their team name is the Holy Rollers! Damn it. No team shirts. Can't tell."

The way the just-mopped, Pine-Sol-smelling linoleum floor tiles gripped the soles of my shoes made me sigh. Familiar, in a reassuring way. I scanned the entire length of the alley and watched balls rolling in two directions. The ones homing in on the pins and the ones returning to their senders. They took straight-as-arrows roads, up hills, bumping and steadying themselves and standing in single rows. The visual noise created by the checkerboard floor tiles was tamed with aqua walls. But not missing an opportunity to add energy to the room, some painters recently added tangerine geometric patterns.

"Hey, Bobby, what lane are we on? And, who are tonight's victims?" I hollered over the stew of bowling noise and shouting-match conversations in the area.

"Lucky Number Thirteen…and you." His laugh was deep and stretched out.

"Wha-da-ya mean?"

"I mean, you're on lane thirteen and your opponents are going to clean your clocks. Your team gets to go up against The

Sledgehammers."

"Shit. Shit. Shit." I dropped my bowling bag. "Really? I guess we all need to take a turn playing with the Devil himself. Well, like they say, if you have to eat shit, it's best not to nibble. Bring it on. Let's get this over with."

"Say, I understand congratulations are in order. You and Marilyn Monroe? Suppose she won't come here and bowl a few frames, will she?"

"I'm sure I don't know. But *never* say never."

Bobby's gaze shifted to the doorway behind me. "They aren't called The Sledgehammers for nothing. Here they come."

I followed Bobby's eyes and turned my head. My bowling-ball and bowling-pin earrings swung like wrecking balls. Together, we witnessed the entrance of the gladiators: one man and two manly looking women. They walked three-wide and wiped out anyone and anything in their path. An open-palm removed a young man from their way with one shove. Otis, the leader of the pack, was a stockman at the dime store and a human bulldozer. We'd been tangling since his grammar-school bully stage. That transitioned to a high-school bully stage. And that transitioned to him becoming a full-fledged, full-time bully.

Otis stopped and stared at me as he ran his beefy hand along the side of his crew-cut, bucket-sized head. He lifted his right index finger to his right nostril, drew in a deep open-mouthed breath and blew a phlegmy rocket out of his nose and onto the floor.

"Hey, Otis. You and your friends should be called The Bulldozers."

"*Penelope*," Otis returned. "Your group of losers should be called The Fat Asses."

"Classy, real classy."

"And don't be calling me Otis. It's Sledgehammer to you."

"Yes sir, Mr. *Sludge*-Hammer."

Bobby handed me the score sheet and a small red pencil. "Brace yourself. You're going to remember tonight for a long time."

"Let's hope for the right reasons." I whispered as I began to leave the counter, "What a hideous human being. I feel filthy just being near him."

Bobby added, "Don't underestimate him. He's someone to be

reckoned with."

"I just pray we can *wreck* him in the process!"

I'd used the bowling alley's ladies' restroom a thousand times before, but as I headed toward it my mind was racing about the potential for disaster once the balls started to roll. I walked into the men's room and jerked when I'd realized what I'd done and where I was standing. But no guys were around, so I checked it out.

There was piss everywhere. My brothers—and father—would've never gotten away with that at home. Maybe that's why bowling alley bathrooms looked and reeked like that.

Thoughts played roller derby in my head as I took it all in. Geez, it's not some rigged carnival game being played in there. It wasn't like archery or sharpshooting. How hard could it be to stand still and start? How hard could it be to not move until you stop peeing?

I was gazing back again to check for incoming pee-dribblers when something stirred up the arresting scent of a room pickled in a brine of man juices. I was suddenly aware of how thick the air was, as if I could grab a handful of it. Not that I'd want to. It was a stink you could chew.

"Hey, babe. You have the wrong room." The brusk voice continued, though I didn't turn around. "Had too much coffee and gotta drop a deuce."

I lifted my free hand and shielded my eyes like the blinder on a horse. "Sorry. I'll just leave you alone to do whatever you need to—"

Before he had a chance to respond, I was out the door, leaving my words trailing behind. I no longer needed to use the ladies' room.

I walked by lane after lane before stepping down into the players' area. That's when I slipped on something slick and jerked to a steady standing position. "Who slopped their damned beer in our area?" I looked around, my eyes like the beams of a lighthouse.

No one responded.

The Sledgehammers had their bowling shoes on faster than greased lightning. Their bowling balls were in the rack, ready to do their damage. "You better not make any smart-ass cracks about our balls," Otis warned.

"Wouldn't think of it. Your balls are the last thing I'd ever want to think about, much less talk about. Besides, you just said *ass cracks*. That's funny enough for me. For now, anyway."

Frankie and Trudy were already sitting down and changing their shoes. Frankie looked over his shoulder. "Where's Paul?"

"Don't know." I adjusted the cuff on the left sleeve of my shirt.

"Um, yeah, about these new shirts." Frankie pulled at the collar of his. Our team's custom-embroidered shirts hollered "Alley Kats and Kittens" in shocking flamingo-pink thread over midnight-black cotton. I designed them, with contrasting pink fold-out sleeve cuffs.

"Calm yourself. You'll get used to them." I pulled at the hem of mine. "I think they make quite a statement."

"Oh my goodness, yes they do indeed." Trudy nodded several times, like making a series of exclamation points at the end of her sentence.

I put my pink ball on the rack, knowing full well that Otis would be compelled to say something he felt was witty.

"Nice ball. Pink, huh? I've got something *pink* you might like."

"Now, now. Otis, that's no way to talk. You don't want to offend me. Do you?" Trudy winked at him. "Remember, I make your lunch most days. It's never a good idea to get on the bad side of the person who makes your food, now is it?"

"Ah, c'mon. Get all your damn shit together. Let's bowl," Otis ordered. Applying bowling-alley etiquette, Otis looked to his right and left before launching his ball. He froze, tightened his lips to a papercut pinch and let his ball-holding right hand rest down at his side. The spectacle that was starting next to him was the last thing he wanted to compete with.

Handy Sandy was showing off his ambidextrous antics on not one, but two lanes. At the same time, no less. Otis waited as Sandy put on his show. He laid on the floor and pushed one ball with his foot and got a strike. With his palm, he pushed a second ball and got a simultaneous strike in the next lane. Then he got up, grabbed a ball with each hand, threw the first one softly and the second one fast and hard in the same lane. The second ball obliterated most of the pins and the first slow-moving ball cleaned up the rest to score a spare. Bowlers from all around cheered. Otis didn't cheer. His reddened scalp and cheeks told how he felt.

Paul rushed in to join us, barely taking a breath to say hello before dropping his ball on the rack and slipping into his bowling shoes. "I'm here."

Trudy replied, "I was getting worried something happened."

"Oh, it will." I had to say it. I knew it was going to be a night with more twists than a bag of candy canes.

"Now that Nosebleed's here—and Handy Sandy finished his show-offy circus act—we can get started. Us against you—a cashier, a cook, a coach and a cab driver. Wanna quit while you're ahead?"

We looked at each other. I spoke up, "Nope. Let's get to it."

"Alright then." Otis cracked his knuckles and raised his hand in front of us. "See this?" He pulled in his fingers one at a time. "This is a fist of dynamite. I'm gonna light the fuse and destroy those pins."

"You could light a fire with the way you smell." I shielded my nose from the pungent stench of hot French onion soup, wet dog hair and burned Brussels sprouts. "Your breath could melt a garage door. And your butt-smoke makes a Porta-Potty smell like potpourri."

"You have no idea," Otis fired back. "I could make something that would really take your breath away."

"Of that I have no doubt. It's hardly a secret that you regularly crop dust aisles at the store with your backfired fumes. We all know it's you. Did you think we were stupid?"

"Stupid? No. Losers? Yes."

"Yeah, we're going to wipe the floor with yous guys," Blanche added.

Delores, who was sitting next to Blanche, corrected her. "How many times I gotta tell you it ain't yous. It's you." She snapped her gum and blew a bubble that she popped and sucked in.

"You two ladies just bowl me over," I said. "What you see in Otis is beyond me. Some gals like a fox. Others, like you two, like an ox."

Otis looked at me with hell in his eyes. He cocked his right arm back before blasting the ball down the lane. The pins must have shivered as they saw the blur of the ball coming their way. It was like they all jumped to avoid the carnage. Otis could throw a ball and make pins fly.

He turned to face me, hellfire still in his eyes. "You're up, fat ass." The two Sledgehammer girls smacked their chewing gum and giggled at Otis's rudeness.

I picked up my hot-pink ball, the only one with gold-glitter swirls and a four-point atomic-looking starburst on it. I planted my feet and centered myself on the brown dots on the alley's glossy wood floor. I pulled the ball up so it rested in both hands above my chest.

"That has got to be the ugliest ball I've ever seen," boomed Otis. "I'm gonna puke a little bit in my mouth every time you pick that thing up. And those shirts. What's the deal with that damned shit on them?" The girls giggled again. Otis grinned at them.

I mouthed the words, "Score tonight. Soar tonight." I swung the ball back, stepped forward and released it. Down the alley it went, with a slight curve to the right at the end. "God Almighty. The first ball and I get a 7-10 split?"

"You can do it." Frankie could be so encouraging.

"Penny, I'll make you some tapioca if you get this. Whipped cream and cinnamon sugar on top." Trudy's go-to fixes and rewards always involved food.

Otis butted in, "Are we here to bowl or what? Next, you two will be taking off your socks and having a bowling-alley puppet show."

"What a great idea." Trudy let the words slip out before she grasped his insult.

My ball came back up into the rack. I retrieved it and fought the urge to look at Otis, not wanting to be distracted by him. I didn't have to look, however. As I wound my arm back and almost released the ball, someone projected a deep, juicy burp. Instead of releasing the ball, I turned to look at Otis swigging on a dark brown beer bottle. He swallowed. He extended his tongue and traced the circular bottle opening with it. Round and round and round. Blanche and Delores noticed the special attention Otis was paying the bottle, looked at each other and giggled some more.

I turned, wound up my arm and sent the ball sailing.

"Otis. Do you have no manners whatsoever?" We all knew the answer to that question, but Trudy asked it anyway.

"Mmmmmmnope. I. Do. Not."

I shouted, "Yahoo." Then I turned to face Otis. "You pig, you missed it. While you were…um…*loving* your bottle of beer, I picked up the split. We'll be drinking your team's tears before long. Ha!"

That hell-look returned to Otis's eyes. I was concerned this

time, but focused on the game instead. Pride was at stake.
"Where's Ralph?" Otis looked at Delores, then at Blanche, who was pulling a strand of her gum out like it was salt-water taffy at the beach.

"Right here. I'm right here," Ralph chimed in with a half-burned cigarette dancing between his lips. A sagging tube of ashes was hanging on for dear life. Ralph was a bag of bones. He didn't look like he had the strength to even lift a bowling ball. But he grabbed one and threw it like a champ. Smashed the pins to smithereens. He didn't even look at which ball it was or have his shoes on yet. And to top it off, he threw a strike ball. I watched as he released a yodel-like scream that made his pointy Adam's apple bounce around his scrawny buzzard's neck.

"How about a pizza?" I raised my hand to flag down a waitress.
"Put that hand of yours down." Frankie looked at me and made a knock-it-off face.

"But pizza might be just the right thing we need." I capped that statement off with a nod.

"If I gotta watch you eat your pizza backwards one more time, well I—"

"Otis, there's nothing wrong with the way I eat pizza. I like to eat the crust first and work my way to the center. So what? I force myself to be in the same room with you at work when you eat those putrid liver-sausage sandwiches smeared with grape jelly."

Otis harrumphed.

"Okay then. No pizza. This time, anyway." I grinned at Frankie, proud of my effective way of distracting and irritating Otis yet one more time.

I leaned toward Trudy and whispered, "I'll bide my time, like the Wicked Witch of the West. I'll let destiny take care of him."

Trudy patted my shoulder.

I added, "You know, karma's only a bitch if you are."

She batted her eyes at me and looked away. She restrained herself and only let the smallest giggle squeak out.

The game became tighter than anyone could've expected. It included three-strike turkeys and even a four-strikes-in-a-row hambone. There were awkward splits that Otis called Grandma's Teeth. I even scored a Turkey Sandwich, with a spare, then a strike, then a spare.

As we neared the final frame of the game, the scores were

close. Otis clinched his so-called fist of dynamite and readied himself to rocket the ball to the pins.

I watched Frankie's leg jiggle wildly until Trudy put her hand on his knee to slow and ultimately stop its movement. Then I glanced at Paul. I licked my lips and raised my arm. I inhaled like a Hoover vacuum. I felt my eyes bulged and my eyelids tightened. Everyone except Otis, whose back was to the two teams, noticed what I was up to. I remember thinking how I'd rather regret what I'd *done* than what I didn't do.

I put my lips on my bare forearm and blew hard. The blast vibrated my lips and cheeks. The air erupted with a fart sound that caused everyone nearby to look at Otis as he was about to release his ball.

He jerked and let go of the ball late, causing it to make a loud "thunk" as it hit the lane and curved off to the left.

"Tit for tat, as they say." I lowered my arm, cracked a small smile and shrugged.

Otis's face flamed scarlet. "Do that again, and there'll be hell to pay." He boiled over and sputtered like Yosemite Sam. "And I mean it. Hell. To. Pay."

I had no response. Nothing sarcastic. Nothing clever. Nothing apologetic. I just stared at him.

Frankie stood up and got in between me and Otis, who had a storm brewing in his eyes. "Okay. Let's wrap up this game and see where we stand."

"Where you're standing is in *my way*." Otis took a step forward.

Delores got up and took him by the arm. "You're scaring me, Sledgehammer. Come on. They're not worth it. Not worth it at all."

"Fine." Otis sounded disgusted. "But I've got my eyes on you two. At the store. At the beach. Sometime, somewhere, I'll get you back. And you, Penny, payback may come when you're playing step-and-fetch-it for Marilyn Monroe. You'll be as useful as a nun's nipples." Otis bugged his eyes and made deep furrows in his forehead. "No one screws with my bowling stats. Not without paying a price. And I almost forgot to ask if you know who's back in town. Someone from your past who—"

"That's enough, Sledgehammer." Delores shook her head.

"I've had just about enough. No, I've had enough. I'm going

to stand outside and get some fresh air." As I walked away, I added, "So, if anyone asks, you can tell them I'm outstanding!"

By the last frame of the third game, I bowled a spare and a strike. Trudy and Paul racked up more points, enough to beat The Sledgehammers. Rather than cheering and clapping, we discreetly shook each other's hands and packed up our gear. I noticed how other bowlers who'd been decimated by The Sledgehammers in past weeks cautiously smiled and nodded to us.

That victory would be the unavoidable topic of discussion at the dime store the next day. And the talk of many Coronado shopkeepers and restaurant workers and bus drivers and hotel workers.

That night was a game changer.

The Sledgehammers were not invincible.

They were vulnerable. For a few brief moments, anyway.

And that was enough for me.

But Otis threatened us, and he was sure to deliver on that promise.

FADE OUT

CHAPTER 13

FADE IN:

- SEPTEMBER 6, 1958, TWO DAYS UNTIL SHOOTING BEGINS
- INTERIOR, CORNET FIVE & DIME STORE (DAYTIME)

With remnants and leftovers from attics and garage sales, the dime-store's breakroom was an island of misfit furnishings. By design, it was not a place to linger. More of a place to take a load off your feet.

I leaned away from the red-and-white checkered cloth that covered the wobbly card table. Frankie flopped onto the unpadded metal folding chair next to me. "If you're too tired to talk, that's okey-dokey. I too am fluent in silence. I don't speak it often. But I can. Right now, if you like."

Frankie slouched forward, elbows on the table and chin resting on his fists. I nodded, which joggled my mismatched pair of earrings: a red die and a green die with all the correct combinations of dots, but filled with rhinestones. I moved a slender bottle of grape Nehi closer to my side of the card table.

"I just got a fuzzy pair of dice like those to hang from my rear-view mirror." He added, "But mine are both red."

"Well, that's just another thing that makes us special. And look at this bracelet. It's just like a roulette wheel."

"You're a walking, talking Las Vegas billboard, aren't you?"

"Yeah, a real show girl." I rolled my eyes and clucked my tongue.

"So, how's your shift going?" He flipped his right foot over his left knee.

"Busier than a one-legged man in an ass-kicking contest. No, busier than a one-armed wallpaper hanger."

He wiped his forehead with the back of his hand. "Why are you so cranky this morning? Who pissed in your Cheerios?"

"I'm not cranky. But you will be soon, I bet. Otis give you any noogies on your scalp? Indian rope burns? Monkey bites? Wet Willies? Leave any fart landmines in his wake?"

"No, but the day's not done yet. He's just being his usual asshole self."

I took a swig off my Nehi bottle, turned my head slightly and burped. "It's so nice to have friends like you. To be comfortable around. Comfortable enough to burp and know it's okay."

"Sheesh. You can be so vulgar, Penny!"

"That's a highfalutin word. *Vulgar*."

"Awe, don't be so sensitive. I'm just giving you a hard time…because I like you so much. That's how boys show it, don't you know?"

Frankie's leg started to jiggle, up and down so fast that it reminded me of the needle on Trudy's sewing machine when it was securing a long seam. He reached over the table and took a long swig off the bottle. He let it bubble and gurgle in his chest. I could hear it. He shot his eyes off to the left and slid them back to center. "Here comes…but wait." He knocked the bottle back and emptied it.

"You are so going to regret that. Besides, there's sugar in there. I thought you stopped eating anything sugary because it will make you fat? Like *anything* could."

Frankie didn't respond, at least not verbally. He just looked at me with eyes that grew larger and larger and larger. It was like holding a lit firecracker in a game of chicken. Hold it too long and there will be consequences. Painful consequences.

"Frankie. Come on. Let it go."

He straightened his back, lifted his chin and parted his lips. "BBBBRRRRRRRAAAAHHHHHPPP" erupted from his mouth. It was long and resonant.

"THAT was the king of burps. Trophy-worthy, I'd say." I bowed my head in reverence.

"That never gets old. I bet you've done that a hundred times. And I'm still in awe of you." I put my hand on his shoulder. When the rush of that awkward good-friends-don't-touch-like-this feeling hit, I patted his shoulder and pulled my arm back. He didn't move.

Frankie peered down at the folded newspaper on the table.

"What's in the headlines today?"

"I mostly read one article. About the cost of living these days. I'm never going to get ahead at this rate. Says here, the average new house costs $12,000. Average monthly rent is $92. And gas is up to a quarter a gallon and could go higher. Really? More than twenty-five cents a gallon?"

"I can see your point. I just priced a case of Halloween costumes. Almost two bucks each this year."

"And get this: a guy invented something called a microchip. Not the chocolate kind." I ran my finger down to the article about it. "It says it has to do with something called integrated circuit boards. They're not sure how these chips and boards will be used, but it's a—let me see the words they used, uh, yes, here it is—a major break-through for science. That'll go nowhere. Just see. Mark my words. That—"

Trudy burst through the swinging stockroom door. "Anyone see my cones?"

Frankie turned to look. "Ice cream or paper?"

"Paper. Did I interrupt something?"

"No. Not at all."

"Just another world-class effort from the belch-master." I raised my empty soda bottle.

"I'll get 'em for you. They're with the paper goods." He disappeared among the mountain range of cardboard boxes.

"Oh-kay. Thank you. I won't be able to serve the cheapskates their free water at the counter without paper liners." Trudy stretched up to see that Frankie was out of sight and hearing range. She mouthed the words, "He likes you."

"Well, of course he does. We've been married since 1948. What we have is special."

Trudy raised her index finger to her lips and shook her head side to side.

"Honestly. We've seen each other through some horrible stuff."

Frankie returned with a cellophane-wrapped stack of white paper cones. "Eureka! Sometimes it's like panning for gold back here. This time, I hit pay dirt."

"Not just this time, Frankie." Trudy gazed at me, then back at Frankie. "Not just this time."

FADE OUT

CHAPTER 14

FADE IN:
- SEPTEMBER 6, 1958, TWO DAYS UNTIL SHOOTING BEGINS
- INTERIOR, CORNET FIVE & DIME STORE (DAYTIME)

Trudy and I were back at the checkered table enjoying a late-afternoon break. It was hard *not* to enjoy any chance to escape from the monotony of the dime store.

"Ywaaaahhhhhhhh!" The screech of an unhappy cat was unmistakable. But in the stockroom? We both turned. Otis. Of course, Otis would be not just part of that situation, but the instigator.

"I got me some pussy." Otis punched his words like a prize fighter.

"Well that explains a lot. Never thought you were much of a man." I knew I'd pay for such an emasculating comment. I braced myself for a verbal barrage.

Otis used his Superman heat-beam eyes to burn me. The cat he was holding by the scruff of the neck squirmed and swiped at the air.

"This kind of pussy, you over-inflated balloon bitch." He gave the cat a spiteful shake.

It'd been a while since he called me that. It secretly stung every time. But I wasn't going to show it. Not to him. Not ever.

"What in the name of Jesus, Mary and Joseph are you doing? What are you thinking, Otis?" Trudy's words had razor's edges. "Apparently, you're not. Give me that cat. It sounds like a two-pound chicken trying to lay a three-pound egg!"

She marched over in full rescue mode. "Give it to me. Give it to me now." As she got her hands underneath the cat, Otis released it like a used paper coffee cup over a wastebasket.

"You want it? It's yours."

"Can we keep it, Trudy? It's not one of the usual strays and I don't recognize it as one of the neighborhood pets. Our house could use a cat. It could be cuddly on those cold, damp nights." I sprinkled a spoonful of encouragement onto my words.

"I suppose." She hugged the cat. It allowed her to. It settled in her arms and relaxed as Trudy moved away from Otis.

"Damn. If you thought me carrying that cat around by its neck was bad, you don't know anything. When I was a kid, I used to put firecrackers in frogs' mouths—live frogs. Lit 'em and stepped back. What a mess. Tied cans to dogs' tails. Pulled twitchy legs out of Daddy Long Legs spiders. One. At. A. Time. Burned ants with magnifying glasses out on the sidewalk. Chased—"

"Oh, geez." Trudy cut him off. "That will be quite enough."

"I better not see that cat back here in this stockroom."

"You won't. You can count on that, Mr. Sledgehammer."

Otis went back in the store through the swinging doors.

"What makes people like Otis so cruel...so violent?" I really wanted to know.

"Some of that is just the stuff little boys do. It's like they're trying to understand how things work—and how they break. Otis never seemed to move beyond that phase."

"I don't think I could *ever* do those things he talked about."

"Don't be so sure of yourself. In time, you'll learn that—given certain circumstances—we're all capable of violence." Her words frightened me, so I changed the subject.

"What should we call him? Or is it a her?" I posed the question but didn't investigate to find the answer. Trudy did.

"Her." That was her one-word response. She stroked the cat's head and behind its ears. Motorboat-like purring filled the stockroom's stale air.

"Her eyes are green. Really green." I studied them. "How about Ivy?"

Frankie appeared through the doors. "Heard you got yourselves a new pet?" He approached Trudy and rubbed the cat's ears. "Good for you...and this cat."

"We're picking out a name for her. How about Ivy?"

"Ivy? No wonder you don't have any pets. You don't know how to name them." He added, "She's kind of ash-colored. Like cinders. What about Cinderella? Ella for short?"

"I like it. Trudy, call her Ella and see what she thinks. That's assuming you like the name too."

"Ella. Ellllaahhhhhhh." Trudy sang it rather than said it.

The cat pawed Trudy's forearm like a baker kneads bread dough. With closed eyelids and fluttering whiskers, she purred and purred and purred.

"I think we saved a cat named Ella from losing one of her nine lives to a bully bone-head named Otis." Trudy hugged Ella tighter.

"I think so too."

I couldn't imagine what Otis was capable of as an adult considering the bullying he'd done as a kid. But I was going to find out, whether I wanted to or not.

FADE OUT

CHAPTER 15

FADE IN:
- SEPTEMBER 6, 1958, TWO DAYS UNTIL SHOOTING BEGINS
- INTERIOR, CORNET FIVE & DIME STORE (DAYTIME)

"There are so many cracks I could make right now. But—"

"But you won't." Frankie put a tower of boxed jockstraps on the check-out counter. "There are twelve. Put them in a bag. Quick. Please."

"Why the hush-hush, super-secret treatment? Everyone knows that during track season you work at the high school too." I smiled. I turned that smile into a Cheshire-cat grin. A wicked grin.

I shouldn't have done what I did next, but I did.

I should've felt bad about it, but I didn't.

"Hey OTIS!"

"Don't you dare—" Frankie's plea drowned out by the quick reply from Otis.

He hollered back from across the store, "Whaddya want now?"

"Price check on jockstraps. Got a customer with a cool dozen of them. Right here. Right NOW." I held one up, reinforcing the embarrassment I was creating for Frankie.

"Those for him?"

"Uh-huh."

"Let's see. The ultra-small ones are eighty-nine cents. No bulk discount." Otis's voice got louder as he neared the check-out stand.

"They're for the high-school track team. Not me." Frankie

cleared his throat. "And they are all size large."

"When I was on the football team, we all wore extra-large."

"Yeah, and now you're just flabby, fat and lazy. Besides, then you hiked the ball and just stood there like a brick wall as guys tried to plow through you."

"What do you know?" Otis turned to Frankie. "I stood my ground and took it. Like a man. You were always running...running away. Those *boys* you still play with—I mean run with—aren't men. They don't have hair on their backs or ball sacks."

I blinked in an exaggerated way.

That last phrase from Otis shut both of us down.

As *ball sacks* lingered around us, Frankie turned to me. "Please charge it to the school's account."

"Your wish is my command. Here's your bag. Tell the boys to wear them in good health—and to have their mothers wash them regularly to avoid crotch rot, because no one likes the stink of a ripe jock. And be sure to tell them jockstraps aren't slingshots. And not to snap them like they do girls' bra straps. Gentlemen keep their hands to themselves."

Otis raised his eyebrows and fluttered his lashes. "Guess that makes me a real gentleman. I've always liked putting my hands on myself."

"That's only because no one else will." I tacked on, "Next please," even though no one else was in line.

I didn't want that conversation to go any farther.

FADE OUT

CHAPTER 16

FADE IN:
- SEPTEMBER 6, 1958, TWO DAYS UNTIL SHOOTING BEGINS
- INTERIOR, TRUDY'S HOUSE (NIGHTTIME)

"You in there, chickadee?" Trudy knocked on my bedroom door a second time. "Penny, my little hen, are you sleeping already?"

"Yes, I'm in here. No, I'm not asleep."

Trudy opened the door and leaned on the door jamb. "It's late. And tomorrow's your big day."

"I know, I know. Thank you for letting Ella come live with us. I feel awful about leaving tomorrow."

"Not to worry. Ella and I will get to know each other in no time at all. And Otis will never carry her around by the scruff of her neck again."

Ella burst out from behind my door and rubbed herself on Trudy's legs.

"What's keeping you up, Buttercup?"

"I can't decide what to wear to The Del. This is a high-stakes game I'm stepping into."

"How so?"

"Let's face it. It's not hard to be mouthy and rule the dime store. The competition—excluding you—isn't that stiff. At The Del, I'm going to have to be on my best behavior. And my best is not all that good."

"Don't underestimate yourself. And don't overthink this, for gosh sake. Let's just focus on one outfit. Just one."

"I'm all packed. Well, mostly packed. I've kept out the navy dress to wear tomorrow. But I don't know if I want to use the red or the white accessories."

"Either will be lovely."

"But I want to be more than lovely. I *need* to be more than lovely." I sat down on the edge of the bed. "When the man in the uniform with that cute little bottle-cap hat opens the door, I want to fit in. Lovely doesn't fit in. Lovely doesn't fit in at The Del."

"First impressions are so important. You're right. But you're worried about a hotel lobby."

"It's not just a lobby. It's a gateway to another world. The world that—up to this point—I'm only part of at the show, watching movies."

"Yes, this is a golden opportunity. *Your* golden opportunity." Trudy sat down next to me.

"I've had opportunities too. Some I took. Some I didn't. Take it from me, unless you want to stand behind the lunch counter at the Cornet Five & Dime with a trail of regrets behind you, take chances now. Blaze *your* trails." Trudy's hands swirled up in a flourish.

"That sounds incredible. You should write inspirational greeting cards. Say, you could be the next Dear Abby."

"Don't flap that smart mouth at me. I'm doing my best to help you see how wonderful your life is right now. You can make it even more wonderful. After my sweet Vernon passed away, I was lost. I had this house. I had stack of bills to pay and an empty pocketbook to do it with. I had a choice to make…and make it fast. Either to get bitter or get better. I chose better." Trudy released the lace-trimmed handkerchief from its prison under her not-so-shiny gold watchband. She rolled it between her fingers.

"If I got bitter, it would've shredded me like cheddar on a cheese grater," Trudy said. "And I would have brought everyone down with me. You know, destiny and fate aren't magic carpets that get us to where we are in life. We do it. Our choices do it."

"That's what worries me." I smoothed out the blue dress next to me.

"Choices?"

"Uh-huh. My track record hasn't exactly been stellar."

"Everyone—I mean *everyone*—has a chapter or two in their stories they don't want to read out loud. And think about this: it's impossible to start the next chapter in your life if you keep re-reading the last one." Trudy paused to let me chew on that. "Have you learned anything along the way?"

"Absolutely."

"Then your track record is better than you think. There's a good man out there waiting for you, but you must *choose* to find him. And if you find, say a professional man, a doctor or a lawyer who's at the hotel for a conference, for gosh-darn sake be friendly. Choose to sparkle the way I know you can."

"What if he's a Hollywood type? A handsome leading-man kind of guy with dreamy eyes and wavy hair?"

"Then you must be on guard. I read how those pretty boys in Hollywood are like frozen lakes in Minnesota: smooth on the surface and dead-cold beneath. You'll need to watch your back. Your wallet. And most of all, watch your heart."

"That's my problem. When it comes to men, my heart gives my head the finger."

"Oh, dear, that's quite a way of putting it." Trudy squirmed in her spot. She released her handkerchief, wove her fingers together and laid them on her lap.

"I have to admit, though, I'm getting more excited about meeting everyone. Especially if I might meet THE one." I raised and lowered my eyebrows three times, like Groucho Marx. "Just picture me, standing with the sophisticated and glamorous people. A stunning…no, a beautiful stranger approaches me. I've been noticed. Not for my earrings. Not for being crude or crass. No one and nothing will be in my way to finding true happiness." I made my words all sing-song and gushy.

"Oh, really?"

"Yes, really." I got serious. "He'll see me…ME…and think I'm special, in a good way…and want me because I'm different and intriguing. I'll be a *surprise*. Like spumoni ice cream."

"How so?"

"It's not much to look at, I know, but it tastes incredible. You can go your whole life eating vanilla or chocolate or strawberry ice cream. Even pistachio. One at a time. Separately." I lifted my shoulders. "But until you've had them all stirred together for you, well, you just haven't lived. This could be my chance…my chance for *romance*."

"If you say so."

"Oh fiddle-dee-dee," I said in my best Scarlett O'Hara drawl. "I'll think about that tomorrow."

The conversation stopped.

I looked over at the dress and jewelry options.

"Red."

Trudy looked over too. "Yes, *red*."

Would the color of blood and fire bring me happiness? I'd know in just a few hours.

FADE OUT

CHAPTER 17

FADE IN:
- SEPTEMBER 7, 1958, ONE DAY UNTIL SHOOTING BEGINS
- EXTERIOR, HOTEL DEL CORONADO (DAYTIME)

If my life had a soundtrack, a full orchestra would've played a swelling, epic melody like the theme from *Gone With the Wind*. It was like a theater's velvet curtain going up as I stepped out of the taxi.

I took it all in.

All of it.

The air was still, like Mother Nature was holding her breath. Something was coming. I felt it. I paused to take it all in. I'd seen that view before, but somehow this was different. Like the first time.

Palm trees fingering the sky stood outside the entrance of the Hotel del Coronado. The afternoon sun was just behind the frilly Victorian roofline, making the huge building glow. I raised my cat-eye sunglasses. With the dark-green lenses out of the way, I could fully see the beyond-its-heyday resort.

The crisp white gingerbread siding and trimming contrasted with the rusty red shingled roof. Some painters were adding another thick layer of paint to a section of the wall nearby. I wondered if the many coats of paint were holding the place up or if the wood structure was still standing sturdy on its own.

The spires and turrets made it look like a wedding cake on the shore of the Pacific. The uniformed staff manned the doorway, as a stream of tourists and businessmen alike came and went.

"Hey old lady, you're still looking good. You've still got it." I whispered words for only the hotel to hear. Everyone in town referred to The Del like a ship with a feminine "her." The Del was a beauty beyond her prime—yesterday's glamour queen—who applies a too-generous amount of cosmetics to blur the ravages and realities of the past. She reminded me of Tilly, without the sparkly brooches and the flashing theater lights.

But I was going to be a guest of the hotel. Not a neighborhood kid on the beach. Not a visitor for a special dinner in the Crown Room. A genuine guest who would have a key and a room and a pillow.

I took a seat on a blinding-white wood bench to soak up the moment. I watched as a woman practically dragged a young boy by the hand toward the hotel's front door. "Look Mommy."

"Not now. We're late."

He pointed his tiny finger toward the tall smokestack of the hotel's power plant. White smoke coughed out of the brick tower. "Look. It's the cloud factory. I wondered where they came from. Now I know."

She wasn't listening. She missed what her child imagined. His spark of creativity was brushed away like dust on a window sill.

I studied the *swans* gliding by—the stylish and graceful women. I could never be one, but I sure could watch them. Fashionable. Beautiful. Proportioned. Balanced. Swans, yes they were swans.

A man and woman walked by, allowing me to hear a fragment of their conversation. He said, "—for God's sake. That's not a hotel. It's termites holding hands in the shape of a sand castle. Why I wouldn't be caught-"

A high-speed chase of thoughts raced through my mind. I didn't fit in. I wouldn't fit in. Or could I? I'd always been alright with not blending in, like a stubborn lump in pancake batter. Lumpy or not, this was my turn. My chance. My ship. And I needed to convince myself that I wasn't going to miss out.

I looked away and straightened my back. I had just as much right to go through that door and enter Marilyn Monroe's world as anyone.

I rose as gracefully as I could from the bench and entered the just-opened doors. I nodded politely to the doorman. He eyed my suitcase and train case. I was carrying them myself.

I paused as The Del gently embraced me. Though I stood alone, I sensed the warmth of hug and, with some imagination, could hear an it's-so-nice-to-see-you-again welcome. It was as if The Del was a living, breathing thing…a place to *linger* in every sense of the word. The lingering spirits with pasts shrouded in mystery could vouch for it. I had an inkling I'd never feel unsafe there because I'd never feel alone at The Del.

Considering how the outside looked, entering it was like being *inside* a wedding cake.

I stepped up to the registration desk. Having rehearsed what I was going to say, I hoped it would come out with clarity and confidence.

"Yes, my good man. I'm Penny Parker. I shall be assisting Miss Monroe during her stay at The Del. That'd be Miss *Marilyn* Monroe. I believe a room has been reserved in my name. Thank you ever so much for checking to ensure my arrangements are in place." I knew I nailed it. I couldn't believe I got it all out. He had to be impressed. Hell's bells, I was. My words—each of them— were delivered with the clarity of sun-catching water droplets cascading in a fountain.

"One moment, Miss Parker," he replied, with the facial expression of someone who'd encountered a bad smell.

I turned to my right and peered down the counter. It was unfortunate and disappointing that no one was there to see me. It was hard to believe: little ole me registering for my room at The Del.

"Ah, here we are. I do hope your room meets your expectations, Miss Penny Parker."

"You'll be the first to know if it doesn't. Not that it won't. But if it did—"

"Yes, miss. Shall I have a bellman help you with your bags or did you plan to continue to carry them…yourself?" I blew that one. A real lady would not have carried her bags. But, who ever said I was a real lady? Or even wanted to be one. Not me.

I turned and scanned the cavernous lobby, skinned in dark stained wood. A massive chandelier with fabric shades on each light bulb hung in the center of the room. The effect was unmistakable. The shades created an amber glow in the room, the warm color of honey as it joins a cup of tea.

"Quite a lobby you have here. I didn't have an opportunity to admire it when I came in. I'd very much appreciate the assistance of a bellman."

"Very good, miss."

A bellman gathered my possessions and directed me to the golden birdcage elevator. The gilt finish made the elevator car and the cage that enveloped its up-and-down path look elegant, in an old-time way.

I entered the car. "Third floor please. Oh, and say, how long's this elevator been here?"

"Since the beginning, miss," replied the small, maroon-uniformed operator.

"That makes it 70 years old. Is it safe?"

"Yes, quite safe, miss." The Chinese man spoke without making eye contact. "I've been traveling in it all my life."

"Is that so, Max?" The man's nametag caused me to pause and think: I wouldn't have expected his name to be Max. I was jolted by an electric shock. A popcorn-popping sound filled my ears and I saw a flash of white light in what was otherwise a dim elevator car. Without thinking about it, I braced myself by placing my right palm against the car's wall.

"Yes, miss. My father helped build the hotel." He looked at me more closely. "Are you quite well?"

"Yes. I'm fine. Just got a little dizzy there for a second."

"That's to be expected. This is your stop. Perhaps we shall see one another again during your stay."

"Thank you ever so much for the lift." I nodded to him. He retracted the cage's door. I wondered what he meant when he said, "That's to be expected?" Did he know something I didn't?

"Your room is just around the corner. Down the hall a bit. And miss, Max is the name I use only here at The Del." He raised a flattened hand to the side of his mouth and whispered, "My given name is Cheng. It means *journey*." He grinned.

"I'll keep that in mind, Cheng. And I'll keep that to myself." I wondered why he felt compelled to offer up that information.

Miraculously, the bellman was standing at attention with my bags as I exited the elevator. I followed him as I studied the meandering hallway. Its aging paint and uneven carpeting must have had stories to tell about the celebrities, the royalty and the riff-raff who'd spent time there. Walking those halls. Stepping on that carpet.

I broke the silence. "Suppose you've seen it all?" I could've asked that in a more sophisticated way.

"Yes, I've seen a lot. But it's not like it was years ago. Some of the old folks like to tell stories about it. No, they *love* to tell stories about it."

He pointed out how The Del was the undisputed queen of ocean-side resorts in her prime. But people no longer spent "a season" at the shore. He bemoaned how they wanted to travel the nation's new highways and see the sights. The Holiday Inn was the hotel of the future. Actually, it was the *motel* of the future. In and out. Back on the road after a good night's sleep and a quick breakfast.

"Allow me." The bellman opened the door and handed me the key. "Bags in the closet or on the bed?"

"Bed, please. That way I can unpack right away and get organized. I'm not sure if you heard. I'll be assisting Miss Marilyn Monroe during her stay."

"I know it now. I believe Miss Monroe is expected sometime today. I shouldn't say it, not to you anyway, but this will be a day I'll never forget. Her. Here. Me. Here too."

"I share your enthusiasm." I glanced at his nametag and added, "Robert."

"And if Kate pays you a visit, be nice to her. Best to stay on good terms with the dead, I always say."

"I know all about her. I've seen her on the beach. More than once."

"We're not to talk to guests about her, but since you'll be working here, you should prepare yourself. Things move. Things flicker and glow. Things, oh, I should stop. Just let me know if there's anything I can do to make your time here pleasant."

"Thank you ever so much, Robert."

He closed the door behind him.

I sat on the edge of the bed, slipped my shoes off and exhaled. There was a three-ring binder and a clipboard on the desk. I looked out the window on to the northern stretch of beach and then back at the binder and clipboard, debating about going through the paperwork or waiting until after I'd unpacked. Waiting won the debate. I opened the window and a fresh sea breeze rushed in to dissolve the musty air that lingered in the room. "That's better."

I put the train case in the bathroom. "No counter?" I looked down at the small white octagon-shaped tiled floor and slid it under the pedestal sink.

Unpacking my suitcase was next. Each skirt, blouse and dress came to life as it was lifted out and hung in the wardrobe. Shoes lined up like soldiers on the lower shelf. An oblong envelope fell on the floor. It must have been tucked inside my clothes. "Penny" was written on the front. I opened the envelope and unfolded its note. My eyes slid down to the bottom and found Trudy's signature.

"My dear Penny. Please know that you have my wishes and dreams with you on this adventure. Take risks. Have no regrets. I'll keep some tapioca and cookie dough in the ice box in case you come back to visit us. With much affection, Trudy. PS: Ella purrs her best wishes to you too."

That was just like Trudy, to do something so sweet. I missed her already, but was comforted to know she was just a few blocks away.

I pulled out my jewelry bag and put it on the small table next to the clipboard and binder. CONFIDENTIAL yelled at me from the cover. Yelled at and enticed me. "I surrender!" I flipped open the binder's cover and sat in an old, but sturdy white wicker chair. Some of the thick paint chipped and fell on the cushion. It may have been sturdy, but its layers of paint were not.

"Miss Parker, congratulations and welcome to the *Some Like It Hot* team."

I looked in the mirror and said in my best breathy Marilyn accent, "Oh, yes. Some like it hot. And some like it *very* hot." My best Marilyn ended up sounding more like a crappy Mae West.

The cover letter went on to describe the contents of the binder. I was to review the information in preparation for the next day, when "your dreams would come true."

How do they know what my dreams were? They must've meant meeting Marilyn Monroe.

I looked at the pages behind the pink tab labeled ABOUT THE FILM and stopped when something seemed interesting or unfamiliar. I noticed that until just a few weeks ago, the film was called *Fanfares of Love* and then *Not Tonight, Josephine*.

I slowed down to read the story's summary. I'd been through some of it before, but I figured I better go over it again.

After two Chicago musicians, Joe and Jerry, witness the St. Valentine's Day massacre, they must get out of town and get away from the gangster responsible, Spats Colombo. They're desperate. The only jobs they know of are in an all-girl band heading to Florida. They show up at the train station as Josephine and Daphne, the replacement saxophone and bass players.

They have no time to get used to dressing as women. However, they enjoy being around women, especially Sugar Kane Kowalczyk. She sings and plays the ukulele. Joe sets out to woo her while Jerry, who's now Daphne, is wooed by a millionaire, Osgood Fielding III. Mayhem ensues as the two men try to keep their true identities hidden. To make matters worse, Spats Colombo and his crew show up for a meeting with several other crime lords.

I flipped forward to a tab labeled, ABOUT THE DEL. A list of milestones and facts about the resort traveled across several pages. The dollar amounts in one entry caught my eye: The Del cost $600,000 to build and $400,000 to furnish. It was a technological wonder of its day as it was lit by electricity. At that time, the hotel was one of the largest buildings in the country to have electric lights. The hotel was heated by steam and fireplaces, and featured elevators and telephones.

I ran my index finger down the list and muttered "blah, blah, blah" then "something, something, something."

I stopped to read that The Del was conceived by two retired businessmen, Elisha Babcock, Jr., and Hampton Story, who became acquainted after moving to San Diego. In 1885, the entrepreneurs bought the entire undeveloped peninsula of Coronado.

The list of celebrities who'd stayed at The Del over the years was impressive. It included Lillie Langtry, Al Jolson, Greta Garbo, Ginger Rogers, Jimmy Stewart, Robert Taylor, Olivia de Havilland, Bette Davis, Mickey Rooney, Judy Garland, Humphrey Bogart, Lauren Bacall, Walt Disney, Joan Crawford and Doris Day.

In a matter of minutes, Marilyn Monroe would be added to the list. And my life would change for-e-ver.

FADE OUT

CHAPTER 18

FADE IN:
- SEPTEMBER 8, 1958, FIRST DAY OF SHOOTING
- INTERIOR, LOBBY OF HOTEL DEL CORONADO (DAYTIME)

It was time. The time. THE time to meet the Hollywood bombshell herself. First, as requested on my agenda for the day, I needed to meet one of Marilyn's regular assistants at the round table under the chandelier in the lobby.

I stood there, doing my best to look like I fit in. Not like an imposter. Not like a fraud. But inside I felt like a third grader on a museum field trip.

"Pleasure to meet you, Miss Parker."

"How'd you know it was me?"

"The binder gave you away." The woman cracked the tiniest slit of smile. "You know what you're in for, right?"

"Yes, I believe I do."

"I believe you *don't*." The nameless woman continued. "Follow me."

I was speechless. A rare occurrence, indeed.

We walked by the golden birdcage elevator I'd just exited. "Cheng, how nice to see you yet again." He smiled in return as the ceiling light flickered and went dark for a few seconds.

"Follow me. Please keep up. There's a reception area in Miss Monroe's cottage where we can talk."

No more words were spoken until we walked through the hotel's expansive, palm-filled courtyard, through a doorway and down a short flight of stairs. The sign next to the building read "Mar Vista Cottage."

A familiar face greeted us. "Miss Parker. We've been expecting you."

"Officer Strong. How nice of you to expect me." He stood firm at the door. His words were warm, but his body language was that of a guard on duty. "And my name is Penny. Isn't that what you call me at the dime store?"

"Yes, it is, but not while I'm here protecting and serving."

He opened the reception area's door. The woman extended her open palm toward a high-backed couch, flanked with two end tables. "Have a seat. We can talk openly here. Marilyn's out on the patio with Paula and the door is closed. They're in their own world now. May I call you Penny?"

"Please do."

"Penny, first off, I need to apologize for how I treated you in the lobby and on the way over here."

"Oh, not a problem. I punch a cash register for a living. I meet all kinds of people who treat me in all kinds of ways."

"Well, we need to project professionalism when we're in public spaces. We're Miss Monroe's representatives. We're here to take care of her every whim. However, when we're alone, we can be ourselves. Are you comfortable with that?"

"I've never been uncomfortable being myself. It's the *projecting professionalism* that I'll need to work on."

"Fine. My name is May. May Reis. I've worked with Miss Monroe on several pictures. I just flew in from New York City to be with her. I'll be in the background this time, though, because you're here. You should know that she's a handful. Lucky for you, she'll rely on Her Holy Highness Paula Strasberg for most things. You get to handle the overflow."

"Overflowing has never been a problem for me. Just look at my waistline." I'd done it again, pointing out my flab.

"You're cute as a button. But I must tell you, working with the most beautiful woman in the world is no walk in the park. Here's what you need to know. You might want to take a few notes in your binder to keep track of the do's and don'ts."

I was about to get a crash course in all things "Marilyn." Seemed like overkill for an eight-day assignment, but I was all ears. I readied my pencil and pad for a workout.

May started with Marilyn's preferences and pet peeves. "Let's start with food." Marilyn loved meat. Her breakfast routine: two uncooked eggs stirred into a glass of warm milk. Lunch and dinner always had meat and a side of vegetables. Grilled steak topped her list of favorites. Favorite drink: Dom Perignon. Favorite dessert: an ice cream sundae, though she'd already discovered The Del's cold soufflé vanilla pudding and she couldn't get enough of it.

"I like pudding." I felt the need to inject myself into the conversation. "I wonder if she'd like my landlady's tapioca? It's the best outside of Minnesota. At least that's what she claims." May went on. Marilyn's favorite perfume was Chanel No. 5. Mozart and Beethoven—as well as Louis Armstrong—created her favorite music. Her favorite store was Bloomingdales and her favorite flower was the rose.

Marilyn was slipping down Hollywood's merciless ladder. She was aware the public was more interested in Liz Taylor and Debbie Reynolds, and how the press loved nothing more than shooting stars and falling stars. "From what you've heard, I bet you know which of those two kinds of stars people think Marilyn is these days." May made a tsk-tsk sound.

"Marilyn has the uncanny ability to pull people in with a grin or a glare. But never touch the talent." She added, "Even if they touch you first."

May reported that Marilyn could be late. Often. Almost always. And she wouldn't appear to be concerned about how her lateness impacted other people.

"Where ever she is and no matter who she's with, all eyes will be on Marilyn. She's a force of nature who has a magnetic pull all her own. And on camera, she's bewitching. Other actors have been known to be bothered by this gift of hers…to steal away every morsel of attention from everything and everyone else."

Marilyn wouldn't have many visitors. She'd rely on few people. Jack Cole was her go-to dance instructor, while Sydney Guilaroff was always on hand to do her hair, which had been recently lightened to what Marilyn called "white blonde."

She didn't often mingle between takes. She prepared her lines privately, emerged from her dressing room, delivered what she needed to and then returned to her dressing room. "You'll find that it requires her many takes to get it right, in her eyes and in Paula Strasberg's eyes. She's her acting coach and she guards the gates to Marilyn. And she's a mighty gatekeeper. You can't miss her. She's all Bohemian and East Coasty in her black clothes—only black—no matter how hot or cold it is. Don't be a nuisance to or make an enemy of Paula. If you do, you're cooked. She and Marilyn go together like Fred and Ginger."

May paused and grinned. "Paula practices *the method* style of acting."

"I've heard about that."

"Yes, it means you tap into your own experiences to help you perform. It's terrifying, I hear, for actors to learn and use. They must be vulnerable. So vulnerable. And Marilyn's already vulnerable enough."

"Hmmmm—"

"She's sensitive and fragile. Sometimes brittle. And the men, well the men sense something else entirely. They want to take care of her and for her to take care of them, if you know what I mean."

"Will her husband be here?"

"That's the plan. Mr. Miller is up in Los Angeles working on a script for her next film, *The Misfits*. They're so in love, until they aren't. If you ask me, he doesn't give her much room to fit in. So, she's left on the outside of things, a lot. He had to know she was the main attraction in their relationship and the bankroller. No man can take that for long. At least I don't think so."

I shot May a curious glance.

"Don't worry about it now. You'll understand soon enough. Anyway, Marilyn's quite nice. Fragile, though. I expected her to be more sure of herself when I first started this job. She isn't. I guess none of us really are if we're honest about it."

"Hmmmm…"

"Although her first instinct is to like everyone, Marilyn is incredibly quick to sense if someone doesn't like her. The minute she gets that negative vibe…BAM…she drops the person immediately."

"Will she talk to me?"

"Yes, but let her take the lead."

"I had no expectations—no expectations at all—of even sitting in her presence."

"Penny, she's not Queen Elizabeth. You'll find that she—"

The patio door opened. A controlled, well-articulated voice announced, "She is ready for you." I jerked myself up to a standing position as if I'd heard a gunshot.

"Ready?" May rose to her feet.

"As ready as a racehorse."

"Then brace yourself. You're about to do something very, very few people get to do in this lifetime: meet the one and only Marilyn Monroe...in her bedroom."

FADE OUT

CHAPTER 19

FADE IN:
- SEPTEMBER 8, 1958, FIRST DAY OF SHOOTING
- INTERIOR, MARILYN MONROE'S COTTAGE (DAYTIME)

"I don't give a good goddamn what he says! Or what that asshole wants! You tell him I'm not like a...what was it he said? Oh, yeah, an *overripe* peach on its way to the trash can. As far as I'm concerned, he can go fuc—" Marilyn's voice was unmistakable. Breathy like in the movies, but with broken-glass edges on her words as she spoke them.

May hesitated at the doorway, looked in and nodded to me as if someone had nodded to her first. "Here we go," she whispered out of the side of her mouth. "She's good now." I told myself to be good too. I also told my lungs to keep breathing so I didn't pass out.

May guided me into the room.

I saw nothing but Marilyn's face.

Everything else faded away.

"I'd like to introduce Miss Penny Parker." May backed away, leaving me front and center. "She's going to be with us during our time here at The Del."

"You're the contest gal...the *winner*." Marilyn blinked in slow motion, just like in her movies.

"Yes. Yes, I am. But I've never thought of myself as much of a win—" I stopped speaking and wished I could eat those last words.

Marilyn hummed as her eyes took a walk all over me. "They told me I'd have an extra pair of hands during this shoot. How lovely."

I glanced down at my hands.

"Not your hands, honey. I meant how lovely to have *you* with us." Marilyn scooped some of her platinum bangs to the side and took a step forward.

I repeated the same words in my head. *Don't blow it. Don't jinx it. Don't blow it. Don't jinx it—*

"The pleasure's all mine, Miss Monroe. Truly."

I was so determined to not come across as some silly star-struck spectator and I was successful for all of about ten seconds. My eyes stretched wide open to the size of hub caps as I added, "God Almighty. You're so much more beautiful than your photographs and movies." My words exploded like popcorn tap dancing in hot oil. Her stunning beauty, however, made me instantly feel the opposite of beautiful. "Did that just come out of my mouth? I'm so sorry. I think and speak at the same time…and usually I speak more than I think."

I'd blown it.

I'd jinxed it.

After a few awkward moments of silence while my heart rat-a-tat-tatted in my eardrums, Marilyn flashed a wedding-dress white grin. "I can see we don't need to coax you out of your shell." She added, "We're going to get along famously. I'm certain of it."

Marilyn turned on the ball of her bare foot. The glamourous, camera-ready waves of her hair followed her with a momentary delay and a slight ricochet effect. Marilyn studied her reflection in the sliding-glass door and then in a floor-length mirror. She peeled open her white terry-cloth beach wrap and dropped it to the ground.

"Penny, give me your first impression. What do you think of this swimming suit?"

A not-so-subtle wave of Chanel No. 5 passed over me, along with an undercurrent of sweet vanilla.

I took a few steps forward and my right foot collided with a coffee table leg that I didn't see because I couldn't stop looking at her. When I did gaze down to see what caused the clinking sound, I spotted three nearly empty white-ceramic custard cups settling back into their places. Oddly, there were no spoons.

"I'm such a klutz. And that just scared the bejeezus out of me." I put some fingers over my lips. "I sure hope The Del doesn't have a you-break-it-you-bought-it policy or I'll be broke before I leave this room!"

I shrugged and squinted like a child who just spilled a glass of milk.

Marilyn licked the spoon in her hand—which I hadn't noticed until that moment—and winked at me. We exchanged a knowing-sort-of look. It was clear who'd emptied those custard cups.

"You'll have to excuse my lack of manners today." Marilyn shifted the spoon to her left hand and reached out her right one. "It's a pleasure to meet you, Penny." Her skin was as soft as a grandmother's kiss.

"Well, what do you think...about this getup?"

I inspected Marilyn's front side, then glanced at her backside. Was she expecting me to say va-va-voom or something like that? I just couldn't. "It's just awful. Doesn't do a thing for you." I shook my head.

"I agree, but I'm going to do my best to sell it out on the beach...and for the cameras. Even for me, though, it's going to be a tough sell." She giggled a bit. "At least I'll look better in it than Jack. He's wearing the same one, with a wig and ghastly makeup." She leaned over and set the spoon down on the coffee table, next to the three custard cups.

A recent newspaper headline flashed in my mind: Blonde Bombshell: Part Little Bo Peep, Part Mae West. Without editing in my head, I said, "More Peep than West, except that arm hole. That's all Mae West."

Marilyn was either confused or had smelled something bad. She must not have followed the Peep/West comment.

"Sorry. Just me speaking and thinking out of order again. I was remembering a headline that described you as part Little Bo Peep and part Mae West."

"I kinda like that." She rested her open palm over her heart. The tips of her elegantly extended fingers touched her chest one at a time. She worked her eyelids like a skilled geisha with two painted-paper fans.

The dark navy-blue wool swimming outfit did showcase Marilyn's legs. As for the middle of her, the swimsuit was a barrier to her beauty and her curves, except for the arm holes which were loose enough to show some breast if she turned just right. "I've always admired Mae West." While gazing at herself in the mirror, she scrunched her nose, making it clear she didn't admire what she was wearing. "Beats being called 'the tart with a heart,' I guess. Hmmmm, girls back in the '20s didn't have it easy." Marilyn pulled at the top's white band of piping. "I don't even want to know what this thing smells like—or looks like—wet."

"You will. We *all* will." I couldn't believe I'd just said that.

"I know, I know. The script calls for me and the orchestra girls to be in the surf this afternoon. Splashing and playing around. Jack too."

A stout woman in a simple black dress came through the doorway. "This is true. You will be in the water. And the wool *will not* smell of violets and roses. But you *will* give Mr. Wilder a performance that will awe him."

"This is Paula Strasberg, my acting coach. Without her, I'd struggle even more than I do. She brings out my best. Don't you, Paula?"

"The talent is all yours...a true gift. I am delighted I can assist you in honing your craft." She turned to face me. We shook hands. It was a limp one. "You work in a dime store. Is that correct?"

"Yes ma'am. I do. But I believe I've been lingering around there far too long. Treading water, you might say. And you know what happens to someone who treads water too long, don't you?"

"No. Tell me, please." Annoyance dripped from her words. I must've been talking too much, at least in her opinion.

"You drown, that's what. Working with you fine folks is just the lifeline I didn't know I was looking for!"

I caught Marilyn as she shrugged and smirked.

Paula continued, "I assume you have been briefed on your role and, more importantly, what your role is *not*." This time she pounded her words like a secretary on a typewriter. Precise. Paced. Punctuated.

"Yes, ma'am. I've been briefed. And I'm a quick study. I promise, you've only seen the tip of this iceberg."

"Iceberg or not," Paula said, "you'll do as you're told."

"I'll do whatever I can to be an asset—and not an ass."

Marilyn giggled. "Now that's refreshing. You keep that up. I need more straight-talking people in my life."

I looked at the floor while my cheeks flamed. I rarely blushed. "People are much too controlled around me. It's not like I'm in control of myself...or much of anything! Besides, I've been getting more selective lately about who I spend time with. You know, I can only give so much of myself. Honestly, I try to give to everyone, but I only have so much affection. I'm not going to waste mine on anyone who's against me."

She blinked in slow motion again, which drew me in more. I couldn't stop staring at her. She was impossibly beautiful, even in that horrible wool swimming suit.

"From now on," Marilyn confided in a girlish whisper with words spoken as if they were floating on pillows, "I'm saving my friendship for people who matter most."

Marilyn's words lingered.

"Okay then. Congratulations on winning the contest that brought you to us. And thanks for making me laugh."

May and I left the room. After the door closed behind us, I turned to May and mouthed the words *HOLY SHIT*. She put her open palm on her forehead. May raised her index finger to her closed lips. She plopped on a chair. I stayed standing.

"First impressions. You only get one. And did you ever make the most of yours."

"I couldn't help it, I—"

"Penny, you're in. It's not like there's a test or anything. But you passed. I've never seen anyone behave the way you did with her. Much less get away with it. No, you didn't get away with it. You nailed it. You could be the secret weapon this film needs to keep her at ease and on task."

"I keep reading about how she slows things down or refuses to show up even for work."

"That's true. But there's more to it than even the columnists know. You'll see for yourself. You'll learn. For now, be happy that you're in the club. Keep playing your cards right."

"But I have a terrible poker face."

"Yes, I've seen that. Remember, though, this is not a poker game. What we're part of has much higher stakes."

The deep voices of two men talking outside stole our attention. A crisp knock on the cottage's door came next. May opened it to find a bellman with a vase of blood-red roses.

"Where would you like them?"

May spoke up. "Over here, on the table by the window." The bellman put them down, turned and disappeared like a phantom. "We're to answer the door." May fluffed one of the blooms. "Marilyn won't and shouldn't, even with the policeman on guard." Marilyn opened her room's door and poked her head around the jamb. "Did I hear someone knock?" She spotted the flowers. "My favorite. Any color will do. I just adore roses, don't you?" "Yes. Absolutely." I accented my response with a nod. Marilyn coaxed the notecard from the envelope. "WHAT'S THE NEXT LINE? WATCHING YOU," she read aloud. "Watching you? That's odd. In all capital letters. No one signed it."

"I wouldn't give it much thought." May turned to me and added, "She gets all sorts of gifts from admirers. From beef steaks to bangle bracelets, we've seen it all. I accept them on her behalf. We can't have just anyone standing in the doorway gawking at Miss Monroe."

"It's Marilyn. May, have her call me Marilyn too." She slid her fingertips around the edges of the card as her gaze shifted out the window. "I'm sorry, Penny, you must call me Marilyn. I didn't mean to talk to you through May. That's something I detest when men do it. They do it constantly at the studio. As if a woman's not sitting right there. Instead men will talk as if you might as well be the salt shaker on the table."

"Call you Marilyn, at all times. I can do that. Yes, ma'am."

"And no ma'ams, please. Old ladies are ma'ams. Just Marilyn. Just plain-old Marilyn."

There was nothing plain about this Marilyn.

But maybe she'd let me see her plain side.

Maybe.

FADE OUT

CHAPTER 20

FADE IN:
- SEPTEMBER 8, 1958, FIRST DAY OF SHOOTING
- EXTERIOR, HOTEL DEL CORONADO (DAYTIME)

For anyone on Coronado Beach without sunglasses, the sunshine had to be blinding. Yet, the stars shined even brighter. Hollywood's machinery was kicked into high gear on the sand in front of The Del despite the breeze.

"Everyone—that includes you spectators—please keep your motion to a minimum." The man with a bull horn warned, "This is highly sensitive and extremely delicate camera equipment. Flying sand will take its toll. And our stars won't like it much either."

"Marilyn. We're ready for you." Billy Wilder reached out to his film's star and directed her to the water. Jack Lemon and a group of girls were heading there also in their wool swimsuits and white bathing caps.

"Now I need you to frolic and play and splash and giggle and jiggle." His German accent was extra apparent when he said *giggle and jiggle.*

"Anything you say, Billy." Marilyn untied the terry-cloth belt on her short white beach cover up. The crowd of rubber-necked onlookers cheered and jockeyed for position. She smiled and raised a hand high to wave and acknowledge them. There I was, right in the thick of it all. Among *the talent*, to use a Hollywood term. Just a whisper away from the most beautiful star in the galaxy.

Jack yelled, "Last one in's a rotten egg." He lifted his fists above elbow height. He stopped to look at his biceps. Then he opened his fists, relaxed his fingers and twisted his hands outward. His biceps instantly slackened and nearly disappeared. He took a step with his right foot and popped out his right hip. Then he stepped with his left foot and popped his left hip out. He shouted "Magic Time!" and dashed off into the surf.

Marilyn stayed where she was. She looked over at Paula. Clad in a black dress, shaded by a black umbrella, wearing oversized black sunglasses and a black scarf that was wrapped around her head to keep her hair in place, Paula nodded and encouraged Marilyn to get started. I was so close that I couldn't help noticing how Paula's lipstick perched itself on the ends of each hair of her not-so-pale moustache, like teeny-tiny red-headed matches.

With closed eyes, Marilyn shook her hands at the wrists, like a baby bird readying itself to take its first flight. She chanted, "Relax, relax, relax."

"May, why's she doing that?" I also asked her, "Won't she dislocate her wrists?"

"Marilyn insists that all actress have their ways to get them pumped up and ready to perform. Shaking out her hands is her way. That's it, far as I know."

I glanced down at my clipboard and then up at Marilyn a couple of times. "Well, it's all just so exciting."

May pushed my clipboard away so I'd look at her. "Marilyn's taken an instant shine to you. Not like I've seen her do before. Please be careful, though. She's fragile."

My eyes followed Marilyn as she joined the other cast members in the water. "I feel a connection with her too. It's strange. I'll be careful. You can count on it."

"I hope so. I just felt like I needed to hear it from you. Everyone seems to want a piece of her and they'll do anything to get it. Makes me sick to watch. She sees it most of the time. But not every time. Mark my words, a second divorce is in her future. We can blame her mother. Her father. Or the studio boys. Or boys in general. Or women for that matter."

I raised my clipboard. My beach ball and beach umbrella earrings danced in the sea breeze.

"I'm sorry. I'm making you uncomfortable." May put her hand on my arm.

"No. Really. You're not. It's just—"

"Just what?"

"It's just—"

"Towel for Miss Monroe. Pronto. Salt water in her eye." The words of the man with the bull horn rose above the roar of the surf.

"That's my cue. See ya, May."

FADE OUT

CHAPTER 21

FADE IN:
- SEPTEMBER 8, 1958, FIRST DAY OF SHOOTING
- EXTERIOR, CORONADO BEACH (DAYTIME)

"Cameras are rolling. Action." The slate boy moved out of the camera's frame. Marilyn's eyes were closed and she shook her hands at the wrists. She snapped out of her actor-prep trance, took Jack's hand, and the pair scampered out of the surf and headed toward some open beach umbrellas. They each picked up a towel and started to dry off. Jack peeled back his bathing cap and luckily his wig didn't come off with it. She didn't wear a bathing cap, which left her hair in a windswept tangle. One of the other girls picked up a beach ball and tossed it to another as the pair passed by.

"You know, Daphne—I had no idea you were such a big girl."

Jack said, "You should have seen me before I went on a diet."

I turned to May and whispered, "Finally. It's about time Hollywood talked about *big* girls."

Marilyn continued with her eyes glittering, "I mean your shoulders—and your arms—"

"That's from carrying around the bull fiddle." Jack turned to face Billy. "You sure you want me to say *bull fiddle* and not *bass fiddle*? It feels more like I'm carrying around a big bird house!"

"Cut. Stop rolling." The bullhorn man halted the production.

"Yes, Jack. Daphne would say *bull*."

"Got it."

Billy instructed, "Take it back to the shoulders-and-arms line."

Jack and Marilyn got back into character, jumping up and down. Marilyn flapped her hands and chanted, "Relax, relax." Jack let out some girlish giggles and a quick "Magic Time!" And they picked up where they left off.

"I mean your shoulders—and your arms—"

"That's from carrying around the bull fiddle."

"But there's one thing I envy you for." Marilyn delivered her lines perfectly.

"What's that?"

"You're so flat-chested."

Jack peered down at the top of his bathing suit and back up to Marilyn's face.

She continued, "Clothes hang so much better on you than they do on me."

His gaze dropped from Marilyn's face to her breasts.

One of the other girls yelled, "Look out, Daphne!" Jack looked up in time to catch a beach ball.

"Sugar, come on. Let's play ball." And the two ran toward the hotel.

"Cut. Let's do it again, from the top this time. Out in the water and up on the beach."

"Yes, Mr. Wilder." Marilyn winked at the director. "Of course, Mr. Wilder."

Comments were mumbled as Jack and the girls put on their caps and headed back out to the surf.

May turned to me. "At least she got her lines right."

But that wouldn't last.

FADE OUT

CHAPTER 22

FADE IN:
- SEPTEMBER 8, 1958, FIRST DAY OF SHOOTING
- EXTERIOR, CORONADO BEACH (DAYTIME)

I pulled at the right side of my too-tight cat-eye sunglasses to relieve the pressure. I loved those glasses, but wished they'd come in extra-large. I slid them up to the crown of my head, but was momentarily blinded as the sun electrified the peaks and ever-moving ripples of the water's surface. The intense glare made tears flow over my bottom eyelids. I had the same sensation on my back as sweat slid down from my neck.

"Why don't you take a break? They'll be at this for a while, up here on the dry sand by the hotel. Then they'll break. Marilyn will rest in her tent. I'll cover for you if anything comes up. Shoo!" May made a sweeping motion with her hands.

I headed straight to the shoreline, to put my feet in the water and cool off.

The moist breeze caressed my face in a familiar to-and-fro rhythm that copied the ocean's rolling surface. The same breeze puffed up my calf-length skirt, making it swing wildly like the Liberty Bell on Independence Day. The sandals that dangled from my left hand helped anchor the free-spirited skirt.

I put my sandals down on the firm sand, and placed my binder on top of them. "Stay." I ordered them as if they were a pair of puppies on the back porch.

It was such a relief to drag my feet through the chilly shallow water. I'd always felt comfortable in the water. I was naturally buoyant. After all, according to my mother, I was "a natural-born fish." She told me about a gazillion times that the kitchen was never so clean as the years I took baths in the sink. I soaked the whole room and she had to wipe and mop even if she didn't want to. From kitchen sink to bathtub to God's great ocean, I never feared water. The only place I felt more at home was a darkened movie theater.

The shoreline was deserted, except for the jittery sandpipers that ran back and forth with each wave in search of tasty tidbits below the sand's surface. The masses were up on the beach, teeming around the filming area like ants around a just-spit-out piece of candy on a hot sidewalk.

A small boy with an oversized sand pail, knee-deep in the water, caught my eye. I scanned up the beach to see who was watching over him. It was only me.

I studied how the surf had eaten away layers and layers of beach near the water's edge, creating a steep ledge and cutoff from where the dry sand stopped and the wet sand started. I watched the water swirl. Black sand danced over the grittier tan sand, with gold flakes shimmering in contrast. Kids in Coronado learned early on that what they thought was gold was mica flakes that washed down from the hills to the ocean.

I reached down to snag a sand dollar out from a tangle of seaweed. There was a familiar tugging at my ankles. The ocean was sucking back its water like a child inhales in front of a candled birthday cake. As I looked toward the sea, an extraordinary swell was forming and about to crest.

The force nearly knocked me over. As I struggled to gain my footing, I witnessed the boy with the pail in the distance being kidnapped by the ocean. Another riot of water and sand, along with seaweed and kelp, exploded on the shore. I steadied myself, moved up to the firmer sand away from the water and ran toward the boy.

"HELP! There's a child in the water. HELP!" I yelled just as the Hollywood man with the bullhorn started speaking again. His words drowned out mine.

The boy's head bobbed up. He gasped for air, never saying a word. Then he slipped under. I ran into the surf toward him, looked back and saw that no one else noticed.

Another wave knocked me over. My skirt drank up ocean

water, weighing me down.

"Damn it to hell!" I swam out to where I'd seen the boy's head. I was nearing the surf line. I knew the water was deep and I was in the crash zone. My clothes—no, my skirt—was holding me hostage. As I watched the surface of the water for the boy, I began to undo the skirt's zipper to free myself from the heavy anchor. His head broke through the foam as water rose to create another wave.

I yelled at him. "Keep your head up!" He didn't say anything in return. He looked at me, straight in the eye. Then his face slid under the surface.

I abandoned my attempt to get out of my skirt and swam toward him, my arms thrashing the water like a speedboat's propeller blades. I could see his face looking up. His hand was even closer. I reached down and grabbed his wrist, then kicked my feet as strongly as I could to keep my head above the surface and pull him up too.

I pulled hard on his wrist, but the drag was overwhelming. Almost as if I was fighting the ocean to release this boy from bondage. His head surfaced. He gasped and coughed. I hollered at him, "What were you thinking?" He wrapped his arms around my neck and nearly choked me. "Hey, it's going to be fine. Not so tight, okay?" A thud hit my thigh. I prayed it wasn't a sand shark.

I looked down to find the boy was still holding onto his oversized metal sand pail. "No wonder. That bucket of yours is dragging us down. Let it go."

The boy didn't let it go. He didn't respond. He just stared at me and shivered and coughed.

"Let's get you—and that bucket of yours—to shore." The waves now worked in our favor, pushing and urging us to the beach. That's not to say that the ocean didn't try to suck us back, but I didn't surrender.

I sat him down on the sand and plopped down next to him.

"I'm Penny. What's your name?"

He reached out to hold my hand. His lips quivered. I wasn't sure if he was cold or if he was beginning to cry. It probably was both.

"Oh, come here." I opened my arms to him. "Well, that's a sight. Between the pail and that forest of seaweed you have wrapped around your feet, it's a miracle I was able to fish you out." I tugged at the slimy green crisscrossed mess that resembled a botched game of cat's cradle.

I scanned the area. Still no one noticed. They couldn't tear themselves away from the cinematic circus that was going on near the hotel.

My temples pounded like a blacksmith after too much coffee in an old black-and-white western. I tried to shake it off.

"Where's your mother? You shouldn't be out here alone."

He pointed to the ocean.

"She's out there…in the ocean?"

He nodded.

"Shit!" I hadn't see anyone out in the water nearby.

"HELP! There's a lady out in the ocean. HELP!" I started to stand up, but the boy pulled me back down. He shook his head side to side.

"You said your mother's out in the ocean, right?"

He nodded and pointed to the ocean.

"But she's not in the ocean?"

He nodded.

"I'm confused. You're alone?"

He shook his head side to side again.

"So, is your father here?"

He nodded and pointed toward the hotel.

"Up there? By all of those people?"

He nodded.

I felt blood skyrocket to my face. My ears burned, from the inside out. I couldn't imagine what kind of parent would leave a child alone by the beach. But I was going to find out.

"Do you think you can get up? I'm not sure I can with this skirt on." I attempted to stand but the soaked skirt had other plans. It dangled around under my bottom and touched my ankles. "It's a miracle we both didn't sink with this skirt of mine."

In the distance, Marilyn's white and yellow striped tent billowed in the breeze on the higher section of the beach. An open window vented the beach side of the tent. I raised my flattened hand to my brow to cut the glare. I could see a blur of blonde hair pass by the window's opening.

Something was missing. "My sunglasses. They're goners I guess. I loved them, but they didn't fit my fat head anyway." He smiled and gazed down the beach. He pulled on my arm and pointed with his other hand. My eyes followed his index finger. There they were, rolling in the shallow edge of the surf. Rhinestones and all. With the addition of some golden dust. "Looks like I'll have some stars in my eyes. The Hollywood kind...and the rhinestone and mica kind too." I swished them in the water.

"Thanks buddy. You have eagle eyes. Speaking of eagle eyes, can you see your father?"

He squinted.

"Well, he must be up there. Wherever Marilyn is, men usually are too."

"Guess I can only ask you yes or no questions. Right?"

He nodded and shrugged.

"So silence is your super power. That's cool. I can do amazing things too. Not just pulling boys and sand pails from the surf." I had his attention. "Let me see. I can choke on air—or my own spit. I can trip over absolutely nothing. And, um, I can fall *up* stairs. Can you?"

He nodded and cracked a grin. The boy was silent as dust in an attic and sweet as a donut.

"C'mon buddy, let's go find your father."

We climbed the steep embankment of dry sand and were met by Marilyn. "God, I saw you two coming out of the water. I couldn't get out of my tent fast enough. You're so brave." I smiled and rolled my eyes. Everyone was staring our way now. Marilyn looking glamorous and star-like. Me looking like I'd been through the washing machine with my clothes on.

"Who's this little fellow?" Marilyn bent down to be at eye level with him.

"Can't rightly say. He's not talking, but he let me know his father is up here somewhere."

"And he's not keeping an eye on you? For shame." Marilyn shook her right index finger.

"Penny, you're a hero...a lifesaver! No doubt about it. Now, let's find his papa." Marilyn stood up and waved her hand toward the sky as a swarm of crew members came toward them. She placed her hand over the boy's hand that the sand pail dangled from. I held his other hand.

"Hold on. I want to take care of this before we do anything else." Marilyn shouted, "Where's this boy's father? We need to have a little chat."

A man stepped forward. My jaw dropped. It had to have looked exaggerated, like Bugs Bunny does in a cartoon. Before any words were exchanged, I studied how the man's loose white linen shirt clung to his physique in the strong ocean breeze. He was so refined. Probably born with a mouthful of silver spoons. The wind swam through his dark hair, making waves. His grey-blue eyes and the ivory of his toothy smile were matinee-idol quality, like Rock Hudson. My thoughts tripped over each other. Being near him made me, well, melty. He was wow-worthy. Unfortunately, he caught me red-handed staring. He gave me a devilish Clark Gable wink. I melted some more.

The boy's grip on my hand tightened.

"Chip. What've you been up to? I see you've found the best treasure on the beach." He came closer. "Every man on the planet would kill to carry a sand pail with Marilyn Monroe."

His insensitive words helped me get a firm grip on my sudden, yet undeniable fascination with this man.

"Wait a minute, buster." The spell he'd cast on me was broken. "You're more interested in who's holding Miss Monroe's hand than the safety of your son?"

Marilyn added, "Didn't you notice that your son and this girl are soaking wet. She saved your boy. SHE saved YOUR boy."

"Thank you, miss. I will forever be in your debt. I don't understand. My son's a fine swimmer, if it weren't for that pail of his." The man stood directly in front of us. Chip stepped back and gripped my hand even tighter.

"Come here, son."

Chip was motionless.

"You'll have to forgive him." The man's voice lowered to a whisper and he attempted to direct his words to Marilyn and me. "Chip hasn't spoken a word since his mother left us—abandoned us—here at The Del. I shouldn't say this, but the note she left broke my heart. And she took a big piece with her, a very big piece."

I looked out to the sea and back at the father. "I know about her."

"How's that possible?"

"Your son told me…in his own way." I shifted my weight from one leg to the other.

Marilyn bent down to face Chip again. "I'm very sorry, Chip. How *wonderful* that your father's here to take care of you—*now* and forever." Marilyn had ladled a layer of sarcasm and suspicion over her words like hollandaise sauce on eggs benedict.

Chip stared down at the sand.

I directed my attention to the father. "You staying here at The Del?"

"Yes. I thought it would be good for him. Even help him heal."

He gazed out beyond me to the crashing surf. "Me, too."

What he did next was too forward, too intimate and too fast.

He took my free hand and smothered it with both of his. They were large and warm. They were soft, unlike most men's hands.

"It's only the two of us now." His words startled me. I thought he was talking about the two of us. But he wasn't.

"No relatives to speak of. So, Chip and I need to stick together."

I filled my lungs with fresh air and held it. He must've noticed. I studied his beauty again. He probably noticed that too.

Everything was beautiful about him, his appearance anyway. His high-waisted pants, cinching in his middle with a narrow, brown alligator belt that matched his alligator loafers. No socks. And as odd and out of place as it should've been, even the rolled-up Archie comic book that was tucked under his arm was strangely appealing.

I focused on his tan hands, plump veins standing at attention like downward-pointing bolts of lightning. Clean fingernails. No jewelry. I couldn't stop staring, and I couldn't stop wondering why he was still holding my hand and why a grown man had a comic book.

"Well, leaving him alone in a riptide is a mighty strange way of *helping* him." I added, "Or maybe that's just my perspective. My soggy perspective."

"Miss Monroe. MISS MONROE!" The bull-horn main was making more announcements. "We're ready for you on set,"

Some of the star's handlers began to whisk her away.

"You can tell Billy I'm no longer ready to shoot." Marilyn dropped her shoulders.

"But, Mr. Wilder is ready to—"

"I don't need to repeat myself, do I?"

"No, ma'am, I mean miss." The handler moved away.

"Chip, it was nice to meet you." Marilyn shook the little hand she was holding. "Please stay away from the water unless your papa is with you. Can you do that for me?"

Chip nodded and slowly released his grip. He stared at me.

"I'm staying at the hotel too, Chip." I didn't release his hand. "I hope to see you around. If you ever need anything or want to talk—I mean, ever want to hang out—you just let me know."

Chip's father handed him the comic book.

"I wondered why you might be fascinated by the prospect of Archie picking Veronica or Betty." I couldn't restrain myself from making that comment.

"It's his escape, I guess. He may be small for his age, but he's smart as a whip. His vocabulary is endless. He reads so much. One of these days, little buddy, we'll find that voice of yours."

I let go of Chip's hand. "Oh, and thanks for the swim, Chip. It was quite refreshing. Next time, let me know in advance so I can wear my bathing suit."

Chip smiled as his father grabbed for his hand.

"Miss Monroe. I've seen all your films. *Gentlemen Prefer Blondes,* that's my favorite. My name's Steele…Steele Wright. At your service."

Marilyn didn't turn to look at him. As she continued to walk, she responded. "Please be of service to your son…and your wife's memory."

Steele turned to me. "May we take you to dinner tonight? It's the very least we can do."

I got lost in his dreamy eyes as he spoke. "Dinner? What about it?"

Chip tugged at my wet skirt.

"Dinner…tonight. I can't. Though I'd love to. It's my parents…my parents' wedding anniversary. It's a big deal. *Every* year it's a big deal. Yeah, that's what anniversaries are all about. Once a year." I kept talking and talking. What must have been running through his mind as I babbled on? "Anyway, it's tonight. In the Crown Room. Been in the Crown Room ever since I can remember."

"Then how about tomorrow? Please?"

I knew I'd been rambling, so I cut my response down to: "Alright."

"How about something less formal. We can walk up the street

and enjoy drinks and a light supper. How's that sound?"
"Like velvet. Oh, not how does your voice sound, right? You
mean how does dinner tomorrow night sound? It sounds great, just
great. See you then."
   I turned away and exhaled in disgust. One moment I was
standing up to him. Challenging him. Then I was a tongue-tied
schoolgirl, gushing to the varsity quarterback for the first time.
Where'd my backbone go? I'd find it again, soon enough.

FADE OUT

CHAPTER 23

FADE IN:
- SEPTEMBER 8, 1958, FIRST DAY OF SHOOTING
- INTERIOR, LOBBY OF HOTEL DEL CORONADO (NIGHTTIME)

Once again, I was going to attempt to master the art of living in the crosshairs of cruelty. The feeling was much too familiar, like I was walking the plank. It was an annual expectation and exercise.

I waited for my parents outside the Crown Room, the hotel's finest dining room. I waited not with excitement, but with dread. Even though my world had become completely unpredictable and my life's script was being rewritten on an hourly basis, there was one sure thing: I was required to celebrate my folks' wedding anniversary at The Del.

The words "Itty Bitty" were sent like a shot across the bow. Actually, they were shot across The Del's lobby.

There was no denying it. They'd arrived.

The way The Commander projected "Itty Bitty" in his unmistakable two-pack-a-day voice made my shoulders rise like the American flag on a windy day. He groaned and cleared his throat. "Put on a few more pounds I see." First assault, right on schedule at 17:00 hours. I could count on him to be all bark. And all bite.

It was effortless on his part. The Commander could twist my stomach into a world-class knot that any sailor worth his salt only dreamed of making. I'd grown tired of attempting to not react that way. I might've been losing that war, but I was winning the battle of not letting the impact of his verbal warfare show.

Still, I'd always be the little girl who was made to feel like a barnacle clinging to the hull of one of his ships.

"Kent. Must you always say such things?" Mom swatted the air in his direction as the speared olive in her martini danced around the glass's glistening edge.

I took a moment to ponder how I survived with those two as my parents. A washed-up warrior without a war. And his damsel in distress. Emphasis on *distress*.

I smoothed out the front of my new dress with an open palm.

"Daddy and Mom, it's so good to see you."

The Commander gave me his full attention. It was the *Daddy bomb* I dropped. That got him.

He leaned in. Everything about him had always been hard. His posture. His expression. His eyes. Even his bristly shipshape crew-cut hair. Especially his ten-hut tone. He was a steel girder of a man.

I shifted my attention to my mother. She was an overripe beauty in love with the corner liquor store, who tolerated whatever The Commander threw her way.

"So good to see you. Happy anniversary. I can't *imagine* what keeps the two of you glued together after falling off the mantle so many times." I was convinced marriage was the wasteland where dreams go to die. Except in the movies.

"Sweetheart, that's no way to speak to us. I'll forgive you this time. But you must be on your best manners for the rest of the evening or I'll-"

"Kitty, that's enough. Let's eat." The Commander pivoted to face the open doorway and began to walk with deliberate steps.

"Your dear brother and his lovely family will be here any time now."

"This evening just keeps getting better all the time." If anyone could have heard it, my rolling eyes sounded like marbles swaying in an empty soup can.

Because it was such an early dinner time, we were escorted to a coveted table by one of the huge windows. The Commander had routines that must not be disrupted. From an early age, I could recite his required schedule. To have food in front of him with military precision by 17:30, he needed to be seated by 17:00, food ordered by 17:15. It was with this type of regimen I was raised in…and rebelled in.

"Another one, if you please." Mom slurred her order to a passing waiter as she raised her emptied martini glass.

"Already?"

"Yes." She looked squarely in my eyes. "Yes."

"So, would you like to hear about my many adventures with Marilyn Monroe? This whole Hollywood circus—"

The Commander broke in, "Itty Bitty, have you found another man yet? You're not getting any younger, you know."

"I still have plenty of bait left on my hook."

"It's the *plenty* that concerns me. You would've had everything with Bradley. But the way you treated him—at the altar, no less."

I glared at Daddy. How dare he bring up Bradley. I had no regrets about adding "runaway bride" to my life's list of accomplishments. Leaving Bradley at the altar was the best decision I'd ever made in my life. Up to that point, anyway.

"I don't appreciate the way you're looking at me." His eyes narrowed. "And I certainly don't—"

Though he technically interrupted us, the waiter introduced himself in a hoity-toity tone as Charles, as if having the name Charles entitled him to interrupt. He congratulated the anniversary couple and offered his recommendations regarding the menu.

Without being prompted, my father spoke up. "T-bone, rare. Potato, baked, dry. Green beans, steamed." He stopped the machinegun flow of his words. "You got that so far? You're not writing anything down."

"I assure you, sir. I won't soon forget what you've just said."

The Commander blinked twice in a big way. I knew this was not the best beginning of a diner-waiter exchange.

"Fine then, I'd like to chase that all down with a triple-Scotch on the rocks."

"Very well, sir." The waiter turned to Mom. "And for madam?"

"I haven't had a chance to look at the menu. May my daughter and I have a few moments to make up our minds? And, as you can see, we have others who will be joining us soon." She waved her open palm across the table to acknowledge the empty seats.

"As you wish." He turned and walked away.

"Mom, he wouldn't have taken our order this soon, especially when not everyone was seated yet. The Commander couldn't wait to give someone orders, could he?"

Mom sighed and leaned toward me. "So are her tits as big as they look in the magazines?"

"Since when did you start using the word *tits?*" I couldn't believe it. "And when did you stop smoking? You don't have a lit cigarette in your hand or the Great Dustbowl of Ashes floating around you."

"Since you left home, I've changed plenty."

The Commander contained his thoughts no more. "Plenty. Yes, plenty for the worse I'd say. Not changed for the better."

"Well, when it comes to change, we can always count on you *not* to. Always the same for The Commander. Always. The. Same." Mom bobbed her head as she pronounced the last three words, her dangly pearl earrings swung in time with the nods.

"Moving out was the best thing I could've done." I might've stopped there, but I didn't. "I couldn't live another day in that house at attention." I was only at-ease when The Commander was away. He didn't leave often. So, I went away.

I heard the all-too-familiar circus coming toward our table. I didn't need to turn and look. I fought the urge to announce, "Batten down the hatches." Instead, I grinned and thought about how a trumpet, a bass drum and a few kazoos would've brought it all together.

The Crown Room was bigger than a football field and every chirp, burp and slurp of my nieces and nephew was amplified like a car horn's blast in a tunnel.

I couldn't help myself. I looked. And it was quite a sight. Lorelei could be counted on for something as impractical as matching outfits for all five of them. She was a prize catch for my brother. Even without children biting at her heels, she naturally drew the attention of men and women alike. She was an eyeball magnet.

The unleashed children were the first to arrive in a blur of red, white and blue, smothering Mom with hugs and kisses. Little dresses, little shoes, little bows. Everything as patriotic as a garish Fourth of July parade float.

The Commander cleared his throat. They all froze, even the littlest one. It was the statues-in-a-museum kind of frozen. There was no messing with The Commander. Their hands dropped to their sides. While not quite at attention, they were as orderly as any kids could be. But it was not to last. That would've been completely impossible with them.

Like getting hit with a blast of icy air when you open a freezer, I realized they were Coronado's version of the no-necks monsters from *Cat on a Hot Tin Roof*. All shapes and sizes, but every one of them had a head on its shoulders, nothing connecting them. That way you can't wring them even if you wanted to.

"Like they say in Ireland, children are the rainbow of life." Mom beamed as she spoke. "But grandchildren are the pot of gold."

"They're a pot of something. But I'm not so sure it's gold." I couldn't resist. That comment earned me a glare, and a twitch of her left shoulder.

My brother was the last member of the circus to arrive. His real name was Morgan, which became Moe when he was a child. Just like the Three Stooges, which is just what his home-appliance store in San Diego was like. A joke. A slapstick, cheap entertainment. Moe's store had inferior products to go along with the inferior service. Everything was inferior. Period.

The all-too-obvious son who would do anything to please The Commander, Moe announced, "Happy Anniversary!" He smoothed his necktie, which was red, white and blue. He kissed Mom and winked at me. "Hey there, Bitty."

Then hell broke loose.

That greeting was like a man being shot out of the cannon. With it, the kids sprung back to life. Arms and legs flying and flinging in all directions. A swirling tangle of elbows and knees.

"Aren't they just the most precious darlings?" Mom posed that question to the waiter as he lowered her next in what would likely be a long line of martinis into her hard-to-target moving hand.

"Yes, ma'am. The *most* precious, to say the very least."

"Lorelei, you sure are living up to your name. I came across it in a crossword puzzle and looked it up the other day. I can't imagine being named after a woman who bewitches sailors by brushing her hair and singing her siren song. They'd get so distracted they'd crash themselves into the rocks of the Rhine River, or even here in Coronado, I suspect."

"How thoughtful of you to share that with us, Penny." Lorelei glared. "So *thoughtful*."

The Commander cleared his throat yet again. All conversation stopped and everyone took a seat.

The waiter took The Commander's cue. "Is there anything I can get anyone?"

The youngest no-neck blurted out, "Wanna Surly Trample. Cherries on a sword."

"Does Mommy's little sweetheart want a Shirley Temple?"

"Now."

"Me too," announced the only grandson. "And there better be cherries on a mini-sword for me. I see a duel in my future." He lifted an arm and pointed the other as if he had a sword in it, Errol-Flynn style.

"No, my darling. Boys have Roy Rogers. Would you like a Roy Rogers?"

"No. I'm a boy and I want a Shirley Temple."

"I'll take his Roy Rogers." The oldest girl let her presence and preference be known. "And I'd like to light a match and set fire to this itchy dress. It's like I have fire ants crawling all over me."

"Don't ask how she'd know what it would be like to have ants all over her. Trust me. She knows." Moe shook his head. "She's never been one for dresses. Never."

The waiter scurried away.

I just let it all soak in. Like a soldier in a battlefield bunker, I had cover. With everything and everyone spinning out of control in front of me, I'd likely not be put in Daddy's crosshairs again for the duration of the meal. I let the whole thing fade away. Flashbacks stepped forward in my head that showcased dinners around our family's table. The sound of another empty booze bottle clanking in the kitchen trash can. The sight of my father's back leaving through the front door. All the horrifying foreshadows of the wear-and-tear of their blistering and blissless marriage.

I must've daydreamed for quite a while. I was brought back to the present when a glass tumbled onto my lap, missing my napkin that was about to fall on the floor. I shot my eyes downward. It wasn't water. It was a blessed Shirley Temple.

"Well, now, isn't this inconvenient?" I stood to let the ice cubes and pink fluid slide off my lap. I caught my napkin before it escaped and blotted my dress. "No harm done. Really."

There was no response from anyone at the table. Each was absorbed in his or her own world or conversation.

I was invisible.

Like always.

Not like when I was with Steele. He looked at me. He touched me. For longer than he should. But I liked it.

FADE OUT

CHAPTER 24

FADE IN:
- SEPTEMBER 8, 1958, FIRST DAY OF SHOOTING
- INTERIOR, HOTEL DEL CORONADO'S CROWN ROOM (NIGHTTIME)

A gentle tapping distracted me from the buzz of my parents' dinner-table bickering and biting. I looked over and found Chip's face. He was staring at me.

"What a nice surprise. Chip, I'd like you to meet my parents." I turned my attention to The Commander and Mom. "We met out on the beach today. In fact, we took a dip in the ocean together, didn't we?"

Chip's upper lip quivered and turned into a smile. He put his closed hand out in front of me.

"Chip is a young man of few words." I looked at his hand. "What've we got here?"

I put my open palm out under his hand and made a squeamish face. "Nothing wet or slimy, right?"

Chip's smile grew. He opened his fist one finger at a time. With the release of the last finger, a roll of Lifesaver mints plopped onto my palm. He pointed at me, then at the word on the candy's package.

"That's so sweet of you. That's absolutely the most thoughtful gift I've ever received from a man...including a *young* man."

"What about me?" The sound of a deep, velvety voice instantly made me feel melty inside. "I don't have candy for you. Perhaps I can surprise you with something tomorrow night." I took my time and gazed up to find Steele. Freshly groomed and freshly scented. He was casting his spell on me again. His words ricocheted in my head like John Wayne's bullets in a barroom brawl.

Mom looked at me with a leading expression. "Sweetheart, you should introduce us to your *other* new friend." She swept her hand outward to point to the grown man, but instead it collided with her empty martini glass and sent it scurrying.

"This is Steele Wright. Chip's his son."

The Commander stood up, extended his hand and attempted to pulverize Steele's hand with one of his memorable handshakes. It didn't work. I could see it on his face. The look of a small defeat, but a defeat none the less.

"Good to meet you, son. Quite a grip you've got there." The Commander slapped Steele on the shoulder. Always one to have the last word or physically punishing move.

"I believe a happy-anniversary wish is in order. Penny mentioned it this afternoon. I'm always in awe of couples who ride the storms of marriage—together—and find safe harbors." He stopped talking and peered down at Chip.

One of Moe and Lorelei's darlings shrilled, "Wanna candy. Me wanna candy. NOW!" She tried to swipe the roll away from me, but was unsuccessful. I glared at her, then caught myself and smiled. "These candies are not for little children. You might choke on it. We wouldn't want that to happen, would we?"

"Safe harbors. Yes, safe harbors. That's what we've found, Mr. Wright," Mom whispered with a slushy wetness.

That was the first time I heard it or even thought it. Steele was a Mr. Right. It was my drunken mother who let me know I'd met my first Mr. Right.

"A handsome catch like you must've avoided lots of storms in life..." Mom's words drifted away like the smoke that no longer lingered from a cigarette butt.

The conversation dried up. Steele took charge. "So, we'll let you get back to it. Again, Happy Anniversary. Penny, I'll see you tomorrow night, right? Dinner?"

I nodded. "With bells on." I could've kicked myself for sounding so eager.

Chip patted the top of my hand and then waved goodbye. My eyes followed the backs of Steele and Chip until they sat at their table across the room.

Mom questioned me with a lilt in her voice, "You're a lifesaver?"

"Uh-huh." And if I played my cards right, there was a chance they could save me too.

FADE OUT

CHAPTER 25

FADE IN:
- SEPTEMBER 8, 1958, FIRST DAY OF SHOOTING
- INTERIOR, HOTEL DEL CORONADO'S CROWN ROOM (NIGHTTIME)

I peeled open the roll of Lifesavers from Chip and placed one on my tongue. It was cool and mind-clearing. I closed my eyes and inhaled.

"So, you must be Penny. Marilyn's Penny." The masculine voice snapped me back into the room. My eyes opened to find Tony Curtis speaking…to me…with Jack Lemmon at his side.

"Sorry for the intrusion, but we heard about what you did today out on the beach. Marilyn told us and pointed you out this afternoon." Tony grinned at me. "How beautiful you look tonight. I almost didn't recognize you."

Jack jumped into the conversation. "Yes, it's amazing what an unplanned dip in the ocean can do to a girl's hair and makeup. That's a little inside joke." He turned to my parents. "We play men dressed as women. Out on the beach. For the movie, I mean."

"These are my parents, Kent and Kitty Parker. It's so kind of you to stop by. I suppose I'll be seeing a lot more of you."

"Yes you will, in a 1920s-wool swimsuit. Women's, of course." Jack double winked and shrugged his shoulders.

"C'mon, let's leave these nice people in peace. How long do you think we're going to be able to stand here before the autograph hounds find us?" Tony barely had the word *autograph* out of his mouth when he saw Mom rifling through her small handbag for what he suspected was a pen.

"Would you like an autograph, hon?" Tony patted Mom's back. She nodded. The Commander was not amused.

"Tell you what. We'll each sign one of our publicity photos and give them to Penny for you. How's that?"

"Wonderful. Just wonderful."

The two moved toward the door and disappeared.

"This place is crawling with gorgeous men. And you're the main attraction. My little girl."

"Don't get too excited. Marilyn is at The Del. She's the main attraction."

"Itty Bitty, you see what these dogs are up to, don't you?" The Commander made a sniffing sound.

"Do you have to call me Itty Bitty? It wasn't even cute when I was little. Sheesh."

The conversation resembled a ping pong game. The heads of Moe's kids shot back and forth in unison as my parents and I lobbed remarks across the table.

"They're all sniffing around you to get closer to Marilyn Monroe. That's all this is. They're using you. Wake up. Smell the coffee."

"Can't you just be happy for me?"

But this is my father. His happiness came from orders given and followed. From saluting and standing at attention. From crisp clothes and spit-shined shoes.

"Can we have some peace and quiet at this table?" Mom tacked on, "Please?"

"Kitty, my darling, you wouldn't know peace and quiet if it walked through your soup. If you had any soup. This dinner is finished."

With that, the celebration could've been over.

Mom rose from her chair, unsteadily. "Dear, you stay right where you are. Penny and I will just go and powder our noses. We'll be fresh as daisies when we return."

I got up and took Mom's arm. "Yes, fresh daisies in a week-old bouquet."

"But what about *our* dinner? It's fine for you all to storm off. What about us?" Lorelei grasped for more words to express her frustration. "After everything I did to wash and dress these children. After getting my hair done. After making an entrance and sitting down at this fine table. After—"

"Lorelei, why don't you just stay put. Order your meals and enjoy them…without us." I gazed forward and directed Mom away from the table.

"My dear, we'll charge it as a business expense. Not to worry. Order whatever you like." Moe added in a hiss, "The old man would just as soon not eat dinner with his loser son anyway."

"I heard that, Morgan. You are not a loser. You're just a disappointment." The Commander could cripple people with his choice of words.

"Really? A disappointment? Just because I can't live up to your memories of Beau. I doubt they're even memories, more like trumped up wishes. He was your heir and I was…I mean, am…your spare. But think about it. Beau didn't start a business. Beau didn't marry and have grandchildren for you. Your precious Beau didn't—"

"Mention Beau's name one more time and it will be your last." The Commander made it clear he wanted to hear no more about his pride and joy, at least not while waiting to settle a bill for a meal he didn't enjoy, much less even get to start.

"How you put up with him, I don't know." I continued to whisper as we took a few steps. "Honestly. He's a real piece of work."

"Yes he is. And he's all mine. *All* mine."

"Not that any woman in the room is fighting to take him from you, Mom."

"Just the same, he's all mine."

My eyes locked on Steele as we went by his table. I was horrified he had to witness me herding my mother away from the dinner table to God knows where. I pushed my shoulders back, smiled at him and kept walking.

"Beau was all The Commander's, until the bombs took him. Moe just couldn't compete with—much less replace—him." Mom's voice trailed off. "Maybe if he'd been able to enlist—"

"Yes. Maybe things would be different."

Either way, I was sure I was going to make things in my life different.

And a man named Mr. Wright was going to have something to do with it.

Maybe *everything* to do with it.

FADE OUT

CHAPTER 26

FADE IN:
- SEPTEMBER 9, 1958, SECOND DAY OF SHOOTING
- EXTERIOR, HOTEL DEL CORONADO (DAYTIME)

I headed back to my room after checking in at Marilyn's cottage. The fog and mist had already burned off. The morning sun was toasty. I found Chip sitting alone on a bench along the sidewalk by the beach, feet flying in opposing directions.

"Hey sunshine." I didn't wait for an invitation, and went ahead and sat down. "I'm going to be straight with you, kiddo. I pretty much think of children as elf-sized, booger-eating fart factories." I waited for a reaction. There was none. "Most kids are grimy germ buckets. Penny-candy shoplifters. But you, Chip, I can see you're different. In a good way." I paused again. "So, what are you doing hanging around on this bench when there's a whole world out there to explore? With your father's supervision, that is."

Chip still didn't respond. I remembered he couldn't answer open-ended questions and that I needed to construct yes-or-no conversations. "How's that comic book? I mean, is that a good one?"

Chip nodded.

"You know, in my other job—my *real* job—I sell those and just about everything else at the Cornet Five & Dime. Kids come in to get comics like addicts, like grownups are about their coffee in the morning."

Chip smiled.

"Does your father buy them for you?"

He nodded.

"Wouldn't you rather read about Batman or Zorro or Mickey Mouse or Woody Woodpecker?"

Chip began to fidget, picking at the nail bed of his right index finger.

"I'm no expert, but it seems to me that Archie's comics are for someone a little older than you."

Chip looked down at the cover of the comic book he was holding. "Archie's Girls" appeared in sunny yellow type against a dark blue background. In much larger letters, "Betty and Veronica" appeared in cherry red over artwork that showed Archie in an unwinnable situation. He'd just carved a heart into a tree trunk, along with the words "Archie loves..." Betty and Veronica looked on, clearly annoyed that he hadn't completed his love message.

"He's in *some* trouble. Who do you think he loves more? I mean, do you think he loves Betty more?"

Chip looked up at me. Then, slowly, he pointed to Betty on the comic book cover.

"You sure? I would have thought it was Veronica."

Chip put his left finger on the drawing of Betty.

"Hey, let's try something." I opened my three-ring binder, pulled out a clean sheet of paper and a small pencil.

"I won't ask you to talk, but can you write me answers to my questions?"

He stared out toward the ocean. I followed his eyes.

"Sun's really sparkling on the water today. It's nice to be seeing it from here, on land. I'm not saying I regret pulling you out. Far from it. You know you can trust me. Is there something you want to say—I mean write—to me?" I stayed focused on the water. "You're looking out there like you see someone. Do you?"

I squinted at where he was looking. A woman in a long black dress and a wide-brimmed hat stared straight ahead as she strolled.

"It's Kate. The mysterious Kate." I kept staring at her until a strong breeze whipped up the sand and she vanished.

"It's like in the desert, when people see palm trees and a pond. Ever since I was a kid I've seen her along the beach or near the hotel. Grownups usually don't see her. But they hear her when she moves things—or breaks things—in the hotel."

I turned to focus on Chip. "You saw her, right?"

He nodded, then took the pencil, paper and binder.
See her lots. He wrote in block letters. *See Mom two.*
"Chip, thank you for telling me. And, it should be t-o-o, not t-w-o." I couldn't believe I corrected his spelling when I should've been head over heels that he was communicating with me. "Now wait a minute. You've seen the woman in black before?"
He nodded.
"And you've seen your mother here too?"
Chip nodded and began to write. *Saw Mom when you saved me. Under water. She helped.*
I gently pulled the paper away and hugged him. I couldn't imagine what that kid had been through. What'd he seen. No wonder he couldn't speak.
His rigid body slackened as I held him. Chip's ear rested on my upper left chest. My heart beat against his temple. A gust stole Chip's comic book, which in turn broke our hug as he went after it.
He came back and pointed to Betty on the cover.
"Yeah, that's Betty. What about her?"
He took the pencil, paper and binder again. *Looks like Mom.*
"Your mother looked like Betty? Blonde hair, with a pony tail and bangs?"
Chip nodded.
"Is that why you read the Archie comics?"
Chip swiveled his head several times. He wrote, *Dad does.*
"Your father likes Betty...because she reminds him of her?"
Chip nodded, then added, *Can't tell him. Can't tell him I wrote for you. Please.*
"It'll be our secret. You can keep secrets, can't you?"
Chip nodded.
"So can I." Boy, so could I.
"How about a cup of coffee?" It was *that* voice again. That breath-stealing voice that brought on a yummy, melty feeling. It was a feeling I could never get used to. And I was more than willing to see if I could. If my life had a soundtrack, the orchestra's entire string section would've been playing a romantic tune that swelled and swelled and swelled some more.
"Surely you have enough time for that." Steele appeared next to Chip and me. It was more like he loomed. I casually folded the paper Chip was writing on and slid it into my binder.

"I don't know about that. I've got a lot to do."

"Please, it's just a cup of coffee. I'd like to spend more time with you, before our dinner date tonight."

He'd said "date." To me. I couldn't fathom that he thought having dinner with me was going to be a date. My head began to spin and I had to remind myself to breathe.

Chip placed the pencil down on the bench's seat and slipped his arm under and around my elbow.

"I don't know." I shoved my excitement down and did my best to act cool. "Gosh, Chip and I were just getting to know each other better. And this time we weren't bobbing in the ocean while doing it."

"Chip, old man, you won't mind if I steal this pretty lady away? Will you?"

Chip swiveled his head.

"Then it's decided." Steele reached out his right hand. Not for a handshake. But to take my hand and raise me up. I hesitated, but obliged. It was as warm and smooth as I remembered it to be. And large...so large that my baseball-mitt of a hand didn't overwhelm his. I knew I could get used to that.

I rose from the bench. "Do you think he'll be alright? He's six, for goodness sake."

"Yes, he'll be fine."

It was against my better judgement to leave him, but Steele was Chip's father and the decision was his, though he'd exercised some pretty lousy judgement in that regard not too long ago.

It was Steele's turn to slide his hand under and around my elbow. We strolled toward the lobby. I felt like a makeshift centerpiece in a cheap Italian joint...a flickering, drippy candle in an empty chianti bottle.

Everything got quiet in my head, which typically was a noisy, chaotic place.

I watched Steele's eyes scan the beach and hotel in a panoramic sweep. "It doesn't get any better, Penny. It's just gorgeous."

"I agree, *you* are gorgeous—I mean the *hotel* is gorgeous. Yes, Steele, the hotel is gorgeous. And the weather and the beach are gorgeous too." I was a blabbering idiot.

He half-grinned and winked at me. That added blushing to my general melty state.

"There's a coffee counter around here somewhere. I'll ask the concierge when we get inside." Steele bewitched me by the time he got to *coffee counter*. He had a way of disarming me. Making me comfortable, perhaps too comfortable and too fast.

I couldn't get over the fact that he noticed me. *Me*. Maybe I had a chance. A beautiful stranger wanted to spend time with Penny Parker. Maybe, just maybe, he could be the one. I couldn't help myself from thinking it…and hoping for it.

I knew of several places to get a cup of coffee at The Del, but I didn't let on, not wanting to be a know-it-all.

After a stroll through the courtyard and brief chat with the concierge in the lobby, we were sipping coffee at a small round table on the deck with an ocean view.

"So, Steele. That's not a common name. Is there a story behind it?" I had to ask.

He took the handle of his spoon, circled it in his creamy coffee, licked it and pointed it at me. "I don't share this with many people. But I sense I can trust you with this secret."

I was thrilled he was going to trust me with a secret.

"My parents named me Shamus Archibald Wright."

"Oh. I see."

"Who wants the word *shame* in their name? Not me. Or how about *bald*?"

"Kinda awkward. No, really awkward."

"I'm glad you agree. I picked up the nickname Skip—and Skipper—and used it until I turned eighteen. That's when I legally changed my name to Steele. I wanted something strong. Solid. Refined."

"And that's what you got, alright. Like Superman. You know. Man of Steel."

"Something like that." He pointed at me with his spoon again. "Say, I know I asked you out for a casual dinner tonight. But let's make it more special. Let's have a night we'll both never forget. Are you game?"

What could I have said? A night we'd both never forget? Hell's bells, yes. Thoughts banged around my head about not having anything to wear, and my hair—

"Hello. Are you in there?" Steele nudged me.

"Yeah. Sure."

"About dinner? Or that you're in there?"

"Both."

"Let's shake on it. I don't want you backing out." He reached his hand out, just as he did at the bench. I pulled in air like a vacuum cleaner before I extended my hand. The warm, smooth sensation of Steele's skin sent a current of electricity up my arm. I gazed down at my hand and then up to his face. My eyes met his. His were ready and waiting. Steele's eyes kissed my face.

I couldn't take it anymore. I flinched and knocked my coffee cup off its saucer.

"I'm such a klutz." I shook out my napkin and began to mop up the creamy brown puddle, which was still forming its edges as it took possession of the glass tabletop.

"After I tripped on a coffee table in her cottage, I was telling Marilyn how I hoped The Del didn't have a you-break-it-you-bought-it policy because a clumsy ox like me would be broke in no time at all."

I must've have frowned at the end of what I'd just said because Steele told me to not make a sad face. "Smile. Like the one on my face."

"With a face like that, you could get away with murder."

"I'm counting on it."

I felt my eyes slide up into my head.

"For goodness sake. I'm just joking." Steele dug into his right pant pocket. "Here. I want you to have this. It's a penny. I carry it around with me for good luck. It's from the year I was born. See? Maybe it'll bring you good luck. It did for me. I found you."

He stopped talking and I didn't know what to say.

"Tonight, then. I'll see you tonight."

I blinked like a schoolgirl who was just asked to teeter-totter with a boy on the playground at lunchtime. He must've been used to that reaction from women. Imagine: Full-grown women reduced to impressionable, dizzy little girls.

That was okay with me.

Being off balance and a bit dizzy was just fine.

So long as I was with him.

FADE OUT

CHAPTER 27

FADE IN:
- SEPTEMBER 9, 1958, SECOND DAY OF SHOOTING
- INTERIOR, MARILYN'S COTTAGE (DAYTIME)

"What's your secret?" Marilyn looked at me in the reflection of her vanity's mirror.

Jesus, Mary and Joseph, she was stunning to look at. Absolutely. Stunning. I wondered what she thought when she looked in a mirror, because I sure knew what I thought when I did.

"I'm not sure what you mean?"

"You and men. I thought I had it. But I'm beginning to question that. Well, not really, but you've got something." Marilyn froze her words and face as she created her signature polka dot. The mole, just to the left and a bit lower than her nose, was almost skin color in the mirror's reflection. But darkened, it became a beauty mark.

"I'm sorry. I still don't understand what you're talking about."

"Penny, already this morning Jack and Tony were talking about you to me. Yesterday, that beautiful man—but not such a great dad—was paying you a lot of attention out on the beach. And I was standing right there. I know what I saw."

"Mr. Lemmon and Mr. Curtis stopped by our table at dinner last night. That's all." I looked down at the floor.

"And what about that man on the beach?"

"Funny you should mention him. His son gave me some candy for saving him. The dad asked me to dinner. Tonight. First it was going to be casual. We had coffee just now and he gave me his lucky penny. Imagine that?"

"I can, honey." Marilyn winked with one eye.

"But now dinner has become something special. Formal. I don't think I'll go. I'm so far out of his league. He's a window-shopping kinda guy."

"I don't follow."

"You know, diamonds like doorknobs."

"Huh?"

"He's like all the sparkling stuff—no, wait, he's like the diamond bracelet I stare at every day when I walk by the front window of The Regal Jewelers. A girl like me can admire. I can even drool. But it's out of my league. Even on my best day I—"

"Even on your worst day, you're beautiful. Believe me. It's taken some time, some broken hearts and some sleepless nights to learn that. But, what's on the outside does count. More than it should." She paused and added, "Here's a bit of advice I was given a long time ago: the knight in the shiniest armor is usually the least brave, honorable and selfless. In other words, watch out for the pretty ones."

Marilyn looked back in her mirror. "He is *gorgeous*. It's hard not to look. But, there's something wicked underneath his smile. Something wickedly good. Or wickedly bad. One thing's for sure, though, he's a chaser...a skirt chaser."

"And I didn't run, did I?"

"No, you stood still and waited for him to make a move. Do you think he's right for you? That he—"

"Well I don't think I have to, *now*. You just made it crystal clear that I should."

"I'm sorry, honey. That's not what I meant."

"But that's how I took it."

Awkward silence hung like a drape over a closed window.

"I can't believe I just said that to you. You. Marilyn Monroe. Please forgive me."

"No forgiveness is necessary. It's been too long since someone disagreed with me and let me know it. It's actually refreshing."

"It's just...this doesn't happen to girls like me."

"Then let's do something about it." Marilyn nodded.

"Let's? As in *let us*?"

"Uh-huh. Tell you what. Tonight's your night. And I'm going to help. Think of me as your Fairy Godmother. I'm going to grant your wish."

"My wish? What wish?" I was talking and thinking at the same time again. "Well, that sounds intriguing." I wasn't sure I'd asked for a wish to be granted, but I knew I shouldn't refuse what was being offered.

I clapped my hands together and let them slowly drop to my sides. "I don't want to sound ungrateful, but this time's been different. He asked me out…when I looked my worst. I'm not so sure a Hollywood makeover is such a good thing for a what-you-see-is-what-you-get kind of girl like me."

"Marilyn, please don't promise anything." Paula Strasberg butted in with authority. "We have a very busy schedule."

"It'll be fine, Paula." Marilyn swiveled around to face me. She put out her hands and I offered mine in return.

"Trust me on this. Mother Nature's work needs a makeover every now and then. Look at me."

"It's hard not to."

"Maybe it's just time for a costume change for you. Be back here at three o'clock. My team and I will wave our magic wands so you have a night you'll never forget. And neither will that cad whose got your attention."

"This is just too much. We hardly know each other. You don't have to—"

"But I insist. I'm the boss. So, what I say goes." Marilyn turned back to face the mirror. "Three o'clock. Sharp. Now, let's run lines. I need to be at my very best out on the beach today. Paula, please begin."

"As you wish." Paula did not look happy.

I reviewed the day's schedule on my clipboard.

"I don't mean to interrupt, but the call sheet has you on the beach until half-passed six."

"I disagree. I have a strong suspicion I may not be feeling well around two forty-five. And I'll need to return to my room for some rest."

"Yes, I see." I grinned at Marilyn's reflection in the mirror. "Then three o'clock will work just fine."

FADE OUT

CHAPTER 28

FADE IN:
- SEPTEMBER 9, 1958, SECOND DAY OF SHOOTING
- EXTERIOR, HOTEL DEL CORONADO (DAYTIME)

"Psst. Psst. Penny Parker!" Schlepping through the sand in her high heels and sloshing around the liquid remnants barely contained in her cocktail glass, Mom made her way across the beach toward me.

"You've got to be kidding."

"Psst. Psst. Penny. Can we talk now?"

"Quiet. Be quiet. And no, Mom, we can't talk now."

"But, Sweetheart. I really need to talk to you."

"Alright." I had to get her out of there. Fast. "I'll meet you on the veranda for lunch. A quick lunch. The kind of lunch you eat, not drink." I shook my head. "I don't know how long it'll be. Just entertain yourself there. You can do that, right?"

"Of course I can. I'm capable of doing anything...at any time. You are too." She grinned and hoisted her cocktail glass to drain its contents.

"Mom, can you stop doing that?"

"What?"

"Saying one thing and meaning another."

"Yes...and no." She turned and headed back toward The Del without uttering another word.

When Billy released the crew for lunch, I checked with Marilyn to be sure she didn't need anything. I got to Mom's table just as the waiter was taking her next drink order. I knew this because of her new collection of sword-shaped olive picks spread in front of her. As he lifted two empty martini glasses, she held her index finger up and—with little grace or care—ordered another. It would go nicely with the half-finished one in her hand.

"I'll have an egg-salad sandwich, please. Wheat toast." I turned to Mom. "Would you like to chew something at this meal, other than olives and ice cubes?"

"No dear. How do you think I stay so fit and slim? You should eat less and drink more. It's been a winning formula for me. For years."

"That'll be all for now. Thank you." I sent the waiter on his way.

"So what's the emergency? I can't remember the last time you asked me out for lunch….to *talk* no less."

"It's your father."

"What did I do this time? And I'm in no mood for any finger waving or tongue clucking."

"That's not why I'm here. I want you to know I made him a fried peanut-butter sandwich when we got home last night."

"That's what you needed to tell me?"

"I knew he felt bad. He didn't—wouldn't—tell me, but I could tell."

"I just don't understand you two. How do you deal with each other?"

"That's marriage, dear. Spend enough time with someone and you know what they're thinking." She drained the martini glass in front of her and rested it on the tabletop. "I wish you could have known him before."

"Before Beau died?"

"No, before that. Long before that. When he came back from the war. When only a piece of him came home. He lived through Pearl Harbor. Everyone waves the flag and talks about how that battle changed the course of the war. It changed a lot more than that. It was about death and mangled bodies and burning ships and bombs dropping. Your father saw it all. He still does."

She swirled a runaway olive in her liquor-less glass. "I've spent all these years settling for what's left of him. You loved him before, but you don't remember it. You were too young. But trust me. Everyone loved him. He was full of fire and fun."

"Now he's hollowed out, like a Halloween pumpkin." That's

how I saw him. "And he's full of smoke, piss and vinegar."

"But when he looks at me, Penny, he sees me when I'm twenty. Not how I look now. Not that there's anything wrong with the way I look now, mind you."

I studied my mother. I'd never talked to her in this serious way. *All I Have To Do Is Dream* by the Everly Brothers played on the patio's public-address system. At that moment, I would've believed I was in a dream.

"Why are you telling me this…about a man who calls me Itty Bitty. In public."

"Because he loves you. And you need to know it."

"Fine way of showing it. I was never itty or bitty. Not dainty. Not delicate. I was chunky and lumpy. I still am. And every time one of you calls me Itty Bitty, I think the exact opposite. Or, I think of *old bitty* Aunt Gertie. How everyone winks knowingly about her losing her man and being a spinster all her life."

I stopped the flow of my words and looked at the men and women eating their lunches around us. "I had a childhood of yes-sirs, no-sirs, ship-shapes and anchors-aways. Did you know I used to think I was allergic to our family?"

I moved the knife and fork in front of me on the table, as if where they were placed was somehow not where they should've been. I tucked the cloth napkin on my lap so it wouldn't slide off and hit the ground. "It's not the words that bother me so much. It's *how* he says them. Always to make me feel small and less than. Except I've always been big and more than."

"Oh?"

She opened the door and I was not about to miss my chance to walk through and let some skeletons out. "It felt like I didn't…didn't exist. Twirling around the living room in my dance-class costumes from Miss Bonnie's. Tapping my feet so hard on the floor they should've heard me in China. And still, it was like I wasn't there. Either invisible or waiting to be yelled at. I never waited to be praised. That was never going to happen. But the boys, they were another thing entirely. Daddy always made time for them. Always."

I tacked on, "I felt like a stain on the rug."

"You're gonna have to make some wine with those sour grapes of yours. To make them go away. Penny, you've got to move on."

"Like you have? You haven't changed your hair style in

decades."

"Why should I?" She smoothed her hair with her flattened fingers. "Everyone always compliments this style. Some things should just not change. Besides, your father likes it this way."

"Has he told you?"

"Not in so many words."

"Then how on earth do you know?"

"I just do."

"You were beautiful. The most beautiful mom on the block. In the whole neighborhood. How was I supposed to compete with that? I heard ladies say how you were too pretty to have a fat girl for a daughter. How was I—"

"Pardon the interruption. Miss, here's your sandwich. Ma'am, your drink." The waiter took a step back. "Is there anything else I can get you ladies?"

"We're good. Thanks." I winked at him.

"I grew up thinking we needed a bomb shelter at our house so I could go there when you and Daddy were arguing, or when you were passed out on the couch and I was supposed to get dinner started. No child should have to want a bomb shelter to be protected from her own family."

I took a bite of my sandwich and chewed.

Mom jumped in with, "You know, he still has nightmares…about things he won't tell me about. Even now. He shakes and sweats. He yells things I can't understand a word of. But we have to cut him some slack. I have to. Maybe you don't."

After another bite, I put my sandwich back down to rest on the plate. I took that moment to consider how I'd never said this kind of stuff to her before. Face to face. I'd thought it to her face, but never dared speak it.

I didn't have much time. And I had a mouthful of sandwich, but that wasn't going to stop me. "It's like Scarlett. You know, Scarlett O'Hara?"

"What?" What is?"

"*Gone With the Wind*," I replied, dabbing my lips with my napkin. "Everyone thinks it's a huge story about the South and slavery and war and love—the right and wrong kinds of love—and all those characters wandering in and out. But it's not. It's one girl's story. Scarlett. Someone we should all hate. She's selfish, greedy and delusional about who she should love and who loves her. Growing up in our house was like that?"

"Like *Gone With the Wind*?"

"Yes and no, Mom. Growing up in that house was an epic survival story. But I didn't have a role...or, at least I didn't feel like I had a role. Not Scarlett. Not her sisters. Not Melanie. I felt like I was in the audience. Watching it all happen. With a bag of popcorn and a Coke. Watching. Just watching."

I paused and studied her face as she looked at the tabletop and not me.

"Grandma Jenny treated me like the star of my own movie. And I guess I did the same for her. We could be anyone we wanted. We could be royal and beautiful and adored...in Paris or Siam. We could be dusty and crusty pioneers in a Conestoga wagon on the Oregon Trail. But when she was gone, I wasn't anyone's star. I was just a shadow. Maybe even a shadow of a shadow."

Her eyes slowly rolled up to meet mine.

I continued. "I know now that it may not have been that way, really. But that's how I saw it. How I felt it. How I *feel* it, even now sometimes. And do you know when it became crystal clear to me?"

"No. When?"

"It was when Lorelei joined our circus. When Moe started dating her, I watched how you looked at her. She was small and she fussed with her hair and handbag and worried about what she ate. Like you. I knew then I was never going to be the daughter you wanted. She was. And before long, you got her."

"I'm sorry you feel that way. It wasn't because—"

"So, I ate and ate." My words spilled out of me like raging water over a broken dam. "I was never going to measure up to you from that point on, not with Lorelei in the picture. And it wouldn't be worth the effort to even try. But you should know that those candy wrappers you'd find in the wastebasket and confront me with, they weren't mine. Moe used to plant his Tootsie Roll and Scooter Pie wrappers there to make me get in trouble. Do you think someone as crafty as me would be that obvious...even stupid? If I wanted to cover my tracks, I'd have done a much better job of it. A much better job than you did with your emptied booze bottles. I guess I got it from you, the hiding gene. Food was my booze...is my booze. Thank you." I pushed my plate away. I couldn't eat after saying that. But I wasn't finished settling the score with my mother.

She scooted her chair back and began to stand.

"I'm *not* done." I stayed planted in my seat.

"Well, I've had my fill. And I'm not talking about cocktails."

"Sit down. Please. I have a few more things to say and I may never have this chance again. Please."

She lowered herself back into her chair, but didn't scoot it back in. My clock was ticking, so I let my guard down and continued. "The other day Trudy asked to see some photos of me as a little girl. She looked stunned when I said I only had three. There are tons of photos of Beau and Moe, but not of me. And definitely not of me alone."

"By the time you came along, I was exhausted." She'd found her voice. "I'm sorry I didn't take more snapshots of you or put together piles of scrapbooks. It just wasn't in me. You need to understand we did everything we could so you and your brothers wouldn't have to live through what we lived through. We wanted something better for you. Everyone did. All of your friends' parents did."

Mom fortified herself with another swallow of numbing nectar from a martini glass. "Your grandmother was so good to you. Not just taking you to the movies. She must have seen something in you in that the rest of us missed."

She swirled the olive around her glass. "I'm not sure we did a good job of it, but your father and I sure tried. We gave you everything we didn't get as children, and somehow that didn't make it any better."

Mom looked away. "Like all newlyweds, I had a fantasy about what motherhood would be like. But my fantasy was all wrong. Instead of the vegetable-loving, chore-loving angels I expected, I got to deal with tantrums, I got to rinse poopy underpants and I got to untangle hair knots. I tried my best to teach you three to use knives and forks, even spoons. But so many meals were eaten without silverware. Despite all that, I loved my imperfect angels, even if it didn't always show."

She was looking at me when she said, "All you wanted to do was go to the movies with Grandma. And after she passed, you spent every penny of your chore money there. Every nickel of your babysitting money. Every dime of your birthday money. All of it went to buy movie tickets. On top of that, your best friend was a washed-up movie star who sold over-priced stale candy at a theater with sticky floors."

"Since I felt invisible to all of you, I went ahead and made myself invisible by going to the movies and being with Tilly. Besides, there wasn't anything or anyone to entertain me here. At the movies, no matter what happens in the beginning or the middle, it always ends well. It ends just swell."

"But that's not life. That's not how it goes."

"That's exactly the point, Mom. Why not escape all of this and sample all of that? Even if it's for ninety minutes? Plus, there's the buttery popcorn and icy Coca-Cola."

"I can make you popcorn."

"But, that's not the point. I just wish—"

"Penny, it's time." May tapped me on the shoulder. "We have to get back to the set."

"Mom, this is May. May, this is my mother."

"Nice to meet you."

"Likewise." Mom looked down at what remained of my sandwich. "You go, I'll finish that up and take care of the bill."

"Promise me. No more drinks."

"Promise."

"Promise me you'll eat."

"Promise."

"Thanks for lunch. And the talk. You aren't going to tell him about this, are you?"

"Who? Your father?"

"Who else?"

"That I can't promise."

"The last thing I want to do is have this talk with him. Not that he ever would."

"He's full of surprises. Why just the other day he—"

"Mom, I have to run. Literally. I have to run."

"Goodbye, Sweetheart." She turned to the ladies at the next table. "That's my daughter. She's working with Marilyn Monroe on the picture they're shooting out on the beach. My daughter may have a promising career in Hollywood. We'll just have to wait and see."

I watched as the ladies politely nodded.

Mom raised her martini glass. "Yes, we'll just have to wait and see."

FADE OUT

CHAPTER 29

FADE IN:
- SEPTEMBER 9, 1958, SECOND DAY OF SHOOTING
- EXTERIOR, CORONADO BEACH (DAYTIME)

"So here's how the whole thing happened. It started at school." Frankie wiped his forehead with the back of his hand. The afternoon sun had heated up the sand, which in turn heated us all up.

"I'm sorry I didn't see it play out." I looked at him and waited to be dazzled.

"I told the guys to run on the beach—up to The Del's breakwater and back—nine times. Not eight. Not ten. Nine. They can be selectively deaf when it comes to instructions. I told them I'd be with them, counting each lap and keeping them in line."

"Then what happened?"

"So David tells me they have a challenge for me. But they're not going to tell me about it just yet. They all laughed and shushed each other. They were up to something. And it wasn't a good thing. Their shenanigans were the talk of the school the other day after they ran their jockstraps up the school's flag pole. All twelve of them."

"I hope they were at least the new ones you just bought."

Frankie's head turned side to side. "Today, they were clustered and some of them watched over their shoulders like prairie dogs. The lookouts were doing their job. The others appeared to be collecting money from each other."

"Then what happened?"

"We got started running near the water's edge, where the sand was firm. The breakwater is always our target. But with the filming, things have changed. People are everywhere. And the guys saw their friends from school standing around, watching."

"You let them watch, right?"

"They asked if they could stop for a while since everyone else gets to watch. I told them 'not today. Maybe tomorrow.' They got all upset. It had to be today. That's when I got suspicious, but I let them stop anyway."

"You're such a pushover." I couldn't help interrupting his story.

"When they got near the crowd, they laughed the way guys do. Not giggling like girls. More of a hey-hey-hey, slap-on-the-back sort of laughing. That's when you waved at me."

"And that's when Marilyn came over, right?"

"Right."

"I couldn't hear what she said."

Frankie continued with his story. "The guys acted like baboons. Jumping up and down. Not at all cool."

"Is that when she smiled and waved at you?"

"Uh-huh."

"Then the guys moved in close to each other, all facing to the center. Marilyn watched. Gregory raised his hand and waved some bills at her. You know, money. She came over and asked, 'Alright boys. What's up?' They laughed. 'Not David's shorts!' yelled one of them as he pulled down David's shorts. They all howled like a pack of coyotes that just made a kill."

"I don't know how you deal with them."

"She was great about the whole thing. She said, 'Somehow, I bet that's not the first time you've done that.' She looked around at them. 'I was wondering what the money was all about. So, what's the deal, boys?' Gregory told her it was for a dare for their coach. They pointed at me. She was still really cool with the whole thing and—"

I interrupted. "Is that when I lifted my hand, shaped like a gun, and shot myself in the temple?"

"Yes, you did that well. Gregory went on to say they collected money for a dare for me to get a hug from Marilyn. She asked how much they collected, and he said fourteen dollars. She smiled and told them that for fourteen dollars, she thought a fella should get more than a hug. They put the cash on her opened palm and she turned to face me. She let the cash fly away in the breeze. Then she pulled my face down to hers and planted a kiss. Not just a kiss. Not a peck on the cheek. The one and only Marilyn Monroe kissed me on the lips!"

"Yeah, I witnessed it myself." I thought about it and remembered how uncomfortable I was with the kiss when it happened. And, as Frankie told his story, I was uncomfortable again. I wasn't sure why. We were lifelong friends. Period. But from that point on, how could any girl's kiss ever measure up to one from Marilyn Monroe? Frankie was ruined. Or was he?

"She slowly pulled away, smiling and looking me in the eyes the entire time. That's when I heard it. 'Coach, looks like you enjoyed that kiss, eh?' I grabbed the tee shirt that was stuffed in the back of my shorts and held it over the front of me. 'Need a few more shirts to cover that tent you just pitched?' The guys chuckled and slapped some backs. She blew me an air kiss. 'See ya later, boys.' That's what she said. And that was that."

"Not really." I grinned at him. "I congratulated her."

"For what?"

"For kissing my first husband."

FADE OUT

CHAPTER 30

FADE IN:
- SEPTEMBER 9, 1958, SECOND DAY OF SHOOTING
- EXTERIOR, CORONADO BEACH (DAYTIME)

"Did I just catch a glimpse of what I think I saw…Frankie kissing Miss Monroe? Oh, geez!"

"Trudy, what are you doing here?"

"I didn't want to be left out. So, was that Frankie?"

"Yes it was, along with his track team."

"Well doesn't that just frost your coffee cake?"

"What do you mean?'

"Your Frankie with a Hollywood star."

"He's not my Frankie. He's our Frankie. He's everyone's Frankie."

"If that's what you think, fine." Trudy folded her arms.

"So, is she going to deliver for us today?" A man's voice came from behind me. I turned around. "Mr. Lemmon and Mr. Curtis, how nice to see you."

"We're placing bets and we thought you'd have the inside track."

"She's good. Shouldn't be any problems. 'Fair weather ahead' as my sailor father would say."

"We're going to hold you to that."

"Pardon me. Let me introduce my good friend, Trudy Vanderhooven."

"Charmed," Tony said.

"Pleasure," Jack added.

"Trudy's the best cook in Coronado."

Trudy beamed. "If you want a home-cooked meal, just let me know. Tapioca is my specialty."

"Sign us up." Tony sounded genuinely interested.

"We better get going. Billy won't wait for us, but he will for her." Jack was dressed as a woman and walked away like a man.

"It's very confusing, isn't it?" Trudy continued, "Men as women, I mean."

"It takes some getting used to. But they're real sports about the whole thing. And it's sure to be a blockbuster."

"If you say so, Penny. If you say so."

As Trudy strolled away, Marilyn waved me over. She was posing for snapshots with fans. The sand was hot, so I didn't dawdle.

When I was about ten feet away from her, I overheard a woman's voice say, "Who's that fat cow?" I was sure she was talking about me.

A different voice said, "No, not that fat cow. That one, over there...the bleached-blonde whore."

I could ignore someone calling me a fat cow. I had two brothers, hung out with boys and worked with a bulldozer named Otis. But no one was going to say bad things about Marilyn within my earshot and get away with it.

I raised my index finger to Marilyn as a signal that I'd be there in a moment. I made a sharp right pivot in the sand and approached the women. My fingernails dug deeply into my palms as I restrained myself. With gritted teeth, I told them, "You can call me anything you want. But what you said about Miss Monroe, those are fighting words in my neighborhood. She's an artist and she's doing her job. Those are two things that probably don't apply to either of you. So, if you're going to suck up oxygen out here, keep your sticks and stones to yourselves. Or, you'll have me to deal with."

Their response was priceless because there was none. They stared at me with blank faces and arms at their sides.

I pivoted again. This time in Marilyn's direction and walked away. She greeted me with, "What did they want, honey?"

"You'd never believe it."

"Try me."

"They called me a fat cow and I took the opportunity to remind them about the manners they were taught in Sunday school."

"Penny, you're so funny."

"I'm sorry. What did you say?" The crowd's cheering and the barrage of requests for autographs drowned out Marilyn's words

"I SAID THAT YOU'RE SO FUNNY."

"Yeah, I would've been a big hit in vaudeville!"

"Now, honestly, what did they say?"

I didn't want to lie, but I couldn't tell the truth…the whole truth anyway. "Alright, how about this? They were admiring your hair and how comfortable you are with everyone on the beach."

"That's better, but *somehow* I don't think that's what they said."

"Just know that I've got your back, Marilyn."

She looked at me with squinted eyes. I could tell she didn't hear me, so I repeated myself. Like only she could, Marilyn grinned and said, "And, honey, I've got yours."

As she finished her words, the crowd went silent and all heads turned. Not in Marilyn's direction, but toward a woman who was coming in her direction. Her steps were smooth and steady, despite the potholed sand beneath her feet. She glided like a goddess: chin up, shoulders back. Her dark-green sunglassed eyes were aimed forward.

It was Tilly.

And she looked grand.

Breathtakingly grand.

Red-carpet grand.

Old Hollywood grand.

I'd witnessed how no one turned heads like Marilyn. But at that moment, Tilly trumped her and proved that anyone who thought stars couldn't shine without darkness was wrong.

No longer just a queen of the silver screen, Tilly was a celebrated Coronado businesswoman who was carrying something that was ablaze in color. Scarlet. Emerald. Amber. Turquoise. And, yes, some black and white.

Tilly's thin frame was draped in a cream-colored, full-length, long-sleeved, cowl-necked, hooded ensemble. As an added measure to keep the harsh sun from her skin, Tilly shaded herself with a vintage black-lace parasol. As she got closer, I could see the sun glisten on the black-jet beads and how the breeze waltzed through the fringe suspended from the parasol's scalloped edges.

Her cloth handbag was glamorously—and stunningly—transformed by a platoon of her cherished brooches. Not a speck of the front panel's fabric showed beneath the thick layer of blinding jewelry. She'd brought the galaxy with her. Tilly swung it ever so slightly in the brilliant sunshine as she walked, which made the crystals and rhinestones shimmer like Fourth of July fireworks, putting Queen Elizabeth's Crown Jewels to shame. At least that's what I thought.

Tilly's entrance stole the show. Even Billy Wilder and the crew stood attentively and in awe. Billy must've thought he was delusional, as if the aging forgotten-star Norma Desmond of his dreams—the character he and Gloria Swanson conjured up in *Sunset Boulevard*—was alive and well.

"That's my friend." I nudged Marilyn. "My *life-long* friend, Tilly." I didn't think I'd ever called her that before, but she was. "You might know her by her Hollywood name: Tallulah Carlisle."

"Of course, honey. I know who she is." Marilyn spoke without looking at me. "She had her days in the sun...and she's going to have another one. Right here. Right now. I'm going to see to it."

Marilyn stepped forward and extended her right hand. Cameras clicked and flashed. Applause from the fans surged as the two stars connected: Tilly's gloved hand with Marilyn's sandy one.

"Miss Carlisle, I'm such a fan. How kind of you to visit. May I offer you a cool drink in my tent."

"You may, my dear. You may. And please call me Tilly. Everyone does these days, at least here in Coronado."

Marilyn led Tilly into her tent. "What a charming surprise. I wish we'd known you were coming. Penny and I would've prepared something special for you."

"It was a spur-of-the-moment sort of thing. I came to see how Penny was getting along. She and I are quite close, and I don't want her to be seduced by Hollywood. She's a terrible mistress. Hollywood, that is. Not Penny."

Marilyn grinned and signaled for me to come with them. Paula and Billy stepped forward, but Marilyn shook her head at them. They stopped and shot each other a look of shock.

Once inside the tent, Marilyn asked me to untie the straps that held the canvas door back.

"Let's have some privacy, shall we?" Marilyn giggled. "My goodness. You've still got it."

"It?"

"Oh my, yes. That thing they say I have. It."

"May I call you Marilyn?"

"Please do."

I handed them each an icy glass of lemonade and a pressed, white-linen napkin.

"Marilyn, you would've been *something* in my day. Like I've read and seen, the camera does make love to you. Those eyes of yours—and everything below them—make magic on film." Tilly paused. "But it's what's above and behind those eyes that counts most. That's why I walked away from it all." Tilly let her words linger in the air like smoke above a blown-out candle. She took a sip of lemonade and made a "mmmm" sound.

Marilyn reignited the conversation. "It is?"

"Yes, the directors and the studios only cared about my looks. My hair. My costumes and headdresses. My hands. My gestures. Not my brains...not the person inside the body."

Marilyn sighed and sipped her lemonade.

Tilly went on. "There was a time when I *loved* to act—to pretend—for the cameras. But the joy of acting slipped away. I decided I better save my life while I still cared about it."

Marilyn sipped, swallowed and sighed again.

"When Mr. Wilder came up with the character of Norma Desmond, gosh, ten years or so ago, he approached me, Mary Pickford and Mae West." Whether she was doing it deliberately or not, Tilly raised her chin and gazed up to the tent's ceiling. She looked as she did long ago in one of her silent pictures. "He had quite a way of blurring fact and fiction in creating Norma."

Tilly smacked her lips and continued, "We all turned him down. However, it was a gold mine for Gloria Swanson. There may have been no Oscar for her performance, but it was a mighty fine performance. Should the occasion present itself, please let Mr. Wilder know how much I admired his direction of *Sunset Boulevard*, but how I take exception to the portrayal of its star."

Marilyn nodded while maintaining eye contact with Tilly.

"But in time, I fear, Norma Desmond—that ghastly monster of a character—will be more famous than the real actresses of my time. That will be ironic, won't it?"

Marilyn had no response other than a slow-motion blink of her irresistibly wide eyes.

"My dear, don't let my experiences frighten you. The Hollywood you're part of is much different, isn't it?"

"No. Actually, things haven't changed at all." Marilyn drew her voice down to a whisper. "It's pretty much still a rich man's meat market. I'm not sure how long *Marilyn Monroe* can take it. Know what I mean?"

"I do. Those bad boys love to play with fire and, sadly, they've not learned their lesson after all these years. They've made the *idea* of Marilyn Monroe something powerful...maybe even unstoppable."

Norma rose from her chair. "I really must let you get back to your work, my dear. You're the star and I'm sure the demands on you and your time are immense."

Tilly handed me her lemonade glass, but dropped her napkin. I started to bend down to get it. Tilly raised her hand in a stop-sign signal.

"You're here for Miss Monroe." With the grace of an angel, she lowered herself and retrieved her napkin. "I'm a woman of independent means who is perfectly capable of picking up after herself."

Marilyn's eyes met mine. Tilly had made quite an impression. At that moment, Tilly had no idea how her visit would impact Marilyn and the choices she would soon face.

FADE OUT

CHAPTER 31

FADE IN:
- SEPTEMBER 9, 1958, SECOND DAY OF SHOOTING
- INTERIOR, MARILYN'S COTTAGE (DAYTIME)

I knocked on Marilyn's door three times. There was no response. I knocked another series of three times. A Coca-Cola and a pair of Scooter Pies sloshed in my stomach. May opened the cottage's door. "They're waiting for you. In her room."

They were waiting for *me*. I liked the ring of that. Marilyn Monroe and a mysterious "they" were waiting for me.

May moved aside and I stepped forward.

"It's time to get dolled up. And you're the doll." Marilyn's voice had a faint schoolgirl squeal to it. "My team is your team. And I'm going to get in on the act too."

"The act?"

"Yeah. You're going to sweep that man right off his feet at dinner, and I'll be there to witness it. I know, I know. I won't create a crowd scene. I'll be undercover. I do it all the time. It's amazing what a scarf on my head and some oversized sunglasses can do. I can be totally incognito, until I don't want to be. And if anyone asks, I'll use the name I use when I travel, Zelda Schnuck. Sometimes I go by Zelda Zonk."

"This is all too much, really. We hardly know each other. Why on earth would you ever want to go through all this trouble? For me?" My pleading eyes locked on Marilyn's excited-little-girl face. "I don't know if I'm ready for this. I want a man to like me for who I am, not how I look made-up or not. Maybe if I—"

"We are—all of us—stars. We deserve to twinkle." Marilyn had a softness in her voice and how she stood. "I have the best makeup and hair people in the business. They're here for you. As for a dress, well, wait until you see what I have for you. We'll have you red-carpet ready in no time!"

I reached out and grasped Marilyn's right wrist with both of my hands. "Just wait right there. Not another word." I closed my eyes and inhaled. "Just let me have this moment." As my eyes opened, I stared down at Marilyn's wrist and my hands. "Just let me have this for five seconds."

Marilyn grinned.

"But—and that's a *big* but—I'll never look like the girls in the magazines and movies, if that's your goal."

"Hell, the girls in the magazines and movies don't even look like the girls in the magazines and movies. I'm living proof of it."

"I'm not so sure of that. If I had my way and I could Frankenstein a new me—an arm from one person, a leg from another—I'd have your body, Katharine Hepburn's cheekbones, Debbie Reynolds' voice and Ava Gardner's eyes. Oh, and I'd want to move like Ginger Rogers. But I've always believed in playing the cards I've been dealt." I put my right index finger to my lips. "But today, with your team's help, I have a wild card to play. Or is it wild cards?"

"So, let's play." Marilyn clapped her hands together.

"Deal me in." My head spun thinking about it all. Makeup. Hair. Dress. Marilyn. Steele.

"Alright then. Sit down and let these artists do their magic."

"They better have buckets of pixie dust, because that's what it's going to take to turn this pumpkin into a coach."

"Coach? Bah!" A woman with a comb in one hand and a can of hairspray in the other stepped forward. "You'll be a princess when you leave here."

Two other women took me by the arms and led me to a sheet-draped rectangular table. "We'll give you a second to undress and lay, face down."

"Undress?"

"Yes, ma'am. Down to your birthday suit. Your private areas will be covered with small towels. We'll take care of that for you. You're in good hands."

The two women turned their backs. I slid out of my clothes and climbed onto the table.

"You ready?"

"Ready as I'll ever be. Do you believe in miracles? I do. Say, did you know that cupcakes are just muffins that believe in miracles...and frosting too? They are. Truly. Now you get to help this muffin believe she can be turned into a cupcake. Better have lots of icing ready to apply!"

I got steamrolled by the two attendants, who had very little senses of humor. One worked my top half. The other focused on my bottom half. "I'll keep my eyes closed. You do what you need to do. Hands. Elbows. Bowling balls. Jackhammers. Whatever you use to relax people, feel free to use it."

With all the pushing and kneading and rubbing and stretching, my body was loosening up. "Are you going to put me on one of those taffy-pulling machines next?"

"Mmmmm...nope," replied one of the girls. "The shower is next for you."

"Alone, or are we all going together?" I wasn't sure if that was a group activity as well.

"Alone."

"Thank you."

When I stepped out from the steam-filled bathroom in a robe, the same two women took me by the arms and directed me to Marilyn's makeup chair. Once seated, I took a gander at myself in the three reflecting panes.

"Look at that fat girl. Well, three fat girls." I shifted my gaze at the reflections of the two women. "Let's get something out of the way. Right off the bat. I'm fat and I know it. You know it. I'm not curvy. I'm not hefty. Not full-figured. Not plus. I'm fat. I have fat. I jiggle even when I'm not walking."

"Are you quite finished?" One of the ladies blinked at me and added, "What will your man think? You want to look your very best, don't you?"

"He's seen me drenched and at my worst down on the beach. And he still asked me out. But I suppose that shouldn't hold me back."

I closed my eyes, shutting down the possibility of seeing myself in the mirrors. "Alright, I surrender. What's next?"

FADE OUT

CHAPTER 32

"I don't do girdles." I put up both open palms in a defensive show of pushing back and taking a stand. "I draw the line there."

"But, we've come so far." The woman's words, and the way she delivered them, egged me on. "This will make a world of difference."

"Speaking of worlds, have you ever tried to squeeze someone the shape of a globe into the shape of an hourglass?"

"Well, this, I admit, will be a challenge. But as I said. Look how far we've come."

I didn't want to look in the mirror. I didn't. "You know, I look really great in a fun-house mirror. Do you have one of those here?"

I gave in. The person looking back was a new and improved model. No doubt about it. My hair was swept back and up, slimming my face. I'd never seen my cheek bones expertly defined by makeup. I'd always hated my chin. My double chin. I'd always had it, and it was the hardest to hide. Thighs and a belly are much easier to camouflage than a double chin.

"I just wish I had a matching set."

"Of what? Earrings? Is that why you were wearing mismatched ones?"

"No, silly. Dimples. I only got one when God was handing them out." I grinned—showing as many teeth as I could like a Cheshire Cat—and pointed to the one I had.

"Your folks got them?"

"Not from my mother, and I can't honestly remember the last time I saw my father smile."

"That's too bad."

The eye shadow and mascara worked as a team to make my eyes inviting. I studied how my newly shaped and penciled eye brows arched and crowned my eyes. The red-wine shade of lipstick made my mouth look like a sharpshooter's target and my teeth were as white as the clouds over the Pacific on a summer afternoon.

The prospect of a girdle popped back into my mind. "Oh, God. I know I'm going to regret this. Please don't make this a Scarlett O'Hara scene. I won't hold onto the bedpost as Mammy tightens the laces. I'm not too girly to be afraid of belching. But I have to breathe."

One of the women came into the mirror's view holding a girdle out in front of her.

"This is what I get for being my family's Clean-Plate Award winner all those years. How are we going to get it on? Over the top? Or up from the bottom? I don't need to say it, but there are some obvious obstacles to either approach."

"This one's a bottoms-up design. We'll use talcum powder."

"A pound of butter might be a better choice. Or a can of motor oil."

"Here, you do it. Sprinkle the talcum. It'll help the girdle slip on more easily."

I dusted, sprinkled and smoothed out the powder on my exposed skin. I stepped into the girdle and began pulling it up.

"Mark my words. Someday a girl who looks like me will appear in *Playboy*. And all of this will be obsolete. Big girls will be hot and skinny girls will not."

"Until that day arrives, we get to do *this*."

"Wait. Let's fold it over a few times at the waistline. It'll give you more to grip. Once it's up at your waist, you can unfold it."

"Easier said than done." I groaned as the girdle's ascension screeched to a halt at my knees. I looked at the vanity's mirrors. "Well, it does make a spectacular hour glass shape...with my calves at the bottom, my thighs and ass at the top and my knees in the middle. But I suspect we haven't achieved our goal yet."

"No. We have not."

"Then, here we go." I sucked in a deep breath and pulled more. Up to my thighs. Up to my ass. I sucked in another deep breath. I pulled. I pulled. And I pulled some more.

Marilyn entered the room. "How's it going? You sprinkle some talcum?"

"Yes, and I've already had a knock-down wrestling match with this damned thing. And I didn't win."

"I see that. It should sculpt your figure. Perhaps the cramming approach is not the best one. Slide it back down." Marilyn studied me.

"I don't mean to sound uncooperative, but I'm not sliding this down after all it took to get it this far."

"Honey, I learned early on that clothes should be tight enough to show you're a woman, but loose enough to show you're a lady. I have to confess that I don't always follow that lesson, however." Marilyn paused and added, "Let me tell you a quick story. When I was twelve, I looked like a seventeen-year-old. The kids at school called me dumb and made fun of my orphan's outfits. I had only two blouses and two skirts, until one day when a girl in the house I was living in loaned me a sweater. Everything changed. Everyone stared at me as if I had three heads. In a way, I had. Two were under that tight sweater. Clothes are important. How they fit is even more important."

I nodded and remained silent. Ironically, she was wearing a sweater. A tight sweater.

Marilyn looked me over. "I'm thinking that a waist cincher might do the trick, without requiring so much effort. It'll whittle your middle. Patsy, please go to Wardrobe and see what they have on hand. There's nothing wrong with a little nip and tuck, right?"

"On my way."

"They aren't going to have my size...my size of anything."

"Sure they will. We have two full-grown men dressing as women in this picture. They'll have all kinds of things they wouldn't normally have on a set, including a waist-nipper for you. It may not be comfortable, but it'll do the trick."

I made a smashed-lips face and bobbed my head a few times in agreement.

"Now, let's see what other magic we can do here. Hair looks perfect. Makeup, yes, striking without looking pushy. Hmmm, let me see your nails."

I raised my hands, palms down. I got tipsy. My center of gravity must've shifted after releasing the girdle at my upper thighs.

"What color's my dress? Maybe they can work on my nails while we wait for the waist pincher."

"It's a cincher, not a pincher." Marilyn corrected me and looked at the rest of the team. "Let's be sure she doesn't see the dress. We're saving that for last."

"I want to say this process is a nightmare. But it's also a dream come true. I don't know how you do it every day."

"I have to admit that dreaming about being an actress is more exciting than being one. Hollywood is like a really, really, really bad boyfriend. Red hot, then Eskimo cold. Full of promises that are never kept. Unpredictable. Loud and then all too silent."

Marilyn left the room through an open doorway. I heard the rustling of fabric, then oohs and awes in tender female voices in the next room.

She returned. "Honey, your dress is perfect, in so many ways. But for now, let's give you a new color on your nails." She walked over to a case of fingernail polish that resembled the paint-sample wall at Hank's hardware store.

"Well, that's overwhelming."

"Not in the least." With one swipe of her hand, Marilyn plucked out a small bottle and showed it to me.

"That's not much of a color."

"You're correct. It's called Nude. And when your man asks about it, you can say that word with all the sensuality you can muster. Try it. Come on. Try it right now."

"Nude."

"No. Hold onto the letters. Like you have peanut butter in your mouth. Smooth and salty." Marilyn cooed her words.

"Noooooooodddddaaahhhh."

"Better, but not quite. Say it laaaaazy."

A new woman entered the room, placed a stool next to me and began to work on my nails.

"I've never had this much attention in my life. Probably never will again."

"Enjoy it. This is *your* night." Marilyn studied me. "You are going to change your bra, right?"

"I wasn't planning on it."

"Stella, off to the costumers with you. Make sure Patsy finds that cincher and pick out a few strapless sweater-girl bras. With what Penny's got, she can rival Jane and Lana any day of the week."

"That'd be Jane Russell and Lana Turner?"

"Yes. It would. They haven't got anything you don't."

"I just have more of it...like two buckets more."

"Wait until you see what a well-engineered bra can do. Uplifting. Shaping. Man eating."

Laughter broke out in the room. Marilyn straightened her back and gazed down at the tight white sweater she was wearing. Her pointy breasts were barely tamed under her top as she shimmied her shoulders.

"Remember what I told you about the boys at school?"

"Sure do. I was listening."

"Well, *men* have an even bigger thing about tits. They *love* my tits. I don't quite get it, but I'm happy they do."

I flashed back to my mother's question at dinner. Even Marilyn described her breasts as tits.

"Photos of these tits have been pinned up and pined for...well, for years!" Marilyn giggled. "Speaking of pine, I've been told I'm single-handedly responsible for producing more wood than all the lumberjacks in the Northwest."

I must not have responded enough for her to notice because she added, "Woodies, you know? Soldiers standing at attention? How about a boney baloney? Stiff one? You must have heard of Vlad the Impaler? Thrill drill? Pocket rockets?"

"Got it." That's all I could get out before snickering like a silly school girl.

"I *knew* you knew. I just wanted to have some fun with you, honey...to get you to relax for what we're about to do to you."

"Mission accomplished," I said as my snickering settled down.

She reached for my hands. "Your nails will just have to wait. Now, suck it in," was the only instruction I got when the waist cincher was being wrapped around my middle. I pulled my shoulders back and sucked in.

"Hey, I can still breathe."

"Not so fast. That was just the *first* pull...the first of many."

Seven pulls later I wasn't breathing as well. My head felt like an over-filled balloon and my vision went out of focus, like cheesecloth over a camera lens.

"That should do it."

"That should do it alright. Kill me. Suffocate me. Break a few ribs. Did the Marquis de Sade design this?" As I rolled my eyes, I added, "I think this thing is so tight it's measuring my blood pressure."

"It'll take some getting used to. Try sitting down." Marilyn patted my wrist.

"Sit? Someone's going to have to pull off that girdle. As it is, I won't be able to reach down there for the rest of the night."

Stella tried to lower the girdle. "It's going to take two of us." Patsy came over to help. They each grabbed a handful of folded girdle fabric. "On the count of three, pull. One. Two. Three."

They pulled like they were shucking the world's largest cob of corn. I started to wobble. "Pull again. Quick." They pulled, but unevenly this time. One side was lower than the other. I wobbled the other way and tippy-toed as I swayed.

"I'm going down. Watch out everyone."

Marilyn pushed a chair behind me.

"Timber!"

Marilyn directed my trussed-up body toward the chair. The twirling and swirling stopped when my ass landed on the chair.

"Lift up your feet." Marilyn's words were mixed with laughter. Patsy and Stella slid the girdle the rest of the way down and off.

"Your shoes, madam." May delivered them like a high-class waiter would say when placing a fancy meal on a white-linen tablecloth.

"Give a girl the right shoes and she can conquer the world. But they're only as good as how she walks in them." Marilyn grinned. "Actresses long before me discovered you have to place one foot in front of the other. It makes your hips and shoulders work and move together. Men can't help but watch. Women can't help but envy."

"May, where have you been? I wish you'd been here through all of this." I smiled at May and sighed.

"This is ridiculous. Why can't I just go as me. Penny. The girl who's been nickeled and dimed all her life. Steele's already seen me soaking wet on the beach."

"That's exactly why he needs to see you like this. I mean, like you're going to look when we're finished with you." May patted one of my cheeks.

"Now, a new bra. Do you want us to leave while you try these on?" Stella laid out several on the counter and stepped back.

"Honestly. At this point, I don't have a shred of modesty left."

Through process of elimination, we determined which bra lifted and shaped best.

"That only leaves the dress. Are you ready?" Marilyn clapped her hands together, like she did earlier.

"As ready as I'll ever be."

"Then close your eyes. Both of them. And no peeking. Promise?"

I ached to peek like never before. And I was a champion peeker. "I promise." I meant it. "But how did they make a whole dress in no time at all?"

"They're the best at what they do. And if we need to sew you into the dress at the last minute, we'll sew you into the dress."

"Alright, then." The whole thing was just so dreamy and amazing.

"Stella, bring it out!" Marilyn sounded like a circus ringmaster calling out the next act to the center ring.

"Arms up, pointing to the ceiling, Penny. Like a torpedo."

"Like my tits. The cones on this bra are pointy enough to poke someone's eyes out."

"Let's all hope that doesn't happen. Now just put your hands up. Please."

Someone got up on a chair and lowered the dress over my hands, arms, head, shoulders and chest.

"Keep those eyes closed."

"Yes, sir." My father barged into my mind. I could see his scowl. I erased him as quickly as I could.

"Now stand up straight so we can smooth it out."

"Easier said than done."

"We'll help you."

I rose.

The dress cascaded down.

I could hear shoes shuffling away from me.

"Hey! What happened? Are you still there? Talk to me. Tell me I don't I look like a wide-screen Cinemascope version of myself?"

Someone sniffled.

"I look *that* bad? Someone's crying?"

I felt several hands smoothing out the dress's lower two thirds. They were swatting, fluffing and picking. It was the sensation of finishing touches.

"You may open your eyes, Penny."

"I'm afraid to. You've all worked so hard. Girls like me don't get Cinderella moments."

"They do—you do—and you will," cooed Marilyn. "Now open those eyes of yours, honey."

FADE OUT

CHAPTER 33

A taxi pulled up to the back entrance for the Hotel del Coronado staff. I looked out the doorway first, checking to see if the coast was clear. I turned off the light that illuminated the doorway so we didn't take any unnecessary risks. We scampered out like two teenagers escaping a slumber party.

"Non-stop trip to paradise. Is that right?"

"Yes, Paul. That's the plan."

"From what I can see, you look incredible Penny."

"Swear?"

"Sure. GODDAMNIT! You look incredible."

"Not *that* kind of swear." I slid across the back seat and adjusted the bottom half of my dress. I turned to Marilyn. "I had no idea how hard it would be to move in a dress like this."

"Honey, I've been in plenty of back seats and no dress or skirt I've worn ever slid very well." She giggled in an excited way.

"I'd like you to meet Paul, our driver tonight. I've known him forever. We bowl together."

Paul closed the back door and sat behind the wheel. "The pleasure's all mine, though I have to say you don't quite look like yourself tonight. Or should I say *yourselves*?"

I replied, "Thanks Paul. I'll assume you meant that as a compliment... to both of us."

"It was," he said over his shoulder.

Marilyn chimed in, "I'm not quite sure how to respond to that Paul. But if you two bowl together, then I'm sure I can trust him with this little adventure of ours. Just like we can trust that sweet old policeman outside my cottage door. He'll keep our secret. I just know it." Marilyn added, "Paul, it's a pleasure."

Paul tipped his hat and winked into the rear-view mirror at Marilyn.

Lonesome Town was playing on the radio. "I just love Ricky Nelson. Can you even imagine a family so perfect that you could have a radio show and then a television show about it?" I shook my head. "They sure as hell couldn't broadcast what went on in the house when I was a kid."

"Mine either," added Paul. "Are you sure you wouldn't rather have a real driver instead of a regular taxi?"

"That would make us stick out." Marilyn patted the top of my hand. "Remember, this is about you, Penny. The *new* you."

"I like the way that sounds. And I don't like the way that sounds. *New.*"

"Now you must do the bushel-basket thing." Marilyn looked out the window.

"Huh?" I wasn't following her.

"You know that song in Sunday school. About never hiding your light under a bushel basket."

"No matter how large the bushel is?"

"No matter. You just shine." Marilyn turned to face me and grinned.

Paul pushed on the accelerator, heaving us against the back of the seat.

"My good man, a tad smoother if you please." Marilyn said that in a nearly unrecognizable voice. It matched her unrecognizable appearance.

Earlier, just as the team finished my transformation, work began on Marilyn. Not to give her the glamor treatment. Quite the opposite. She got the dowdy treatment. The spinster transformation. They had experience at it. This was far from the first time they helped Marilyn venture out incognito. A short dark wig with a black skullcap hat and netted veil. Black cat-eye glasses. Very little makeup. No lipstick. A dab of foundation to mask any hint of the trademark mole on her lower cheek. One of Paula's black dresses and an overcoat. Dark leather lace-up orthopedic shoes. A plain handbag. A white, lace-trimmed handkerchief tucked under her wristwatch band on her left wrist.

Marilyn brushed off the sleeve of her coat with the back of her hand and then pushed up the cat-eye glasses. "You know, looks aren't all they're cracked up to be. It's just *another* set of problems."

I didn't respond.

"When I'm in New York City, I can walk right down the street and no one notices me. But when I walk like Marilyn and talk like Marilyn, then it's a mob scene."

The way she said *Marilyn* made it sound as if she thought of Marilyn as someone else entirely.

"You're a real scene stealer, Penny. Tonight, let me fade into the scenery."

"If you say so."

"I picked out a dress in those shades of blue because they brought me good luck once."

"They did?"

"Ever see *There's No Business Like Show Business*?"

"Sure. You were great with Ethel Merman, Donald O'Connor, Mitzi Gaynor—"

"Thank you. I liked making that picture. My character's name was Vicky Parker. Say, that's got to be a sign, Miss Penny *Parker*."

She patted my hand again. "And the dress I wore in the finale, that's the one your dress looks like, made everyone else disappear on screen. That's what I've been told. This dress is not exactly the same, but those silky shades from arctic blue to azure, well, the camera just loved them."

As I adjusted my dress's shoulder strap, I studied the clear crystals that encrusted it. "The camera loved—loves—you," I added as I smoothed out the dangling blue rhinestones that shifted on my lap with Paul's sudden lane change.

"Penny, I'm going to tell you something not many people know. In that film, there was this enormous staircase we had to walk down—together. Of course, you had to look forward the whole time. Never down. There were rehearsals to make us all feel comfortable doing it. My dress had this cascade of puffy, sparkly tulle along the left side and then down around the bottom. It was like I was going to be walking in a shimmering cloud. My own…personal…shimmering…cloud." Her voice faded away along with her gaze.

She eased a sigh out. "It was long enough to trip on, especially on stairs. But don't you worry. I made sure yours wouldn't be too long."

Marilyn added. "I didn't go to any of the rehearsals. Not one. When the time came to shoot, I just showed up and went down those stairs without a hitch. Mitzi told me later that Ethel was livid I pulled it off. And that film helped push my career forward. So, I want the same for you. No rehearsals. Just you and Steele and a shimmering blue dress. I hope it all goes without a hitch."

I grinned. My head swiveled side to side.

"What? You don't believe me?"

"Of course I do. I just can't believe you told me that story."

"Well why ever not? I'm just a girl like you. Trying to have a good time."

"But you're Marilyn Monroe. You don't have to tell me anything."

"I'm here with you. Right now. This could be a night you'll always remember. I have a feeling I'll remember it."

"There's no chance that's not going to happen. And if it does— if this is a dream come true—I won't know what to do next."

"Silly, you just go out and find a new dream. We always need a dream…all of us." Marilyn gazed down at the handbag on her lap and slid her index finger along the strap's edge.

"How do you do it? Keep going? With a smile on your face?" I genuinely wanted to know.

"Honey, I'm not always smiling. You know that." She kept her eyes on her handbag and her finger sliding along its strap. "I fake it. I bluff. Part of acting is being an imposter. Honestly, most of acting is being an imposter. Sometimes it's hard to turn that off."

"So how do you cope with it all?"

She lifted her gaze to my face. "I hope for the best. I try to, anyway. But people always expect me to fail…or fall down…or trip up. They say I'm a has-been. They compare me to an overripe piece of fruit. That can wear a girl out until you do exactly what they expect. You fail to deliver. I don't want that for you."

"Neither do I. With your help, Marilyn, that won't happen."

And it didn't. Well, not exactly.

FADE OUT

CHAPTER 34

FADE IN:
- SEPTEMBER 9, 1958, SECOND DAY OF SHOOTING
- INTERIOR, PAUL'S TAXI CAB (NIGHTTIME)

I watched Marilyn stare out the taxi's side window at the flashes of passing street lights.

Dark. Light.

Dark. Light.

Dark. Light.

It was hypnotic.

Dark. Light.

Dark. Light.

Dark. Light.

It was like a get-ready-for-this transition to a dream sequence in a schmaltzy movie.

"This is such a charming little town…what I can see of it."

"Yes. I suppose it is when compared to New York City, London, Paris, Rome and all the places you've been."

Marilyn nodded.

"Yikes. Perfume. We forgot to spray some." She looked through her handbag and fished out a small bottle. "Put out your wrists."

I did.

"Chanel No. 5. You can't go wrong with Chanel No. 5."

The perfume was intoxicating. Its floral-citrus-soapy scent masked the musty smell of Paul's cab.

The taxi was quiet for a long minute.

"Don't be nervous. Don't be nervous." Marilyn's voice was heavy with concern.

"I'm not. Not much." I admitted it out loud.

"I wasn't talking to you. I was talking to myself."

"What do you have to be nervous about?"

"I hope this disguise works for as long as we need it to. I've done this lots of times, but you never know if or when the charade will end."

"That's something to be nervous about." I paused. "Marilyn, I have to tell you something."

"You do? Go right ahead."

"I'm not me. I mean, I feel like I'm wearing someone else's skin. And it's too tight."

"I understand, honey. Believe me. I do. But let's give it a try. Let's not be ourselves tonight."

I turned to look at Marilyn. "I hope I don't regret this."

"You won't."

I wasn't so convinced by Marilyn's delivery of that line.

"Paul, for tonight, Marilyn's going by the name Zelda Schnuck. Be sure to call her that if you need to get her attention…outside of your taxi, that is."

"Sure thing."

"Now, like we agreed, I'll get out first." Marilyn sounded firm about her instructions. "I just have to see you coming out of the car and going into the restaurant."

"Are you sure? I've never done anything like this before. God, I hope it works." My gaze moved from the windshield to my side window.

Our conversation screeched to a standstill while lights continued to race by.

And everything got blurry. *Everything.*

I asked myself whether it was all just a daydream I hadn't woken up from. And would I even know it if I did?

My world stayed blurry until the Red Rose Supper Club came into view. My eyes darted to Marilyn's. Then to Paul's in the rearview mirror.

"It's show time." Paul punched the words like a trumped-up radio announcer.

"Penny, this is what you've been waiting for."

Paul stopped his taxi as smooth as silk. A uniformed doorman opened my door to reveal a red carpet.

"Marilyn, it's not just a red carpet." My hushed words escaped my lips in a rush. "There are rose petals scattered on it. I can't believe it. I'd ask you to pinch me, but I think you might just do it."

Paul added, "And look at that sign. The place is closed to the public tonight. He bought out the restaurant...just for you."

I put my gloved hand on the doorman's hand. I knew I was supposed to let Marilyn go first, but I didn't.

My dress cascaded down as I stood. I didn't take any steps though. I closed my eyes to savor the moment. I tipped my head back and slowly opened my eyes to find a field of stars, like sparks in the sky. I lowered my chin and caught a glimpse of Steele standing in the club's doorway, waiting for me to arrive.

"Move. Walk to him and show off the new you." Marilyn encouraged me not only with words. She nudged my bottom to push me forward.

"I've got to just stand here. Take it in. This may never happen again in my lifetime."

Steele came toward me.

"See, he thinks you're afraid. Stand up straight and walk to him." Marilyn pushed my bottom again.

"Alright already." I said the words like a ventriloquist. No lips moving, at least not in plain sight. I placed one foot in front of the other, just as Marilyn taught me. It made my hips and shoulders move as a team like never before.

Steele stopped in his tracks, watching me as if I was the only thing on the face of the earth worth his attention. He was at his most chocolate-box-enchanting so far. I wondered if it could get any better than that.

"You're stunning. Beautiful. Breathtaking." Steele's satiny voice caressed my heart.

Strains of *Bewitched, Bothered and Bewildered* swirled on the air around me. It was like a scene out of a movie, with a sound track to swell with the emotion of it all.

"Do you like it?" Steele used his hand to gracefully point out the speakers stashed in the potted ferns along the red carpet. "I wanted you to be serenaded by Frank Sinatra and have the scent of roses perfume your pathway."

"I don't know what to say. I just—"

"Then don't. Let's not let words limit how we feel." Steele approached me with an extended hand. "Let's go inside. Just the two of us. We'll dance. Drink. Dine. And see just where the evening takes us."

I placed my hand on his and moved toward the club's front door.

I gazed over my shoulder and winked at Marilyn and Paul.

I mouthed the words, "Thank you. Bye."

It was all so dreamy. In fact, it was *too* dreamy. That's because it was a day dream. Just another one of my strolls down Dream Street.

It was just too good to be true for a girl like me.

FADE OUT

CHAPTER 35

FADE IN:

- SEPTEMBER 9, 1958, SECOND DAY OF SHOOTING
- INTERIOR, PAUL'S TAXI CAB (NIGHTTIME)

"Hey! Princess Penny! We're heeeeeere!" Paul's heavy foot on the brake pitched everyone forward. "Penny. Are you listening to me?"

"What? What? Oh." My words conveyed how I was startled and then disappointed.

"Stop daydreaming and looking out the window with your mouth open. You might drool on yourself. I haven't heard you be so quiet—for that long—well, for quite a while. What were you thinking about?"

"You know I have a rich fantasy life. I guess I went on a little excursion. But I'm here now. Right. Here."

"A girl has to get herself mentally ready too." Marilyn nudged me with her elbow as she shook her hands. "Come on. Shake out your hands too. It'll get you all set for your big moment. Your big reveal."

"Yeah, your big moment. I'll be waiting to take you back to The Del when you two are ready."

"I feel like I should give you some advice." Marilyn placed her index right finger over her closed lips. "I've got nothing. How about, have a good time?"

"Works for me." I leaned in and confessed, "I'm afraid."

Marilyn whispered back, "You?"

"Yeah, me. I'm just Penny the Cashier."

"And I'm Norma Jeane, just a girl who grew up in an orphanage and foster homes. Relax, honey. Enjoy this while it lasts. Few things do, you know…last." She grinned and added, "I've always loved what Mae West said about how you only live once. But if you do it right, once is enough."

I grinned back at her.

The Red Rose Supper Club's neon sign glowed green and red. As agreed, Marilyn quickly got out first and waited in the doorway. By the time Paul got out and came to my door, I had my right gloved hand out.

Marilyn encouraged me with a series of nods. I looked around for Steele. He wasn't waiting outside. I took Paul's hand and, as gracefully as possible, rose from the taxi.

"Thank you, Paul. Thank you ever so much." I closed my eyes and opened them in slow motion.

It was a warm evening. I didn't need a wrap. Besides, I wanted the crystals on the upper part of my dress to glisten like the evening lights. My necklace—a simple strand of rhinestones—and matching chandelier earrings must've shimmered like the wishing star. I wished I could've seen them.

As I stood up straight, I raised my chin and looked toward Marilyn. I was casting a spell on everyone who could see me. I was the bombshell of the moment, while Marilyn lurked in the shadows.

When I passed her, Marilyn whispered, "I hope you're ready. Because it all starts now. Right. Now."

Without looking in her direction, I whispered back, "I'm ready."

Once inside the club, I was greeted by the hostess. Before she finished speaking, I blurted out, "Has Mr. Wright arrived yet?"

She gave me the once-over and tightened her lips into a grin that I suspected had suspicious motives. "Your Mr. Right? Here?"

"That'd be W-R-I-G-H-T." I spelled it out for her.

She checked her list. "No, he has not. May I suggest you wait for him in the lounge. You might enjoy one of our signature cocktails."

"Thank you. That's exactly what I'll do." I crossed the lounge and stood at the bar.

"Perhaps you'd like a seat at a table." The bartender's eyes traveled my body.

"I don't think so, but thanks for the offer." I wasn't about to add any more wrinkles to my dress before Steele saw it. Not a chance. Besides, I was enjoying breathing normally again. I gracefully rested my left palm on the side of my newly defined waist. While the cincher did its best to create an hourglass figure, it was a bear hug to my lungs, especially when I was sitting.

"Then a barstool?"

"No, thank you."

"A cocktail for you?"

"Martini. Shaken briskly. Two olives. Not one. Not three. Two."

Marilyn moved in closer. She snickered at my last remark.

"You got it." The bartender pointed an imaginary pistol at me and made a click sound with his tongue and cheek.

A man sitting two barstools away joined the conversation, uninvited. "Did it hurt when you fell from heaven?"

"I don't remember. Did it hurt when hell coughed you up?" I grinned at my cleverness.

Marilyn made a small "o" shape with her lips. I was sure she was bug-eyed behind her cat-eye glasses and the net veil.

The voice of the hostess caught my attention. "She is here, Mr. Wright. You'll find her in the lounge."

"D-Day!"

"D-Day?" The bartender questioned me as he dropped a square napkin on the bar before he placed the martini glass down.

"Oh, never mind. But keep talking to me. There's a tip in it if you look fascinated by our conversation and laugh every now and then."

"Your date's here, right?"

"Yes, and I want to make a good impression."

"I'll play along, tip or no tip. A really good game of cat and mouse—"

"Fine, just play along."

The bartender looked over my shoulder to see if he could spot my date. "No one new is in here."

"There has to be. I heard the hostess say his name."

"There's a guy who sorta looks like one of them Hollywood movie stars standing over there. Doesn't seem like he's finding what or who he's looking for."

"That's him. But he may not recognize me. I put a little extra effort into my appearance tonight."

The bartender looked at me again. "Yes, I can see that."

"Whaddya mean? I mean, what do you mean by that comment?" I corrected my tone and pacing the second time.

"I mean, you are a vision this evening. He's a lucky man to have you with him. That is, when you join him...which I would recommend doing soon. The women without dates tonight are circling their wagons around him as we speak."

I made a fist with my gloved hand and gently pounded the bar in frustration.

"Not to worry. He's coming this way."

I felt a wildfire rage from my chest to my ear lobes. I was hot. I was cold. My heart sped up. My stomach dropped.

"Excuse me." Steele spoke up to get the bartender's attention. "Has a Miss Parker come in?"

"I don't know anyone by that name—"

"But *I* do." I turned. I shimmered.

Steele stared and studied.

"I don't quite know what to say, Penny. You're a whole new and improved you—"

"Nope, it's just me with a fresh coat of paint."

"Don't sell yourself short. You look stunning. You look like a...um...a movie star."

"Well, that's something *this* girl has never heard before. Thank you."

I caught Steele looking at my breasts. I didn't know how anyone could avoid them. They were like two gigantic snow cones mounted to my chest.

"Your dress. It's so flattering...yes flattering."

"Oh this little thing. I borrowed it for the evening."

Nearby, Marilyn spun a swizzle stick in her drink and smiled. She made a shooing motion with her hand, encouraging me to get on with my evening.

"Would you like to stay here or move on to dinner?" It was kind of Steele to ask my opinion.

"Dinner please. It's been a long day."

"Bartender, bring the lady's martini to our table...and bring one just like it for me."

"You got it."

I winked at the bartender and turned to take Steele's arm. He escorted me back to the hostess and on to our table. He pulled out my chair. I wasn't used to that kind of treatment, much less from a man like Steele. The evening was intoxicating. *He* was intoxicating.

I scanned the room for Marilyn as I adjusted my dress and sat down, but she hadn't been seated yet.

He sat down and outstretched his hands. I looked at them. I eased in a lung-filling breath and rested my hands on his.

"Now tell me. Everything." He sounded genuinely interested.

"About?"

"About you. I want to know everything about you. We can start with your family."

"Trust me, you don't."

Steele was unfazed. "Then we can move on to your favorite color. Your favorite book. Your favorite flavor of ice cream. It may take an hour. An evening. A month. A lifetime."

I couldn't believe he wanted to know that stuff. I looked in to his eyes. He was serious. He did want to know. I smiled and moved my shoulders to make my necklace, earrings and bodice sparkle ever so slightly.

"Should I order for you?"

"That'd be wonderful." I hoped I wouldn't regret that decision.

Steele opened the menu, ran his finger down the column on the left side, then the right. He closed the menu and placed it on the white tablecloth.

"My, my, that was quick. You make up your mind—our minds—fast, don't you?"

"It's simple. We're at the beach. We should have something from the sea." He directed his next comments to the waiter. "We'll start with calamari and mussels in that creamy tomato bisque you're known for."

"Sounds absolutely divine." It didn't. But I said it anyway.

"Then a Cacsar salad, extra anchovies."

"Mmmmm." I flashed my eyes and grinned at Steele.

"I can't get over it. I can't stop staring at you. You were beautiful before, but now, well—"

I looked down at my dress and patted my necklace.

"I tried to tell you earlier, it's like you're a new woman."

"Nope. Just a dime-store dolly dressed up for the ball. You, on the other hand, look very nice. A dark suit suits you well."

"Thank you. We're quite a pair tonight."

"Yes we are."

"I almost brought Chip with me. He said he wasn't feeling well, but he'll be fine with a hotel nanny. Heck, he'd be fine *alone*. He's a real trooper that way." Steele rested his elbows on the table's edge, raised his hands and steepled his fingertips. He leaned in. "He's an apple that didn't fall far from the tree. He's been through so much lately. But other than not talking, he's doing fine, just fine."

"Does he ever try to talk to you? Does he write you notes?"

"No. He's in his own world now and he only swoops down to our world when he wants to. Like his famous relatives."

"Who's that?"

"The Wright brothers, of course. Of plane and bicycle fame. They're family."

He had to be lying. The other day he said he didn't have any relatives...that he and Chip were alone together. "Impressive!" I lied too. "Now, back to Chip. He seems like such a bright boy. I'm sure that someday you'll help him open back up again."

"I can hope so."

"There's always hope, isn't there?" I moved the knife and spoon a bit at my place setting.

"Not long ago, I didn't think so. But I do now."

I caught myself grinning and raised my palm to cover my mouth. I couldn't believe he was talking about me.

"Penny for your thoughts. Where are you?"

"I'm right here. With you. Only you." Marilyn, who was sitting against the wall at a small, badly lit table, caught my eye. She gestured to me to sit up straight and push my chest out. She used hand signals to tell me to open my eyes and smile. If anyone noticed what Marilyn was doing, they would have thought she was nuts and looked the other way for fear of connecting with her. I looked around the room and it appeared that Marilyn, this version of Marilyn, was going unnoticed.

"Did you know The Del is haunted?" My voice wavered on the word *haunted*.

"You don't say."

"Yes, I do. A woman—or at least her ghost—roams around the beach. Her name's Kate and she died at The Del. I've seen her myself. In fact, I saw her the other day."

Steele adjusted the napkin on his lap.

"It was the most amazing thing. I've asked people about it at the hotel but it's very hush-hush. The bellman told me that people commit suicide at hotels all the time. It's the murders that hotels don't like people to know about."

"Murders?" Steele looked over my shoulder, at the doorway and at his martini, fingering the olives.

Marilyn nodded and encouraged me to go on by making more hand gestures that I couldn't decipher. If only she knew our conversation was about ghosts, she might not have been so encouraging.

"Kate Morgan is her name. The papers said she shot herself, but people around here think she was murdered."

"You know a lot about her, don't you?"

"Well, I grew up in Coronado. We may not have any headless horsemen here, but we do have Kate. I'm kind of an expert on her. She-"

"Pardon me, your soup is ready." The waiter lowered two bowls of aromatic seafood bisque onto the table.

"Wish me luck." I lifted my spoon and aimed it at the bowl.

"Luck? For what. I'm the luckiest man in the world to be sitting here with you, right now. There's enough luck here for both of us."

"You may not say that when I slop this soup down the front of me."

Steele grinned. His eyes twinkled like I'd seen a thousand times in the movies.

"Give me your hand." His voice was deep and breathy. I'd have given him more than my hand if he'd asked for it that way.

"Penny, you've cast a spell on me."

"I could say the same about you."

"Yes, a spell. For me, it started on the beach after you saved Chip. You were upset with me, but I could see through it. I could see *you*. The real you. The way you looked at me, even though your words said something else. Penny, something's happening here. Between us. A warmth. Do you feel it too?"

"I do. I *really* do."

I froze and panicked the way only a woman can. And I instantly doubted Steele felt the *same* warm sensation I was feeling at that moment. In fact, it was impossible.

FADE OUT

CHAPTER 36

FADE IN:
- SEPTEMBER 9, 1958, SECOND DAY OF SHOOTING
- INTERIOR, RED ROSE SUPPER CLUB (NIGHTTIME)

A warm feeling. A warm *wet* feeling. It was that most-unwelcomed sensation every human with ovaries knows. I inhaled and made fish eyes. I'd known that alarming sensation since I was innocently sitting at my sixth-grade desk.

My period.

My super-scary, oh-so-mysterious *first* period.

That warm wet feeling was the first of several gory tidal waves.

In my twelve-year-old head I screamed, "Run for the bathroom! Run for the bathroom! RUN FOR THE BATHROOM!" And I screamed it the same way—in my grown-up head—while sitting across from Steele at the supper club.

"Steele, if you'll excuse me. I need to powder my nose. I may be gone for a while, but not to worry. I'll be back—"

My words trailed me. Steele didn't even get to respond. Or stand up. Or pull out my chair. My mind was filled with a vision of my mortified sixth-grader self, when I was standing at the school office's counter and not-so-sensitively handed a cotton brick that passed for a sanitary napkin. As I neared Marilyn, she made the fish-eye face back at me. I pointed at the restroom sign.

I was awake in a nightmare.

Marilyn whispered as I passed, "I'll be right there."

"My new blue dress. Not on my new blue dress!" I chanted the words as I entered a stall. "Please. Oh, please. Oh, please." I took a deep breath and twisted to see the back of the dress. No blotch. No spot. Not even a polka dot. I eyed the ceiling and declared, "Thank you!"

"You in here, Penny? If you don't want to talk, just poke your shoe out under the stall door."

"I'm here."

"What's wrong, honey. Your stomach upset?"

"No, what's upset is farther down. You know, Miss Scarlett has returned to Tara. It's time to ride the cotton surfboard."

Marilyn was silent. Either she understood, or she didn't and was still thinking about it.

"It's my period. Auntie Flo decided to visit. Unannounced and unexpected. It's time to ride the cotton pony. My tomato soup is boiling over."

Marilyn snickered. "I've never heard some of those."

"How about, my pipes have burst again? Or, I woke up and found the Japanese flag under me on my sheet. Or, there are too many Communists in my fun house." Leave it to me to find humor in such a disaster. It did diffuse my fear, though. "I have to admit this wasn't the surprise I was expecting tonight. But here it is. And here I am. Do you have anything in your purse to help?"

"No, I didn't pack for that. And I have this *huge* purse. Bigger than any I would normally carry. It's more like a piece of luggage."

I heard water running in the sink.

"Here, this should help."

I looked down. Marilyn was passing some wet paper towels under the stall's door.

"Is there much to clean up?"

I couldn't believe I was talking about menstruation with Marilyn Monroe in a public bathroom. No one would've believed it if I told them.

"Give me a second to get this dress out of the way and...um...assess the situation." That was something The Commander would say in a challenging predicament. He was the last person I wanted to be thinking about. "Get out of my head!"

"What was that, honey?"

"Sorry, I was thinking out loud."

"Napkin or tampon? What works best for you?"

"Both, I guess. Just to be safe."

"Coming right up."

I struggled to get my purse open and to fish out some coins. I took a moment to study Steele's lucky penny, which I'd tucked in a separate compartment for safekeeping.

I whispered, "You're more like an *unlucky* penny than a lucky one." As odd as it sounds, I was talking to a coin.

"What's that, honey?"

"Oh nothing. I was just getting some coins for the—"

"Don't worry about anything." Marilyn tried to reassure me. "You just wait right there."

"And my options would be to—"

"Don't get sassy with me. Just hold on a second."

"Thank you. Really. Thank you, Marilyn."

"That's what friends are for, right?"

My face tightened as I grinned. Marilyn had just called me her friend. "I can't believe this. For I don't know how long after I had my first period, my mother made me take a belt and a sanitary napkin in a brown-paper sack in my school bag...just in case my period came. One time it fell out in the hallway and the boys kicked it around like a playground ball. I was mortified. Still am, I guess."

I heard some coins drop with a metallic clink.

"Whew. It's stocked. Nothing worse than an empty dispenser when you're having a crisis. I hope these do the trick."

"So do I." I thought for a moment, and noticed a tickle in my left nostril. "No, please no."

"What's going on in there?"

"I think I'm going to sneeze...not just think...ACHEW!" A momentary silence hung in the air as I gazed down again. "Sweet Jesus, it looks like Jack the Ripper was in here."

I heard Marilyn rifle through more paper toweling.

"They sure don't tell little girls about this...that on your Cinderella night, blood might gush out of your bottom and turn your dream date into a bloody nightmare."

"No, *they* sure don't. Say, do you want me to go back out to my table now or wait for you?"

"Wait please. We have to talk."

"I'll just wash my hands and give you a little time to—"

"That'd be great. Thanks."

After a few minutes, I opened my stall's door. Luckily, no other women had come into the bathroom.

I started washing my hands. "So, he's a prince, after all. Charming as they come."

"They usually aren't. Come to think of it, they *never* are, honey."

"He's a god! A gorgeous god who's so connected to me. Like I'm the only girl in the room. Like I'm the most important person in the world, not the overweight personal assistant to the most beautiful woman in the universe."

"He is easy on the eyes. I'll give you that. But he's moving fast. Too close. Too attentive. You sure he's not up to something?"

I wiped my hands on a paper towel as I swirled around to see my backside in the mirror.

"Disarming. That's what he is." I threw my paper towel into the wastebasket and turned to face Marilyn.

"He looks like he's had plenty of practice disarming women. Trust me. I know the type."

"I suppose you do. It's like he casts a spell on whoever he's talking to, except Chip. His son doesn't buy it, does he?"

"He's like the wolves of Hollywood. On the prowl. Out for the kill. And then they move on."

"But I like the way this feels. I *love* the way this feels."

Marilyn advised, "If it's real, you'll feel the same tomorrow. Now let's get you out of here before Old Faithful erupts again and ruins your dress this time."

"I just wanted to be pretty. For once. Me. Pretty."

"Beautiful is not always pretty. Honey, there are all kinds of beautiful."

"True, but you're the new gold standard."

"I guess I did kind of mess it up for everyone else, didn't I?"

"Yes, you did. But I don't hold it against you." I added, "What am I going to say to him?"

"Just tell him you're not well and need to head back to the hotel. You have a big day tomorrow and need to be at your best. And keep moving. If you sit down, he'll convince you to stay and talk some more."

"Okay. I can do that."

Marilyn left the restroom first to return to her table. I looked at my reflection in the mirror. "Damn. It's not even midnight and this party's over."

As I neared our table, Steele stood up and stepped to the side to pull out my chair.

"No need for that. I really must leave. Now, in fact. I hope you understand. I've had a lovely time, but I'm not well and need to get back to The Del. Big doings tomorrow. And I need to be at my best."

"Will you at least let me take you back to the hotel?"

"No. But thanks. I'll be fine."

Marilyn moved toward the door and out of my sight.

"If it's alright, I'll say my goodbyes here." Before he could respond, I added, "Maybe we'll see each other at The Del some time." I pivoted on the slippery soles of my new shoes and walked away to join Marilyn outside.

The ocean air caressed my face. "That's better." I looked for Paul and his taxi. Marilyn and I held each other's arms as we walked out to the curb.

"Shit." I collided with Marilyn's shoulder.

"What's the matter, honey?"

I reached down and took off what was left of my defective pump. The heel played dead on the pavement. "Now what?"

"You don't want to leave that behind like Cinderella did. Do you?"

"Fat chance." I slipped off my heelless shoe, which had become a slipper. "That is, unless Steele's right behind us and ready to scoop it up and hand it to me on bended knee." I turned to check. He wasn't there.

I bent down again, picked up the heel and stuffed it in the broken shoe. We hobbled to Paul's taxi.

"To The Del. Pronto!" Marilyn spoke to Paul in an uncharacteristically deep voice.

"Once you're in my cab, you won't have to talk like that anymore."

"But I kind of like it." Marilyn released a squeak of a giggle.

"I don't think the millions of red-blooded American men would." I cleared my throat. "Say, are you up for one more stop before we go back to the hotel?"

"Sure. What do you have in mind?"

"Putting our feet up in a real house. In a real living room. With real people." I winked at Marilyn.

"Absolutely. I'm all yours."

Before long, a disturbing thwack-a-thwack-a sound came from the rear of the taxi.

"Ladies, it sounds like one of the back tires is coming apart and slapping the fender." Paul maneuvered the car to the curb.

We watched him get out, bend over and start laughing.

"Have you *ever* found anything funny about a flat tire?" I looked at Marilyn with a screwed-up face.

"Not me." Marilyn's head swiveled side to side.

We watched Paul continue to laugh until he stood up with a shiny silver fork in his hand. He came over to the window, which I was lowering.

"It appears we've hit a fork in the road. Literally." He started laughing again. "Won't take but a minute to change the tire. But that's a first for me. A fork!"

A fork in the road, I thought. I was facing one too. But not a piece of silverware.

"It's a first for me too." Marilyn went on, "I didn't think there were any *firsts* left for me in this life. Go figure."

She wouldn't have said that if she knew what was going to happen to her in just a few short days.

FADE OUT

CHAPTER 37

FADE IN:
- SEPTEMBER 9, 1958, SECOND DAY OF SHOOTING
- INTERIOR, PAUL'S TAXI CAB (NIGHTTIME)

"You remind me of Shelley. You know, Winters. You have her edge. She's quirky and outrageous. Did you know we shared an apartment for a while?"

"No, I didn't."

Paul's taxi started out on the road again.

"One day, when we had nothing else to do, we made a list of men we wanted to sleep with. She had all the young, beautiful stars like Errol Flynn and Laurence Olivier. Directors too. There was no one under the age of fifty on my list. I even had Albert Einstein on mine. Funny, we've never compared lists to see who's checked off more names."

"Really?"

"Really."

We passed a donut shop and glanced at each other. We both must've been thinking about how good a donut would be at that moment.

"Shelley always battled her weight. The studios hounded—absolutely *hounded*—her to lose weight. They always wanted to shove that poor girl into revealing dresses." Marilyn grinned and laughed to herself.

"She'd tell people she wasn't overweight, just nine inches too short. She told me about gobbling jelly donuts and guzzling cold lemonade as a kid with her sister on their front porch in St. Louis.

How she loved that part of her childhood. But they went without, like everyone else back then. When we were rooming together, we had practically nothing. Get this: we shared a bathing suit for photo shoots and a mink coat for dates."

"You don't say."

"We were that close. You'd have to be to share a bathing suit. But she's like the little girl with the curl in the middle of her forehead. When she's good, she's oh-so good. And when she's bad, she's horrid." Marilyn nodded as she completed her sentence. "She's one of the unforgettables. You know what I mean?"

"Sure. Well, no."

"Honey, everyone in this world is replaceable. But not everyone is unforgettable."

I let her words sink in. "Now I got it."

"I think of her all the time. Especially when I'm with guys."

"You do?"

"Uh-huh. She taught me how to be sexier. Come on. Try it with me. Tilt your head back."

I did as she instructed.

"Now lower your eyes."

Paul watched me in the taxi's rearview mirror. I lowered my eyes.

"And, ever-so-slightly, open your mouth."

I cracked my mouth open.

"Works every time."

"What do you think, Paul? Sexier?"

He didn't say anything. With words, anyway. But he winked at me in the rearview mirror.

"Look. There's Tilly's theater." Marilyn watched as we drove by. Paul slowed down so we could see the neon glow, the light bulbs flash, and, most of all, Tilly beam as she sold tickets to a snaking line of customers.

"I like her. I could learn a lot from Tilly." Marilyn's words were pillow soft and wispy.

When we pulled up to Trudy's house, the front-porch light was on. Like it always was in the evening. I could count on it to welcome me like a lighthouse in a squall.

"Come on in. Make yourself at home." I waved Marilyn in.

"I've pretty much forgotten what *home* feels like. And because I've lived in so many other people's houses, I guess I don't know how to make myself at home anymore. Imagine that."

"I certainly feel that way at The Del. It's nice there. But it's not home. And there's no Trudy."

"No *Trudy*?"

Trudy entered the living room from the hall just as the two of us sat down. Ella followed her, making figure eights between Trudy's legs with each of her steps.

"Who's this glamourous movie star sitting in my parlor?" Trudy used her I'm-so-surprised voice that sounded like she was encouraging a pampered poodle in need of attention. "Is that you, Penny? Under all that makeup? Honestly, is that necessary? And, will you kindly introduce me to your friend here?"

"Yes, this is Marilyn...Marilyn Monroe."

"T'aint nice to tease your landlady."

"I'm not teasing. This is Miss Monroe. Though she doesn't much look like herself, does she?"

Frankie followed in Trudy's footsteps, entering the room with a half-eaten slice of cherry pie on a plate. He stopped abruptly and his fork fell on the floor. I wasn't sure if it was because he saw me or Marilyn.

"Penny, you look so...um...so...you've changed." His voice cracked on the word *changed*.

My cheeks warmed and I grinned.

He'd seen *me*, not Marilyn.

"I mean...um...changed in a *good* way." Frankie stared at me. Not the way a good friend does. Or a brother. This was different. More like when we were on the beach together and things got all awkward.

I felt pretty.

I *was* pretty—in his eyes. In mine, too.

His eyes kept roving over me. Down and up. Up and down.

It'd finally happened. He was looking at me the way all girls want to be looked at by a man at least once in their lifetimes.

"Your hair...that dress. Where's the girl with scabby knees and goofy earrings?" Frankie didn't move. He didn't pick up his fork. He stared at me in an ogling sort of way. He didn't even acknowledge Marilyn or Trudy.

Trudy broke the silence. "Frankie, don't just stand there like a snowman in Minnesota. For gosh sake, pick up that fork and skedaddle yourself back into the kitchen."

"Yes, ma'am." Frankie added, "Good to see you, Penny. No. It's *great* to see you." He still didn't move.

"You might as well see the whole thing." I turned half-way around and peered at him over my shoulder. "Take a good, long look. This dress goes back to where it came from when I get back to The Del."

"Nonsense." Marilyn used her natural voice, even though she was still in her disguise. "It was made for you. Please consider it a gift...sort of like the gift I gave this young man out on the beach."

Frankie continued to stand motionless. The fork still rested on the floor, waiting patiently for Frankie to pick it up and return it to its friends in the kitchen.

"Hello again." Marilyn cooed her words to Frankie. After all, they did know each other. Even smooched on the beach in public. Marilyn looked more like herself then, however.

This time it was Frankie's turn to blush. "You remember me?" I could see his cheeks and ears turn scarlet.

"How could a girl forget when an entire track team of strapping athletes pays her to hug...or was it kiss...their coach?"

"Hug, I believe," Frankie replied. "But somehow it ended up being a kiss."

"Funny how things just happen, isn't it?" Marilyn grinned.

"Speaking of things that just happen, on the way here we hit a fork in the road." I knew what I said had a double meaning.

"What's so special about that?" Trudy's eyes had a curious look about them.

"No, we hit a fork in the road...a piece of silverware. It stuck right in the tire!" I wanted to say that I'd hit a fork in my life's road with Steele, but I held back.

"Paul was such a sweetie," Marilyn said. "He changed the tire and gave Penny the fork as a souvenir."

I held up the mangled fork and waited for a riot of laughter that never came.

"I better go. Thanks for the pie, Trudy." And with that, Frankie disappeared like the Road Runner in a cartoon. The fork remained an orphan on the floor.

Trudy turned her attention back to me. She put an open palm on her temple and the other on her apron. "Well, heck. I wasn't expecting any proper guests. Just Frankie for a bit of dessert. He's such a sweetheart. Anyway, you'll have to pardon me for my appearance. Penny, a bit of warning would have been nice, don't cha know. It's a pleasure—a real pleasure—Miss Monroe, to make your acquaintance."

"There really wasn't any time to call ahead. She and I were…um…conducting an experiment tonight."

"You were, were you?" Trudy bent down and retrieved Frankie's fork. "And was this experiment of yours a success?"

"We're *here* aren't we?"

"And from that I'm to take that it was *not* a success."

"Yes and no."

Marilyn chimed in. "But Penny showed grace under pressure— the kind that crushes coal into diamonds." She paused. "And we all know what girls think of diamonds." Her eyes bulged when the word *diamonds* passed her lips.

"Were men involved?"

"Why yes, they were. Well, one man. A man I'm head over heels for." I looked down at my bare stocking foot and then at my shoe on the coffee table with the broken heel tucked inside.

"Someday this will be the makings of a very funny joke, I suppose, about heels," Trudy said. "But I sense you're in no mood for a funny joke."

"Oh, no. We're very much in need of a good joke." Marilyn adjusted her coat.

Trudy looked more carefully at me. "Would you like to run yourself upstairs to wash your face and change out of that glamour-gal dress of yours?"

"That sounds wonderful. If you ladies will excuse me, I'll be right back."

I climbed the stairs and closed the bedroom door behind me, the knob made a quiet click. I crossed the room over to the mirror. "Just one more look before it all vanishes." I said the words to myself, and to the glittering girl in the looking glass. I hadn't seen her in a while. She used to look back at me from every mirror when I was a child. She used to be my pretend best girlfriend.

"It's not even midnight…but you're missing a shoe." A little girl's voice came from behind me. I saw a much younger version of myself in the mirror sitting on the edge of the bed in a sequin-encrusted, stiff-tulle-skirted tap-dance costume. The girl had Shirley's curls and ringlets. Knobby, skinned-up knees. "Yeah, it's you...me...us."

I turned to look at the bed, to be sure that no one—no one *real*—was there. In the mirror, however, Little Penny was staring back with scissors in her hand and blonde curls scattered all over the bedspread like confetti after New Year's Eve.

"Who cares? So, we didn't turn out to be the next Shirley Temple. At least we got rid of those curls, but kept the sparkly stuff."

"That's just for tonight. And it's about to come off."

"That costume you have on would look real fine on stage, I bet."

"Costume? It's not Halloween. It's not a movie musical. It's not a dance recital. But I must say I felt special in it tonight. Even though it's just a disguise."

"My outfit makes me feel special too," replied Little Penny. "Different from my brothers. More like Mommy and the movie stars."

"You'll never believe it, but we're working with one of Hollywood's biggest stars. She's downstairs right now."

"I know. I'm with you all the time. When you wake up and when you go to sleep. Even when you put on the day's earrings or when you're at the beach with Frankie looking at his—"

"That's quite enough, young lady. Thanks for tagging along and helping me to—"

"Penny, are you coming down sometime soon?" Trudy's voice carried up the staircase and into my room. "We have company, as you well know."

"Be down in a second."

Trudy didn't know it, but I had company upstairs too.

FADE OUT

CHAPTER 38

FADE IN:
- SEPTEMBER 9, 1958, SECOND DAY OF SHOOTING
- INTERIOR, TRUDY'S HOUSE (NIGHTTIME)

My bedroom was right over the kitchen. The furnace vents created an eavesdropper's dream. So, I listened in to what was going on below.

"So this is the heart of your home, Trudy. Am I right?" Marilyn's voice got louder with each word. I suspected they must've left the living room and were moving through the kitchen.

"Miss Monroe. Is there anything I can get for you? A cup of tea? Coffee? Some cookies? I've got some snicker-doodles…baked fresh today." Trudy played the part of a gracious hostess with ease. "Don't mind the cat. We're still getting used to her. And she's getting used to us. You had dinner, didn't you?"

"I'm fine. Not a thing for me. But Penny might want a little something."

"Let me help you with those things."

I imagined Marilyn was removing her disguise—the borrowed coat, hat, wig and glasses—and Trudy was gathering the items. "Now you look more like yourself," Trudy said. "What did Penny have you up to? This *experiment* was her doing, right?"

"Once she told me about her admirer, I wanted to help. I may have helped a little too much."

"I'm sure Penny appreciates all that you've done. Was he worth the effort?"

"She thinks so. From where I stand, no, he wasn't worth it. I've learned a thing or two about men. There are lots of fish in the sea and lots of frogs out there to kiss. My gut tells me he's a toad in a prince's package."

"Penny's special to me." Trudy's words had a mother's tenderness to them. "I can see she is to you too."

"It was the strangest thing. We hit it off right away. I find myself telling her things I don't tell many people. I love how she's always so sure of herself, at least until I dressed her up and took her out tonight."

"She'll be fine. You're a dream come true for her. She's spent most of her life at the movies. And with you here, she's living in a movie."

"Living in a movie. That was something I did as a little girl. But I had no choice. You see, my mother—and her friend Grace— would take me down to Grauman's Chinese Theater. We'd put our hands and feet in the stars' prints in the cement. But sometimes my mother would drop me off there—alone—when she had to work a weekend shift. She was a studio film cutter. I'd spend the whole day by myself."

I heard Trudy ask, "Really?"

"Yes. She'd say I 'was in good hands' in the courtyard. She'd tell me that someday I'd walk in their footsteps and that my footprints would be there in the cement too, for other little girls to stand in. As crazy as my mother was, she was right. I was maybe ten years old and I had a hundred movie stars as babysitters. Imagine that."

"I can't believe she left you on your own." Trudy's voice had a worried tone to it.

"She did. I made the best of it. A couple of coins lasted me the whole day." Marilyn paused. "Now, just listen to me going on. Like I do with Penny. I won't bore you with any more of my memories."

I came out of my room and to the top of the stairs. "Trudy, I could use a hand up here, please."

Trudy poked her head out from the kitchen. "Sure thing, chickadee. I'll be right back, Miss Monroe. Make yourself at home."

"Thank you ever so much. And please, call me Marilyn."

When Trudy found me, I was half undressed. "It's stuck. And now I'm stuck."

She steadied me onto both of my feet, smoothed out the dress's fabric in the back and slid the zipper down.

"What relief. Now the girdle has got to go. I know it's not a real girdle. Marilyn called it a cincher...a cincher that's really a pincher, I'd say."

"Sure thing. She's nice. I mean really nice." Trudy grinned and her eyes got squinty.

"I know. I can't believe it either. She's so powerful and somehow, when we're alone in her room, she seems almost powerless. Insecure. Unsure. Vulnerable. That's it. Vulnerable. And scared. Sometimes she has scared eyes. Right before the cameras roll. She has that scared-eye look kids have when they get lost at the dime store."

"The cincher's off. Need help with anything else?"

"No. Thanks. You better go back down. It's not every day Marilyn Monroe is under your roof."

"Alright then," Trudy said. "Take your time. Let your dream come to an end."

"An end? Who said anything about something ending?"

FADE OUT

CHAPTER 39

FADE IN:
- SEPTEMBER 9, 1958, SECOND DAY OF SHOOTING
- INTERIOR, TRUDY'S HOUSE (NIGHTTIME)

I'd left my bedroom door open so I could hear what was going on downstairs. Trudy must've come across Marilyn in the living room.

"It's not much, but my late husband and I were happy here. And now I'm happy here with my girls."

"It's lovely, truly lovely."

"Like I said, it's not much, but it *is* enough for me. On this rug, I can stand on my own two feet or kneel to pray. On this windowsill, I can look out at a storm and know I'm safe. On this chair, I can nod off and dream about the past…or the future. And on this mantle my man is always with me."

"Is that your husband?" Marilyn pointed to the sepia-colored photo of a uniformed man above the hearth.

"Yes, that's my Vernon. I came here from Minnesota to be with him. Left everything. And everyone. And the ice and the moose and the mosquitoes. For him. And I'd do it again. In a heartbeat. Yes, in a heartbeat."

"Sounds like quite a guy."

"Yes, he was. You could make a movie about what he went through, and what we shared. He was no saint, though. But he was mine. And living with him—and loving him—taught me something everyone should know and not have to discover for themselves the hard way."

"What's that?"

"Give me a second to get this straight in my head so it comes out right." Trudy blinked a few times. "We came to love not by finding the perfect person, but by learning to see an *imperfect* person, perfectly."

"That's so true. I'm going to remember it." Marilyn continued, "Mind if I use it in the future? You're so smart!"

"I'm not smart at all. But sometimes I guess I do amaze myself. Then I'll do something stupid, like putting the laundry in the oven. Nobody's perfect, that's what I always say."

I came down the stairs into the living room. "Didn't interrupt anything, did I?"

"Not a thing, honey. Feel more like yourself now?"

"Yep, just Penny from the five and dime." I looked over at my broken shoe. "I even had my fairytale moment. But I'm not sure a broken heel really counts."

"How about some tapioca? Won't take but a minute to dish it up?"

"Sounds wonderful." It did sound wonderful. "I didn't get a bite of dinner. We ordered, but then my lady parts ordered me to the ladies' room. And now me—and my parts—are here. Thanks to Marilyn, a real crisis was averted." I stopped to laugh. "Oh my gosh. You should have seen us. Imagine me. In a bathroom stall. Bleeding. In my dream dress. And Marilyn dressed in that get up helping me deal with it all."

Marilyn confessed, "I've been in some memorable situations. That was one…well, I'll always remember it."

"Hard to believe, right? Me and Marilyn having an adventure in the ladies' room. And now we're here with you. Say, are there any leftovers from dinner?"

"Sure. Miss Monroe, are you sure you won't have something to eat?"

I eyed Marilyn and winked that it was okay.

"Sure. I'd love whatever you have. This is Penny's night. And please call me Marilyn."

"Come with me then. You don't mind being in the kitchen, do you?"

"Of course not. I love being in my kitchen, but I'm never home."

I chimed in, "I hate it when I go in the kitchen looking for food and all I find are ingredients." I poked at my stiff hairdo with a pencil from on the counter. "That's why I love living with Trudy. Well, one of the reasons."

"You two can eat in the dining room." Trudy's head was in the refrigerator.

"Nonsense. The kitchen table will be fine." Marilyn pulled out a chair. Before she sat, she asked, "Is there something I can do to help?"

"Nothing at all," Trudy replied. "This lady-boss of yours is not what I expected, Penny."

"No, she's not. Thank goodness." I sat on the chair next to Marilyn's. "Say, how's about we start with the soup of the day: whiskey with ice croutons?"

Trudy revealed her face from around the refrigerator door. Her eyes were sharply aimed at me.

I grinned in return. "That was meant to be a joke."

"I'm a Midwestern cook. I know my way around a kitchen. Potatoes. Ketchup. Butter. That's all I need." Trudy pulled out a casserole dish. She lifted the tin foil that acted as a lid. "I call this Desperation Hot Dish. Look good?"

"Delicious." Marilyn's eyes sparkled.

"Serve it up." I couldn't wait. "I'll even eat it cold."

"Nonsense." Trudy turned on the stove and placed the dish on the burner. "Just so you know, there's macaroni, hamburger, corn, kidney beans and a can of tomato soup in it. All we do back home is stir it up and let it bubble and bake in the oven. Some shredded cheese on top and voila."

Trudy went back to the refrigerator and pulled out a cut-glass salad bowl. "How about some Ginger Ale Jello Salad to go with your hot dish?"

Marilyn and I smiled at each other.

"Please don't go to any trouble."

"No trouble at all, Marilyn. I do this for a living at the dime store. I don't know if Penny told you I run the lunch counter…for people who appreciate a nice meal and a nice conversation. And for those who gobble and go. Human wood chippers, that's what they are. Anyway, I make a mean grilled-cheese sandwich."

"Yes, she did tell me that. And I can grill a mean beef steak, for dinner or for breakfast." Marilyn nodded. "But a roasted chicken for lunch, that's something I get a yen for. When I was little, we'd go to church and then have a chicken lunch at home. We'd go for strolls afterward. Holding hands. Looking in the fancy store windows at things we couldn't afford. We were dreamers. When you don't have money, you dream." She grinned again and turned her attention to Trudy. "You dream and you eat a lot of grilled-cheese sandwiches."

"Grilled cheese and tomato soup was one of my husband's favorite meals. He was simple that way." Trudy made her way to the sink and rinsed her hands, then dried them on her apron. She leaned against the counter.

"They say that every woman has two true loves in her life—one that makes them, one that breaks them. For me, it was the same man." Trudy shrugged. "And I wouldn't have had it any other way. For me, Mr. Right—my first real love, or what I thought was love—was also Mr. Wrong."

She dropped her hands to her sides. "But, odd as it sounds, I'm one of the lucky ones. With my Vern, I've known the kind of love that songs are written about. Now, I'm a landlady, a lunch-counter waitress and a widow. Stir all that together and I've been able to make my way in life."

I got up, stepped over and put my arms around Trudy. "What would I do without you and the rest of The Blessed Sisters of My Jelly Belly...Sara Lee, Betty Crocker and Aunt Jemima?" I pinched Trudy's cheek.

"I'm good enough for now. But you'll find a man and move on." Trudy gave me a side eye. "One day you'll kiss a man and know—absolutely know—his are the lips you want to kiss for the rest of your life. He's out there. You'll see."

Marilyn added, "Is that what you're hoping for, honey?"

"Well, if I'm honest, he would just be the first part. A big part, mind you. If I got a home and a family of my own making, that would make me even more happy. Oh, and throw in a best, best, best girlfriend."

Trudy stirred the contents of the casserole dish on the stove. "It's as ready as a Minnesota lake frozen enough to drive on and fish through." She spooned some on two plates and put them on the table in front of me and Marilyn.

We didn't miss a beat and started to eat. I kept the conversation going. "You'll never guess what my mother did the other day. She asked me to lunch and went on and on to apologize for everything she and my father did wrong."

"You don't say." Trudy leaned against the counter.

"I do. And she did. Mom talked about him before the war—and after the war."

"So many boys came home men." Trudy whispered, "And so many men came back wounded."

Marilyn nodded.

Trudy added, "And not the sling, cast or crutches kind of wounded."

"Breaks my heart." Marilyn put her fork down on her plate and glanced at me. "Penny, can I have her? I need a Trudy in my life too."

"What a sweet thing to say." Trudy smoothed out her apron and looked at Marilyn. "Not to worry. There's plenty of me to go around."

"Hey, that sounds like something I'd say." I put my fork down too. "There's more than plenty of me to go around."

When the time came for us to leave, Marilyn was the first to speak. "Thanks for everything, Trudy. Now this evening's finally over and done."

Marilyn reached out for Trudy's hands.

"Nothing is ever over and done." Trudy finished her thought, "Except a fried egg." She hugged Marilyn for an exceptionally long time instead of accepting a mere touching of the hands.

"And with that, we're on our way." I gave Trudy a quick goodnight hug and patted Ella on her head.

Sitting in the back of Paul's taxi, Marilyn prodded, "So tell me about that boy of yours. The one from school. The one you were once married to."

"Frankie? We've known each other since we were kids. We've been through a lot together. Isn't that right, Paul?"

"Yep."

After a momentary pause, Marilyn said, "Keep going."

"His parents were a mess. They still are, just like mine. We were married and we made it work. It was just a school project, but we learned how to pay our bills, how to raise a baby. Well, the baby was just a five-pound bag of flour. But it was more of a responsibility than either of us thought."

"He sounds sweet."

"Yes, he is."

"And he's a good kisser. Even with an audience on the beach." Marilyn splashed some sass on her statement.

"Now that's something I can't comment on."

"You never kissed him? Ever?"

"Nope." That was my one-word answer.

"Well, you're in for a treat. Every couple must start somewhere. It's like buying your first bra. You wish there was more there—and there will be if you're lucky—but you have to start somewhere."

"I can't say I've ever heard kissing and buying a brassiere in the same analogy before, but I follow you."

I looked forward and met Paul's eyes in the rear-view mirror. He announced, "I'm not saying a thing. In fact, I'm not hearing a thing. Besides, you're home. Here's The Del. Miss Monroe, it's been my pleasure to be your driver tonight. May I help you to your room? Carry anything for you?"

"Thank you for your kind offer, Paul. But I think the two of us will be just fine. Yes, we'll be just fine."

However, I had no idea how *not* fine I was going to be in just a few hours.

FADE OUT

CHAPTER 40

FADE IN:

- SEPTEMBER 9, 1958, SECOND DAY OF SHOOTING
- INTERIOR, HOTEL DEL CORONADO (NIGHTTIME)

The rhythmic clickety-clack sound of a movie projector came at me in waves as I staggered down The Del's hallway. In a sticky molasses-like slow motion, I passed numbered doors. All of them closed. I was alone.

The hallway sconces flickered in sync with the clickety-clack movie projector sound. Without warning, everything sped back up to normal when I found myself standing in front of the opened door of the bird-cage elevator. The lone light bulb mounted in the car's ceiling glowed gold.

The car was empty. *He* wasn't there. But then he was. "Cheng, you look...um...younger."

"I should," he replied.

Party sounds traveled up the elevator shaft. My ears told me there were happy people nearby who were celebrating and blowing noisemakers. Someone sloppily cheered, "Happy New Year!"

I entered the elevator. "Cheng, I know your name means journey, but this is—"

The gate closed by itself and the floor dropped out from beneath me. As I reached for the handrail, the car jerked to a stop. The collapsible door creaked open.

"This is your floor."

"But I don't remember you asking or me telling you where I

wanted to go."

"You did not," Cheng said. "But I know, just the same."

Trudy was standing with open arms. I blinked a couple of times, gazed down to find that I was wearing my nightgown and, of all things, black pumps. I looked up and stepped into Trudy's embrace.

"What the hell is going on?"

"Oh, Penny. You should not use such language, especially at a time like this. And with what you're going to see."

"What I'm going to see?"

"Yes. Put your hand on mine." Trudy's raised hand and arm extended before us.

"Alright. If you say so."

Paper streamers hung from the lobby's enormous chandelier. A sea of partiers filled the room. A banner over the registration desk announced, "Happy New Year 1935!" I stared at it. A woman bumped me and broke my concentration. I scanned the room, hoping to find a Hollywood production crew in action. It had to be a hot set. Someone else bumped me from behind. A slosh of an iced drink splatted on my shoulder. I turned.

If I'd had a drink in my hand, I'd have dropped it for sure.

It was my mother. A younger version—much younger—and clearly pregnant. Our eyes met. "I am sooooooo sorry, miss. I don't understand how I could be so clumsy. That was my first drink of the night." She was beautiful. Prettier than in the old scrapbook snapshots. Prettier than in the studio portraits of my parents' wedding on their living room's mantel.

She stared at me with questioning eyes. She didn't recognize me. It must have been what I was wearing. My nightgown and black pumps, that had to be it.

"You'll have to excuse my little lady. She's not quite herself tonight." It was The Commander in his dress whites…a younger version of him too. But he wasn't cranky and there was no ten-hut tone in his voice.

"Excuse me," I replied as I smoothed out my nightgown to make sure I was as presentable as possible. Trudy stood in the background.

"Come along, my precious Kitty Cat." He held Mom around the waist. "We've celebrated quite enough already. You and your precious cargo need some shut eye. Let me help you." He was caring and comforting and chatty. The Commander turned to me. "I didn't catch your name."

"It's Penelope. But most people call me Penny."

"Isn't that a coincidence, Kitty. Out of all the people here tonight, we meet someone with the same name you picked out for our third bundle of joy. Well, we best be on our way. Happy New Year's to you, Penny."

"And to you."

I turned back to see that the elevator door was still open. Cheng stood straight, eyes forward. Trudy took my hand again and headed back over to the elevator.

"What's going on here?" I had to ask. "Am I dreaming?"

"A New Year's Eve celebration. That's what."

"Yes, I can see that. I can even feel that." I pulled at the wet spot on the back of my nightgown to let it air out a bit. "How did I get here? To 1935? I'm not even born yet."

"This birdcage brought you. Ready to go back?" Trudy smiled.

"I guess so."

"Then step in and hold on, please." We entered and the cage door closed itself again. The elevator took off, shooting upward as if it was going to burst through the roof and head for the stars.

"CHENG!" I wasn't prone to screaming, but at that moment, I screamed.

The door opened.

"Next stop, Penny my dear." Trudy took my hand.

It was a wedding. Shit, it was *my* wedding. Bradley stood at the altar. He looked dreamy. Definitely better than he did any other day. As Trudy walked me up the aisle, I stared at his hands. The fingers on both were fluttering. As I got closer, his fingers pulled into fists.

"Brace yourself." Trudy's words had icicles hanging from them.

In an instant, Bradley's balled-up fist was coming straight for my face.

Everything went black. Inky black. But that changed as flickering lights flashed at an increasing pace. The clickety-clack sound of a movie projector was back and got louder and louder until it filled my head. There I was: in total darkness surrounded by the repetitious machine-gun sounds of a movie projector.

With the crisp crack of thunder everything stopped.

I was back in my bed and it jolted like it was dropped from the sky.

My arms and legs were cocooned in a tangle of sheets and blankets. My head was under the covers at the foot of the bed. I thrashed my way out and, in the process, kicked off a black pump. The other one stayed on my foot. I swept the sweat off my forehead, then my upper lip.

"What the hell was that?" No one answered. I was alone in my room but I was talking as if someone was there.

"That messed-up version of *A Christmas Carol* didn't really happen, did it?"

Again, no one answered.

FADE OUT

CHAPTER 41

FADE IN:
- SEPTEMBER 10, 1958, THIRD DAY OF SHOOTING
- INTERIOR, MARILYN'S COTTAGE (DAYTIME)

"Special delivery for Miss Monroe." A maroon uniformed bellman passed a fruit basket to May. I'd just arrived and was setting down my purse and clipboard. "You have yourself a pleasant morning, ma'am." He placed his fingers on the front of his bottle-cap hat and saluted.

"And you do the same." May turned with her hands full and left the cottage's door open behind her.

"By the way, my name's Nick. I'll be the one delivering packages here."

"Fine. Thank you, Nick."

He saluted the Coronado police officer assigned that day to keep an eye on Marilyn's cottage door. "Bet you see all kinds of people—and packages—come and go out of here, eh?"

"It's not my place to discuss it." The officer leaned forward. "But if it was, my answer would be *yes*."

Inside, May placed the basket on a round reception table.

"Can I help you with that?" The least I could do was offer since my hands were free.

"No. I'm fine. So how did it go last night? Was it a dream date?"

"In some ways it was."

"Penny, you looked like a million bucks when you left here."

"Thanks. That's the way I felt too." I eyed the puffy gathering of cellophane and the red ribbon that held it together at the top of the basket. "Are we supposed to open cards for her or is that something she prefers to do?"

"For a basket of fruit, we can do it. Boxes that look like they hold jewelry, she opens." May handed me the basket's card. I broke the envelope's seal and slid the card out. I mouthed the words, "Saw you masquerading last night. Let's you and me have a party all by ourselves."

"And what does *this* admirer have to say?"

I didn't respond. My mind was preoccupied with the possible meanings of the message.

"I'll ask again, Penny, what does this admirer have to say?"

I forced the card back into the security of its envelope. "Nothing worth repeating." I put the envelope under the first page of my clipboard. "I'll share it with her when she's awake."

"Then you better head out to the patio. She's doing her breathing exercises."

"At eight fifteen?"

"She said she's starting something new as part of her daily routine. Not that she has a routine or even keeps one."

I opened the patio door. There she was. Breathing in the fresh air as if it was a Thanksgiving spread. "It's good for the baby." She devoured another serving of ocean air. "It's time you knew—especially after everything we went through last night."

"Baby?"

"Shush. Keep it down. Billy and the rest of the crew don't know yet. I'm keeping it a secret. This is the second time this year and I don't know how many times I can go through this. But I'm determined. Now if my body would be determined too and plant that egg in the right spot so I might be able to keep it."

"I'm so happy for you. Truly happy."

"Thank you, Penny. I could stay here forever. Away from it all. A quiet life by the beach. Me and my little family."

"Sounds wonderful. I know exactly what you mean. I'm happiest when I have a seashell in my pocket and sand between my toes."

"Funny you should say that. It reminds me of the times my mother took me to the beach. That is, when she was able to. She was in *the industry* too. At Consolidated. As a film cutter. I was telling Trudy about this just—"

"What was her name?" I interrupted Marilyn so I wouldn't let it slip that I'd been eavesdropping on their entire conversation.

"Gladys Pearl Monroe Baker."

"But I thought you were in an orphanage?"

"I was. And foster homes. My mother couldn't take care of me…at least not all the time. That made the world around me pretty grim." Marilyn let her words hang. "I was a lonely little girl. I learned how to pretend to block out how grim everything was. The whole world seemed like a closed door to me. Like I was always on the outside looking in. Not allowed in. Not good enough to come in. What I could do is pretend. And did I pretend."

"You must have been a beautiful little girl. Look at you now."

"Ha! No one—and I mean no one—ever told me I was pretty when I was just Norma Jeane. Not even once. I used to think I was a weed in a sidewalk crack…stretching to catch any patch of sun." Marilyn paused and appeared more focused. She moved her lower lip to the left and bit down for a moment. Even without her trademark ruby-lipstick coating, the fleshy tone of her lips still showcased her gleaming front teeth. "I believe all little girls should be told they're pretty. Often. Even if they aren't…so they know they're loved. Then, and forever."

"I second that." I raised my hand as if I was voting. "Is there anything I can get for you? A basket of fruit was just delivered. But I wouldn't eat any of it. Let me go and get the note."

I came back with the envelope. "Tell you what. I'll go back inside and take it away so no one gets into it."

"Whoa. What's your hurry?" Marilyn read the card. "I see. I mean we were *seen.*" She lowered her dark sunglasses and looked out over the ocean. "I understand the first line. But not the second."

"Me too. Do you still have the note that came with the red roses?"

"Sure, honey. They should be with the flowers inside."

"We should keep them together, with any more you get. They might add up to something. That's usually how it works in the movies." I rolled my eyes. "Honestly. Here I am, telling you about how things are done in the movies."

"That's a good idea…to keep them together."

"And maybe I should show them to the officer outside, so he's aware and keeps an eye out." I started to step inside.

"That would be a *bad* idea. Let's keep this to ourselves for now. I get gifts and messages from cranks and creeps wherever I go."

"It's your call. I'll ask again, is there anything I can get for you?"

"Please ask May to bring me something to pep me up."

"I can get you a steaming cup of coffee."

"That's not what I had in mind, but thank you just the same. May will know what I need. Some orange juice would be nice though. It's like a sunrise in a glass. Probably good for the baby too."

I smiled and went in to speak to May and get some juice.

"Penny, can you bring me the script for today? I need to get it down. We're going to be in the water today and I don't want too many takes. I'm sure Jack and the girls don't either."

"Will do." I could hear Marilyn lah-dee-dahing the melody to *By the Sea*.

"She's in fine spirits," said May as she shook a few pills out of an envelope and into her hand. "You don't need to tell me. I overheard. These should do the trick."

I returned with the script and pills.

"Sit with me. Penny, I can't tell you how much I enjoyed last night."

"The makeover and beginning of dinner were incredible."

"They were, but I'm talking about going to the house and talking with Trudy. She's really something. Is she always so—"

"Uh-huh. When she tells us we're her chicks and our rooms are our nests, she means it. That's even how it feels. Not like it felt at my parent's house. It's nothing like that."

Marilyn popped the pills in her mouth and took a swallow of juice. She cleared her throat and asked, "Your mother wasn't the best?"

"She loved a bottle of booze, my brothers, my father and me. In that order."

"I'm sorry. But I understand. Probably better than most."

"Frankie understands too. He hardly eats and never stops running. He can thank his family for that. The only good thing his father did for him was bring home broken clocks, by the box load."

I could tell by the curious look on Marilyn's face that I needed to explain what I'd said. "Frankie was a curious kid. He'd take those clocks apart and try to figure out how they worked. His dad bought the guy who ran the clock-repair store beers in exchange for broken clocks. That's got to be the only good thing to come from drinking too much."

"You like him, don't you?"

"Sure. I told you we've known each other—"

"Yes. And you were married in school. But you *like* him. I can see it. I can hear it in your voice when you talk about him."

"He's not like Steele...not at all."

"Guys like Steele are a dime a dozen."

"Maybe in your life. In mine, he's one in a billion."

Marilyn opened her script. "May, I know you're listening. Is Paula here yet? I need to run my lines."

"Not yet, but I'll send her out as soon as she arrives."

"Thanks. You're a doll." Marilyn opened the script, but turned to look at me. "I've just got to get better at this?'

"This?"

"Acting, of course. When I started out in this business I knew how third-rate I was. It was like I could feel my lack of talent...as if it were cheap clothes I was wearing on the inside. But, my God, I wanted to learn. And I've been doing it ever since."

"It's certainly paying off. Hard work usually does." I didn't know what else to say, so I added, "I'll just go inside and leave you to your work."

"Thanks. You're so sweet...like cotton candy."

I whispered to myself as I walked away, "I could get used to hearing things like that."

FADE OUT

CHAPTER 42

FADE IN:
- SEPTEMBER 10, 1958, THIRD DAY OF SHOOTING
- EXTERIOR, CORONADO BEACH (DAYTIME)

"Honestly? Tony's going to trip me so I fall—to the ground?"

"Yes. That's how we've planned it." Billy Wilder didn't make eye contact with Marilyn. Instead, he kept staring down at his notes. "Do you want to rehearse it or just jump right in?"

"Let's just do it."

May and I stepped back and watched.

Tony Curtis sat in the high-backed wicker sun chair. He wore a blue blazer, captain's hat, silk scarf, white pants and Coke-bottle-bottom glasses. "Ready when you are, Billy." He punched key syllables to achieve his character's Cary Grant impression.

Marilyn flapped her hands and chanted "Relax, relax." Jack grinned and announced, "Magic Time!" A chorus of girls' voices started singing, "I love coffee, I love tea, how many boys are stuck on me? One? Two? Three? Four? Five? Six—" The group was standing, wiggling and jumping in a big circle as they tossed a beach ball between them and counted out loud.

One of the girls threw the ball over Marilyn's head and she took off after it toward Tony's chair. He was pretending to read a newspaper. He lifted his left foot, over which Marilyn tripped and fell, knees and palms into the sand.

"Oh, I'm terribly sorry," Tony said.

"My fault." Marilyn brushed the sand off her legs. She froze. No words came. Her hands fell to her sides. Her eyes shot from the right to the left, then she zeroed in on Paula. Just as a coach should do, she smiled encouragingly at Marilyn.

"Cut. Set it up and do it again." The director's familiar German-accented voice rode the sea breeze.

"Yes Billy. I'll do it until I get it right, but if I end up with scabby knees, I don't want to hear any complaining about it."

"You'll hear no complaining from me."

May turned to me and whispered, "He says that now to get what he wants. Then he forgets and makes new demands. Scabby knees, that's a new one."

I whispered back, "Well I hope so."

"Isn't that every red-blooded American man's dream: to have Marilyn Monroe on her knees?"

"If it is, Tony's dream is coming true today."

FADE OUT

CHAPTER 43

FADE IN:
- SEPTEMBER 10, 1958, THIRD DAY OF SHOOTING
- EXTERIOR, HOTEL DEL CORONADO (DAYTIME)

"Oh, Sugarplum. There you are!" If my life had a soundtrack, the unmistakable screech of a record-player's needle sliding abruptly across an LP would've filled the air. Lorelei was surrounded by beautiful women, wearing beautiful clothes, living presumably beautiful lives. The round table on The Del's porch was shaded by an umbrella with fringe that moved with the ocean breeze.

"Lorelei, I didn't know you were coming for lunch today." I faked a friendly tone.

"Well, I called last night and asked for the front desk to hand-deliver you a message. It seemed that you weren't picking up the phone in your room."

"For that to work, I'd have to be in my room, now wouldn't I?"

Several of the ladies at the table snickered. Lorelei put a stop to that with a quick glance in their directions.

"Please pull up a chair and join us. We're all feeling just *bridal*!"

"Bridal?"

"You know, we're as giddy as brides. Anyone who's *anyone* is saying that these days." Lorelei scanned the faces around the table for reinforcement. She got it. "Penny, let me introduce you to the wives of some of San Diego's leading businessmen. Let me start with Trixie here on my right—"

"I'm so sorry. I wish I could. But Marilyn asked me to have

lunch with her today. We've been shooting out on the beach and we have scads of things to catch up on." The women ooooed and ahhhhed. "I'm sure these fine ladies will understand, won't you all?"

They nodded and winked at me. Lorelei didn't.

"Before you run, could you at least tell us a few tidbits about what it's like to be her servant…I mean to serve her. You know what I mean."

"Why yes, Lorelei, I know *exactly* what you mean." I could count on her to do her best to make me feel like a toad among a flock of swans. "Quite frankly—" I held the word *frankly* as I rolled my eyes up as if I was searching for just the right gossipy thing to say about my employer. The women all leaned forward to savor every syllable I uttered next.

"I'm not at liberty to share anything about her. I signed a non-disclosure agreement. I'm sure you understand. Everything she's told me and everything I've observed and—" I stopped and raised an open palm to the edge of my mouth. "And everything I've been asked to do is *strictly* confidential. Hush-hush, you know."

Sharing nothing was almost more powerful than telling something. The women appeared thrilled to know there were secrets they couldn't know, but that they were chatting with someone who did.

"I really must be going now." I used my right hand like a cat uses its paw to push something away.

"You run along then, my sweetest of sisters." She was such a big, fat, *skinny* liar.

"Lorelei, always a pleasure." I was just a big, fat liar.

Despite her polished façade, I was certain she was sizzling inside like a pound of bacon in a frying pan.

I may never be a swan like them. And after everything I was going through, I was pretty sure I didn't really want to be.

I turned and walked away.

And didn't look back.

FADE OUT

CHAPTER 44

FADE IN:
- SEPTEMBER 10, 1958, THIRD DAY OF SHOOTING
- EXTERIOR, CORONADO BEACH (DAYTIME)

Marilyn was wrapped in her white beach cover up, her arms folded in front of her. Tony was in his wicker sun chair, still pretending to read the newspaper. The Del loomed in the background along with a smattering of palm trees and beach umbrellas.

Billy Wilder approached her. "I know you aren't used to working this way, but I have to ask you to try. Jets take off from the nearby naval base about every ten minutes. This is a long scene to shoot. About three minutes, uninterrupted. So, we must watch the clock when we start. Are you with me? Can we do this?"

Marilyn stepped over to Paula. They chatted in hushed tones. I wished I was closer to listen in.

"I can do it." Marilyn repeated, "Yes, I can do it."

After a jet ripped the sky, Billy checked his watch. The crew quieted the onlookers.

I didn't usually look at the crowd. I always tried to keep my eyes on Marilyn. But something unmistakable just beyond her distracted me: Otis' unmistakable bucket-shaped head. I guessed he must've snuck out from the dime store. It was too late in the day for a break and too early for his shift to be over. I watched him as he skulked a few rows back in the crowd. I swore I saw Bradley too.

I focused back on Marilyn as she started to rev up her getting-ready-to-shoot ritual.

"Action" was announced and the slate boy moved away with his clapboard. Marilyn's left hand demurely tugged at the hem of her beach cover up and she lowered herself to her knees on the sand next to Tony's chair.

"How's the stock market?" Marilyn got the first line down on the first try.

I listened carefully to how her words were delivered with her trademark breathiness. I watched as the wind rippled Marilyn's hair and made her look less glamorous and more approachable. I made a pouty-lips expression as I mouthed the scripted words.

May elbowed me and whispered, "You look like a fish. Not a sexy siren."

"Great, that's exactly what I was going for."

We smiled at each other and turned our attention back on the actors.

"Up, up, up." Tony's delivery was crisp.

"I'll bet—just while we were talking—you made like a hundred thousand dollars."

"Could be. Do you play the market?"

"No—the ukulele. And I sing too." Marilyn was on a roll.

"For your own amusement?"

"A bunch of us girls are appearing at the hotel. Sweet Sue and Her Society Syncopators."

"Oh, you're society girls?"

"Oh, yes. Quite. You know—Bryn Mawr, Vassar." Marilyn straightened her back and spoke with a slightly snooty air. "We're only doing this for a lark."

"Syncopators—does that mean you play that fast music? Jazz?"

"Yeah. *Real hot!*" Marilyn almost growled like a tiger as she delivered the line. Her eyes enlarged and her toothy grin sparkled in the sunshine. She snapped her fingers as she swung her arms in front of her chest.

"Oh. Well, I guess some like it hot. I personally prefer classical music." Tony spoke a line—and the name of the film—in one fell swoop in his best Cary Grant impression.

A man behind May and me said in a not-so-quiet voice, "This movie's gonna be lousy. I could eat a bowl of Alpha-Bits and crap out a better script." We didn't dare turn around to see who said it.

Marilyn and Tony exchanged several more lines.

"Jesus H. Christ. I bet that babe gets more ass than a truck-stop toilet seat. Penny, how's about introducing us to your new friend." I didn't need to see the face the voice belonged to. It was Otis. I wasn't sure how I'd react if Bradley was there too. We hadn't spoken since I turned and walked away from him at the altar. Childish of me? Perhaps. Childish of him? Perhaps, but not unexpected.

"Sure, Otis. Allow me to introduce you to May. And keep your voice down. This is a live set and we have work to do." I nodded at Otis and then at May. I knew he wasn't referring to May as my new friend, but I couldn't resist taunting him before I turned him down.

"That's not who I was talking about." His words sagged with disgust. "And you know it."

Bradley was there, standing next to Otis. He was silent up to that point. I decided to break the iceberg between us.

"Bradley, it's good to see you."

He swept over me with his eyes and locked his gaze over my shoulder. "It's *her* that we came to meet." He might have greased the skids with something a little friendlier. But that was Bradley. It shouldn't have surprised me. But it did. He hadn't changed. Not one bit. He watched Marilyn like a dog watches a pork chop.

"The short answer is *no*...the long answer is *HELL no!*" I brought my voice down. "Meeting her is *not* going to happen. Not on my watch. Miss Monroe is—"

"Cut the crap. We'll wait here." Otis twisted his feet into the sand, grinding himself a firmer stance."

"You. Will. Not." May cut her words sharply like she was slicing a carrot with a dull knife. "This is not a tourist attraction. This is a place of business. Shoo."

"May I be of assistance?" Steele's voice never sounded so good.

"I don't believe so." My eyes ping-ponged between Otis and Bradley. "These two visitors were just about to step away." It may have only been three against two, but with Steele on our side we had a better chance of controlling the situation. At least I hoped so.

"No. I think I'll stay right here." Otis turned to Bradley. "How about you?"

"I'm good. This will be just fine." Bradley's voice made the hair on my arms stand up, and not for a good reason.

"You guys have to leave. Now!" I delivered my words with all the strength I could muster while keeping my voice down to avoid causing a scene. "If you don't, I'll give my secret signal to the security team—and the Coronado Police Department officers—and you'll be hauled away. Do you want that?"

"Not the secret signal." May eyed the two brutes.

Steele took a step closer. "Trust me, you two. It's time to leave."

Otis and Bradley swiveled their feet in the sand. I wasn't sure if they were digging in deeper or squirming.

Otis started to move away, but turned his head to face me. "You'll regret this, Porky." I couldn't believe he said that in front of Steele and May. His voice had the same threatening pitch it had at the bowling alley. But then again, his voice was always marinated in a brew of threat and disgust.

Though Bradley was silent, his eyes were screaming at me. I knew the look. But he held back his words and his fists. That time, anyway.

I watched their backs move away from us.

"You sure know how to pick 'em." May elbowed me.

"Uh-huh, it's a real gift."

"Are you two talking about me?" Steele grinned.

"No." I quickly added, "And yes."

"Cut. Print it." Billy's words shocked the entire crew. Their faces showed it. Marilyn's especially. "Thank you everyone. That was perfect. Besides, we're picking up long shadows and need to stop for today."

A jet flew overhead, scratching the sky.

May pointed to shadows stretching out to the right of Tony's chair and the umbrellas behind them. "See? That's why location shooting is so hard. And why they need Marilyn to deliver...every time...on time. Back in the studio, everything's controlled, or at least controllable. Not out here."

I watched Otis and Bradley continue to walk away. "Controlled and controllable. Sounds good to me."

But Otis and Bradley were neither of those two things. They never had been and never would be. It just wasn't in the cards for them. And I'd soon discover—the hard way—that someone else was neither controlled or controllable.

FADE OUT

CHAPTER 45

FADE IN:
- SEPTEMBER 10, 1958, THIRD DAY OF SHOOTING
- INTERIOR, MARILYN'S COTTAGE (DAYTIME)

"Come on in, honey." Marilyn's voice sounded relaxed, not like before.

I stepped into the bathroom to find her sliding into a bubble bath. "Oh, gosh, I'm so sorry to catch you—"

"Don't be silly. I haven't got anything you haven't."

"But mine's just arranged differently…and there's enough for two." I looked down at my chest and toes.

"You're too funny. My bare tits and ass are plastered all over garages and bars from Syracuse to San Francisco. Between that calendar I did and that edition of *Playboy*, well, there's just not much of me that people haven't seen."

"And now I can say I've seen it too. Lucky me. Right?"

"Right. It's not like you're out for my job."

I must've looked stunned.

"You know what I mean. Like in *All About Eve*. When Anne Baxter clawed her way into Bette Davis' affairs, not to mention her circle of theater friends. I've never had an assistant who wasn't from the industry—you know, film industry. You won a contest. An innocent contest. So, it's not like you're after my job, right?"

"You have nothing—and I mean *nothing*—to worry about with me." I turned my head side to side and blinked in an exaggerated way. "Now, Paula, she's a different story. I caught her holding up one of your dresses against her chest and looking in the mirror.

And it wasn't a black dress either."

My eyes slid from Marilyn to the mirror over the sink, then back again. "Pardon me for saying it, but you're way too smart to play dumb."

"I agree." Marilyn's head bobbed as she continued, "And I'm doing something about it." She wrung out a large sponge and ran it over the length of her arm. "That's so kind of you to say."

"If you'll excuse me, I'll let you enjoy your bath. Alone. As in, with me *not* being here."

"As you wish, Penny. As you wish—" Marilyn's words turned into bubbles as she slid down beneath the soapy water's surface.

FADE OUT

CHAPTER 46

FADE IN:
- SEPTEMBER 10, 1958, THIRD DAY OF SHOOTING
- INTERIOR, MARILYN'S COTTAGE (DAYTIME)

There were three confident knocks on the cottage's door. "Delivery for Miss Monroe." Then three more.

As I walked to answer it, I asked myself out loud, "A delivery this late in the day?" I opened the door to find the bellhop with an enormous frilly box of candy. A pink fabric rose rested on top of a rippling bed of red satin.

"You again. What's your name?"

"It's Nick. At your service." He bowed. "I don't mind coming over here at all. Beats schlepping luggage. New guys get to start doing that."

"Well that's just dandy." I took the box. "Thanks. See you soon."

I pointed to a red envelope. "May, do I open it?"

"Yes. I'm sure it's harmless."

After I broke the seal, I slid the card out. "You and Tony on the beach. We can do better. We'll show them!"

"Okay. Now I'm getting creeped out. Does she get notes like these all the time?"

"This group of messages has got my attention. Penny, thank you for sharing them with me even though Marilyn wanted to keep a lid on them. There are some crazy people out there. This one—he or she—is definitely persistent."

"He or she?"

ɪme women are totally annoyed by her. She makes most gals
ɣ comparison. If you were a cheerleader then a prom queen
aɪɪu ...en married the football star…and twenty years roll by, you'd
get insecure when Marilyn's pictures and calendars are in your
man's hands."

"Insecure around her? Hell, women have been insecure since
Eve traipsed around that garden of hers."

"You're in good company then." May looked over at Marilyn's
bedroom door. "Even she's insecure."

"About what? She has everything."

"You'd think that, wouldn't you?" May ran her fingertips over
the box's red satin frills. "They're the most insecure. Hollywood
people, that is. I think they're more unhappy than regular folks. I
know they are. Unhappy with happy faces on."

"I don't get it. When I go to the movies, there's always this
magic. Even during a crappy picture. I know they're acting. I
know it isn't real. But just like the audience gets to escape in the
dark, they do it for a living. They get paid to get lost. To be
someone they aren't. To be something they dream they could be."

May's fingers slid off the box and onto the tabletop. "You're
getting an inside look, one that few people get. I hope that won't
ruin it all for you."

"No, I'll always have the movies. Even when life gets me
down. Or pumps me up."

"Yes, but the stars don't. At some point, Marilyn won't either.
They never watch their films. It must remind them too much of
how they looked when they were younger."

"But that makes them forever-young."

"No, my little sugar cube, that makes them forever *trying* to
stay young. And that's not possible. Unless you find the fountain
of youth."

"I heard that someone did, and it tasted a lot like vodka."

May did a double-take at me and snickered.

"I'm going to get some air." I opened the patio door and a blast
of ocean air hit me. "That's better. You can keep your conditioned
air. I like my air natural. The way God made it. I like the doors
and windows wide open. That's the way I see it." I sucked in two
lungs full and eased it back out ever…so…slowly.

"Speaking of seeing, my little friend is out on the beach again."

"Alone? This late in the day?" May already knew the answer.

"Yes, he is. Mind if I make sure he's okay?"

"Not at all. But you should talk to his father about that. It's good for kids to have some freedom, but that kid has far too much of it."

I waved as I left the cottage and headed toward Chip.

"Say buddy, what you up to?" I fluffed his hair with my fingertips.

"Marilyn just got a box of chocolates. Want some?"

Chip didn't respond.

"Want to see if there are any good shells out today? I see you've got your sand pail. Could be some pirate treasure out there. You just never know what will wash ashore."

He nodded and slid his hand in mine. It made me smile. Instantly. I was connecting with him…really connecting.

I let him have the water side as we walked next to each other at the ocean's edge. I took smaller steps so he didn't have to struggle to keep up.

"There's one. Look at that. A perfect sand dollar." As I bent down to pick it up, Chip picked up a piece of frosted, rounded green glass. He held it up to the late afternoon sun.

"I love beach glass, don't you? Makes me wonder who threw the bottle into the ocean, and where they threw it. How long it ground around the bottom of the ocean against the sand so that it's broken edges got smooth. And the shiny glass turned hazy. Do you think about that too?"

Chip nodded and gently placed the glass in his pail.

"What if there was a message in the bottle? Now that bottle's gone. The message is too. All that's left is this bit of glass." My words stopped flowing. I just looked out at the surf.

Chip did the same. His fingers made a fist that cocooned the piece of green beach glass.

It was safe with him.

I could tell he wasn't about to let it go.

I began to doubt that I could ever let him go.

FADE OUT

CHAPTER 47

FADE IN:
- SEPTEMBER 10, 1958, THIRD DAY OF SHOOTING
- INTERIOR, LOBBY OF HOTEL DEL CORONADO (DAYTIME)

"Tonight. It's got to be tonight. A late dinner. With me. Say yes." Steele didn't need to bring out all his usual ammunition. Right there. In the hotel lobby. His request left me like a pool of melted butter on a surf-and-turf platter. "By the way, you look *amazing*. Love the earrings. They really sparkle and...um...dangle."

It was an awkward comment at best. But I didn't miss a beat and replied, "Down to my shoulders, almost. They're called shoulder dusters. Anyway, about dinner, sure. What time?" I completely wasted the opportunity to hesitate and at least appeared disinterested. Make him work for it. But he was all Errol Flynn hair and Paul Newman stares. Irresistible. He knew it too. He had to.

"Something less formal?" Steele checked his wristwatch. "Say, seven-thirty? We can meet here in the lobby. I'll take care of the rest."

"Yes, you take care of the rest." I just stood there and looked at him. "Speaking of taking care, did you know Chip was out on the beach alone again. I took him down by the water and we collected shells and sea glass. And then I sent him back to your room."

A bellhop's voice broke through the lobby's buzz. "Mr. Steele Wright. Phone call for Mr. Steele Wright."

"I'm right here."

"You can use the house phone over there." The bellhop made

a sweeping motion with his arm to direct Steele to a pair of parlor chairs separated by a small table. The phone rested on the marble tabletop.

"Thank you. I'll be there in a moment." Then Steele turned to me. "If you'll excuse me. It must be an urgent matter of some sort. Business, you know. It could take some time. Why don't you run along?"

"Sure. Goodbye." He'd never mentioned business before. And, I'd never asked.

Steele walked away. He picked up the phone's receiver, nodded, stepped to the right, stepped to the left and wrapped the phone cord around his left index finger. He turned to look back at me and began to walk. But he stopped just around the corner of the elevator door out of sight.

I moved closer and leaned against the wall. I listened for anything I could overhear. After all, it was a public space.

Just as I began to pick up a few of his words, the elevator door opened, releasing several hotel guests from the car. "Do you wish to continue your journey, miss?" Cheng's face peeked around the corner of the wall.

"How did you know I was here?"

"This old elevator's a cage. I can see quite a bit through it. I can hear things too."

"That must come in handy." I tilted my head and studied Cheng. "Guess my work is finished here. I'll go back to my room." I entered the car, but kept on eye on Steele, who was still talking on the phone. He ran his fingers through his hair and stopped the motion, with his opened palm creating a skull cap.

"You watch him. You like him." Cheng closed the car's door. "He is not all he appears to be."

He sounded like he knew something. "Why would you say that?"

"He is *more* than he appears to be."

"Now what's that supposed to mean?"

Cheng opened the collapsible door. "This is your stop. Is there anything else I can do for you?"

"No. I don't think so." I stepped out and headed down the hallway that was becoming more familiar and welcoming.

When I opened my room's door, an ocean breeze stole my breath. It was good to be there. My home away from home.

I showered, dried off and stepped back into my bedroom area. The red dress, red patent-leather pumps and red-plastic heart-shaped dangle earrings—mismatched heart-shaped earrings, of course—looked like a deflated version of me laying on the bed.

"Two hearts? Too obvious." I opened my jewelry bag and pulled out a pair of oversized pearl dangle earrings. "That's better. One heart. One pearl."

I fished out a strand of fake pearls, long enough to double up and create the appearance of two strands.

"That should do it."

Down at the restaurant, Steele held my hands across the table. Like he'd done before. His penetrating eyes had full control of me. My eyes. My thoughts. My heart rate. My heart.

"You aren't what I expected...what I expected *you* to be."

"Oh?" I pretended I was coy.

"You're so much more."

"I am?"

"Absolutely. While everyone is falling over themselves around Marilyn, it's you that I see...and watch...and daydream about."

"I hear that all the time. *Really.*"

"I'm sure you do." Steele was so polite.

"No, I don't. I really don't."

"Well, now you have. And I'll say it again if you'd like, if that will make you happy. I want you to be happy. And I want you to always smile so I can see that dimple of yours."

I put my palm over my cheek. "I want to make *you* happy." I realized what I said. Out loud. "You'll have to excuse me. Everything I think falls out of my mouth."

"Some would call that honesty."

"My father, The Commander, would call that being sloppy. You know, the whole loose-lips-sink-ships thing. He was Navy. He *is* Navy." I looked down at our joined hands. "That might be part of the reason I like you so much. Because you talk and you let me talk. He rations his words like bacon and coffee during the war. It's like he only has so many to use each day. Like he's cheap with his words. He's always thought I talked too much."

"Well, I want to hear what you have to say. All of it."

"Are you sure about that?"

"Mr. Wright." The waiter presented Steele a phone. The long extension cord made it possible to take the call at the table, as well as trip any unsuspecting pedestrians in the restaurant. The waiter took several steps backward, running his fingers along the chord and elevating it like the poles and telephone lines that ran parallel to every street in America.

"Pardon me, Penny." Steele lifted the receiver and cupped his hand next to the mouthpiece and his mouth. "Yes. Uh-huh. No." It went on like that for several minutes.

"I really must go. I trust you have all you need to proceed." He paused. "Fine then. Thanks for the call." He placed the receiver back into the phone's cradle. The waiter stepped forward to take away the phone and gather up the extension cord.

"Should I be concerned?"

"About what?" Steele returned a question with a question.

"You. And these phone calls. Are you a gangster? A brain surgeon? An FBI agent?"

Steele grinned. "No, I'm none of those things. What I am is an extremely successful—"

The waiter interrupted by asking, "May I take your order now?"

FADE OUT

CHAPTER 48

FADE IN:
- SEPTEMBER 10, 1958, THIRD DAY OF SHOOTING
- EXTERIOR, CORONADO BEACH (NIGHTTIME)

"I knew a stroll along the beach would be perfect." His voice was velvety.

I swung my pair of pumps from the hand that wasn't holding Steele's. "I didn't know that things were wrong."

"Just a figure of speech." Steele gazed at the stars. "There's nothing like the moon and the stars and the sand and the surf and you. Most of all, you."

He stopped walking and twisted me toward him. He slid his left arm around my waist and pulled me in close like a boa constrictor. In the same abrupt move, his right hand cupped and rubbed my boob. He groped me right there on the beach. Like he was entitled to. Then, he had the nerve to tilt his head and come in for a kiss.

It was like he flipped some switch. His aggressive handling took my breath away. And not in a good way.

He'd blindsided me. I goddamned him in my head.

"Hold on a minute, buster. I don't remember giving you the green light." I couldn't deny that I'd been wanting to kiss him. Badly. But I didn't want to kiss him *then*. Not if I was being forced to.

Within a few heartbeats, the soundtrack of my life went from seductive samba bongo beats to screeching violins, the kind of music to have a nightmare with.

"I didn't know I needed a green light." Steele's words were

prickly. Even though he was smashing his body against mine, his hungry hand released my boob, slid down my ribs, over my belly and headed south for my Fun Zone. Copping a feel was one thing. A hand below the waistline was entirely something else.

"No!" My word—that single word—could not have been misunderstood. Or so I thought.

He ignored everything and just kept going.

He was taking over my body.

"I said *no!*" I tried to push away, but he wouldn't release me. "Who are you? Has your evil twin brother taken over?"

"Come on. You know you want this. Look at me. Just do it. Look at me."

His wandering—and demanding—free hand gripped my wrist. I glared over his shoulder, not at his face.

"These eyes. Look at *these* eyes. You want me. I've known it since we first met."

"I've looked at them enough. Maybe too much. Now let me go."

He squeezed me. He snapped his head to the side and jerked forward, making another attempt at a kiss. "You'll see. Just relax. It'll be the best you've ever had."

Clearly, he was unaccustomed to rejection and it stirred something in him like wasps from a nest hit with a rock.

"I said no. Don't. Ever. Do. That. AGAIN." I punched my last word like a prizefighter in the ring.

He slackened his grip and I fell backward into the damp sand. The whole scene was unbelievable. Unexpected. Un-Steele. Or at least the Steele I thought I knew.

"What's wrong with you?" He didn't help me to my feet, so I managed it myself.

I raised my fist and swiveled it in the moonlight. "Oh, there's plenty wrong with me. I admit it." I filled my lungs. "And there's plenty wrong with you too. You're a coward. That's at the top of the list. Why does this keep happening to me? You're just like all the bullies my life." Visions of Otis and Bradley filled my mind until I swiped them away. "Who—or what—messed you up?"

Another couple was close by, near enough for Steele not to try anything more.

"Don't embarrass me, you walking freak show," he whispered in a failed attempt to be discrete. "You've ruined everything. My plans to-"

He severed his words. I could feel his rage, his flames.

Then he bellowed, "Suit yourself. Don't let me—or anyone—get in your way." He capped off his rant with a crisp "Good NIGHT." He turned toward The Del and headed inland.

I stood there.

Stunned.

Relieved.

Stunned.

Rejected.

Stunned.

How could I have picked a loser again? But wait, he picked me, didn't he? I cut off my thoughts when I belted out, "STAY AWAY FROM ME!" I kept shouting at Steele's back. "And don't try that again with me. Or with any girl for that matter. You're a bully. A selfish sonofabitch. And you'll get yours, in the end. JUST YOU WAIT, MR. WRIGHT."

"Yeah, yeah, yeah," he muttered.

After I reassured the passing couple that I was okay, I brushed the sand off my palms and dress. I reached into my purse and pulled out the penny Steele gave me...his so-called *lucky* penny.

"Hey, Steele! WATCH THIS!"

He turned.

I held up the coin and then threw it with all my might into the surf. "So much for your LUCKY PENNY."

Steele swung around to face the hotel.

"BETTER LUCK NEXT TIME!" I yelled loud enough for him—and everyone else on the beach—to hear.

It felt good. And it felt bad.

I faced the open sea and inhaled.

I knew that would calm me down.

The waves rolled in with their own pace and rhythm, like the hot tears that escaped and slid down my cheeks.

One wave after another glistened in the moonlight, almost like stars on the earth's surface instead of out in the galaxy. There was something bobbing just off shore, where the waves were crashing. I stared at that area with each passing wave.

And then I saw it. Saw her. A face and a hand. A hand that glowed. A hand that *sparkled*.

I squinted and put the edge of my flattened palm against my

forehead, like a sea captain peering at the dark horizon.
    She was gone.
    The woman of the sea.
    Gone.
    But not gone from my memory.

FADE OUT

CHAPTER 49

"It's me. Penny. I'm just checking in to be sure you don't need anything." I spoke through the door to Marilyn.

"Actually, I do need something. And I think you might be just the person to help me." Marilyn opened the door. I smiled at the officer on duty as I entered the cottage. "I was just running through some lines for tomorrow. Hell, I was even looking ahead at what we'll be shooting in the studio too, when we're back in LA."

"Anything interesting."

"Very. At one point, I'll say to Tony, 'I'm tired of getting the fuzzy end of the lollipop.'" Marilyn paused. "Ain't, I mean, *isn't* that the truth?"

"It is. And I just took a lick off the fuzzy end of my lollipop." I released a breath of air and rubbed my right eye, which I suspected was pinkish from crying. "Actually, it was more like an ammonia moment."

"What do you mean?"

"Like when you get a whiff of ammonia. Or smelling salts. Your head's instantly on fire. You're more aware than you've ever been in your entire life."

"Sit down. What happened?" She squinted at me. "Was it him?"

I tripped on a throw rug but landed on a chair. "Will I ever grow out of this klutzy stage?"

"I don't know, but go ahead and tell me about Mr. Wright."

"I think I'm beginning to see *him*. The him that all of you have been seeing. The man I was blind to."

"Did he say something?"

"Yes, and he did something."

"Honey, there are men out there who will teach you wrong from right."

"You mean right from wrong?"

"No. They start with the *wrong* and you have to end it *right*. Besides, I'm used to getting manhandled. It's practically what I do for a living."

"Not me. Not ever. Well, there was this one time when—" My words dried up as a single tear rolled down my cheek.

"Oh, sweetheart. He's not worth it. Most of them aren't. My goal was to find a gorgeous man who didn't ruin my mascara, just my lipstick. Now, I've got him. And Penny, he may not be gorgeous in some people's eyes, but he can mess up my lipstick anytime."

I wiped away the tear and grinned, just a bit.

Marilyn passed a tube of lipstick from her vanity to me. "Here. Keep this. It'll remind you of this moment. Kisses, not tears. Got it?"

I took the tube from her.

"Trust me on this one, Penny. Some things fall apart—even good things—so better things can fall together. You'll see."

"I'll try."

"Do you want to tell me more? Or would you rather go and blow off some steam?"

"Steam." I said it fast, without any thought.

"Then I've got an idea. Can you talk with a deep voice?"

"Sure. I mocked my brothers plenty of times."

"Can you walk and stand like a man?"

"I'm The Commander's daughter, aren't I?"

"Then we're going to have a boys' night out."

"You mean a *girls'* night out?"

"No. Boys. Tony and Jack have been having all the fun. They're getting to be women. Me. I get to be Marilyn. All lips and hips. But that's going to stop. At least for tonight."

"I'm not following you. I mean I'll follow you, but I don't understand what you're saying."

"When people look at me all they see is her, Marilyn. They don't see me. They don't even look at me like I'm a human being. So, if they aren't going to see me anyway, why not be a man for the night? Or at least for a couple of drinks. And a couple of laughs."

I nodded. "If our two guys can be girls, we two girls can be guys. I got it."

"Good. I'll get one of the bellhops to sneak over to the employees' locker room and snag us some men's clothes. Then we're going out. We'll return the clothes before anyone knows."

"Where'll we go?"

"To that dark Mexican pick-up joint you told me about. Where the fortuneteller is. We should be able to blend in there. It's dark, right?"

"Yeah."

"Say, what do think of asking Jack and Tony to go along? In drag? We can all go incognito."

"Won't that make us all stick out. If it's just the two of us, we stand a better chance, wouldn't we?"

"No, I don't think so." Marilyn rolled her eyes around as she thought. "What if we kept apart? I know. We could dare them. No. Bet them. We could see who's the first person to get picked up by someone of the opposite—I mean same—sex. I know they'll do it. This is just what we all need."

"What'll we wager?"

"It's got to be something…something…uh, something really tempting. We'll figure that out later."

FADE OUT

CHAPTER 50

FADE IN:
- SEPTEMBER 10, 1958, THIRD DAY OF SHOOTING
- INTERIOR, MARILYN'S COTTAGE (NIGHTTIME)

"Well this is something I've never had to do." Marilyn smashed her breasts down as she unrolled a wide ACE bandage around her chest.

"Here. Let me help you. But let me finish this first." I sculpted a rolled pair of socks and stuffed them into the unzipped fly of my suspendered trousers.

"No, you're not doing it like them. All they want to do is take it out to play, not put it away." Marilyn burst out laughing.

"Right or left? Don't they dangle it one way or the other?"

"Uh-huh. I vote for right."

"Me too." I squashed it in place and safety pinned it. I looked up at Marilyn, who was standing motionless with the ACE bandage hanging down. "I don't want it to fall out while we're there."

I zipped up my pants and helped Marilyn suppress her breasts.

"Funny, we're getting into *their* pants this time." Marilyn giggled.

"Do you think we'll get away with it? Honestly, do you believe anyone will think you're a guy?"

"The boys are getting away with it in the movie. But they aren't exactly pretty, like us. We'll just be pretty men. They're out there, you know."

"I know all too well. Steele is pretty."

"Pretty shitty, if you ask me."

"I didn't. But I agree now. I'm sorry I didn't see it before." I exhaled and slouched a bit.

"Honey, they don't say love is blind for nothing."

"But for me it was deaf *and* dumb too."

"You've learned your lesson." Marilyn looked at herself in the mirror. "We'll just have some fun with these getups. Then we'll hightail it out of there and come back here for a nice bottle of champagne."

We—all four of us—arrived at the Village's front door together. The guys as girls. The girls as guys. "Now remember, the first to get picked up wins." Marilyn used a deep throaty voice. "And *no* cheating."

"Not bad." Jack responded using his perfected falsetto. "If I wasn't looking at you, I might think that voice belonged to…to…to—"

"To a man?" Tony added, "Five o'clock shadows. Nice touch."

"I know a thing or two about makeup, but usually for women." Marilyn adjusted the brim of her baseball cap.

We walked in together and headed for the bar. A disheveled man took Tony's arm. "You look familiar. Didn't we take a class together? I could have sworn we had chemistry."

"Yes, definitely *had* chemistry. Now let me go or I'll—"

Jack interrupted, "Now, now. You just leave my sister alone and let us get a drinkie-poo." Jack pulled Tony over to the bar, leaving the drunk no time to consider what Jack said.

"Does that count? It was a pick-up line. Did I win? Already?" Tony looked eagerly for an answer.

"Too soon. You've got to let us warm up first." Marilyn licked her lips and smiled at me.

"Hey, knock that off. Men don't do that." I didn't want our covers to be blown so quickly.

"Oh, yeah-yeah. I'll do better, honey."

As I looked over her shoulder, an oversized painted clay statue of a Mexican diablo grabbed my attention. Bulging eyes. Horns. With both hands, he was holding an enormous snake that was either his tail or something else that I didn't want to look at closely enough to figure out. "Don't look now. The Devil has his eye on you!"

Marilyn started to turn around.

"Hey, I said *don't* look."

"Alright then. But that just means you're going to have to protect me all night."

"Deal."

She and I used our best swaggers to get over to the fortuneteller's area.

"Well I'll be goddamned." I pointed to Steele inside Esmeralda's tent. The front-flap door was still pinned back. "After everything that happened tonight, he's here."

"So are you, honey…I mean buddy." Marilyn corrected her word choice.

"I just wonder—"

"Wonder what?"

"I wonder if she'd help me get revenge." I was a woman scorned, dressed as a man. I wondered if that made me a man scorned.

Marilyn asked, "Who?"

"Esmeralda, the fortuneteller."

"Most people will do just about anything for cash. I'm guessing she's not a woman of untainted scruples." Marilyn delivered her words as if they were scripted.

"Those are some highfalutin vocabulary words. Impressive. Anyway, anything's worth a try." I stepped next to the tent. I didn't want Steele to see me or Marilyn. Esmeralda was telling Steele that life is what you do while you're waiting to die. Not exactly a customer-friendly thing to say.

"Hey, gypsy woman. Get out here." I used a deep, edgy voice. "I gotta bone to pick with you."

Esmeralda went on to tell Steele, "And that's why I keep the door closed…except for people who don't like to be closed in, like you." She poked her head out the doorway and saw me using a wild gesture with one hand to draw her close, while my other hand's index finger was over my closed lips in a shushing way.

"Let's go over here." I mouthed the words so Steele couldn't hear.

Esmeralda poked her head back in the doorway. "Pardon me, sir, for a moment. Close your eyes and relax so the spirits feel welcome in your presence."

The fortuneteller whispered to me. "So how can I help you?"

"That man—" I realized too late that I was talking in my normal voice. Esmeralda looked at me with questioning eyes. The manly appearance and the womanly voice didn't connect.

"Anyway, that man just treated me like shit. Out on the beach. Will you help me get back at him? Woman to woman, please?"

"If he's an asshole, I'm happy to help. There are too many assholes in this world who never get their comeuppance. Tell me what he did and I'll twist it around to scare the tar out of him."

We shook hands. "Say, I remember you. The energy. It pulsed right from your hand to mine. Welcome back."

I told her about what had just happened on the beach. Marilyn stepped over, lifted the front brim of her ball cap and added, "Give it to him good. He's pretty on the outside, but ugly on the inside. And nobody treats my friends, like this girl...er, guy...um...like that. Her name's Penny. That might make this easier."

Esmeralda nodded with a slow gaze. Her brain's gears must have been turning.

"I have what I need. If you want, you can stand behind my tent and listen. No one will see you two and suspect anything. But don't make a peep. Not a snort. A gasp. Silence. Agreed?"

I nodded. Marilyn shook Esmeralda's hand and slipped her some crumpled paper money.

"Pleasure doing business with you two." Esmeralda went back into her tent as we went behind it.

"Now, give me your hands. I need to feel your passion, your drive." She paused. "Yes, now I can see more clearly. You're a man with much, much heat. Much strength. A man women are easily attracted to. They lower their guards. You're always in control. But—" She stopped speaking.

"What? Do you see something? Feel something? Tell me." Steele's words were punctuated with question marks and curiosity.

"There's a woman. No. There are women. On the beach. At night. One is standing by you. Arguing with you. Another is in the water. In the surf. She appears to be warning the woman on the beach. Waving her arms. She's coming closer. And closer. And closer."

"What's she doing?"

"She's coming out of the water. Not onto the beach. She's rising out of the water. Over the water. I can see through her. Do you want me to ask her name?"

"No. Don't do that."

"She's saying Gloria...no, it's Glow...just Glow. Please, do not release my hands or the vision will vanish."

I heard heavy hands hit the tabletop. "Here are the five bucks you asked for. I'm outta here."

I peeked around the edge of the tent to see Steele's back as he hurried away, clipping the shoulders of several people. One of them was Tony, who replied, "Watch where you're going." He said it in a loud, male voice. Steele did a double take as he moved toward the entrance.

Jack sashayed over. "Nice. Blow our cover why don't you."

We joined the guys. "Any luck?" Marilyn rubbed her hands together like a cold person.

"Not yet, but the night's young." Jack raised his shoulders and winked with both eyes.

I spotted a woman who was alone at the bar. She raised her almost-empty glass of beer and nodded at me. "Um, guys, I think I might have a live one on my hook." I stepped to the side and added, "Watch me."

I swaggered over to the bar, said a few words to the woman and then hailed the bartender. He poured another glass of beer and put it in front of my new friend. We chatted. I cautioned her not to judge me by my wrapper, and I wasn't talking about a candy bar. I put my hand on her shoulder and whispered something in her ear. She giggled and playfully slapped my shoulder. Then I came back to my Hollywood friends.

"You won. I can't believe it? The three of us, actors, who get paid to pretend we're someone else. And she not only sells herself as a man, but she picks up a woman."

Marilyn shook her head. "You know what? Let's have a party of our own. That'll be everyone's prize. I've got some champagne waiting for me at The Del. Care to join us?"

"Sure," replied Tony.

"What the hell. Let's go," added Jack. "Tony, I can't believe it. You make such a pretty dame."

"You're not half bad yourself, buddy."

FADE OUT

CHAPTER 51

I was pretty sure my sanity was playing hide and seek with me.

"Cheng? Where are you taking me? I don't remember even getting in your elevator. It's been such a long day and night. I'm exhausted. Really exhausted." I rested my back on the cage's wall.

"You are here with me. That is all you need to know." Cheng stood in his usual front corner with the control panel, arms folded in front of his chest.

"And you are also here with me." A woman whispered the words, but only Cheng and I were in the car. "You...are here...with me." The voice became more direct.

I studied Cheng. With his eyes, he nudged me to look in the car's other front corner. I followed his lead and found a woman standing there, where no one had been standing a moment ago. She was my height, though her wide-brimmed hat and draping veil might have made her look taller than she was. Her black-lace dress had a high neck and long sleeves. Her skirt touched the floor.

"I have been waiting for someone...like you. A very long time I have waited." Her voice was comforting like a mother's. Not my mother, but other mothers.

I stared at Cheng. He blinked and gazed forward.

"You are the one. Yes, you *are* the one." The woman spoke with confidence, clarity and conviction.

"I'm what? The one what? And you, are you Kate?"

I shifted my weight and put my right foot out in front of the left. I was dizzy and started to lose my balance. I poked my fingers through the cage's wall and held on.

"Here, you need this more than I do." The woman held out an unwrapped lollipop that looked like it had been dropped on the floor more than once. Its sticky surface had collected things like fly paper collects flies.

"What's that?" I could see what it was, but asked anyway.

"It is the fuzzy end of the lollipop, of course. You have heard about it. Now it is yours."

"No, thank you. I don't want it."

"Want has nothing to do with it." Kate moved it closer to me. "It is yours. The fuzzy end—"

The floor of the elevator car dropped out and I fell, reaching out for something to hold onto, but nothing—

I woke up taking heaving breaths. My bed's sheets looked like an army had marched through them.

Was it another dream?

Was it real?

It was Kate, that was for sure.

I checked the clock on my nightstand and saw something that didn't belong to me.

A lollipop.

An unwrapped lollipop.

A *fuzzy* lollipop.

FADE OUT

CHAPTER 52

"I am *not* moving. Not now. Not ever. I mean it. I really mean it."

"Marilyn, you have to get up. Everyone's waiting." I was just doing my job. A sheet of paper on the nightstand caught my eye. "Is that something you want me to put in the mail?"

"Sure. Fine. It's to Norman. You know, the poet. Norman Rosten. May's got his address. She's the one who typed the letter."

The solitary piece of stationery had a sketch of the hotel and beach printed on it.

Marilyn's eyes closed and her breathing got heavy. "For as long as I can remember, my body's been a toy box. One day, it's going to be a crime scene."

I had no words to respond with. I held the letter close enough to read and noticed someone had added a tiny figure in the artwork of the surf, with the word "Help!" being shouted.

"Don't give up the ship while we're sinking." The typed letter went on, "I have a feeling this boat is never going to dock. We're going through the Straits of Dire. It's rough and it's choppy, but why should I worry? Marilyn."

Below the word *Marilyn* a short message appeared. "I would have written this by hand but it's trembling."

I put the paper back on the table and nudged her shoulder. "Marilyn. Get up. Please."

"I've been thinking about our chat with Tilly." She paused. "If she could walk away from Hollywood, so can I. I think that's just what I'm going to do."

"But everyone's counting on you. Their livelihoods depend on it. What you do or don't do touches so many people. Please."

"No, my mind is made up."

I had to think of a maneuver or bribe fast.

"How about you plan your escape *after* finishing this project? Uh?"

She didn't respond. I needed to sweeten the deal.

"I'll help you. Promise. Say, how about we have dinner with Trudy and the girls tonight? That would be a nice way to end the day. Now come on. Let's get going."

May cleared her throat as she leaned on the room's doorjamb. She shook her head. "Good luck with that."

"Alright already. I'll do it. But only because I want one of Trudy's meals. You strike an unfair bargain, Miss Penny Parker. And don't you dare tell Billy why I'm so cooperative today."

"Don't jinx yourself by saying that." I started shaking out my hands, like Marilyn did before every take. "Sheesh, you've got *me* doing it now."

FADE OUT

CHAPTER 53

FADE IN:
- SEPTEMBER 11, 1958, FOURTH DAY OF SHOOTING
- INTERIOR, TRUDY'S HOUSE (NIGHTTIME)

Marilyn's elbows were resting on the edge of Trudy's dining room table. She was bright and attentive. "Now what?"

"Poker?" Bootsie batted her eyes to make her idea irresistible. It didn't work.

"Dominos?" Trudy didn't embellish her suggestion.

"How about the Ouija board? Let's place a call to heaven and see who answers?" I got up, opened the buffet's center door and pulled out a board-game sized box. "These things creep me out. Well, at least they used to. It's been years since I've touched one. After everything I've been through lately, it may be a piece of cake now."

"Piece of cake, does anyone have room for cake?" Leave it to Trudy to offer more food.

Groans were met with more groans. "Not now. But maybe later." I was never one to pass up her cake. Any flavor. But I was stuffed at that moment.

Marilyn slumped back in her chair. Elbows were off the table.

"Are you uncomfortable with this?" I put the box down on the table.

"I was always told they were the gateway to hell...that you shouldn't open any doors for demons to come through. But then again, my mother had demons that she carried with her. Kind of like her own personal club." Marilyn rubbed her chin.

"Alright. We can play dominos." Bootsie turned to the buffet's open section and brought out the oblong box of domino tiles.

"No, go ahead. Do the board. I'll watch." Marilyn pushed her chair away from the table. "Really. Go ahead."

"My two cousins—Elma and Dorothy—could make that board speak. Oh, could they make it speak. Scared the tapioca out of me." Trudy pushed away from the table too. "I'll watch from a safe distance."

"What does it say on the back of the box?" Marilyn showed more interest.

I flipped it over and scanned the text. "Says they're called Spirit Boards and Talking Boards. Blah blah blah. Oh, it says the heart-shaped piece of wood with the window in it's called the planchette. Players put their fingers on the planchette, concentrate and the planchette moves across the board to answer questions by pointing out letters, numbers or words. There are four words on the board: yes, no, hello and goodbye."

"Okay." Marilyn nodded.

"It says the Chinese used planchettes 800 years ago to contact the dead. Blah, blah, blah." I skipped ahead. "And, similar activities occurred in Rome, Greece and India."

"Alright already. Let's get on with it. Penny, you and I will go first. We'll show them how it's done." Bootsie's voice was bouncy with excitement.

Bootsie placed the board on the table, the planchette on the board and her fingertips on one half of the planchette. I took the chair next to her and placed my fingertips on the other half of the planchette.

"We used to do this at every sleepover when I was a kid." Bootsie seemed more than eager to get started. "Now we need to light a candle and turn off all the lights...and anything electric. The current disturbs the spirits."

"Now how do you know that?" I cocked my head and waited for her response.

"I just do. What should we ask?"

"Let's see if Kate is here. You know, the ghost at The Del."

"That won't work. She's at The Del. You just said it yourself."

I cleared my throat. "Trudy, what about Vernon? Can we reach out to him?"

"My Vern is here all the time. I don't need some voodoo board to talk to him."

"But we do. Can we? May we?"

"I suppose it'll be alright."

"Then you take my place." Bootsie stood up and stepped away from her chair. "The two people who are touching the planchette must close their eyes. No cheating is allowed."

Marilyn watched from her vantage point, with wide-open eyes.

Trudy sat down, put her fingertips on the planchette and even before she took a deep breath and closed her eyes, there was movement on the board. I peeked. I couldn't resist. I didn't move the planchette on purpose. Our hands slid as a team across the board to the word "Hello."

"Vernon, you could at least wait until we called you." Trudy talked to him as if he was sitting across the table.

"So, let's ask him something. Like, is he happy?"

Our hands and the planchette moved to the upper left corner of the board to the word "Yes." I was still peeking, but let the other girls announce what was happening on the board.

"I've never done this before. I've only talked to him while I cooked or washed dishes or folded laundry."

I spoke up. "Vernon, do you know what year it is?" Our hands slid from number one to number nine to number five and then number eight.

The girls' eyes darting back and forth.

"Vernon, what do you think of having Marilyn Monroe in our house?"

Our hands moved to the letter "w" and then the letter "o" and back to the letter "w." The girls announced each letter as it appeared in the planchette's window.

"He said, *wow*. Marilyn, what do you think of that?" I had to ask.

"It's not the first time a man has said wow around me, but I have to say it's the first time a dead one has."

We all laughed, but I couldn't help but notice a nervous edge to it.

Trudy removed her hands from the planchette to wipe away tears from each of her eyelids. Instantly the planchette and my hands shot across the board to the word "Hello."

My eyes opened wide. I raised my shoulders to signal that I didn't know what was going on. My fingertips went cold. Not all at once. But as if the cold was going up toward my wrists. I pulled my fingertips off the planchette and raised my open palms. The planchette trembled...on its own. Then it started to move around the board in a figure eight.

"Saints preserve us. That's what my cousins said happened to them once. They said it was a sign that someone—or something—was trying to get out of the board."

Then it shot off the table and into Marilyn's lap. She jumped to her feet. "Get it away from me. I don't want to touch it."

The planchette fell to the floor.

"Burn it. We have to burn the whole thing." Trudy got up and grabbed a dish towel from the kitchen sink, along with the metal wastebasket. She returned to the dining room, placed the box, board and planchette in the basket using the dish towel. We followed her through the house to the back door. "Penny, bring some newspaper. And matches."

"Sure thing."

It was a backyard bonfire unlike any I'd ever witnessed.

"We have to close that door. Maybe fire will do it. At least no one will *ever* use that board again...not in this house, anyway. Never."

"Never." I said it with conviction.

"Never," added Bootsie.

"Never, ever." Marilyn turned away from the fiery newspaper. The board didn't appear to burn. "Never, ever."

FADE OUT

CHAPTER 54

FADE IN:
- SEPTEMBER 11, 1958, FOURTH DAY OF SHOOTING
- INTERIOR, MARILYN'S COTTAGE (NIGHTTIME)

"Penny, you grew up here, right?" Marilyn laid her head back on one of the couch's pillows in her cottage. "What do you know about the ghost that people say haunts the hotel?"

"I know the whole story. It always bothered me. Not because I'm afraid of ghosts, because I'm not." I shook my head. "It's because the stories never really added up. I know a thing or two about stuff not adding up. For instance, no one—and I mean *no one*—believed me when I tried to—" I caught myself before going on.

"Tried to what?" Marilyn prodded me.

"I might as well put it all on the table for you. I left my fiancé at the altar. I just walked out. Dress, bouquet and all. He exploded. Why wouldn't he? Then again, as a kid, Bradley was kicked out of the Boy Scouts for buying his badges. I should've considered that more before saying yes to him. Anyway, that's the kind of person he was."

I caught myself darting my eyes, but then focused on Marilyn. "I knew it wouldn't work out. Bradley was a brute. He treated me like dirt. But that wasn't something new in my life."

I bit my lower lip and continued. "He was almost always angry and mean with me. But he was all charming with everyone else—Cheshire-Cat smiles and crushing handshakes. When I think about it, though, I bet he didn't ever like anyone, not really. I don't think he liked himself. I saw that and learned that just in time. He told me—no, convinced me—he was my last chance. It was him or be a spinster. I think my parents agreed."

"Did he hit you, honey?"

"Why would you ask that?" I tilted my head and blinked a few times. "It started slowly. But a push became a shove, and a shove became a choke, and a choke became a hit. I blamed myself and it was awful. But I couldn't tell anyone. They would've thought I mouthed off or just had it coming to me. So, I did something to change everything. And it happened on my wedding day. At the altar."

"Good thing you didn't go through with it." Marilyn nodded.

"On some level, I loved him, as crazy as that sounds. The problem was I didn't *like* him. To make things worse, I still work with his best friend at the dime store. Otis, that's his name, is just like Bradley. So, I never really escaped from him. But, you know, I used to think the worst thing in life was to be alone. It's not."

"It's not?" Marilyn looked puzzled.

"No. The worst thing in life is to end up with people who make you feel bad about yourself. They *make* you feel alone."

I gazed at the ceiling. "I read something—I don't remember where exactly—but it said, if you can't love yourself, how can you expect to love someone else. That hit me right between the eyes. Do you understand?"

Luckily, Marilyn changed the subject. "What did you mean about things not adding up about the ghost? Was there a murder or a suicide?"

I turned in my chair so I was facing Marilyn. "So do you want to hear it...hear it all? Because I know an awful lot."

"It's that or learn my lines. Since Paula's not here, you can fire away."

So, I did. "It was 1892. That's when she checked into The Del and never checked out." I enlarged and then squinted my eyes several times, followed by a dramatic, "Dun...dun...duuuuun" in a deep voice.

Marilyn smiled.

"It was Thanksgiving Day. She was twenty-four. By all accounts, she was unhappy. On top of it all, she was alone. And you know how questionable it appeared for a young lady to travel and check into a hotel alone back then. Plus, she had no luggage."

Marilyn pursed her lips and slightly raised her shoulders, crushing the pillow behind her head.

"She came in the ladies' entrance to be discreet, being an unescorted woman. Can you believe that? The hotel even had a dining room just for single women who were uncomfortable eating in mixed company."

"I believe it."

"She signed the register Lottie A. Bernard. An alias. Her room cost three dollars and eighty cents a day. She told hotel employees she was waiting for a gentleman to join her. Five days later, she was dead outside on a staircase leading to the beach."

Marilyn placed her right index finger beside her nose. "I hope I go fast like that. I don't want to end up an old mummy in a hospital bed, like I'm waiting at a bus stop for God to come along and take me away." She stared at me. I assumed she wanted to hear more. Before I could start up again, like some storytelling tour guide, she asked, "You certainly know the facts, but is that it?"

"Hardly. The police couldn't positively identify her. They ended up telegraphing a description of Kate around the country. They even had a sketch made of Kate's face based on witness descriptions. She had two moles on her left cheek."

Marilyn slid her finger over to touch the beauty mark on her left cheek.

"The newspapers started calling her the 'Beautiful Stranger.' One of the stories is that once her identity was confirmed—she was married but estranged from her husband—they figured she'd arrived at The Del hoping to rendezvous with a lover."

"You weren't kidding when you said you knew a lot about this woman's story."

I grinned.

"Here's where it gets even more interesting. Kate was employed as a domestic in a hoity-toity Los Angeles mansion."

"Ohhhh!"

"She traveled here by train. Passengers later said a woman matching Kate's description argued—as in a lovers' quarrel—with a male companion who then deserted her on the way to San Diego. While she was here, Kate looked sick and sad. She even went across the bay to San Diego to buy a handgun."

"Really?" Marilyn leaned forward.

"Uh-huh. The San Diego coroner said Kate died from a self-inflicted gunshot wound."

"Wow."

I continued. "Early one morning an electrician found her, clothes soaking wet, on the stairs leading to the beach. Blood was on the steps and her feet were pointing to the ocean. A pistol was next to her body."

Marilyn blinked in an exaggerated way.

I went on to tell her another story about how Kate came from Iowa and she was the wife of Tom Morgan, a gambler. Then another story had her pregnant and abandoned. "Funny thing is, they never did an autopsy on her. There was even talk of her having stomach cancer and that her brother, who was a doctor, was to arrive any day to help her. He never showed up. Guess what? She didn't have a brother."

"So where does the ghost part come in?"

"You do like this story, don't you?" Considering all the people Marilyn had met, the places she'd been and the roles she'd played, I was shocked she found Kate's story so interesting.

"Yes, so get on with it, please."

"Ever since then, hotel guests—and lots of hotel employees—keep reporting ghost stories. Usually about her room on the third floor. Number 302. Lights flickering. The television set turns itself on and off. Breezes come from nowhere. There are unexplainable smells and sounds. Stuff moves when nobody's moving it...at least anyone who can be seen. Doors open and close themselves."

"You don't say."

"She doesn't like men. Pulls off covers and rips their clothes. And the housekeepers say they make the bed, only to come back and find it messed up. Or there are dents, like someone laid on top of the bed."

"My word."

I saved the best for last. "And get this, she walks the hallways. And outside along the shore. I've seen her myself. Just the other day."

"While we were filming?"

"No, my full attention is on you then." I winked at her. "If you go to the gift shop, just off the lobby, watch out. Things fly off shelves. But usually they don't crash. The shop ladies find them upright and unbroken on the floor."

Marilyn stared at me. I stared back.

"So, you believe in ghosts?"

"Sure, why not?" I was matter-of-fact about my answer. I'd just told her I'd seen Kate myself. I knew she heard me, but she asked anyway.

"I do too. Someday, I think I'll be one. A nice one. Maybe I'll move things too. Like in the gift shop."

"Maybe we should get a new Ouija board and see if Kate will talk to us." I really didn't want to, but I made the suggestion anyway.

"We should."

The conversation stopped. We exchanged glances.

"Maybe not." Marilyn's voice was wobbly.

"Uh-huh, maybe not."

FADE OUT

CHAPTER 55

- SEPTEMBER 12, 1958, FIFTH DAY OF SHOOTING
- EXTERIOR, MARILYN'S COTTAGE (DAYTIME)

Birds flittered and chirped as I passed a group of gardeners in the hotel's courtyard. The morning sun was still low in the sky. Cool shadows filled more than half of the space. It was the kind of morning I expected to find Marilyn on her patio sunning herself and her unborn baby. That is, if she was conscious. Not lulling in the lingering effects of sleeping pills or jarred awake by coffee and her get-up-and-go pills.

Just as I raised my knuckles to knock on Marilyn's door, it opened and a man backed right in to me. The first zone of impact was my unavoidable pair of breasts. He turned to face me with a jerk.

"I am so sorry, my dear. Must run." After those eight words, Tony Curtis dashed away.

Marilyn was standing in the doorway leading into her bedroom. "Come in. You might as well know."

"Know what?"

"When a girl has a collision with a man who's leaving my bedroom in the morning. That's what. The conclusion to be drawn is pretty easy." Marilyn fluffed her hair.

"You could have been running lines or—"

"I invited him in. We ended up in the sack and fuc—" Marilyn didn't complete her last word.

To me, the "f" word was a thief. It always stole my breath. My eyes shifted right and left as I searched for something to say.

"You don't have to act surprised."

"But, I—"

"That's all I'm good for. All any man wants. And I deliver it. On a silver platter. A goddamned silver platter."

That was more than I bargained for with this eight-day job. I was supposed to fetch lemonade and beach towels. Not walk into the end of a tryst.

"Is there something I can get you?"

Marilyn lowered herself on the couch, raked her fingers through her hair and motioned me over. "Sit. Please. Years ago, we dated and got close. Last night was a dash—not a stroll—down Memory Lane for us. It shouldn't have happened. But it did. And now I need to tell Arthur about it. He won't be surprised. Disappointed? Sure. Surprised? No."

"You don't have to tell me this. I—"

Marilyn interrupted me. "Have you ever disappointed someone you loved?"

"Guilty as charged." I raised my right palm.

"I have too. And I read about it in Arthur's journal. We were in London shooting *The Prince and the Showgirl*. Everything was going just swell. Then I looked at his journal. I read how I sometimes embarrassed him in front of his friends and how I disappointed him. He used the actual word *disappointed*. It about killed me to read that and-"

This time, I interrupted her. "Really, you don't need to tell me—"

"Just shut up and listen to me!" The words exploded out of her mouth, like a chain of men out of a circus cannon.

I tightened my lips and braced myself.

"Let me say this. Not to get your pity. Not for me to feel ashamed. I've found it helps me to talk about things. Bad things. Talking about bad things kills them. Sort of. And it lets the truth be out in the sunlight…out in the air."

She gazed away from me, then slid her eyes back to focus on mine. "Look. I'm no angel. Never claimed to be. Never behaved like one. You just walked in on the tail end of another one of my bad choices."

Her words stopped. I fought the urge to let mine loose.

She studied me and glanced off in the distance again.

I studied her. Was she a victim? Was she a victor? Powerless or powerful? A few things were clear. She had demons and monsters as too-close-for-comfort companions. She may have slept her way to the top, but she made the choices. She drove her own destiny. She wasn't a victim. And she wasn't powerless.

"See those flowers? That box of chocolates? They came from someone who wants me. Someone who can't have me. Because of that, he or she wants me all the more. Know what I mean?"

I took that as permission to speak. "Like a diabetic wants a donut."

"Yes, except plenty of diabetics sneak a donut or two." She focused back on me. "I'm not a donut. Marilyn may be. A cupcake even. But not me."

She was talking about herself as if there were two of her. I didn't respond. I didn't get the sense that she invited me to.

"You must hate me." She got up and headed back to her bedroom.

"No, I don't." I spoke without permission. She turned her head and said over her bare shoulder, "Good. I couldn't bear that."

I had no idea about what she was going to be capable of bearing in just the next few hours.

FADE OUT

CHAPTER 56

A sheet of The Del's stationery crawled under my room door. I put my tube of lipstick down, took the few necessary steps away from the vanity and picked up the paper.

"Please be aware that significant wind and rip current, commonly called 'riptide,' have made our beach unsafe. Hotel management asks that no one swim in the ocean until further notice. Please keep small children away from the water entirely. As always, you may enjoy our swimming pool, with lifeguards on duty until 10 p.m."

I released the paper over the wastebasket. "Nothing to worry about with me. No more beach for me today." I looked at the note in the basket, sighed and went back to the mirror.

"Anchors away," I said to my reflection. I picked up my handbag and headed down to the hotel bar. My father's mysterious invitation to have a drink had me on guard. That was a first. And I had my guard up.

The Commander was waiting in the lobby, under the chandelier. His hands were behind his back.

"Hi Daddy." I pecked him on the cheek. He was never one for the public displays of affection. So, I knew a kiss and saying "Daddy" would grate on him.

"Penelope. Thank you for meeting me tonight. Let's get a drink. There's something I need to tell you. And a drink will be required to get through it."

He gently took my elbow. In his other hand a gold-foil wrapped gift box glistened as we passed each table lamp and wall sconce. I couldn't help but remember what my mother once told me: A man with a gift for no reason usually has a reason.

It was a long walk from the lobby to the beachside bar. Down a flight of stairs. Down a hallway lined with boutiques and shops that were closed for the evening. No words were exchanged, but my mind was spinning with questions. Were my parents getting divorced? Was he dying?

We stopped at a small round table. Within the blink of an eye, a waiter approached us. "Your best whisky. Straight up. And a Shirley Temple for the little lady."

I knew not to engage the conversation until the drinks arrived and he'd knocked one back.

"Your mother and I had a long talk this afternoon. And you know I don't talk much."

He didn't wait until he had his first drink. I figured it had to be a divorce. I looked at the gift box, but realized that people don't give presents to announce a divorce.

"She said you two talked. She said she told you about me before the war. And before you were old enough to remember." His eyes dropped and he began to pick at one of his fingernail beds. "And how you thought you were invisible to me." His eyes darted, but didn't stop on my face.

"However, there's more you need to know. I did things. Saw things. Well, let's just say no one comes back from war the same as when they left for it. Do you understand?"

"Uh-huh."

"There's more." The flickering flame of the candle on the table revealed sweat forming on his upper lip. He was way outside his comfort zone.

The waiter set down the drinks. The Commander poured the drink down his throat while holding up his index finger to the waiter. Once he'd swallowed and made his usual "ah" sound that comes after a stiff drink, he lowered his hand and ordered a second one.

"Penny, when you get right down to it, my father wasn't anything more than a frown in overalls. I grew up with brothers. No sisters. I went to war with men who became brothers. I barely had the skills to talk to women, much less little girls. Not a chance. Are you following me?"

"Sure, Daddy. But why are you telling me this now?"

"Because it needs to be said."

"You aren't dying, are you?"

His darting eyes froze on my face. "No. Nothing like that. Can I go on?"

I nodded and took a sip of my sugary drink.

"You know I grew up in Chicago. And how—"

Chip approached our table. Alone. Panting. With an envelope in his hand.

"What are you doing out wandering alone again?"

He pushed the envelope at me.

"Alright already." I broke the seal and slid out the card. "Meet me at the breakwater. Come alone. Now. Please. Now!" It was signed by Marilyn.

"Since when do you deliver notes for her?"

Chip ran his finger over the word *now* on the card and raised his chin several times as if to nudge me in to action.

"Daddy, something's wrong. I have to meet Marilyn out by the breakwater. Wait right here. Please. Wait here so we can finish this."

As I got up to leave I noticed Chip pulling another note out of his pocket.

He turned and bolted back into the hotel.

FADE OUT

CHAPTER 57

FADE IN:
- SEPTEMBER 12, 1958, FIFTH DAY OF SHOOTING
- EXTERIOR, CORONADO BEACH (NIGHTTIME)

I paced where the soft, loose sand met the firm wet sand, waiting to meet Marilyn in what I expected would be a frantic state. At least that was the sense I got from her note.

What I did find below a darkened, starless sky was a familiar mountain range of rocks jutting out from the beach and into the surf. Wisps of fog had already eased their way ashore, followed by sound-muffling heavy air. I turned to see The Del struggle to sparkle like a grand paddle-wheeler in the Mississippi moonlight.

I was alone on the beach.

Just me and the breakwater.

That is, until I spotted a woman in a long black dress walking toward me. "Kate, is that you?" There was no response other than her raised hand.

My thoughts were broken when another figure appeared in the ghost-grey mist. This time in regular clothes. Nice clothes. But it wasn't Marilyn. It was two people walking so close they seemed to be one. The figures held hands as they strolled away from me, up the beach and away from the hotel.

"Penny, what's the matter?" Marilyn, who'd come up from behind me, was breathless as she reached the breakwater.

"Geez, you scared the shit out of me." I turned to face her. "I was going to ask you the same thing. You shouldn't be running around the hotel alone."

I held up her note.

"But I got one from *you*." Marilyn let her head dip to the side. Her eyes told me she was confused.

"Chip brought me a note from you. It said to meet you out at the breakwater. That I was to come alone. And do it now."

"But I didn't send you a note," Marilyn said. "You signed your note, Penny. I told the guard at my door I was going out slip out for some ice cream and that I'd be alright without an escort. Chip vanished before I could thank him. That little scamp."

I was flattered she cared enough about me to risk dashing around The Del unescorted—and not in disguise—but I was frightened that someone was playing with us. And not in a good way.

"I ran down here like my hair was on fire when I got your note. Left my dad sitting alone up at the hotel bar. Something's up." I looked around. "Did you see them?"

"Who?" Marilyn's head swirled around as her body caught up.

"The two women who were holding hands and walking toward me."

"No. I only saw you and the rocks."

"Hello, ladies." Steele's greeting came from the rocks and murky mist.

We turned to follow his voice.

"I'm right here." He climbed over the top boulders and smiled at us. "I've been looking for you everywhere."

"Funny, I've been *avoiding* you everywhere." I didn't want to look at him again…ever.

"Anything I can do to help? You shouldn't be out here." Steele went on, "Didn't you get the message about the riptide tonight? I had one that was slid under my room's door."

"I got one too." I didn't want to keep talking to him, but I did. "So, then what are *you* doing out here?" A surge of fear raced through me. I was on guard and readying myself for whatever happened next.

I checked the water's edge to see if the two women were there. They weren't. "Hey, tell me something. Why exactly are you out here, especially when Chip's out wandering around the hotel in the dark? He delivered a note to me."

"He did? Well, that's just fine. Yes, just fine." Steele moved toward us.

"What's fine?" Marilyn took a step backward.

"That you both showed up." Steele sounded creepy, like after he tried to kiss me.

"Wait a minute. What's going on here?" I took a step back to be closer to Marilyn.

The surf crashed behind me, but I stayed focused on Steele. The water swirled around my feet. I didn't budge.

"I wanted some *special* time with you." Steele glared at Marilyn. His words rang dull and flat, the way fog has a way of doing to a conversation. "But I had a feeling I also needed to share this special time with *you* too."

I watched him.

He stepped toward Marilyn. "You've been haunting my days...and my nights...for years. Ever since I saw you in *Gentlemen Prefer Blondes*, this gentleman has preferred blondes...one blonde in particular."

"Stop it, Steele." I'd had enough. "I'll go get the police if I need to."

"No. You won't," Steele commanded. "You're going to stay right here."

"I will not. And neither will Marilyn. Come on. This is some kind of sick joke and I won't be part of—"

"Sick? Perhaps. Joke. Not at all." Steele pulled a hand gun out from the back waist of his pants. "Why did you do it, Marilyn? Why both of *them*? You could have any man on the planet—even the President—and you pick a homely writer and a buck-toothed baseball player. Look at me. We'd be great together. Why them?"

"The fact that you even have to ask that question should tell you why." Marilyn folded her arms in front of her chest.

"My dear Marilyn, despite your unwise choices in the past, tonight you're going to be all mine. All. Mine. You're going to *choose* me." He turned slightly and pointed the gun at me. "And you, Penny, you're going to watch."

"Steele—" I started to speak, but got cut off.

"Marilyn and I have so much in common. You know, being the pretty ones. In my family, I was the pretty one." Steele kept his hand on the gun. "My brothers were athletic. My sister was the smart one. Me, with my eyes and this hair and these broad shoulders. No one expected much from me. Other than to look good. But they're all dead now. Dust and ashes. Good riddance, you know?"

"Dead?"

"Yes. It was so unfortunate. My parent's house mysteriously caught fire one night. I was the only one to survive. Imagine that."

"What's wrong with you, Steele?"

"Wrong? Me? I'm perfectly fine." He leaned forward as if he was about to share a secret. Despite the thickening fog, the lights of the hotel gave his eyes a fiery blaze. "I'm a gift, you know. And I give and I give. Think about it. How did it make you feel when I noticed you and paid attention to you? When I bought you coffee? When you were getting ready for our dinner date? Like a princess…like Cinderella, I bet." He nodded and waited for me to say something, but I didn't.

"My mother—rest her soul—told me my looks were not only my meal ticket, but my passport. To the world and everything I wanted in it."

My brain raced. I had to admit—only to myself—there was truth in what he said. But that lasted only a few confusing seconds. No, he was wrong. Completely wrong. Clearly, Steele was beautifully broken. He was like a Hollywood set piece. A facade. Stunning and convincing, but nothing behind it or inside it. And, I hated to admit, Marilyn was the same, in some ways. But she was no façade. There was something incredibly special inside her.

"Focus on me, Penny. Wake up!" Steele's words brought me back. I couldn't believe I let my mind wander.

"I'm here…right here."

Marilyn was silent.

"Let us go. We promise not to tell anyone. Will we?"

Marilyn moved her head side to side without uttering a word.

"I wish I could believe that. But we're at the point of no return. Geez, I like how that sounds. No. Return." Steele's eyes went from fiery to fizzled. He had dead eyes…black and burned out. "Gloria and I were at this very spot. It was windy and there was a riptide. And she just…*disappeared*."

Marilyn cocked her head. "Gloria?"

"Wait a minute. Your wife?" I paused. "You didn't. Did you?"

"She disappeared. Just. Disappeared. A riptide and fog have a way of doing that." Steele's voice got wispy and harder to hear over the surf. "Was it an abandonment of her responsibilities and child? Or an unsolved missing-person's case? The world may never know. But now it's your turn, Miss Marilyn Monroe. Archie and Betty have been telling you all along."

"The roses? The candy? The notes…those notes that didn't make sense?" I was trying to connect the dots.

"Like I said, Archie and Betty were telling you."

I was still confused. "What were two comic-book characters telling us, Steele?"

He extended his arms and moved us so our backs were to the rocks. He faced us.

"Lines of dialogue from the comic book. They were telling you." Steele's eyes pierced mine. Sliced right in. "Betty's a blonde. I like blondes. I *really* like blondes."

"What's wrong with you? You had Chip reading and walking around with a comic book you…fantasize about…" I noticed someone running toward us on the beach. I also noticed how the ocean had darkened, making it look deeper than it was. Like some mysterious abyss loomed offshore. Superstitious people might've involuntarily held their breaths at that sight, felt woozy in their guts and thought evil was on the horizon and in the ebony depths. They'd have convinced themselves that it was coming our way. Good thing I chose not to be superstitious at that moment.

I figured my goal at that point was to keep Steele talking long enough for that running person to see us.

"I'm done with you, Penny. Actually, I never even started with you." Steele's voice had become acidic. "You were pathetically easy to seduce. The easiest of all my conquests. And there have been many. Many. Me attracted to you? That's pathetic. Before you know it, you'll be some dried-up old bitch of a spinster." He was a boiling pot—no, a pressure cooker—and he no longer tried to keep his lid clamped on tight.

"Please let Penny go. It's me you want, right?"

"That's right. It's you I want. I want to preserve you…for the world…for history. You'll always be remembered in your prime. I was hoping to be more discrete. Or at least as discrete as last time. But Penny is too involved now. And she's putting all the pieces together. She knows about Gloria. She's got to go too."

Marilyn's eyes shot from Steele's face to mine. She must've seen the running figure coming toward us.

"You don't want to do this. Let's talk…talk about your wife, about Betty, about me. Let's just talk." Marilyn was drawing out our conversation.

"I'm going to let *this* do my talking." Steele held up the gun. "Quietly. Silently even. That's right, silently. The silencer on this pistol will make sure there's no commotion. The riptide will make sure there's no evidence. No evidence of either of you."

I moved in front of Marilyn. "Let her go. Steele, let her go. Then we can talk. Talk this all through. Think of Chip and what will happen to him. He—"

My words were sheared off when Steele whipped his pistol against the side of my head. The ground sped toward me for a what I knew was going to be a painful embrace. When I hit the sand, my lungs emptied. My heart stopped. My world spun.

I laid there, playing dead, swirling in my own secret storm. Blood raced to my temple and everything else pulled away from me. Maybe I could surprise him at just the right time. A surge of ocean water shocked and soaked me, but I didn't react. Not a twitch. But   in   my   head,   I   was   shrieking, "ohmygodohmygodohmygod."

"NOW IT'S YOUR TURN MISS...MARILYN...MON—"

"No, it's YOUR turn!" Frankie bashed Steele in the back of the head with a hand-sized rock from the beach. I peeked in time to see the whole thing happen.

"GODDAMIT!" Steele didn't fall. He didn't teeter. Without flinching, he turned to see who attacked him, holding out his silencer-tipped gun. "It'll take more than that to take me down."

Frankie dove for Steele's knees, which threw him off balance. Then, from the side, another body collided with Steele's, nearly missing me.

"Daddy!" I unleashed my fear and it pounced, landed in my gut and did its best to claw up my throat. I kept it down, but let my words explode as I took in the unfathomable sight of all three of them wrestling and thrashing in the wet sand and crashing surf.

"Frankie, try to get the gun away from him." The Commander was in charge. Daddy put Steele in a vice-like headlock. His elbow was right under Steele's chin. "That silencer won't do you any good. People will still hear it." Daddy squeezed Steele's head tighter. "We used to call those suppressors, not silencers. But Frankie and me, we're going to do both to you."

"LET ME GO, OLD MAN. You'll both pay for this." Steele growled. All three were forced to roll over each other.

"Marilyn, run for the hotel!" I kept yelling. "Go! Now! Nobody should find out you were here."

"I'm not leaving you. Not after the way you stepped in front of me to take—"

There was a sharp "twerp" sound. Steele's gun had gone off.

Frankie rolled off the human pile. Daddy pulled away. Steele was left. Shivering. Recoiling. Then he was motionless. Lifeless. A wave surged up and lapped at his back.

I knelt by my father. "Are you alright? What do we do now?"

"Let me think a second." Daddy started to stand.

Marilyn knelt by Frankie. "You okay?"

"Yeah." Frankie was breathless from running and wrestling. "I think so."

Daddy—with his militaristic cool head and pent-up emotions—looked toward the hotel which had nearly disappeared in the fog. No one was near us. "The riptide warning must be keeping everyone away." He checked Steele's neck for a pulse.

"Riptide." I repeated my father's word as I scanned the crashing and swirling water. "Mother Nature can take over...and she can finish the job."

"Why would we do that? This was self-defense. I'll go up and call the police." Daddy had a ten-hut, harrumph in his voice.

"I don't know—" Marilyn started talking.

"But what if—" Frankie started too.

"Wait," I blurted. "Everyone shut up but ME!"

I had their attention. "Let's think this through. Yes, it was self-defense." I watched Marilyn, who had gotten up and was pacing. "But think what *this* will do to *her*. Marilyn can't have this kind of publicity. Not now. Not ever. She can't be blamed or hurt by any of this."

"Gosh, don't give me a second thought...not at a time like this." Marilyn's soft murmuring was almost lost under the sound of the waves hurling themselves at the breakwater's boulders.

"And I'll be damned if that sonofabitch Steele gets any headlines over this. No one should know about him or his story." I inhaled as my eyes darted between us. "Besides, he doesn't *deserve* a proper burial, after all he's done. He should just disappear in the undertow. Vanish."

"But what about Chip?" Frankie winced as he spoke. "Won't they throw him into an orphanage?"

"Enough already." Daddy's voice broke the conversation like a miner's pick-axe. He looked down at Steele's body and then at us. "You win, Penny. You don't play fair, but you win." He threw the gun up on the dry sand. "Help me, son. Let's get him out into the surf." He waved at Frankie to come over, not knowing Frankie was afraid of the water.

"If we get him out beyond where the waves are breaking and let him go, the current will take care of the rest." Daddy took Steele's feet, while Frankie grabbed his shoulders. "See...over there...where the water looks smoother. That's our target. It looks safer there, but that's where the pull is strongest."

They sloshed out into the water, released Steele's body and waited to see if Daddy's plan worked. Sure enough, the body bobbed, rolled and was swept away into the hazy darkness.

Frankie turned to head to shore. "Commander. You alright?" There was no response. Daddy was caught in the ocean's pull. His head was above the surface but he was being pulled away, like he was on a high-speed conveyor belt.

"Frankie, the tide...Daddy—" I started to get into the water.

"You stay there. I can't deal with both of you."

"But I can—"

Before I could get anything else out, Frankie was swimming toward Daddy. Through what had been a veil and quickly thickened to a shroud of fog, I witnessed Frankie getting a firm hold on Daddy and swimming parallel to the shore. "You can do it, Frankie. You can do it." Before long, he headed back toward the beach.

"Can you believe Steele did that to his wife? Slipped her body out into the current?" I looked at Marilyn. "Now that it's happened to Steele, is that justice or what?"

"I don't know, honey. I don't know." Marilyn's voice was more breathless than usual. "Honey, I don't—" Marilyn collapsed into unconsciousness.

"Daddy!" I shouted to the surf where my father and Frankie were coming out of the inky water. Daddy turned and shushed me. When he saw Marilyn on the ground, he grabbed Frankie's shoulder and pushed him in our direction.

I patted her cheek a few times, but it didn't help. She was out. By then, Daddy and Frankie were with us.

A suffocating grey blanket of fog tiptoed in. Like a giant eraser, it rubbed out all the details and smoothed out the rough edges of everything in sight. It wasn't the least bit comforting, though it did create a secretive barrier from the world…a barrier the four of us would need to guard the rest of our lives.

"Let's get her up to her cottage. We can walk along the shore, holding her up so it looks like the four of us are taking a stroll. But what about the policeman at the door?"

"She has a patio, right?" Frankie knew the hotel well.

"Let's get her there. I can go around to the front door and get by him." I looked down at my wet and sandy dress. "I'll have to explain *this*. Oh, I'll think about that later."

Frankie stood there, staring at me.

My eyes met his. I don't know why, but I blinked slowly, the way Marilyn taught me. "I'm so proud of you. Who knew there was a lifeguard hiding in you all this time?"

FADE OUT

CHAPTER 58

FADE IN:
- SEPTEMBER 12, 1958, FIFTH DAY OF SHOOTING
- EXTERIOR, CORONADO BEACH (NIGHTTIME)

Even though we'd made it to Marilyn's cottage undetected, there was still work to be done.

"We've got to get Chip. He's alone." I couldn't bring myself to even imagine how what happened on the beach would impact him for the rest of his life.

"But what are we going to tell him? That his father's dead." Frankie had a point. "That he got shot and we dumped his body into the sea?"

"I dunno. But he needs to know his dad's not coming back. Ever." My fingers pulled up into fists and I tightened my lips.

"What about the bellman, the one who's always delivering those gifts here?" Frankie's leg started jumping. Slow at first, then like a piston.

"You mean Nick?" I thought about it. "Yeah, he'll help us. I'm sure he'd help Chip."

After thinking some more, I added, "I can tell Chip that his dad's left. And that until we know for how long, we'll stash him and take care of him. Nick must know of a place where Chip can go unnoticed…for a while anyway." My fingers relaxed out of what had been fists.

"There have to be a million places to hide at this big old hotel." Frankie stood up and started to pace.

"Let me take care of the rest of it." I knew this was something

I could take care of. "I'll use Chip's room key. I'll mess up the place and make it look like they skipped town in a hurry without settling the bill. No one will suspect Chip's still here."

Or would they?

FADE OUT

CHAPTER 59

FADE IN:
- SEPTEMBER 12, 1958, FIFTH DAY OF SHOOTING
- INTERIOR, MARILYN'S COTTAGE (NIGHTTIME)

"Who's got the gun?" No one answered me. "Come on, who's got the gun? Jesus, Mary and Joseph!" I ran for the patio door. "I'll go. You stay here and keep her comfortable."

"No, you stay here." Frankie stepped forward. "I can get there faster than anyone in this room, and get out of there faster too. The fog should give me all the cover I need."

"What should he do with it?" I looked at Daddy. "Any ideas?"

"Just to be safe, take it to the trash bins behind the dime store." Daddy's voice exuded confidence and clarity. I watched him as he was about to say something else. "Wrap it in some garbage and push it down deep. It'll get hauled to the dump and no one will be any wiser."

"This is insanity. Unbelievable insanity. Listen to us!" I let my mouth catch up to what was racing in my head. "We're cleaning up a crime scene. Not watching it in a movie. This. Is. Real."

Daddy took my cheeks in his palms. "You're in shock and you need to hold it together. I know you can. We'll think it all through…calmly…later…yes, later…and figure out how we go on. Like good soldiers. Like even better sailors. Like survivors."

Frankie bolted out the door.

"That Frankie, he's a good man." I was shocked. Daddy praised someone. I witnessed it. Something must've been changing in him.

I had to focus on Marilyn next. "I don't know how, but you've got to get some rest. Can I help you? Let's get you to your bedroom, turn the lights down low and see what happens." I did my best to sound reassuring.

"Penny, I've been around some gutsy women." Marilyn drew in a weak breath and continued to whisper, "But what you did for me tonight, well, I've must say you've got some lady nuts on you...and they're the size of beach balls. I can never repay you...never...."

"Just relax. We can talk about this another time. Are you sure I can't get you something?"

"Get May. Get Paula. They'll know what to do." Marilyn's eyes were needy. Her fingers brushed the length of her neck.

"Do you want me to get your pills? I can do that for you."

"Yes. Yes, please."

I left the room and became all too aware that my temple was throbbing. Maybe it'd been throbbing all along and I'd just noticed it again.

Pain—and her cousins Panic and Guilt—chased each other in my head. I did my best to push them away and keep a clear mind. But after all I'd just done and seen, I was sure my soul must've shriveled up like a wad of day-old Bazooka gum on a park bench. I was going to spend eternity making S'mores around a ring of hellfire.

I came back with several envelopes and pill cases. "Here, I got you a glass of water too." The cool liquid sloshed over the rim and streamed down my wrist.

Marilyn dumped one case onto her palm. She fished out three pills and dry swallowed them. "Here, use some water the next time." I handed her the glass and added, "Pardon me while I go and I'll send my father away."

"Thank him for me. And thank Frankie, too. I don't know what this is all about, but I'm sorry you got dragged into it."

As I stepped toward the doorway, I heard Marilyn fuss with the second pill case. I didn't look back.

"Thank you." I hugged Daddy and pulled away. "Thank you." I hugged him again. "That was from Marilyn. Now you need to get out of here. Go home and try not to think about what you saw...or did...or didn't do. You know what I mean."

"Yes, I know what you mean." He started to walk away. "I'm

proud of you. And Marilyn's lucky to have you as a friend."

"Now I've got to find Chip. What must be going through his little mind?"

"He'll think his father abandoned him."

"But Steele made him deliver those notes." I shook my head. "Maybe Chip knows. What if he watched from a distance?"

"For now, he'll be fine," Daddy said. "He seems to know his way around The Del...alone."

"I have a bad feeling about this."

"*This*? I'd say you should have a bad feeling about something else that happened on the beach tonight." Daddy was right.

I hugged him one more time and nudged him out the patio door. I sat down on a cool, damp chair. I tried to clear my head and failed, miserably. I could hear myself breathing, slower but still too fast.

As I let my shoulders slump down and rest against the back of the chair, Marilyn called for me from inside her cottage. I didn't know how she did it so fast, but Marilyn was already in a pilled-out haze of grief and silk.

"How'd you change your clothes so—"

Marilyn hunched over. Vomiting. Retching.

"I'm going to get May and Paula right now."

"Thank you. But first, I have to tell you something." She paused. "You need to stay away from me."

"Puking doesn't bother me—"

"That's not what I mean, honey. You need to get away from me. I hurt people. Badly. I don't mean to. But I do. And you'll get hurt too. You'll see—"

She used the wastebasket I passed to her. Her aim was not good, though.

May, Paula and a doctor were in the bedroom in no time at all. They were probably quite practiced at dealing with this scenario. Marilyn vomited again and again. Violently. I watched the star's triage team help her. "I've called Cedars of Lebanon Hospital. We'll take her there as discretely as possible."

There were perfectly good hospitals in San Diego, but they insisted that only Cedars of Lebanon would do.

And with that, Marilyn was gone, racing up to Los Angeles.

What would happen next with Marilyn, the movie and me? That question couldn't be answered. At least not that night.

FADE OUT

.

CHAPTER 60

FADE IN:
- SEPTEMBER 13, 1958, SHOOTING CANCELLED
- INTERIOR, HOTEL DEL CORONADO (DAYTIME)

I tracked down Nick at the hotel and explained what happened. I held back a few details—a few rather significant details. Instead, I focused Nick on what needed to happen next. And as I expected, he came through.

"I know just the room to put him in. It's a servant's room that used to be connected to a full-sized guest room, but the doorway between them has been walled over. It's too small to rent now. Employees sneak away to take naps there from time to time. Don't ask how I know that."

I grinned at him.

"But it has a bathroom and a small window. I'll make sure he has everything he needs until you figure out what's next."

"Nick, I'm counting on that." I wrapped my arms around him. "Thank you. I'll be back with some extra clothes, toys and snacks for Chip. Oh, and my best friend Frankie will be stopping by too."

With Chip's situation taken care of, I could turn my attention back on Marilyn and the movie...and me.

The producers told the press Marilyn was suffering from "nervous exhaustion." Among the crew, there were rumors about the stress in her marriage, the stress of a location shoot and the stress of carrying a motion picture. And then there was simply the stress of being Marilyn Monroe.

While no one—except Marilyn—knew exactly what caused

her to overdose, three people had more insight than most: Frankie, Daddy and me. Make that four: Steele.

Billy Wilder made it clear the future of the project was in jeopardy. There was next to nothing he could do without Marilyn in Coronado. He shut down the location production, not knowing when she would be fit for work. The plan was for everyone, except me, to get back to work in the studio and shoot scenes without her.

When May told me about the interruption in the location production, she mentioned rumors of replacing Marilyn. Mitzi Gaynor, who'd been a strong contender for Marilyn's role earlier, was a likely candidate.

I was thanked and told I'd be notified if or when location filming would begin again.

I hoped it wouldn't end this way.

FADE OUT

CHAPTER 61

FADE IN:
- SEPTEMBER 13, 1958, SHOOTING CANCELLED
- INTERIOR, HOTEL DEL CORONADO (DAYTIME)

My life's script took another unpredictable turn. I couldn't be sure what to expect at any given minute. What I should've expected, but didn't, was how I'd feel physically after everything that happened.

My brain hurt. My body hurt. It was like I'd been a piñata at a four-year-old's birthday party.

When I felt unsteady stepping out of my hotel room's bathroom, I was reminded just how beaten up I felt. I spotted it when I made a towel turban to swaddle my wet hair. And it stopped me in my wobbly tracks. The swelling and bluish-green bruise on my right temple demanded a bag of ice, followed by a generous amount of foundation cream before I left the room.

A crunchy sound came from the bottom of my room's door that led to the hallway. As odd as it sounds, an Archie comic book came through. I opened the door.

"Chip! Are you there? Out in the hall?" I looked right and left down the hallway. No one was in sight. "Chip? Chip, come out. We need to talk." I couldn't believe I yelled at him about talking. "I want to make sure you're okay. Please, Chip. Please." Like so many times before, there was no response. "Nick, you know, the bellman, is looking for you too."

I closed the door and started flipping through the comic book. My fingers shook so much that the pages vibrated.

I leaned back, resting my shoulder blades on the door. I let my arms hang down at my sides. I was horrified that it might be the one Steele talked about at the breakwater…the comic book he said had the lines from Archie and Betty that he used in his notes to Marilyn.

Someone made the search easy, circling each of them with a red crayon. I didn't know if it could be anyone except Steele.

The first circled passage said, "It's a secret?"

Then came, "Fat chance."

"The heck with them."

"Let's you and I have a party all by ourselves."

"We'll show them."

"You're a darling."

"All to myself."

"Poetic justice."

I threw the comic book onto the bed. "Geez, he was nuts."

A wildfire of emotions swirled in me. Sadness. Frustration. Fear. Outrage.

One of Hollywood's greatest stars—and my newest friend—had almost been publicly executed in the most brutal way. And no one else would know this part of Marilyn's story, except Frankie, Daddy and me.

FADE OUT

CHAPTER 62

After gently knocking three times, I turned the key Nick gave me in the doorknob to Chip's hideout room.

"Chip. It's so good to see you again." I did my best to sound like a good friend, not a witness to his father's grotesque death. "Nice place you've got here, young man. Nick really set you up."

His hug was vice-like. I dropped the shopping bags to better embrace him. I scanned the room. Nick did a good job of making it homey. Chip's beloved sand pail—the one he was holding when I dragged him out of the ocean—had a place of honor on the table.

"Are you alright?"

He still didn't speak. His sobbing spoke, though.

I hugged him until his breathing settled down. I eased him away from me, wiping his tears and fluffing his hair.

"I've brought you all kinds of things from the dime store. Just look."

I pulled out some t-shirts, packages of underwear and socks, several pairs of shorts and a thick writing tablet, along with sharpened Crayons and pencils.

"This should tide you over until we figure out what's next for you. Don't you have any aunties or uncles? Cousins? Grandparents?"

Chip swiveled his head side to side.

I placed a hand on each of his shoulders. "Chip, I'm here for you. And I always will be. Frankie and I will do our best to get this all sorted out. You're going to have to be patient. This may take some time. Are you okay with that?"

He nodded and raised an open palm to my right temple. He patted it gently and blinked repeatedly. So much for expecting the foundation cream to fully conceal my rainbow bruise.

I wondered how patient he would be and how much time it was going to take. While I did that, he opened the tablet and started to write. He lifted the pencil when he completed the word *sorry*.

"Whatever are you sorry for, Chip?"

He wrote *Dad*.

"It's not your job to be sorry for your father."

He continued to write, *His messages. Notes.*

I wasn't sure how to respond to that.

He began to write at a feverish pace. *Said Mom left because of me. I told him she was out on the beach. I told. Then she was gone. All my fault.*

No wonder he'd stopped speaking. In his little-boy logic, he thought her disappearance was because he told Steele where Gloria was. He carried the burden—the unnecessary burden—that his words caused her disappearance.

"Chip, your mother loved you dearly. I'm sure of it. And she still does."

He started writing again. *Dad is crazy. Not my fault?*

"Of course, it's not your fault." I patted his knee. "He appears to be gone. Will you be alright here alone?"

Chip responded with two words. *Not alone.*

"I know you're not alone. Nick brings you food and spends time with you during the day. Always remember, Nick's here for you, especially if you get lonely."

He wrote more. *Kate is here. Mom too.*

"Oh. That's nice."

I wasn't sure if I should've been horrified or comforted.

I chose to be comforted.

FADE OUT

CHAPTER 63

FADE IN:
- SEPTEMBER 15, 1958, SHOOTING CANCELLED
- INTERIOR, CORNET FIVE & DIME STORE (DAYTIME)

Banging a cash register was bad before. But after everything I'd been through, it was even worse. A man, a home and a pack of wild kids—even the no-neck variety, like my nieces and nephew—was sounding better all the time. I wanted the whole American dream that everyone else wanted.

"Penny. Penny Parker. Where are you?" Trudy slammed her metal spatula against the stainless-steel cooktop. That yanked me out of a perfectly good daydream and forced me to look at the Luncheonette counter.

"It's still early in the day and you're about as fresh as a week-old loaf of pumpernickel bread. My little chickadee, what's going on in that head of yours?"

"Everything. It's a very busy place right now, even if it doesn't show on the outside."

Trudy reached for bright red-and-white can from the Heinz Soups display next to her grill. I avoided having to continue the conversation by reading the display's signs. Large Bowl 15 cents. 2 Minute Service. Cream of Tomato. Old Fashioned Bean. Genuine Turtle. It wasn't like I hadn't seen it before—like ten-thousand times before—but I still marveled at the display's two soup-warming pots built right in. Could it be any more self-sufficient? Then my eyes shifted over the gleaming chrome and glass case that kept the flies off the pie slices and onto the

Kellogg's Cereal stand that housed tiny individual-serving sized boxes. Corn Flakes. Rice Krispies. Wheat Krispies. PEP. Krumbles. All-Bran. I couldn't believe Trudy hadn't nailed me yet. I thought I was so clever, that my strategy to out-fox her had worked. Once she'd opened the can of soup, sloshed its contents into a warming pot and turned the dial on the timer, she was all mine again.

"You didn't think I'd forgotten about you, right?"

She wasn't going to miss the chance to nail me.

"You were saying something about how busy your brain is today?"

I didn't respond immediately, but when I did, I said, "I was thinking about what you told me not so long ago. About violence. About how given the right circumstances, we're all capable of violence. I'm worried about—"

"You've never been a worrier." She'd hardly let me get any words out. "But you've heard me tell this to the girls at home to stop worrying about the crazy things they worry about: Worry is like a rocking chair on the front porch. It may give you something to do, but it gets you nowhere."

"Well, *I've* got something for you to do. You can ring me up."

"My goodness, Madge. When did you sneak up? I haven't seen you in ages."

"While you were out being all hoity-toity with the Hollywood elite, I was wiping noses and butts at home. That's why I'm here today...for a treat."

Madge studied the cobalt-blue bottle of Evening in Paris perfume in her hand. "My husband adores it on me. Really gets his engine racing, if you know what I mean. But maybe it's too much of a luxury right now."

"Only you could say." I gazed at the bottle and then up to Madge's eyes.

"I just love saying it in French, though. *Soir de Paris*. Oh, I'll take it. And this too."

She handed me a Hula Hoop. I put my open hand next to the side of my mouth and spoke in a hushed tone. "Don't Hula Hoop without wearing a bra. Trust me on this one."

Madge did a visual double take and cocked her head to stare unquestioningly at me.

"Penny! Finish that order. Quick. They're here." Frankie

frantically motioned with his hand for me to leave the cash register and come to the backroom.

I wrapped up the sale and sent Madge on her way as politely and briskly as I could.

"Who's here?" I made my way over to Frankie.

"The garbage men." He slid his eyes to the right and left. "Come with me, and don't make a scene." He hushed his words. "With any luck, you-know-what will be off to the dump. Never to see the light of day again."

"Stop it. You sound like a thug in a gangster movie."

He shushed me and added, "Hey, I'm just trying to speak *your* language…like in the movies."

I cracked a nervous smile and patted his shoulder.

He took my hand and led me to the backdoor and pinned it open with the brown rubber doorstopper. We didn't go out. We stayed back in the shadows to watch the evidence of the crime—our crime, Steele's crime—being whisked away.

The filthy vehicle pulled up, carrying filthy men with it.

"What a job. I think mine's bad. Can you even imagine the shit they deal with?" I shivered and shimmied.

In what must've been a mindless routine, the men lined up the truck with the bins. Within a few seconds, the questionable—and criminal—contents were stuffed into the belly of the beastly truck.

"I don't think I'll ever look at a garbage truck the same way again."

Frankie wrapped his arm around my back and whispered, "Nice shiner. Makes you look tough. Except it should be under one of your eyes." He quickly added, "But I can barely see it. Hardly at all. That makeup of yours…"

"Pardon me for the interruption, Romeo and Juliet." Otis bellowed for everyone within an earshot to hear. "What are you gonna do now? KISS HER?"

"Yeah, I am." Frankie's words startled me. "If she wants me to."

"Frankie's gonna kiss Penny." Otis sing-songed his words like a school girl on a playground. He stood in the doorway and continued. "Frankie and Penny are gonna smooch."

I turned to look at Frankie's face.

He was serious.

"I do. Want you to kiss me."

What happened next, well, it wasn't the romantic moment I'd dreamed about. Instead, it was something I wished I could've forgotten.

He missed my mouth.

"Uh, that was nice, but why did you just kiss my ear?"

"I had to. You turned your head." I couldn't believe I messed up our first kiss by reacting to the garbage-truck driver honking his horn as he pulled away. I just knew, that once the gun was gone, I wouldn't be distracted again. And I was right.

When the truck was out of sight, I felt lighter. It was like I'd been holding my breath for days and finally I could exhale. And breathe.

The garbage men took the pain and heaviness—and suffocating darkness—with the gun. But had they really?

Frankie bit his lower lip. "I guess I need some practice. Can—*may*—I try again?"

"You're such a gentleman. Such good grammar—"

What happened next was something I'd never forget.

Before I could even close my eyes, Frankie's lips were touching and then gently—ever so gently—pressing against mine.

His chest rose and fell as he drew in a breath. His boney-ribbed hardness pressed against my fleshy squishiness. His lips traveled over mine and I tasted Juicy Fruit gum. He was delicious.

Frankie's warm fruity breath caressed my cheek. Banana, pineapple and peach all mingled together. I felt melty. My whole body tingled. We were breathing the same air as his kisses consumed me. His fingertips traced the back of my neck with a trail of electricity. Even in the blur of it all—like riding Alice's Tea Cups at Disneyland—I recognized there would never be another moment like that one. Never again would a spark...a flame...a blaze burn so hot in us. If it did, there'd be nothing left of us but ash.

The stubble on his upper lip was a sandpapery contrast to the velvety softness of his lips.

He started to pull away, but I moved my hand up behind his head and pulled him in so we could keep kissing. My heart hammered in my ears and sounded like the flapping wings of a bird taking off. My veins pulsed with honey and hot sauce.

And then it happened.

My busy brain, the one that never stopped buzzing, went quiet.

Silent.

It emptied out.

I'd surrendered to what I was feeling and didn't want or need to think about it.

It was glorious.

It was clock-stopping.

It was intoxicating.

It was addicting.

It was a prelude, no, a preview of coming attractions, like at the theater.

My buzzing brain sprung back into action. And what I thought was profound: that it may not have been my first kiss, but it was the first kiss with someone who mattered—who mattered most.

I whispered into his ear, "That was the best kiss ever."

"Good. Then you'll never forget it."

"That'd be impossible."

The magic of the moment was interrupted by, "Well, it's about damned time!" Otis clapped his beefy hands together several times. It sounded like he was genuinely happy for us. I chose to think so, anyway. But then he threw in, "How'd it stack up against Marilyn Monroe's kiss, buddy-boy?"

Leave it to Otis to add a sour note to such a sweet moment.

Frankie wasted no time responding. "Best ever. BEST. EVER!"

"Yes, it is about time!" Trudy joined Otis in the doorway. "It absolutely is. And things will *never* be the same again."

She was right. We could never go back to the way things were.

Nothing ever would be the same.

And I had a strong hunch that kiss from Frankie would be my last *first kiss* ever.

FADE OUT

CHAPTER 64

FADE IN:
- SEPTEMBER 15, 1958, SHOOTING CANCELLED
- INTERIOR, CORNET FIVE & DIME STORE (DAYTIME)

Frankie came up to my checkout counter late in the afternoon with an armload of items. I helped him disassemble the teetering stack. "You know, we have carry-baskets and push-carts. They make shopping so much easier."

"Yeah, I know all too well. Seems like I'm the only person around here who stacks the baskets inside the store and rounds up the carts out in the parking lot."

I lowered my voice. "Going to see Chip again?"

"That obvious, huh?"

"Last time I checked, you didn't have much use for coloring books, green plastic soldiers—" I swam my fingers through the items on the counter. "Or checkers, Hershey bars. Do I need to go on?"

"No. Thank you." Frankie reached for his wallet. "I should get something for Nick too, to thank him for everything he's doing for Chip. Stowing him away at The Del can't be easy."

"Has he talked to you yet?"

"Nick?"

"No, Chip."

Frankie leaned in. With a hushed voice, he said, "I've been there to visit him practically every day—and I know you have too—since you-know-what happened and still not so much as a peep out of him. He seems to like having company around. It's too bad. He's a great kid…a great kid who had the bad luck of getting a shitty man for a father. And now he's got a great big question mark for a future."

I rang up the items and arranged them in one of the store's brown-paper shopping bags.

Frankie grabbed some candy from the shelf in front of my register. He scattered a variety of Tootsie Rolls, Bit-O-Honeys, Slo-Pokes, root-beer barrels, Charleston Chews, Clark Bars, Necco Wafers and Chick-O-Sticks on the counter.

"What, no Mary Janes? You've got just about everything else." I smiled at him enough to make my single dimple form.

He reached over and added a fist-full of Mary Janes to the candy on the counter.

"We do owe Nick something." I tightened my lips and studied the ceiling. "I don't know what. I'll think about it. And I owe you something too. You've been so good about spending time with Chip. It seems to come naturally to you…being with kids, that is. You make it look easy-peasy, lemon-squeezy."

A man holding a bottle of Old Spice in front of his chest stepped up behind Frankie.

"Be with you in just a moment, sir." I made eye contact with the stranger as I hit the total bar on my register. The bell rang and the cash drawer jumped out at me. It always made me jerk, like when the *Pop Goes the Weasel* song of one of those hand-crank jack-in-the-boxes is over. I knew that creepy-clown puppet thingy was going to burst out. But it surprised me every time.

"That'll be three dollars and seven cents, please." Frankie passed me the correct amount in bills and coins.

"Say hi to you-know-who for me. Tell him I miss him, and that I'll be by later."

"Will you be wearing this pink smock or that fancy new blue dress of yours? I like you in both, by the way. Or even better in your bathing suit." Frankie dazzled me with his flashy, frisky eyes before he headed toward the front door.

"Is that your husband?" The Old Spice man stepped forward and repeated his question because I didn't respond the first time. I didn't quite know how to respond.

"Yes, *you* could say he's my husband."

Maybe I'd be able to say that soon too with no doubt in my heart or mind.

FADE OUT

CHAPTER 65

FADE IN:
- SEPTEMBER 16, 1958, SHOOTING CANCELLED
- INTERIOR, CORNET FIVE & DIME STORE (DAYTIME)

"Daddy, what are you doing here?" He'd rarely come into the dime store when I was working.

"Can't a guy buy a girl a cup of coffee every now and then?" He had a needy look about him.

"The last time you did that we were…um, interrupted."

"But I need to finish what I started to tell you," he said and cast his eyes to the floor. "Do you have a break coming up?"

"Sure. I'll meet you at Dixie's Donut Den in ten minutes."

When I arrived, Daddy was already at a table on the patio with two cups of steaming coffee in front of him. The reflection of my pink smock in the window was blinding enough. But the afternoon sunshine made my eyes hurt. I squinted as I poured cream in my cup.

"Sun in your eyes?"

"That obvious, uh?" I reached in my purse for my cat-eye sunglasses, the ones I almost lost while saving Chip from the surf. His face flashed in my mind as I shielded my eyes. "Much better."

"I need to finish what I was telling you the other night. You know it won't be easy for me. But, you'll give a guy a break, right?"

"Right." I sipped from my cup and swallowed. "Absolutely."

"So, as I was telling you, I grew up in Chicago. I started my life on a nickel and a crumb. But things got better. Sort of. I worked with your grandpa in the Union Stock Yard slaughterhouses. I was a real son of a butcher and bitch too, if I'm honest with myself. But you don't know what it was like…what it did to me."

"You don't have to—" I clipped my words and put my cup down on the table.

"Yes. Yes, I do. War changed me. But before that, the slaughterhouses changed me. I can still see it. Smell it. Hear it. Conveyor belts constantly moving. Blood everywhere. Death everywhere. And we were part of it. The guys didn't call your grandpa Three-Fingered Jack for nothing. Almost everyone was missing a few parts."

"You can stop—" He didn't hear my words. He was looking off into the distance, as if he was picturing the whole thing again.

"Hogs crossed to eternity over a big wooden bridge. We called it the Bridge of Sighs."

"Like the one in Venice?"

"Yes. Once they got up there, chains were attached to their hind legs and they were swept away. Squealing. Screaming along an overhead track. I was waiting for them and—"

"Stop. Please stop."

He took a long drag on his coffee cup, swallowed and exhaled. "I have to tell you, there were times when I just stood there, frozen. Like I was playing possum. Eyes closed. As if I was dead…couldn't see it…that it might go away. But it didn't. There's no playing possum in a slaughterhouse or on the battlefield."

He'd never talked—about anything—for this long. Much less about his feelings. Something else had to be going on.

"I need to apologize, Penny."

"Why?"

"You never got an Easter ham. Or bacon and eggs. I couldn't be near it. Smell it. I went without eating sometimes during the war when Spam was all there was to eat."

"You don't need to apologize for that, Daddy."

"Yes. I do. And I need to apologize because I treated you like your brothers. No. Not even like your brothers."

It was too much to take in. It was true though. When people would ask me who I was like most in my family, I'd reply, "Nobody." And I'd think to myself about how I was the family shadow. Just a shadow.

"I'm sorry," he added. "For the confusion."

"Confusion?"

"Your mother said you don't like it when I call you Bitty or Itty Bitty."

"I don't. I never have. Would you like it if someone called you teeny tiny all the time, when you look like me? I guess it's better than Dumplin' or Fatso or Porky or Humpty Dumpty."

"You've forgotten. And we should've been better about reminding you. Before Beau—"

I broke in by saying, "Died?"

"Yes, before then. You used to prance around the house singing about animal crackers in your soup. You were obsessed with Shirley Temple. And your mother, what she went through. You had wet rags rolled up in your hair every night to make those curls of yours. The same ones you cut off with your mother's sewing scissors. You were still so cute. And small, compared to your brothers. So, I called you Itty Bitty. It's that simple."

I thought his words had dried up. But I was wrong. Even though he'd used up his daily ration of words, he went on. "For all those years, no matter what I was saying to you, I knew I was talking to the second most beautiful girl or woman I knew. But if I told you that, would you have believed me? Would you have thought I was mocking you? What would your brothers have added to whatever I said and teased you endlessly?

"No, I wouldn't have thought you were mocking me. I'm sure Beau and Moe would not have been any less merciless to me, Daddy."

"Whether you had Shirley Temple curls or not, you need to know how I saw you with the eyes of a proud father. I'm sorry I didn't tell you. I should have. I really should have. I hope you can forgive me someday. When I saw what you were trying to do to help Marilyn out on the beach the other night…damn, you were a true friend. It was like being on the battlefield where you've got to know and trust that everyone has your back. I bet Marilyn's not used to that in Hollywood. And I have to say, Frankie proved his mettle out on the beach too. There's steel in his spine. He's a warrior. He's a keeper. Yes, he's a keeper."

"I'm not quite sure how to respond to that, Daddy." The word *steel* robbed the air out of my lungs, but I fought the urge to show it.

"Then don't. Besides, I have something for you."

He placed a small gift box on the table and nudged it toward me. "Here. Open it."

I'd never gotten a gift from him. Just him. I looked at it. Then at him. I untied the ribbon, pushed back the crisply folded gold-foil paper to reveal a box of animal crackers. Drawings of circus animals were printed on the sides and a soft-string handle was on the top.

My lips quivered and I couldn't make them stop, even by putting a finger over them. It was like someone was yanking the air out of my lungs. The roof of my mouth burned and wetness pressed against my lower eye lids. I opened my mouth but choked on the words that couldn't fight their way out. My throat slammed shut, like a bedroom door after a teenager's fight.

"Are you alright?"

I nodded, tears jumping out of my eyes like paratroopers.

"I'll never call you Itty Bitty again. Unless you want me to."

"Don't stop, Daddy. Please don't stop."

"As you wish—"

He smiled. At me.

"You have a matched set."

"Huh?"

"Dimples. You have two. I only got one. Someone asked me about it the other day and I said I couldn't remember the last time I saw you smile. I didn't know if you had dimples at all."

"They're your grandma's. We have her to thank for the dimples in our family."

He reminisced a while longer. I absorbed it all, like a slice of white bread sopping up the last shadows of gravy on a dinner plate.

FADE OUT

CHAPTER 66

FADE IN:

- SEPTEMBER 17, 1958, SHOOTING CANCELLED
- INTERIOR, HOTEL DEL CORONADO (DAYTIME)

"Chip, I love coming to see you. I don't mind doing all the talking. But I want to hear your voice too. We've got to get you talking again."

He sat, motionless. No sign of agreement or disagreement.

Before that visit, I did my best to figure out a way to get him talking again. The fact that he was writing his responses was fine. No, it was great. But if he was ever going to get on with his life, spoken words would need to be part of it.

I came to his room prepared this time. And armed.

I'd been thinking about how I got kids to put their faces in pool water during swim lessons. That could be a real hurdle for some of them. They were convinced water was going to rush in and drown them.

So, I brought a box of striped-paper drinking straws.

"Here." I handed him the small bag from the dime store. "Open the box and pick the one with your favorite color on it."

He pulled the box top open and slid out a straw. A red one.

"Nice choice!"

He looked at me with a suspicious smirk.

"When I'm teaching kids to swim, they use straws. They blow bubbles into the water with their faces up high at first. Then lower and lower until their noses and later their faces are in the water. Before they know it, they're not afraid of going under water."

Chip stared at me, not making any connection to his situation.

I slid a blue straw out of the box and blew air through it. "Now you blow air through yours."

He did.

"Now think of it as a harmonica. Have you ever played a harmonica?"

He nodded in agreement.

"Great, that will make this even easier." I started to hum into my straw. "C'mon, join me. You hum too."

No dice.

"Please. Can you try?"

He blinked and drew in a breath.

Nothing happened after that, other than him pulling the straw out and crumpling it up.

"Let's try something else." I licked my arm, applied my lips and blew. The fart sound made him smile. What boy his age— well, any age—isn't entertained by farting?

"Now you try."

I hoped this might be more up his alley.

He licked his arm, applied his lips and blew. The first attempt was a bust. But the second was stellar. He was a natural. I laughed loud at first, but remembered we had to be quiet in that room…his hiding place.

"Do it again."

He did.

I silently laughed, holding my belly and slapping my knee.

"Now do it without touching your arm. Just blow raspberries, like this."

I inhaled and shot the air back out in a slobbery lip-vibrating stream.

He copied me with great success. I was on a roll. Could a breakthrough be far behind?

I jumped up on the bed and squatted with my arms curled up into my armpits. I made monkey noises. I hopped. I made the bed springs screech.

"Join me. It's okay to jump on the bed, just this time."

Chip hesitated, but I suspected he'd jumped on this bed plenty of times already during the days of his confinement.

I made more monkey noises.

He didn't make any.

I jumped harder and higher. I made sillier monkey noises.

He jumped harder and higher. But he didn't make any noises.

And then it happened. The bed broke and crashed to the floor, with the two of us slamming into each other. I covered my mouth, a stupid thing to do as if the noise had come out of there. He covered his lips too.

"Monkey see, monkey do. What a pair we are!" I giggled in a hushed way. He did too. Finally, noise was coming out of that little boy.

If it took breaking another bed, I'd do it.

Chip was finding his voice.

His words and wishes might never go unspoken again.

FADE OUT

CHAPTER 67

FADE IN:

- SEPTEMBER 17, 1958, SHOOTING CANCELLED
- EXTERIOR, SAN DIEGO ZOO (DAYTIME)

"It's just not right to lie. We'll both burn in hell for this."

"Calling in sick to work when you're not sick is hardly a go-to-hell offense," Frankie said as he sat down next to me on the park bench. "Considering what we've done in the past week, I'm pretty sure our passports have already been stamped for an eternity of hellfire and brimstone and..."

"Alright already. I got it." I poked his ribcage with my index finger, but didn't let him squirm away. The grasp of my other hand was firm on his wrist.

"Kiss me you fool!" My eyes widened with excitement.

"It'd be my pleasure, ma'am." He put my half-eaten Hershey bar that he was carrying and his bag of peanuts down on the bench. A few nuts spilled out and dropped to the ground.

"*Ma'am*? I'm not our parents' age. You may call me Miss or Princess or Empress."

"It'd be my pleasure...Miss." As Frankie leaned forward, one of the elephants trumpeted. I fought the urge to look and I triumphed, keeping my attention on my favorite man and not one of my favorite animals.

His lips were heading for mine until he took a surprising path south. Swirls of emotion triggered me to gasp for an extra bit of air. Frankie nuzzled my neck with delicate kisses. If kisses could be whispers, those ones were. Maybe he was whispering. I couldn't tell because my eyes were closed and everything got melty. My mind repeated the same words, "This is not a daydream. This is not a daydream." But the sound of my heart pounded so loudly I couldn't concentrate. I didn't want to concentrate.

Each kiss had its own flicker of warmth that coursed and curled inside me. And those flickers combined to form flames. His warm lips left a trail, like footprints in the sand that I knew no tide would ever erase. His kisses were obliterating my thoughts.

When my brain kicked back in, I found myself wondering who taught him to kiss a girl's neck like that. Then I pushed that thought out of my mind and simply enjoyed the sensations. Waves of heat rolled through me and my breathing became uneven as the world slowly disappeared around us.

Everything started to blur and race at the same time as Frankie lips moved up to my jaw, kissing a pathway to my lips…closer and closer…my lips parted and I didn't do it, at least consciously…our breaths mingled, mine chocolatey and his like peanuts…together, we were a human Reese's Peanut Butter Cup and we tasted mighty fine…I was becoming addicted to Frankie…I didn't just want to be around him, I craved him…he covered my mouth with a hungry kiss…not demanding, but hungry…I drew my tongue over his teeth and swallowed his groan of pleasure…and I wished for it to never end…I knew a kiss like that was a beginning, a promise of much more to come.

In the heat of the moment, I was melting. Or *something* was melting. The scent of hot-candle wax—no, melted Crayons—got stronger and stronger. The unmistakable squeal of a toddler and the unmistakable warning of a woman broke into my hazy-with-love mind. "That's *very* hot, let Mommy blow on it." I couldn't believe some lady was letting her kid eat a hot Crayon. I had to look.

There were no words exchanged as we separated, but the smirk on his face said everything. I smiled back and scanned the area for the mother and child. They were standing in front of a clear bubble-topped machine that had a Mold-A-Rama sign over it. She was holding and blowing on a gray plastic elephant that I guessed came from the machine. The toy-making vending machine, and the one next to it, must have just been installed because I'd never seen one before, especially there by my beloved elephant enclosure. And I would've noticed.

"I gotta have one of those."

"Not me. No thank you," added Frankie. "I want one of those." He pointed to the other machine which, for a quarter, would make an "Earth Invader" called a Purple People Eater. Not exactly a zoo-animal souvenir, but since he liked the song on the radio it'd be meaningful to him.

I dug in my handbag for my coin purse as an elephant trumpeted again, demanding attention. Was it sounding an alert? An alarm? Or was it calling out for a snack? Peanuts perhaps? I reached for the peanut package next to Frankie. But he intercepted my hand and pulled it up to his face so it cupped his jaw and cheek. His head tilted slightly and rested on my palm. His eyes closed and he was irresistible. Simply irresistible.

"Why did it take us so long to figure this out?" My words were tender and hushed and carried the tinge of regret.

"I don't know. But I'm glad we did."

Again, an elephant trumpeted. But this time it had a higher pitch. When I looked over, I discovered it wasn't alone. Its pachyderm pal raised its trunk and sprayed us with a geyser of water from the pool it was wading in.

"That's a first for me. Now I can say I took a shower with an elephant!" I wiped moisture off my bare arms.

"Not exactly," Frankie said. "You were showered *by* an elephant."

"A minor technicality."

We got up, brushed off and placed a few of Frankie's peanuts on the extended trunks of both elephants. We didn't share my chocolate bar with them. It was much too rich for elephants.

We held hands and started walking. He swung me around and said, "I have something to confess."

Confess was always a loaded word. Loaded with guilt. Loaded with pain. Loaded with secrets.

I noticeably inhaled.

"Oh, it's not a life-or-death kind of thing," he added.

That somehow wasn't reassuring.

"Let's sit down again over here on this other bench...out of the soak zone of those elephants."

Soak zone made me smile awkwardly, but a smile nonetheless.

It was his turn to inhale. And I noticed it.

"I have to confess...."

FADE OUT

CHAPTER 68

Frankie cleared his throat with a cough. It sounded not quite like a sea lion, but more like a goose. He started talking again, but stopped walking. "I have to confess that…that I was running on the beach and came up to The Del to say hi. I saw you with Steele. Having coffee on the patio."

"That was nothing." It was my best attempt to brush off any concern he might've had.

"I *saw* you," he repeated. At that moment, he didn't see me. He saw my feet. We weren't making eye contact. At least he wasn't. "And you looked happier…happier than you ever look with me. He said something and you laughed."

His head rose. *Oh, God. What was he going to say next?* The words raced across my mind like a news-ticker sign in Times Square.

His eyes matched mine. "Your grins were three times as big as ours."

"That's not possible. I have a big mouth, but not THAT big."

"Penny, I'm serious. You looked…*happier*." He cleared his throat again. "And I was happy for you. If it was time for you to meet the man of your dreams—or whatever you'd call him—I decided I'd be happy for you. But I wasn't happy for me."

That was it. His words ended. It was up to me to respond. "I'm sorry you saw us and that it bothered you. I was happy, or I thought

I was. Man, was I wrong, as you well know. He was a smooth talker. A charmer. And I ate it all up and licked the plate. But that's all water under the bridge."

He winced.

"Bad analogy. Got it." I shoveled through my brain for something else to say. "It's all in the past. Our past. And it'll stay there. Hidden away. Far, far away."

"You've always made me happy. And I'm the happiest I've ever been. Right here with you…in the zoo."

"Nice alliteration."

"Actually, it's a rhyme. But who really cares? I care about you, Frankie."

"I care about you too. And I'll care for you, for-e-ver."

I couldn't top that, so I stayed uncharacteristically silent.

After a few minutes of watching people and pachyderms, I directed Frankie to the Mold-A-Matic machines. He dropped a quarter in each of them and we watched the show. Like magic, when the two halves of the metal molds opened, there stood an elephant in my machine and a Purple People Eater in Frankie's. I fished out my coin purse and raised a quarter. "This one's for Chip."

When we left the zoo, I bought Chip an animal-picture book to go with his molded-plastic elephant. "I wish we could've brought him along, but it's just too soon."

Frankie squeezed my hand. "Yes…too soon. But someday."

He wasn't just growing fond of Chip. He was getting attached. That made me happy. And it made me worry.

FADE OUT

CHAPTER 69

FADE IN:
- SEPTEMBER 18, 1958, SHOOTING CANCELLED
- INTERIOR, TRUDY'S HOUSE (NIGHTTIME)

"I agree to do this article on one condition: that you focus on the contest and what it was like for me as the winner. Not about Marilyn…the movie star." I used my firm voice and nodded for emphasis, sending my earth-globe earring and my crescent-moon earring into orbit.

"Agreed," replied Stan Drake, the reporter who set the whole adventure into motion when he'd told me I'd won a contest I didn't even enter. "And don't mind my photographer. He'll be shooting while we speak. Now, let's get started. The valued readers of the *Coronado Eagle & Journal* want to know exactly what Miss Monroe is like."

"Stan, what did *you* just agree to? Because *I* just agreed not to talk intimately about her."

"I didn't say anything about being intimate, did I?"

"No, I guess not." I weaved my fingers together and rested my hands on my lap. I filled my lungs and unfortunately sucked in his spoiled-milk and sauerkraut scent. "She's dazzling. And somehow she's down to earth. She's a one-of-a-kind star. A star who's set a high bar—a dizzingly high bar—for beauty in Hollywood. America. The universe."

"Right. I see. How has this worked out for you?" He scribbled notes with his pencil and pad.

"It's been great. Everything I expected and more. Though I

really didn't know what to expect. Sometimes fate takes you where you never expected to go."

"Like Miss Monroe's bedroom?"

"Yes, something like that."

"Is she difficult? To work with and work for, that is?"

"She's an artist, not a machine. Things don't always go right. Or to her satisfaction. Or Billy Wilder's satisfaction. Making a movie is incredibly complicated. More than you can imagine. And everyone must do his or her part. Me, I do whatever I'm told to do. Get a towel. Accept a gift from a fan or admirer."

"Sounds exciting for a cashier from the dime store."

"Absolutely. I'll never forget a single moment of this."

"Has Kate Morgan made herself known on the set or around the hotel?"

"I couldn't really say."

Stan went on to ask about Tony Curtis and Jack Lemmon, and about the work hours and the crowds on the beach.

He thanked me for my time.

His photographer wished me well.

Stan said an article would appear in the next few days and that I should look for it.

I couldn't believe he thought I wouldn't.

FADE OUT

CHAPTER 70

FADE IN:
- SEPTEMBER 21, 1958, SHOOTING CANCELLED
- INTERIOR, TRUDY'S HOUSE (DAYTIME)

"Have you read it yet? Did you really say those things?" Trudy sat at the breakfast table, the paper unfolded in front of her. Ella was lounging at Trudy's fuzzy-slippered feet, licking her paws and smoothing her whiskers. "Sunday edition. Front page, no less. That makes you a cover girl. Dern tootin' it does."

I'd never been a fast-start-in-the-morning kind of girl. Trudy's questions and comments changed that. Instantly.

"Let me see. Did he twist my words? You know how close I've become to Marilyn. I'd never say anything bad about her."

"Brace yourself. I believe this is called a *hack job*." Trudy pushed the paper in my direction. "I'll get you a cup of coffee."

There it was. On the cover. A large photo of me, with my mouth open wide and in mid-sentence. "Oh. My. Lord. I look like one of the hungry, wide-mouthed hippos on that jungle ride at Disneyland. Shoot me now."

The headline seared my eyes. "EXCLUSIVE: INSIDE MARILYN'S BEDROOM." The smaller headline tucked under it didn't help my cause. "DIME STORE CASHIER PENNY PARKER WINS MORE THAN SHE BARGAINED FOR WITH CONTEST."

I filled my lungs and began to read the article:

When Penny Parker, long-time Coronado resident and cashier at the Cornet Five & Dime, learned she'd be Marilyn Monroe's go-to girl, she was shocked. But she was in for a real shock when the blonde bombshell invited her into her boudoir.

During an exclusive interview with the *Coronado Eagle & Journal*, Parker described containers of pills, bottles of champagne and racks of glamorous getups.

"I really didn't know what to expect," admitted Parker. "It was nothing like a normal bedroom."

Parker is getting an up-close and personal view of Hollywood's inner workings. "She's an artist, not a machine. Things don't always go to Billy Wilder's satisfaction." That has been made abundantly clear out on the sands in front of The Del. Onlookers have grown concerned about the star's behavior, especially before the cameras begin to roll.

"Yes. She shakes out her hands at the wrists. Yes, she tells herself to relax. Yes, people stop and stare." Parker explained it was Monroe's way of preparing for the cameras. Others on the set said it looked like she was having a breakdown.

In fact, production has been shut down indefinitely here in Coronado. The film's producers have alerted the press that she is suffering from "nervous exhaustion." Parker reports otherwise. "She loves a grilled steak and baked potato. She gets gifts of roses and chocolates and fresh fruit. It's like an endless party in her cottage."

Because of the reported "nervous exhaustion," the film's crew is back in Los Angeles and is expected to shoot interior scenes in the coming days, without its most brilliant star.

Is Monroe's marriage on the rocks? Parker answered with a shrug and opened palms. Is Monroe sick? Again, Parker shrugged. Is there a big secret to keep the lid on? Her shoulders raised a third time.

Only time will tell when and if the *Some Like It Hot* cast and crew return to Coronado. Parker would not comment about the project's future other than to point out, "If they're back, I'm back."

The *Coronado Eagle & Journal* will approach Parker for further comment as this bombshell of a story continues.

A sidebar article featured comments from Tilly and a photo of her shaking hands with Marilyn on the beach.

The headline made my blood boil. "CREATURES OF THE DARK." A smaller headline added, "CORONADO'S VERY OWN HOLLYWOOD LEGEND COMMENTS ON BLONDE

BOMBSHELL."

I prepared myself for more of Stan's twisted journalistic trash:

Tallulah Carlisle, better known as "Tilly" to the locals, knows a thing or two about Hollywood. She qualifies for the title of "expert," considering how she runs the town's movie house and that she ran away from Hollywood at the zenith of her career.

Next to Mary Pickford and Gloria Swanson, Carlisle was perhaps the most glittering goddess of Hollywood's golden youth in the 1920s.

Carlisle visited the sandy-beach set of *Some Like It Hot* recently. She spent time with the film's star and was eager to share her insights with the *Coronado Eagle & Journal*.

"Miss Monroe is an extremely talented performer. She can act with her eyes and subtle gestures. That's mighty difficult to teach. It's impossible for some to do. I found her to be a force, on screen and off, with inescapable gravitational pull. In other words, she's magnetic. Out on the beach, I witnessed how her fans were like iron filings trying to organize around her. It was fascinating and familiar."

She continued, "I see a lot of myself in her, and that worries me. For all its pomp, powers and promises, Tinseltown is a place where dreams are made. And, sadly, where they're dashed."

With conviction and without hesitation, the Coronado businesswoman advised Monroe to not be seduced by "the glitter, bugle beads and ostrich plumes," and to be leery of "the wear and tear and glare of Hollywood."

She described actors and actresses as "creatures of the dark." Carlisle explained, "Not monsters or vampires. But performers who tell stories of love and loss to millions of viewers in the comfort of a darkened theater. Miss Monroe's abilities are among those of our time's greatest storytellers. How her story ends, that's entirely up to her. And I've told her that."

Carlisle said she has no regrets about abandoning Hollywood. "I had my day in the sun."

For the fortunate residents of Coronado, Tallulah "Tilly" Carlisle's star continues to shine in sunlight and moonlight.

FADE OUT

CHAPTER 71

FADE IN:
- SEPTEMBER 22, 1958, SHOOTING RESUMES IN LOS ANGELES
- INTERIOR, TRUDY'S HOUSE (DAYTIME)

"Yes. Mr. Drake's office, please. No. I will not hold. Tell him Penny Parker's on the line. Yes. Uh-huh. Now, please connect me to Mr. Drake."

Trudy stood at the sink, washing breakfast dishes. "Be polite." She whispered, "You've already seen what a newspaper man can do with your words."

I began to think the phone line was disconnected. I folded my arms in front of me while still holding up the earpiece to the side of my head.

"Hasn't he picked up the phone yet?"

I shook my head in response to Trudy's question and covered the phone's mouthpiece with my palm.

"Nothing—and I mean *nothing*—is easy these days. I swear there have been more twists in my life than in a bag of pretzels."

Trudy blinked and nodded. "Then eat the pretzels. Life is short. You know what I always—"

"Ah, yes." I responded to the man's voice on the phone. "This is she. I will never speak to you again. How can you manipulate a person's words the way you do? Journalistic integrity must not be valued at your newspaper."

Trudy turned and leaned on the counter. She wiped her hands on her apron and listened to my side of the phone conversation.

"Yes. Uh-huh. Well, I really don't care if the night editor sliced and diced the article you turned in. But I do care what people think of me. What are Marilyn and Mr. Wilder going to say about this? No. Yes, I'm sure they're used to this kind of treatment. I won't— no, can't—speak to you anymore. Just know that I will be writing a strongly worded letter to your superiors and demand that it be published in the next edition. Good day!"

Trudy didn't miss a beat. I hardly had the phone's receiver back onto its cradle before she said, "That just stinks to the high heavens, chickadee. Is there anything I can get you?"

"Like I told you when this whole Marilyn *thing* started and you asked the same question: you can get me a husband, a home and a family of my own making? And it would be nice to get a best, best, best girlfriend."

"And like I told you then, those things are *not* on my menu today. But I have an inkling those things are in your future. Be patient…like tapioca."

"Tapioca?"

"Yes, indeed. Tapioca's got to sit in the frig to cool. Folks don't usually like it hot. But patience brings you a cool, tasty tapioca treat. Trust me. You'll see. Be patient."

FADE OUT

CHAPTER 72

FADE IN:
- SEPTEMBER 23, 1958, SHOOTING CONTINUES IN LOS ANGELES
- INTERIOR, TRUDY'S HOUSE (NIGHTTIME)

May telephoned to let me know Marilyn was back to work at the studio. It was the first time I'd spoken to her since Marilyn was whisked away from Coronado.

"Let me talk to Penny." I could hear Marilyn in the background. "Are you on the line?"

"Yep. I'm here."

"It's so good to hear your voice. I've missed you." She paused and her volume went down to a hush as she said, "Nobody treats me the way you do. No one makes me laugh. No one sneaks out with me."

"That makes me happy and sad...that you missed me and that you aren't having any fun. If it means anything, we aren't having much fun down here either."

"Honey, I'm sorry you got pulled into all my drama...especially down on the beach. I won't say anything more about it. Not on this phone anyway. I never know who might be listening in."

"Understood."

"Before I go, tell me how Chip is holding up. Is there anything I can do to help?"

"Nick, that nice bellman who delivered a lot of the gifts from your admirers, including you-know-who, checks on him during the day. And Frankie and I take turns going over in the evening. But I don't know how much longer we can pull this off."

There was an audible sigh on Marilyn's end of the line. "He's got no family? No one?"

"Nope."

"He's got you, Penny. The ocean brought you two together. You saved his life and now you're connected. Maybe you always will be."

I didn't immediately respond.

"I have to run. I'll see you in a few days. Can't wait!"

May came back on the line to tell me the crew would be coming back to Coronado to finish the film's exterior shots. I was to report back to The Del on Monday and pick up where we'd left off.

May had no idea where Marilyn and I'd left off before her hospitalization. At least I didn't think she had.

FADE OUT

CHAPTER 73

FADE IN:
- SEPTEMBER 24, 1958, SHOOTING CONTINUES IN LOS ANGELES
- INTERIOR, THE VILLAGE THEATRE (NIGHTTIME)

I needed to get away. Badly. And only The Village Theater would do. Tilly was at her post, encased in glass with a heaven of flashing lights above the main doorway.

"You're looking fine this evening. New broach, Tilly?"

"You have the eyes of an eagle, my dear. Yes. Sparkles so nicely, doesn't it? How are you?"

"The filming started again, but up in Los Angeles…"

Tilly interrupted. "That's not what I was referring to. How are people reacting to your newspaper article?"

"You mean, *our* newspaper articles?"

"Yes. I stand corrected."

"Let's just say that I'm not ready to pack my bags and head to a new life in Hollywood. I think I'll enjoy it all from my comfy seat in your movie house. I see you've got *Damn Yankees* on the screen tonight. Any good?"

"Pfff. It's a musical. Light weight. But Tab Hunter is yummy and Gwen Verdon bumps and grinds like the best of burlesque. But what do I know? I'm a dusty relic, drenched in rhinestones and marinated by the past." She knew how to pick her words for the ultimate impact. "My solution to most anything is more mascara and brighter-red nail polish."

She waved her hands with the grace of a ballerina and framed her face with her then-still hands. She posed as if for a lobby card or a glossy still shot that she could autograph for her fans.

I loved Tilly.

I loved who she was.

I loved what she was.

I loved what she did for me.

I.

Loved.

Tilly.

I couldn't help but compare her to Marilyn. Would Marilyn make movies in her seventies or eighties? Would she retire from the screen and own a movie palace like Tilly? Would her jewels be gemstones or glass? Would she be trapped in the past?

I'd heard it said that Memory Lane was a nice place for a stroll, but you wouldn't want to buy a house there. So far, Tilly continued to win the battle of becoming Memory Lane's most famous homeowner, unlike all the war veterans in Coronado who couldn't seem to move on.

Tilly motioned me to come around and sit with her in the ticket booth. It'd been a while since she'd done that.

"How's it feel?" Her words were direct.

"Fine. No, it feels *wonderful*." And it did. "Every time I come to your theater, it's like filling up a car with gas. Movies do that for me. But here in the ticket booth, with you—and these photos of you in all your glory—well, it feels like I'm part of the show. Is that what it's like for you?"

"It is. I'm so glad you feel the same way, Penny. Because one day this will all be yours."

"I don't understand."

"I'm not the spring chicken I once was. At some point—not too soon, mind you—my make-up and jewelry will go on strike and this Hollywood look will vanish. I have no husband. No children. But I have you. And you will have *this*. All of this." She swept the air with her palms in the direction of the lobby and the flashing lights. "Every week when you slid me some coins for a ticket, I set it aside. Year after year, I saved it all for you when you might need it most. The theater will be your nest, and the money will be your egg to go with it."

"*My* nest egg?"

"Yes, my dear."

My mind should've been blank after hearing that news, but it wasn't. Frankie would inherit Green Gables and I'd just been offered the theater—not to mention a stash of cash. Our future was becoming clear and secure. It was being served up to us on a silver platter. Or was it?

"Are you sure, Tilly?"

"Yes, my dear, I'm sure. I've thought about this since you were a little girl and you came here with your grandmother."

"Really?"

"She had so little money, but she had so much hope for you. I never charged her for your tickets or snacks."

"But I saw her pay you."

"Yes, but you didn't see me give the money back with the tickets or after you were digging your hand into a bag of popcorn. It was something I wanted to do for her…and you."

Tilly went on. "When I left Marceline, I'd never known hunger. My parents' farm in Missouri always kept our bellies full. But when I got to Los Angeles, I learned about all kinds of hunger."

She took my hand in hers. "The *hungry years* of the 1930s— and the war—reminded us all to live in the moment and not take anything for granted. Your grandmother knew what it was like to go without. But she didn't want you to feel that way. Ever. Like so many women, she let her grandchildren eat first. Bowls of soup. Toasted-cheese sandwiches. And if there was anything left, she had that when you weren't looking. I bet, if you think hard, you might remember her telling you she wasn't hungry or she'd already eaten."

I looked down at the silvery metal countertop and dug into my memory banks. Sure enough, Grandma Jenny had said those things. I'd been so naïve and completely selfish. What I was thinking must've shown on my face.

"Don't be hard on yourself. You were a child. All children— and most of the *adults* in Hollywood—think only of themselves. She loved you. That was just one of the ways she showed you."

"I'll never look at a Coca-Cola or a bag of popcorn the same way again."

"In time, you will. But now, before I get any older and wiser…or, perhaps, un-wiser, I need to teach you the business of running a theater…the business part of show biz. The upkeep of the building. Ordering supplies for the concession counter. Hiring and keeping employees…"

She kept talking while my mind became preoccupied with connecting dots. I could see what I'd known—but kept down deep—all along. Starting with Grandma Jenny, food was tied to love and feeling loved. In her kitchen. At the movies. Holidays. On Saturday afternoons. When I had a good day. Especially when I had a bad day. Food was present…and it *was* a present. And when Grandma Jenny was gone, the food-love connection lived on.

"…all of this you must learn." Tilly's words came back into my awareness. "And I will teach you."

"This is all too much. You've been so kind…all my life. And I've been learning so much from Marilyn about *making* pictures."

"Now, my dear, Tinseltown will always be yours," Tilly said. "Safely tucked away here in Coronado."

FADE OUT

CHAPTER 74

The day had dragged by at my cash register. But I'd had something to look forward to: I was going home for dinner. Amazingly, I did look forward to it. I'd never expected to look forward to going home. Not in my entire life.

"That was delicious Mom. I'd forgotten how good your meatloaf is. All I ever seem to eat these days is Trudy's cooking. Thanks for having us over."

"Nonsense," she said from her place at the end of the table. "This is your home. You're always welcome here. Anytime. Anytime at all."

Mom picked up and passed the mashed potatoes to me. A flashback of a dinner-table scene from *Leave It to Beaver* played in my head. All she needed was a string of pearls. Like Mrs. Cleaver's. I almost said, "Golly gee." But then she knocked over her wine glass—not a martini glass, since she announced she was cutting back on the booze—and brought me back to the reality of my imperfect family. Imperfect, yes. Mine, absolutely.

"Would you like a bit more? I added sour cream and some onion. Just the way you liked them when you were little."

"I couldn't. I just couldn't."

"But I can." Frankie took the bowl from Mom. His leg started to jiggle, rubbing up against mine under the tablecloth.

I nudged his ankle with mine, in hopes that he'd stop his jiggling, and whispered with a sideways mouth, "You don't have to. You won't hurt her feelings. You've already eaten more than I've *ever* seen you eat. When did you start gorging yourself like a truck driver at a greasy spoon? I'm going to tell your mother the next time—"

"Mrs. Parker, would you pass the gravy, please?" Frankie winked at me.

"Hold it right there, young man. I'm going to state the obvious…at least the obvious to me. What's up with all of you?" Mom continued with her questioning. "Who are you people? Seems like overnight you're all getting along. No one's fighting. No snotty comments or stinky faces." Her pupils pinballed between the three of us as she spoke. "Don't misunderstand me. I like it. I like it a lot." She smiled in a loving way that I couldn't remember the last time I'd seen. "And, on top of that, Frankie's eating seconds!"

We exchanged glances. Three of the four of us at the table shared a secret. A terrible secret. A transformative secret. We'd changed alright. But was it for the better?

"We're heeeeeeere! Don't mind us. Finish your dinner. Go on. We've brought dessert." Lorelei was nearly bowled over by her no-neck children as they poured through the doorway and into the dining room. "Penny, everyone's talking about your newspaper article. The girls in my card club would *love* to have you join us sometime. When your schedule allows it, that is."

"That sounds *wonderful.* I'll get back to you on that."

"Moe will bring the dessert in just a minute. He's out talking to old Mr. Pendleton next door. Probably apologizing for breaking something of his when Moe was just an *adorable* little boy."

The noise level in the house quadrupled. And Daddy didn't flinch. He didn't wince. He didn't holler in his ten-hut way. He just smiled at me. Dimples and all. Then at Mom.

The phone rang in the kitchen.

"I'll get it." It was only a few steps away. I cleared my throat and said, "Hello. What? I can't hear you. Please repeat that…I still can't hear—"

"They hung up. The nerve! And now I get to straighten out this cord." I dragged some of it over to the dining room archway.

"Someday, my privacy will not be measured by the length of

the telephone cord. Someday, telephones won't even have cords. Mark my words."

Mom responded. "Duly noted. Oh, there's an envelope on top of the toaster. It's for you. I found it in the back of the desk drawer the other day. I have no idea how long it's been there, but it's yellowed. I guess it's been a while."

I instantly recognized the handwriting as Frankie's. It was no longer sealed. Not ripped open. Perhaps it separated over time.

"Did you read this, Mom?"

"Of course not. Your name is on it. I guess it fell in there and hasn't seen the light of day since."

"Letter to my wife, Penelope" appeared on the outside of it. I read on. "This isn't part of our project, but my mother made me write you this letter. She said it's what a good husband should do. So, here goes. I'm supposed to tell you that you make my world complete. Even though you'll always be in my dreams, I would die if I didn't see you in the morning and at night before I go to sleep. I'm supposed to tell you that my life began when I met you and that we'll be together until the end of time. And then some. I guess that's it. If the junk and stuff I wrote creeps you out, I'm sorry. Your husband, Franklin Holland. PS: It doesn't creep me out."

My arms went limp and dropped to my sides, along with the letter. The kitchen felt like the oven was on fire. It was so hot. I was so hot...from the inside out.

Frankie came into the room. I showed him the envelope and letter, but I didn't hand them to him.

"You never got that?" Frankie's eyes dodged back and forth. "You really *never* got that?"

"No. Apparently, it was stuffed in the back of the desk drawer. Mom used to put important mail in there, like bills. I guess she thought this was important. I have to say I agree."

"Yeah. Me too."

"Did you mean it then? Could you mean it now?"

"Before I answer, I better read it. You know, so I don't agree to something I'm not sure about."

I handed him the letter he'd written long ago. His eyes slid back and forth with each line he read. He licked his lips and swallowed. He swallowed hard like a peach pit was lodged in there, next to his Adam's apple...like he had the makings of a fruit salad in his neck.

His eyes stopped following the trail of words on the paper and met their destination: my eyes.

"Yes." He smiled, radiantly. "Yes, I do."

He reached out, wrapped his arms around me and whispered, "I've waited a lifetime to love you. And I'm not waiting any longer."

FADE OUT

CHAPTER 75

FADE IN:
- SEPTEMBER 25, 1958, SHOOTING CONTINUES IN LOS ANGELES
- INTERIOR, PENNY'S PARENTS' HOUSE (NIGHTTIME)

My brother interrupted the love-letter conversation I was having with Frankie. I should have seen that coming. Moe swung the back door while he cradled an armload of his favorite hard candies, mostly sour balls and chewy soft-center raspberries.

"A bag or box or tin would be a politer way to bring dessert to a dinner party." My sarcasm was abundantly apparent.

"Well, I did, Miss Queen of the Checkout Stand. But the bag broke when it landed on the sidewalk. I was talking to Mr. Pendleton. Old people, sheesh. Always living in the past."

"What do you mean?" I couldn't resist asking.

"He told me about the day you almost died on a piece of hard candy."

Frankie spoke up. "That's a story I haven't heard."

"That's because I was too little to remember."

"Well, Mr. Pendleton remembers," Moe added.

"So tell us." Frankie seemed intrigued.

"It was Penny's big day and her birthday party was in full swing. She was little. Three or four. Apparently, she snuck a hard candy from the dish in the front room...the one that only company got to choose from. Not us kids. Not ever. She got it stuck in her throat. She probably tried to swallow it whole when The Commander caught her in the kitchen."

"Then what?" Frankie was intrigued.

"As Mr. Pendleton tells it, The Commander grabbed Penny by the ankles and shook her upside down while Mr. Pendleton slapped her on the back until the candy popped out onto the kitchen floor. And do you know what Itty Bitty did after she stopped crying?"

Frankie stared at Moe, waiting for him to answer his own question. Moe obliged. "My little sister picked up the candy and asked if she could finish it."

I couldn't help but add, "Well, why let a perfectly good piece of candy go to waste? I was thrifty even at such a young age."

"Somehow, I'm not surprised," Frankie said. "Not surprised at all."

But there were other surprises coming our way…surprises that would take Frankie's breath away.

FADE OUT

CHAPTER 76

FADE IN:
- SEPTEMBER 29, 1958, SHOOTING RESUMES IN CORONADO
- INTERIOR, TRUDY'S HOUSE (DAYTIME)

When Marilyn returned to The Del, she had her husband with her, along with May and Paula. The weather was typical for San Diego in autumn. Sunny. Warm. Not hot. I had just three days left with my new friend, Marilyn. What a thought: *my friend*, Marilyn.

Her hug was a thief. It stole my breath. She didn't release me as she whispered, "I hope Chip is okay. I've worried ever so much about him. But I don't dare talk about or visit him. Understand?"

I nodded gently and said nothing.

"Oh, Penny," she belted out, "I've missed you…missed you ever so much. Let's go for a little stroll. Together. Just the two of us." She took me by the arm and directed me out to her cottage's patio and through the gate. Marilyn waved off the man standing there to secure her living space.

"Billy knows," Marilyn said. "Arthur told him about the baby. And that I need to work shorter days."

"That's a relief, isn't it?" I waited for a response.

"I guess so. Billy said if I came to the set before noon, I could leave earlier. Seems fair to me."

"Me too."

"Speaking of fair, I have to apologize for how unfair the newspaper was with the article they ran. You have to know—"

"Honey, it comes with the territory. I'm used to it. I don't like it. But I'm used to it. Besides, it's me who should be apologizing to you…and Frankie and your father…and poor little Chip. You'd only known me for less than a week when I ruined your life…all of your lives."

"You did no such thing. My life isn't ruined. Changed? Yep. Ruined? Nope. Back to that article, though, it would've been one thing if it only appeared here in the local paper. But the Associated Press picked it up—I think that's the phrase they use—and it ran across the country. They twisted every…single…thing…I said. Please don't hate me."

"I could never hate you, Penny. Never. Got it?"

"I guess so."

"We go together like a wink and a smile." To make her point, Marilyn winked in slow motion and grinned at me. "And I hope we always do."

I did too.

FADE OUT

CHAPTER 77

Marilyn was to be out on the beach at nine o'clock. But we all knew that wasn't going to happen. It wasn't likely, anyway.

I was inside the cottage with her. Paula was helping her rehearse lines, mothering her and reassuring her. "Use your talent...your splendid talent, my dear. Bravo. Let's run it again Remember, true artists must make mistakes...until they do not."

Marilyn had her lines down cold. In fact, I'd heard the lines so many times I was sure I could deliver them. But I kept my thoughts to myself. This time, anyway.

After delivering a series of excuses about an hour apart to Billy that ranged from Marilyn needing to wash her hair to it's too hot in the high-noon sun, I fought the urge to applaud when Marilyn agreed to appear on the beach at two thirty. I would soon discover that applauding at that moment would've proved to be premature.

Marilyn had one line to deliver. And she couldn't do it, at least not in combination with the other instructions from Billy and the crew. In the end, after what I counted as fifty-eight takes, the day's work was done.

Back in the cottage, I found it hard to reconnect with Marilyn. Arthur created a buffer zone, keeping everyone except Paula away. And her sparkle was gone. Like something had wiped it away or sanded it down.

"Penny, are you there?" Marilyn's voice came from her bedroom.

"Just a second." I got up out of my chair and stood in the doorway. "What can I get for you?"

"Come and sit down. We haven't really talked since—"

"Marilyn, they're ready for you outside."

Marilyn squished her lips together and rolled her eyes. She didn't verbally respond to May's request.

"They're waiting for you." May repeated it.

"Alright, I'm coming." Marilyn pushed back from the vanity. "Penny, we'll talk about *that* when we get back. Come on. Walk with me."

I was speechless. It was like she'd turned on a light switch. She transformed. Marilyn looked better than she'd ever looked on the screen, on the beach or in disguise on our adventures. She was luminous.

"You like it? It's an original by Orry-Kelly." Marilyn twirled in a circle. Long strands of beads shook and trailed her movement. It was skin-tight. Marilyn was a curvy vision in white, topped off by a white-fox stole. Even to another woman, Marilyn's breasts were beacons. More than usual. They were bigger. I wondered how they were going to explain the changes in her appearance in the final cut of the movie, especially considering scenes were shot out of order. It would take Hollywood magic, I guessed.

"I'm stunned and it's stunning." I kept talking as we walked. "No one's going to be able to take their eyes off you."

Marilyn twirled around again. "One time, when Orry-Kelly was measuring with that tape of his, he measured my chest. Then my waist. Then my hips. He smirked. Do you believe it? He smirked at me and said, 'I was just measuring Tony and he's got a better-looking ass than you do.'"

"No, he did not." I couldn't believe someone in the industry would say something like that to a star like Marilyn.

"He did. And I opened my blouse and said back, 'He doesn't have tits like these.' We both laughed. And, I suppose we were both right. Tony does have a nice ass."

I thought Marilyn's pregnancy, for those who knew about it, had to be obvious. For those who didn't know, like the tourists and gawkers on the set's edge, her appearance was sure to raise questions.

The scene scheduled to be shot that day involved Tony dropping off Marilyn at the hotel's front door at the end of their date on his character's yacht. It was to take place in the wee hours before dawn. To get the best light, it was to be filmed in the afternoon, when the height and spires of the hotel created lots of shade. I was told that in post-production the images would be darkened to make it look like night time.

Marilyn appeared and took everyone's breath away. The crew. The crowd. The cast.

She closed her eyes, shook her hands at the wrist and told herself to relax.

Marilyn was back.

And she was red hot.

And everyone liked it.

FADE OUT

CHAPTER 78

FADE IN:
- OCTOBER 1, 1958, LAST DAY OF SHOOTING IN CORONADO
- EXTERIOR, HOTEL DEL CORONADO (DAYTIME)

I dreaded that day coming: the last bits of time I'd have with Marilyn. If my life had a soundtrack, the most mournful death-march dirge would've filled the air. Angels would've wailed and their tears would've showered down.

The crew was ready to shoot the scene in which the all-girl band arrived in a touring bus at The Del's front porch. The porch was lined with elderly men rocking in chairs, presumably wealthy and available. They were all in resort clothes topped off with Panama hats. They stopped rocking as the bus came into view.

May and I watched from the sidelines.

"This ought to be good." May folded her arms. "We're in the home stretch. She better not fall apart now."

Marilyn didn't.

She walked toward the cameras the way only Marilyn could, taking tiny steps, pushing out each hip blade with each step. Her shoulders were back and down, elongating her neck. Her arms were limp and her hands were open.

She climbed the stairs and said a few lines as Jack, dressed as Daphne, carried an enormous load of luggage. All of it captured the interest of Osgood Fielding III, the character played by Joe E. Brown.

The scene was rehearsed without any hitches.

It was time to shoot.

Jack yelled, "Magic Time!" Marilyn closed her eyes, shook her hands at the wrist and told herself to relax. Her husband and Paula were in the wings. In sight. In control.

And Marilyn delivered.

I took it all in, with lingering wide-eyed glances that swept across the scene.

May noticed what I was doing and said, "You can wait around a lifetime, but you'll never see the likes of this again."

"I know. That's why my heart is soaring." I added, "And breaking."

FADE OUT

CHAPTER 79

FADE IN:
- OCTOBER 1, 1958, LAST DAY OF SHOOTING IN CORONADO
- EXTERIOR, HOTEL DEL CORONADO (DAYTIME)

The last big exterior sequence to be shot before the crew's time in Coronado came to an end was across the street from The Del, at Glorietta Bay. Marilyn needed to follow Tony and dash—in heels—down a pier to Tony's character's speedboat. Like before, they had to shoot it as a day-for-night sequence: shot during the day with special filters to simulate night. It was to be the final sequence of the film.

Marilyn was wearing a sheer black dress that, in the previous scene in the ballroom, she sang a torchy ballad in. As noted in the script, at the end of the song, Tony was to step on stage and without uttering a word, take Marilyn in his arms and kiss her.

I helped Marilyn put on a sparkling diamond bracelet. It was so sparkly it made my eyes water. I started singing—in my head— the line for *Diamonds Are A Girl's Best Friend* about Tiffany's, Cartier and Harry Winston.

"It's not real, is it?" I had to ask.

"I'm sure I don't know. But make sure the clasp is tight. I wouldn't want to lose it." Marilyn's eyes grew large. "And I wouldn't want to shake it off either." She began her hand-shaking ritual. It didn't fall off.

"Thanks, honey. Wish me luck."

"Good luck. Oh, not just *good* luck. Great luck."

The cameras began to roll and Marilyn was given the signal to start.

I watched as she scampered down the wooden pier shouting, "Wait for Sugar!" Marilyn nearly flew down two sets of stairs to arrive at the boat. Tony, Jack and Joe were waiting in their seats for her.

She climbed into the boat and Tony asked, "Sugar! What do you think you're doing?"

Marilyn responded, "I told you—I'm not very bright."

I didn't pay attention to see how many takes it took to satisfy Billy. I didn't want to. Counting them would lead to an end. An end of it all.

However, counting or not, Marilyn delivered and Billy accepted.

That was a wrap.

THE wrap.

The crew could pack up.

The cast could head north.

I'd be left behind.

When Marilyn walked back up the pier she stopped and gave me a hug. I had the overwhelming sense of Tilly's movie screen fading to black and the velvet curtain coming down. But this time, it was a scene in my life. Not a movie.

"I wish I'd never met you." I blurted the words out over Marilyn's shoulder.

"But, honey—"

"Oh, I don't mean it *that* way. I meant I don't want it to end. This. All of this. Coronado will never be the same. *I* won't be the same."

Still hugging me, Marilyn replied, "Then come with me."

"No. Really. I couldn't."

"To be honest, I don't want to leave either. But just think of the fun we'd have in Hollywood. Come with me. There's nothing to hold you back here, is there?"

Neither of us spoke.

"Or is there?" Marilyn asked a second time.

"There is."

"Frankie. Am I right?"

"Yes. He's the one. The one for me."

"Then you should stay here." Marilyn hugged me tighter. "*Absolutely,* you should stay here."

"You stay too. We'll figure out a way to make it work. We can—"

"I have to go. Hollywood's waiting for me." She continued softly, "I'm afraid Marilyn is not a Coronado girl...but Norma Jeane could be."

She pulled away and then pulled me back in. She whispered, "Remember me, will you? Please, don't *ever* forget."

I wanted to say, "As long as I breathe, you'll be remembered." But the only word I could whisper back was *never.*

I knew it was the end of something.

But what?

FADE OUT

CHAPTER 80

FADE IN:
- OCTOBER 2, 1958
- INTERIOR, HOTEL DEL CORONADO (DAYTIME)

My suitcase yawned open on the bed and was just about full. An ocean gust made the hotel room's sheer curtains dance. They fell back into place as the wind settled down. My life was about to do the same, although I'd learned new vocabulary words: slate boy, cincher and scene stealer. A bonus word was suppressor, rather than silencer.

I had a sadly familiar feeling, like the one I had while hugging Marilyn the day before…just like when the velvet curtain closes at Tilly's movie theater. Marilyn was gone. Hollywood. Gone. The bright lights and the sneaky shenanigans. Gone. And the closing credits looked and sounded a lot like the cash register that was waiting for me back at the dime store.

I had a brainstorm: what if I wrote my thoughts down on paper. Then they'd be out of my head. Plus, I could crumple them up and throw them away. I grabbed a pen and a sheet of stationery.

"Marilyn: All those unfinished conversations. All those knowing looks you'd give me. Silent signals passed so easily between us. When I'm out on the beach, I miss you. In the morning, in the afternoon, in the evening, I miss you. It's like you took my days and my nights with you and—"

"Package for Miss Parker." My blood turned to ice water. In a flash, my lungs were heavy. Like concrete. I couldn't breathe in. A package? For me? What if it was from Steele? How could that have been? Did he have one ready to go…for delayed delivery?

Three knocks rattled the door. "PENNY, IT'S ME. NICK. I'VE GOT SOMETHING FOR YOU!" Then he whispered, "Open the damned door already."

I fought it, but lost and opened the door. "This time it's for you." Nick grinned. He handed it to me and bowed his head slightly. "And for Chip."

"Thank you ever so much." My voice trailed out. What was I holding? Maybe I should've given it back to him. To take it away.

I sat next to my suitcase. The first envelope was addressed: To Penny Parker, in care of—and to care for—Chip." I broke the seal to reveal a neat stack of one-hundred-dollar bills. A paperclip held the money together, along with a small note in Marilyn's handwriting that read, "This should help. There's always more where this came from."

Then I moved on to the package. Like I'd done so many times before at Marilyn's cottage, I slid the card out of the envelope. I could hear her voice as I read the words she wrote. "I swiped this for you. That makes me a criminal. In the script, when I get this bracelet, I say, 'Real diamonds. They must be worth their weight in gold. Are you always this generous?' Then Tony says, 'Not always. But I want you to know I'm very grateful for what you did for me.' Are they trying to make me and Sugar sound dumb or what? Anyway, I wish it was earrings. I know how much you love them. But I think you'll love this too. I wish it was Tiffany's or Cartier or Harry Winston…and not dime-store diamonds. I will always, always, always miss you, my dear Penny. You know what they say about diamonds, but I think *you're* my best friend."

My hands went weak and fell to my lap. I looked out the window to savor the moment and the sentiment.

I coaxed the small box from its silver-foil wrapping-paper cocoon. After fumbling with the box's spring hinge, I opened it to reveal a stunning diamond bracelet. The one she wore in the last scene on the pier.

It was garish and gaudy.

I could hear Marilyn's breathy voice say, "dime-store diamonds." That was me, a dime-store diamond.

It was *perfect.*

FADE OUT

CHAPTER 81

FADE IN:
- OCTOBER 2, 1958
- INTERIOR, HOTEL DEL CORONADO (DAYTIME)

The last thing to pack was a Ouji board. Why I bought another one and brought it to my room I'd never know. It beckoned me to come to the table. Not teased. Beckoned. I complied. "Okay, one more time. But there's only me here. This will be a solo flight."

I sat on the chair next to the table and placed fingertips from each of my hands on the planchette. "What's next?" Looking up at the ceiling and then closing my eyes, I asked, "What's next for me?"

I filled my lungs and slowly let the air escape. The planchette began to move. I watched the window in the planchette to capture the letters and piece together the words. Once again I asked, "What's next for me?"

The planchette slid over *L*. Then *O*. Even though I was alone, I announced to anyone who might be watching, "I'm not doing this. I'm not pushing this thing. Really."

Then the planchette slid over *V*. Then *E*.

"Holy shit. Is that you, Kate?"

It went over the word *No*.

Chewing my lower lip, I asked, "Um…is that you, Gloria?"

The planchette slid over the word *Yes*. As if it electrocuted me, I took my hands off the planchette and board. I leaned back in my chair. "I wish I could have met you. Chip's a great kid, despite that louse of a husband you picked. Oh, sorry I said that. Damn, what if *he's* listening? What if he's here? Please tell me he's not going to haunt me. Tell me he's not here."

Without me making any physical contact, the planchette made its way over the word *Yes*.

"Does that mean yes, he's here? Or yes, he's not here?"

Under its own power, the planchette moved from *N* to *O* to *T*.

"Whew! The last thing I want is to be haunted by him. Wait a minute, I'm talking to you. Like we're having a conversation." My words dried up, along with all the spit in my mouth. I stood, pulled back the sheer curtain and looked out the window. I pivoted around and laughed. "I can talk to dead people. Not just see them. I CAN TALK TO DEAD PEOPLE!"

Then I talked to the board. "This changes everything. Everything. Will you always be with me?"

The planchette went to the word *No*.

"Will you always be with Chip, wherever he is?"

The planchette did not move.

"Will you come to us and talk to us when we call out to you?"

It moved to *Yes* on the board.

"I can't tell you how much—"

A loud rapping on the door broke our conversation.

"Who is it?"

"It's me, Frankie. Time to go."

"Fine. I'll be right there."

"Say, who were you just talking to? Someone on the phone?"

"No one was on the phone. Well, not on a phone like you and I talk on."

"Huh?"

"Never mind. Let's get out of here."

I laid the Ouji board and planchette in my still-open suitcase. "You're coming with me," I whispered to the board.

My life's script was about to be rewritten yet again...and I never could've guessed what was going to happen next.

FADE OUT

CHAPTER 82

FADE IN:
- OCTOBER 2, 1958
- EXTERIOR, CORONADO BEACH (DAYTIME)

"Is this what life's gonna be like now? Because if it is, I'm going to need to start taking Geritol and fistfuls of vitamins to keep up." I let an exaggerated gust pass my lips as I melodramatically put the back of my palm on my forehead. I was like a balloon without any air in it.

"Beats me. But it sure beats life before Marilyn came to town." Frankie brushed the sand off his bare feet before he put them on the blanket. He sat next to me. His leg immediately began to jiggle, brushing against mine. "Your suitcase, bags and boxes are all in my car."

"Thanks. You're the best. Honestly. You're the best." I put my hand just above his knee cap and squeezed. "And I'll like you even more if you sit still. Just this one time."

He stopped moving and started humming. Quietly at first. Then louder.

"Okay. I'll ask. Why are you humming *Found My Million Dollar Baby at the Five and Ten Cent Store*?"

He grinned.

"Oh." I got it.

I looked out to the surf, the sand, the sun. I breathed it all in. "This has got to be the most beautiful place on earth. I'm never leaving. Never."

Frankie joined me in watching the edge of the ocean kiss the shore, again and again. "You'll get no argument from me."

"It feels like the whole thing was a dream. Well, except that one part." I let my head roll back so my face was in the sun.

"You're gonna miss her, aren't you?" Frankie's words stabbed at me.

"Yes, I am. And I'm going to be afraid for her. She's so fragile."

"You mean broken?"

I considered the word *broken*. After a few beats, I responded. "Not broken. Damaged. And needing to be rescued."

"I'm not sure anyone can rescue her." His words cut more wounds in me. They were truthful. Not unfeeling or uncaring. But full of truth.

"I wouldn't be so sure. Someday, someone will find a way to help Marilyn. Or maybe help Norma Jeane let Marilyn go."

I had no more words or thoughts to share.

We let the surf speak to us, like it had all our lives.

It wasn't long before my words and thoughts needed to be shared again. "I feel like an egg."

Frankie didn't respond right away. "You're hungry for an egg?"

"No, that's not what I mean."

"Okay then. I'm not sure I want to know, but why do you feel like an egg?"

"I'm changed...and I can't change back, even if I wanted to."

"So where's the egg come in?"

"I was raw and in my shell before." I kept my eyes closed as I raised my outstretched arms to the sky. "Now, I'm a sunny-side-up fried egg being lifted out of the frying pan. And—"

"And what?"

"I'm still an egg, but a different version of myself."

"I see what you mean. We're the same, but not the same."

I slid my hand onto his, weaving our fingers together. "When we're a hundred or so years old and I'm still holding your hand, I want to say, 'We made it...to the finish line.' What do you want, Mr. Holland?"

"I want to be waiting at the front of a restaurant and hear the hostess say, 'Holland, party of two, your table is ready.'"

"I want that too." I turned to look at him, but instead another boy stole my attention. It was Chip.

"What are you doing out here?" My voice strained as my throat tightened. "Get your sweet self over here. We've got to—" I stopped speaking when I saw a woman in a skirted, navy-blue suit—holding an official looking briefcase—standing on the paved sidewalk in front of The Del. Behind her, Nick was watching. I mouthed the words *thank you* to him. He waved back and scooted out of sight.

Chip moved toward me, raking his toes through the sand, chin down. He grappled with his sand pail and a shopping bag in the same hand. His other hand was tightened into a fist. The breeze danced in his hair, pushing it in all directions. When he got to the edge of the blanket he looked up, into my eyes. Piercingly. Longingly. He held out his fist.

"What's in your hand, buddy?" I asked casually and flashed back to when he did this in the Crown Room.

Chip raised his chin sharply.

I took that as a sign to lift my hand, confidently putting my open palm under his fist.

Chip's eyes overflowed.

Mine did too.

Frankie's eyes ricocheted between Chip and me.

Chip dropped a shiny-new roll of Lifesavers in my hand. No words were needed. Lifesavers. That's what we were. Frankie and me. Lifesavers.

He dropped the pail and shopping bag and stood there, emptyhanded.

I pulled myself up to my knees and hugged Chip. I hugged him like I'd never hugged anyone before or likely ever would again. My hot tears were joined by erratic breathing. My chest heaved as I sobbed.

Chip broke down.

It was time to say goodbye.

I knew it.

I dreaded it.

"Chip, I met you on this beach and I'm not about to say goodbye here too. I don't ever want to say goodbye to you."

Through my flooded eyes I studied the woman in the much-too-serious, official-looking navy-blue suit.

There had to be a way to keep Chip from going to an orphanage or getting shuffled around in the foster system.

There just *had* to be.

Thoughts screeched in my head like a fork making friends with a garbage disposal.

I whispered to Frankie over Chip's shoulder, "He's got no one."

Frankie put his palm on Chip's back and the other around on mine. "Yes. He does have someone. He has two someones."

"Please." The word sounded weak and rusty.

"Chip, did you just say something?" I eased him back enough to see his face.

"Please…can I stay with you?" He paused. "It would be the wonder-fullest thing ever."

"Oh my God. You're talking!"

Frankie watched with blinking eyes.

"And if you keep me, I'll never stop talking. Ever."

My leaking eyes met Frankie's. I held up the roll of Lifesavers. It shimmered in the sunlight. "Frankie, could we? Could we make it work? Is it time to save another life?"

"I believe it is. No question about it." He grinned and exhaled a puff of air. "I guess I need to change what I said a minute ago."

"What's that?"

"What I want now is to be waiting at the front of a restaurant and hear the hostess say, 'Holland, party of *three*, your table is ready.'"

I grinned back at him. "Three's a good number."

"It's not just a good number," Chip added. "It's the *best* number!"

If my life had a soundtrack, a hallelujah chorus would've cascaded from the heavens.

I ran down the checklist in my head: I got a man. I got a home—Green Gables, no less. I got a movie theater. And most importantly, I got a family of my very own…plus a best, best, best girlfriend.

I turned to face Chip again. "Everything's going to be great—no, perfect. You just wait and see."

Frankie whispered, "Maybe you should say *imperfectly perfect.*"

"You guys, nothing's perfect." Chip glanced down and then back up into my eyes. "Well—*nobody's* perfect."

FADE OUT

EPILOGUE
September 12, 2018

A blustery ocean breeze ushered him through the glass doors of the Coronado Historical Society's lobby. The building's stale smell welcomed him like the scent that's unavoidable in antique stores and a grandmother's attic.

"Hello there. Anything I can help you with today?" The woman behind the reception counter spoke like an old friend, greeting him warmly and making strong eye contact.

"This may sound a bit crazy—" He didn't get to finish his thought.

"Nothing's too crazy to handle around here."

"Alright then," he said as he neared the desk and extended his hand. "Name's Calvin. Cal for short. I'm a writer. My wife and I are staying at The Del, celebrating our anniversary and Valentine's Day. I've had the strangest series of…*things*…happen to me in the past few days. Things are telling me to stop writing the book I'm working on and instead start a new one that takes place at The Del."

"That's not crazy at all. Coronado and The Del speak to many people. They inspire people to do and say things they wouldn't normally do. But how can I help you?"

"I need to learn about this area during the late 1950s. Actually, the fall of 1958."

"You've come to the right place. And the right woman. I was here then. Well, not at this desk, but here in Coronado. I was a senior in high school. The fall you said? That was when

Hollywood came to our own backyard. Actually, it was the beach!"

He smiled and pulled out a pen and writing tablet from his backpack. "I'm thinking my story is going to take place at The Del during the filming of *Some Like It Hot*. Do you have some time to talk now?"

"I volunteer here, so this is my time. And now it's *your* time. Ask away. When we're done, I'll give you my husband's number. You *must* talk to him. He volunteers here too. Should show up any time now. His claim to fame: he kissed Marilyn right out on the beach."

"No way."

"Yes sir, my Billy not only kissed Marilyn but was kissed *by* Marilyn. It's quite a story. You should include it in your book."

Cal took notes in his own sloppy shorthand. He didn't want to be too focused on the tablet or lose the connection he felt with the woman behind the counter.

"I'm sorry. I don't think I got your name."

"It's Bess. Say, you know who else you should talk to, but now you can't since she just passed away. Cancer stole her from us. Damned shame. Anyway, her name was Kathy Clark. She was Miss Coronado in 1958. She may have lost the Miss San Diego County Fair title to that actress from La Jolla, Raquel Welch, but it was Kathy who was picked to be Marilyn Monroe's assistant. She had lots of stories. I remember her telling me how she thought Marilyn was timid and shy, but always thankful for any glass of lemonade or pool towel she brought her. She had a huge crush on Tony Curtis. Kathy was doubly disappointed that she wasn't asked to be his go-to gal...and that he never hit on her!"

The receptionist broke into a disruptive belly laugh. Other people in the lobby turned to look and see what the commotion was about.

"After the filming was done and the Hollywood folks headed up the coast, Kathy became a junior high school teacher. She did that for decades. *Everyone* loved her."

"I'm sorry my timing isn't better." Cal put his pen down.

"You can go to the library up the street. They have truckloads of old stuff. I'm sure there are newspaper articles about Kathy and when the filming was going on."

"Did you watch? The filming, I mean?"

"Sure. Like I said, Billy and I were seniors. The minute school got out in the afternoon, we all came down to the beach to watch. Of course, we came down to the beach most days, filming or not. When the surf was up, we were out. That's where my husband got kissed by Marilyn Monroe. I told you that already, didn't I?"

"Yes." He nodded.

"Let me tell you my version. Then you can compare it with his. He's a bit of a storyteller. Over the years, his version has been— shall we say—embellished."

Cal grinned and readied his pen and paper.

"On one of those afternoons, Billy and his group of guy friends were horsing around on the sand when—"

"Hey there, sweetie. Ready for a break?"

"Billy, I want you to meet Cal. Go on. Tell him about when you got kissed by Marilyn."

Billy reached out and shook the writer's hand.

"Okay. Here goes. I was dared to kiss Marilyn. All the guys pooled their cash and it came to something like fourteen dollars. She saw the commotion the guys were making and came over. At that point, they'd shoved the money in my hands. She asked me what we were up to. I told her the guys had dared me to kiss her and, if I did, I'd get the money. She asked how much they had. I told her. She said that for that much money, *she'd* kiss me and not just have me kiss her. Before anyone could do or say anything, she took me and kind of dipped me down and kissed me on the lips. Everyone applauded and she went back to filming."

"That's incredible." Cal blinked in an exaggerated way.

"I told the guys I'd never wash my face again. Of course, in time, I did."

Bess went on to tell Cal stories about what it was like to be in Coronado in the late '50s: what The Del was like to the local kids; the ever-present naval personnel; the shops and restaurants along Orange Avenue; and the Cornet dime store.

"Thanks for telling me all of this. Fate connected us. I'm sure of it. Just like so many other things in the last few days."

Bess asked, "Did you come across any ghosts yet?"

"Not personally, but I spoke to a clerk in the gift shop who swears Kate keeps knocking down all of the Marilyn Monroe merchandise. She was certain Kate didn't like the competition."

"Sounds about right."

Bess continued, "Have you gone down to Green Gables? There's plenty to learn there too. If you see a woman on the front porch—and she's got some crazy earrings on and answers to the name Penny—tell her what you just told me. She's been waiting for someone special to come along. For a long time, I suspect. She may be ready to tell her stories now. The historical society has been after her for years. But, she's been closed-lipped. We're sure she's got some secrets. Some big secrets."

"I'll go there now. Penny, is that what you said her name is?"

"That's right," Bess replied. "And when you finish your book, bring some copies to us. We'll sell them for you."

"I'm sure we'll talk again soon. Bye for now."

Cal pushed hard on the doors to get out. The ocean winds fought him momentarily. He headed toward the beach and Green Gables. Just as Bess described, a woman was sitting on the porch. Her hair was pulled up into a tight bun. Her crimson-sweatered arms swaddled an ash-grey cat as she looked out to sea.

"Pardon me."

There was no response.

Cal tried again. "Pardon me, ma'am."

The woman looked down her front sidewalk to find the source of the voice.

"Are you Penny? I'm Cal. Bess down at the historical society thought it would be good for me to talk to you about a project I'm working on. It's a novel about the filming of *Some Like It Hot*. I'm hoping it will turn out to be a love story. Could we talk now?"

The woman still didn't respond.

"If not now, is there a better time?"

She focused on him. "You want to know about Marilyn, don't you?"

"Well, yes. But everything must've already been written about her. I can get that by researching online, or going to a library or bookstore. I want to hear about what it was like to be here—and live here—during the filming in 1958. It must've been incredible."

Her eyes were like an FBI agent's, scanning and studying Cal as he continued to talk. "But truth be told, I do want to uncover stories about Marilyn…the real stuff. You know, real people telling real stories. Not a *National Enquirer* story about how she, Elvis and JFK are living the good life in Cuba. Or were abducted by space aliens."

"Come up here and have a seat. Don't mind Ella the Eighth. She's an old girl, but she comes from a proud line of feline companions." She stroked the cat's neck and rubbed its ears. Penny smiled with her eyes and shook her head side to side. Cal watched as the movement made the old lady's mismatched beach-ball and flamingo earrings waltz.

As he climbed the eight steps to the porch he kept his eyes on Penny. He stopped between the seventh and eight step when something in the large picture window stole his attention. In addition to the reflection of the Pacific Ocean beach with its strand of gleaming sand and blurred azure water and sky, Cal watched a stooped-over woman with a walker moving by the window's frame. She'd stopped to fiddle with some pieces of frosted sea glass that were on the lace-covered tabletop, around an overflowing metal sand pail. The sun lit up the glass like a Tiffany lampshade.

He squinted and watched how she ever-so-slightly turned to gaze at him. She tilted her head. Winked with her right eye and fluffed her puffy white hair with her left hand, which she freed from the walker's handle for a few brief moments. Her lips thinned up into a smile…a knowing sort of smile.

"She's there, isn't she?" Penny asked. "Behind me?"

"Yes." He closed his eyes and inhaled. "Chanel No. 5." His eyes opened as he said, "It's my wife's favorite."

From inside the house, the words "He's the one" passed her lips, through the sheer curtain and the window screen.

Penny replied with a question. "You certain?"

"Ever so."

His eyes darted from the woman in the window to the woman in the chair. "Is that—"

"The one and only."

"You mean—" He still hadn't moved from the seventh and eighth steps leading up to the porch.

"It wasn't the Secret Service. It wasn't the Mafia. Not the Kennedys. Not a conspiracy. And it wasn't the drugs."

"It wasn't?"

"She and I became friends—good friends, the very best of friends—long ago. We learned that without her platinum hair, ass-hugging skirts and beauty mark, she could blend in. Hard to believe. I know, I know. She once said she'd love to get away from it all and live a quiet life here someday. When it was time for Marilyn Monroe to go, she went. She went out big time. Not with a poof. But with a bang."

Cal looked at Penny with studying eyes. She reached out her right hand. He focused on it.

"I don't want to shake your hand and send you on your way, if that's what you're thinking. Two crazy old broads living in a beach house with a stash of *Wizard of Oz* stuff. We're not the Wicked Witch of the East or West. We're not Glindas either, though. Frank L. Baum visited here. Frequently. But that's an entirely different story. For another time." She paused. "I just want to hold your hand. Is that alright?"

"Of course it is." She patted his extended left hand. She rubbed it. "Geez your hands are cold."

He shrugged. "Warm heart?"

"I'm—we're—counting on that," Penny said. "You know the saying about how desperate times call for desperate measures? It was never more true for her in Hollywood at the end. With the studios. With her doctors. With her men. All her men. She'd run her marathon. So, in a mish-mash of circumstances, she and her housekeeper made it look like a drug overdose. You'll never guess who's really in her casket." Penny's eyes got big like a goldfish's.

"She's been hiding in plain sight, as they say, and no one's been the wiser. Except for me and my late husband. He went and picked her up in 1962 and brought her here. More than fifty years ago. Imagine that."

"I can't. I mean, I can, now. I guess."

"Where are my manners? You better come up here and sit with me. This is going to take some time."

He slid into the white Adirondack chair and set his backpack down on the porch.

A uniformed mail carrier made his way up the walkway and went right up to the door. "Hey, Mom."

Penny didn't blanche. "Hey, Chip."

"I stopped by the theater and made sure the concession-stand supplies were delivered. Oh, and the new ticket-seller was there training. And before you ask, yes, she had on a few of Tilly's brooches. I told her the story about how she gave you the theater all those years ago."

"All those years ago, pish-posh," the old woman said.

"Anything interesting in the mail today?"

"Yeah." He held up an envelope as he entered the front door. "Another *Some Like It Hot* stamp. Not every day you see Billy Wilder, The Del and you-know-who strumming a ukulele."

Cal looked stunned and Penny didn't miss it. "You mustn't tell anyone. Not yet anyway. After Zelda—that's the name she goes by—is gone, you can. You look like someone I can trust. And I'm an awfully good judge of character."

"Thank you."

"After she's gone, then the end of the story can be told. Her story. It'll be yours to share. Chip and I will be here to back you up."

"Why me? After all this time. I stroll up. Sit down. And you hand this to me?"

"Life does that sometimes." Penny went on, "Something just like this happened one day when I was cashiering at the old dime store. A man from the newspaper told me something that changed my life. Forever."

"Well, I can't believe it. God, no one will believe it."

"They don't have to. You'll know the truth. She's had an unbelievable life. Actually, she's had three lives if you think about it. Before Marilyn, Marilyn and after Marilyn." Penny leaned back in her chair. "People used and used and used her. Others tried to rescue her. In the end, she had to rescue herself. By disappearing. Not in death. But into the shadows. Back to the beach. Back here."

"But—" Cal interrupted his train of thought and looked down the beach at the Hotel del Coronado's adobe red shingled spires and turrets and its blinding white lacey ginger-breaded woodwork.

Penny's eyes followed his. "Nice view, huh? Hasn't changed much, not really. Now sit back. We've got some bombshells to discuss."

THANK YOU FOR READING

Dear Friends:

Thanks for spending time with Penny and Frankie and Marilyn. I hope you enjoyed their journey in *My Friend Marilyn*. There are many movies I can watch over and over again. *Some Like It Hot* is one of them. If you told me even two years ago that I'd write a book that's centered on the making of this film, I'd have laughed. Inspiration can come from anywhere. I'd love to tell you what inspired my current works-in-progress, but you'll just have to wait a little longer.

As a storyteller, my books and my day-to-day life are full of adventures. It would be great to have you be part of them. If you'd like to get to know me better, please connect with me on Facebook at Christopher Lentz or Twitter at @AuthorLentz. Another way to connect is through my website at www.christopherlentz.org.

I'd love to hear what you think about *My Friend Marilyn*. When you have a moment, please help others enjoy my books by leaving a rating and short review at your preferred e-tailer. Feedback from *you* inspires *me*.

I truly believe love changes everything. I hope you agree.

Thanks for reading and, in a way, spending time with me!

Chris

Christopher Lentz

EXCERPT FROM

Blossom

and Blaze

Brock couldn't believe his eyes, and he did nothing to conceal his reaction when he met Blossom at the ladies' shop door. "You...you look incredible. But wait. Don't talk," he instructed. "Just stand there."

"Really, Brock, you're going to do this again?"

Flora, the shopkeeper, squinted at Brock and tilted her head.

He looked to the ground and slowly closed his eyes. With a grin, he announced, "Okay. I've got it."

"Flora," Blossom said in a hushed tone, "this is something he does—well, I've done it too—to capture a moment,"

"Well this definitely is a moment to capture," Flora said with revved up eyelids.

Blossom turned to face Brock. "When I was in this shop and looked in the mirror, I saw the same girl I saw staring back at me in the window of the Tie Yick general store. You know, that day you took me up to Twin Peaks for the first time? Not the Chinatown girl with flour on her face from making fortune cookies. Today, this feels like 'the *real* new me.' Not an imposter in borrowed clothes."

"Well, if I might add," Flora said, "you not only look stunning, but you've learned to move like a real lady. You're going to give Velvette what she's looking for in her shop girls, and then some. You're going to go over like flood water!"

Brock added, "I agree."

"Don't forget to wrap and keep your hair in place while you sleep tonight," Flora said as Brock and Blossom began to leave the storefront.

"I will, and thank you so much."

"Ready for dinner?" Brock reached for Blossom's gloved hand.

"I'm exhausted—and exhilarated—at the same time. Hungry, I'm not so sure. But we better take care of dinner before it gets too late."

"Exhausted *and* exhilarated. Wow," Brock said. "I found a place I hope you'll like. It's called The Cherry Blossom. It's a Chinese restaurant, just around the corner. Sound good?"

"Yes, actually it does. I've never gone this long without rice and chop sticks...and fortune cookies."

Brock grinned when she said "fortune cookies."

*****

The Cherry Blossom's décor was nothing like its counterparts in what used to be San Francisco's Chinatown before the earthquake and fire. But just the same, the familiar smell of broth and fried vegetables stirred Blossom's senses and memories.

"Two, please," Brock said to the white-aproned man who greeted them at the door.

"Very best table for you here by window," he asked in broken English. "You have Chinese food before? Need help to understand menu?"

"I think we'll be alright with the menu," Blossom said.

"Good, good, good, ma'am. I be back to take order soon."

While Blossom and Brock had eaten in a few restaurants since they left San Francisco, this was the first time a restaurant felt homey.

After they'd ordered and silently studied the restaurant and its customers, Blossom asked, "See her over there in the yellow dress and green hat?"

"Yes."

"Her name's Paulette Smythe...not Smith. She does secretarial work for the mayor at City Hall. However, she has *eyes* for a police officer named Bruno." Blossom winked at Brock when the word "eyes" passed her lips.

"Really! You don't say!" Brock said playfully. Blossom nodded as if she was adding an exclamation point to the end of her previous statement.

Their order arrived in no time at all and it was greeted by the couple's grins. To Blossom, it was more of a home-cooked meal than restaurant food. She lifted her chopsticks and scooped a heaping amount of steamed rice. Her eyes slowly closed as she chewed it, savoring its taste and texture.

About midway through the meal, Brock said, "See that man in the booth with the blue tie on? His name is Waldo Potts, and he's a professor at the college. He teaches English Literature and he's just about to finish writing his first novel. It's a love story. As you might guess from his unkept appearance and lack of social graces, he's never been in love before. That should make the novel quite interesting. Or not."

"Oh, I couldn't agree more!"

The two went on making up stories based on imaginary backgrounds and circumstances of the people around them. They'd played this game in eateries and along the road as they travelled to Pasadena.

Brock yawned. "Let's get back to our home away from home. We're both going to need a good night's sleep. No nightmares tonight, right?"

"I'll try my best, but no promises."

"Tomorrow's going to be a turning point for us. I just know it. Everything's going to change for the better. You'll see."

"Not everything."

"What do you mean?"

"One thing couldn't get any better." She reached across the table and intertwined her fingers with his. "Us."

The waiter brought their bill on a small plate with two fortune cookies and some orange slices. "You have fortune cookie before? Some say Japanese make first. I say fortune cookies Chinese...come from China."

As Blossom was about to answer, he added, "Must be offered to you so you pick your own destiny."

"Oh really?" she replied with widened eyes.

"We just started giving cookies out." He paused with a sense of pride in offering what he thought must be a "first" in the Los Angeles area.

Blossom added, "I've never seen such a thing before." *I've only spent a lifetime making about a million of them by hand and stuffing those paper strips in each and every one of them,* she thought.

"Well then, I must pick wisely," she said. "Shay Shay."

"You speak Chinese?" The waiter's voice had a sparked sense of interest.

"Oh, no. I just know how to offer my thanks and appreciation. We had a Chinese maid when I was a child." She'd betrayed her Chinese upbringing. In a Chinese restaurant, no less. Her physical transformation—and the way she embraced her just-discovered Irish heritage—was coming together.

The waiter bowed respectfully and left the couple.

Brock opened his wallet to pay the bill. He pulled out the fortune Blossom gave him the very first time they met at The Golden Palace...when she was making cookies.

He read it aloud, "Confucius say, 'Wherever you go, go with all of your heart.'"

Blossom glanced down. She held back tears of joy by blinking rapidly like the fluttering of two painted-paper fans.

"I came to you with all of my heart," Brock said with clarity and confidence. "Now it's yours. And it always will be."

But would it? He left his fiancée to be with me, she thought. *Could I ever really trust him? My heart says 'yes.' But my head's not so sure.*

She gazed into Brock's eyes. "And my heart is yours too." Unlike Brock's confession of eternal love, Blossom omitted "and it always will be." Would she come to regret that?

This is an excerpt from *Blossom and Blaze, Book Two of The Blossom Trilogy,* by Christopher Lentz. It may not reflect the book's final content.

READING GROUP QUESTIONS

These suggested questions are offered to help you and your reading-group members discuss *My Friend Marilyn*. Though the story takes place more than half of a century ago, there's much to relate and react to today.

1. How did your family—as you were growing up—define "beautiful"?

2. Has "The F Word" ("fat," that is) ever been used to describe you? What about "bag-of-bones" or "bean pole"? How did it feel?

3. Do you think you would have been successful as Marilyn Monroe's personal assistant in 1958? Why? If not, why?

4. How and why do you think men and women view their body images differently? Do the media, peer groups and Hollywood feed that difference?

5. We often don't see the world as it is. For good and not-so-good reasons. Sometimes the stories we tell *ourselves* prove that. Do you think Penny is delusional? Is she as confident and together as she wants everyone else to believe? Why do you think that?

6. How would you describe the relationships between:
   - Penny and Frankie
   - Penny and Marilyn
   - Penny and Steele
   - Penny and Chip
   - Penny and Tilly
   - Penny and Trudy
   - Penny and her parents

7. Have you experienced a close friendship that moved beyond friendship? How did it turn out?

8. Penny fell hard for Steele. It blinded her to some important signals. Have you or anyone you've known slipped into this kind of romantic situation? How did it turn out?

9. Penny and Marilyn came from different worlds. What do you think brought them closer than employer and employee?

10. Marilyn and Tilly came from the same world. How do you think Marilyn reacted to the choices Tilly made by leaving the screen and becoming part of the business of showbiz?

11. Do you think Penny and Marilyn would have ended up with the same kind of relationship had they met under other circumstances?

12. Penny got what she longed for: a man, a home and a family of her own making. Do you think that was enough to make her happy?

13. Penny also longed for a best, best, best girlfriend. She got more than one friend. Who were they?

14. Do you think this novel should have ended differently? How would you have wrapped up the story?

A CONVERSATION WITH CHRISTOPHER LENTZ

Why did you choose to write this story?
It wasn't a choice as much as it was a need. I was in the middle of writing The Blossom Trilogy series of historical romances when karma or fate or destiny pushed this project at me. And there were too many signs to ignore. So, I shifted gears.

First, my wife and I were staying at The Del, celebrating Valentine's Day. We walked over to the Coronado Historical Society's museum and met a man who was kissed by Marilyn Monroe, on the beach, during the filming in 1958. He told me his story. My imagination took it from there. That was the spark that lit the blaze!

Back at the hotel, a shop clerk told me about ghosts moving and throwing things in the store. I bought a book about the history of the hotel and began writing out on our room's sunny balcony.

Then, back at home, karma kept pushing. My daughter, Allison, and I were at Disneyland, waiting in a line as you often do at the Magic Kingdom. I struck up a conversation with a woman who turned out to be the only female concierge at The Del. And on her cellphone, she showed me photos of ghostly guests at the hotel.

Finally, I knew I had to write this novel when I was roaming an antique store in Orange, California. A book about Marilyn Monroe was being showcased on a bookshelf. I already had a stack of books about her, so I didn't reach for it immediately. But when I pulled back the cover of *Marilyn: Norma Jeane,* I discovered how it was dedicated: "To Chris." It was signed by journalist-feminist Gloria Steinem and photographer George Barris, who's well-known for taking the last photo of Marilyn on July 13, 1962.

Some things you best not ignore. And because I didn't, you got to read this story.

What's your "elevator pitch" for this novel?
When people ask what *My Friend Marilyn* is about, I say it does two things. First, it explores the unique kind of friendship that forms between women. Second, it explores body-image issues that everyone faces whether they're famous or not.

Then I add, the story is about—in an imaginary way—an unlikely and unbreakable bond between Marilyn Monroe and a Melissa McCarthy-ish woman. To make that description a bit tighter, I say it's a mash up of *Some Like It Hot* and *Bridesmaids*. That pretty much always gets the desired ah-ha nod!

Do you like or hate doing research for your books?
I don't just like it. I *love* it. I've always been the kind of person who was drawn to old people and talking about "the olden days." Not because I wanted to live then, but because we can learn so much by hearing about them. Not to mention, appreciate what we have today.

When I'm researching a place or character, I can't wait to dive into "History's Dumpster." There are treasures a plenty for those who like the hunt. It all makes the storytelling richer.

Why ANOTHER book about Marilyn Monroe?
This novel is not about Marilyn. It's not a high-gloss love letter to the memory of Hollywood's most explosive bombshell. It's Penny's story, with Marilyn helping her realize who her real friends are. This book falls in the historical-fiction category. That's because it's based on history—real people, real events, real locations—but the story, for the most part, is made up.

I've heard it said that memories can be more like prisms than panes of glass. When people look back at Marilyn, they often see what they *want* to see. And that's not always positive or kind. I wanted to show her making a real connection with another woman. Someone she could talk to and go on unexpected adventures with. That's why she and Penny have so much fun, as well as pull each other through some tragic situations.

Marilyn had to be more than the breathless blonde who appeared on screen. I wanted this story to focus on how she might've lived, rather than how she died.

Who would be in your dream cast of the filmed version of **My Friend Marilyn?**

Many authors say they write their stories with celebrities in mind to help them visualize their characters. And, I suspect, sometimes authors think of these stars as members of the fantasy cast for filmed versions of their books.

I don't normally work that way. But this time I did. For me, Melissa McCarthy *is* Penny Parker. Her comedic timing and delivery, along with her vibrant sassiness shaped Penny. I even had a photo of her in the corner of my laptop screen when I was writing. I admit it.

I never thought of anyone but Marilyn when I was writing her fictional lines of dialogue or when I was describing her. She was—and is—a one-and-only.

Steele Wright was inspired by the way Rock Hudson looked in his heyday, while Frankie Holland and Richard Chamberlain had a lot in common in my 1950s-mind's eye. I should point out that my mother had a major crush on Richard Chamberlain "back in the day," so that's kind of a shout out to her.

That would be my dream cast, with great emphasis on the word *dream*.

Isn't the last line of **My Friend Marilyn** *the same as the film's last line?*

Yes, it's the same. "Well—nobody's perfect" is such an iconic piece of Hollywood dialogue that I knew I had to find a way to use it to wrap up my story too.

Ironically, the line was only meant to be a placeholder—a throwaway line—in the script until Billy Wilder and I.A.L. Diamond came up with something funnier.

They never did.

And those three words become what most film historians would call the most famous last words.

Do you have any personal connections to your characters?

Yes. All authors do, whether they admit it or not. My strongest connections are to Penny and Frankie. I've been both of those characters. It's a Goldilocks kind of thing. In elementary school, I was Penny. Too heavy. Too slow. Bullied. Last to be picked for a team, and that was understandable. Now. Not then.

During the summer of seventh grade, I became Frankie. Too thin. Bullied. Still last to be picked for a team, but for another set of reasons. It looked as if I'd break, like the see-through unicorn in *The Glass Menagerie*.

So, who's "just right" in the story? I bet you'd think Marilyn was. But I'm pretty sure she wasn't.

During my life, I've worn JCPenney's "Husky Pants" as a kid and skin-tight Angel's Flight polyester disco pants in my twenties. And daddy jeans too.

What's important to realize is that no matter what size I was, I was me. And had I not looked in the mirror over the years and seen the reflection of different versions of me, I don't think I could've told Penny's and Frankie's story very well.

Why have a plus-size protagonist?

All good stories have conflict and tension of some kind. For this story, I wanted an outwardly confident fluffy girl to make friends with the most beautiful woman on the planet...who, by the way, had major body-image issues.

You never say what size Penny is or how much she weighs. How come?

I want readers to see Penny the way *they* want to see her. If I wrote she weighed two-hundred pounds or one-hundred-and-fifty pounds, would it make any real difference? It's Penny's perceptions about body image and beauty that matter.

She tells us she's overweight and always has been. This battle is hers.

But, in fact, it's everyone's. No matter what your size or weight, I'd bet dollars to donuts (perhaps a bad phrase to use) you wish you were a size smaller or a few pounds lighter. We share Penny's experience and, hopefully, chuckle with her when she's making fun of herself.

And here's something to consider: What if Penny wasn't obese? Only muffin-top thick-waisted? What if she's an unreliable narrator? What if it was only in her mind? What if it was just how *she* perceived the world and her place in it?

Did you learn anything new about Marilyn while you were researching the book?

Lots of it's in the book, but what I couldn't smoothly incorporate includes:

- When she was younger, she feared blemishes so much that she washed her face fifteen times a day
- She never graduated high school
- She used petroleum jelly as a moisturizer, as well as Nivea
- She thought the right side of her face was best
- She wore glasses
- She often didn't wear undergarments in public and when she was home, she preferred to wear nothing but a bathrobe
- According to her dressmakers, her measurements were 35-22-35; she was five feet five-and-one-half inches tall; her bra size was 36D; she weighed between 115-120 pounds
- In 1946 alone, she tried nine different shades of blonde hair color before settling on platinum
- She was known to sip vermouth out of a red coffee thermos while on set

Were you tempted to include real quotes from Marilyn Monroe?
I considered it, but because this is a work of fiction, I chose not to, with the exception of a few that I altered slightly.

Here are some quotes I came across that are pretty telling about the woman she was:

- "I'm selfish, impatient and a little insecure. I make mistakes, I am out of control and at times hard to handle. But if you can't handle me at my worst, then you sure as hell don't deserve me at my best."
- "I believe that everything happens for a reason. People change so that you can learn to let go, things go wrong so that you appreciate them when they're right, you believe lies so you eventually learn to trust no one but yourself, and sometimes good things fall apart so better things can fall together."
- "Hollywood is a place where they'll pay you a thousand dollars for a kiss and fifty cents for your soul."
- "If you're going to be two-faced at least make one of them pretty."

- "It's better to be unhappy alone than unhappy with someone."
- "All little girls should be told they are pretty, even if they aren't."
- "I don't mind living in a man's world, as long as I can be a woman in it."
- "It's not true that I had nothing on. I had the radio on."
- "If I'd observed all the rules I'd never have got anywhere."
- "What do I wear in bed? Why, Chanel No. 5, of course."

There are some wild rumors about Marilyn Monroe. Which ones intrigued you the most?

For decades, people have been fascinated by and have fantasized about Marilyn Monroe. I wouldn't be telling the truth if I didn't admit to being a member of that special club. But when I started writing *My Friend Marilyn*, I knew I wanted to tell a story about who she was—and could've been—with a happy ending. But not necessarily a storybook happily ever after.

This is a novel. Not a biography. Not a memoir. Not a tell-all. So, it includes truths, half-truths and not-truths. It explores what-ifs and offers an alternate ending.

However, I did run across some amazing claims about the star's life and death. I avoided them, but some are just too intriguing not to mention:

- From her earliest days, she was rejected, neglected and abused. She was only 12 days old when her mother, Gladys, couldn't afford to quit her job as a film cutter for a movie studio. A schizophrenic who was institutionalized on and off throughout her adult life, Gladys handed her baby over to virtual strangers, paying them $5 a week to look after Marilyn.
- While still in a foster home, she was raped, got pregnant and delivered a baby boy. The child was whisked away.
- In a town where looks reign supreme, starlets and full-fledged stars alike go to extremes to change their faces. It's been reported that Marilyn had a nose job, a chin implant and breast augmentation, as well as electrolysis to remove her widow's peak.
- She'd long been in the crosshairs of ruthless FBI director

J. Edgar Hoover, especially after she got involved in a dizzying round of musical beds with the three Kennedy brothers.

- Frank Sinatra was her protector, playmate and even her pimp.

- She was known to have had sexual encounters with Joan Crawford, Marlene Dietrich, Judy Garland, Barbara Stanwyck and Elizabeth Taylor.

- The final weekend of her life was a nightmare of emotional collapse, loneliness and betrayal. She'd been fired by her studio, rejected by her lover Robert Kennedy and thrown out of a party given by her friend Frank Sinatra.

- She knew better than to kiss and tell. But when she threatened to break Hollywood's golden rule, Bobby Kennedy and his bodyguards reportedly attempted to silence her with a barbiturate-laced enema. She didn't die. Kennedy quickly helicoptered to San Francisco and ordered Marilyn's psychiatrist, Dr. Ralph Greenson, to finish her off. He came to her house and administered a fatal shot of barbiturates directly into her heart.

- Ex-husband Joe DiMaggio was planning to propose to her again. Lovesick and devastated by her death, he banned the Kennedys, Frank Sinatra and many Hollywood cronies from her funeral. For decades, he had fresh-cut red roses delivered to her grave three times a week. He died in 1999 and his last words were, "I'll finally get to see Marilyn."

The movie had another name and almost had a different cast, right?
Penny's background binder notes that until August, the film was referred to as *Fanfares of Love* and then *Not Tonight, Josephine*. In August 1958, United Artists got a waiver from MCA to use the title *Some Like It Hot* (the title had been used for a 1939 Paramount Film), from the line in the child's nursery rhyme.

The primary cast was to include Tony Curtis, Frank Sinatra and Mitzi Gaynor. Ultimately, the casting team brought together the winning combination of a sex symbol (Marilyn Monroe), a matinee idol (Tony Curtis) and an emerging comic (Jack

Lemmon).

Did L. Frank Baum write books while in Coronado?
Yes, he visited the area a number of times between 1904 and 1910. He would stay at the Hotel del Coronado for months at a time. It's believed that he wrote at least three books in his popular Oz series at The Del. They include: *Dorothy and the Wizard of Oz, The Road to Oz* and *The Emerald City.*

Why did you include a mute character in the story?
I needed a way to show—not just tell—how much Chip was impacted by the actions of his parents.

Chip's silence was inspired by a video I came across, in which poet Maya Angelou tells about being raped as a child by someone her family knew. The rapist was found dead, appearing to have been kicked to death. When she learned this, she stopped talking for five years. She said that with the logic of a seven-and-a-half-year old, she thought he died because she spoke his name.

She said that out of evil there can come good. In those five years, she read every book at her black school's library and whatever books she could get from the white school's library. Not Mother Goose rhymes, but the works of Shakespeare, Longfellow, Poe, Kipling and Balzac. She memorized much of it.

When she decided to speak, she had a lot to say. And many ways to say it. She said she was saved in her muteness. She was able to draw from human thought and disappointment and triumph…enough to triumph herself.

That's what I wanted readers to come away with after they met and got to know sweet—but oh-so-traumatized—Chip.

Why include the Archie comic book?
I never spent much time with Archie comic books. I did watch *The Archie Show* cartoon in the late 1960s. I included it in the book as another way of connecting readers with the past, and beginning to show the creepier side of Steele.

It's worth noting that Archie first appeared in Pep Comics #22 in 1941. It was hoped by his creators that he'd appeal to fans of the Andy Hardy movies that starred Mickey Rooney.

Where did Trudy Vanderhooven come from?

I was raised in Detroit. My wife's family is from Wisconsin. As a result, we spend time each summer in the upper Mid-West and soak up all of its color and quaintness. The Scandinavian influences are inescapable. And the kitchens of many homes are equipped with Lutheran church cookbooks that are regularly the sources of savory hot dishes and creamy tapioca puddings.

I thought a displaced Mid-Westerner would make an interesting landlady and lunch-counter waitress at the Southern California dime store Penny works at. That's how Trudy was born. The recipes in the back of this book came from vintage church cookbooks. Go on and give them a try!

What or who inspired Tilly the ticket seller at The Village Theatre?

I worked at Disneyland in the 1970s and 1980s. Tilly is the mannequin who's always ready to take your coins at the turn-of-the-20th century Main Street Cinema. However, the multiple screens in the classic movie palace entertain all who enter, free of charge. No tickets required. Like all "cast members" at Disneyland, Tilly's nametag features the name of her hometown: Marceline, Missouri. Not-so-coincidentally, that happens to be Walt Disney's boyhood hometown.

Her character grew in importance as I developed the story. I needed a character to counterbalance Marilyn in terms of Hollywood and history. Showcasing a silent-film star who bolted out of Hollywood in her prime could force Marilyn to take a harder look at her career and its trajectory.

As a side note, the fortuneteller at the Mexican Village in the story is named after the mechanical fortuneteller at the Main Street Arcade: Esmeralda.

Is the Hotel del Coronado as incredible as it sounds?

I think so. My wife and I spent our wedding night there, and many anniversaries since then. This book resulted from a Valentine's Day stay in 2016. But that's another story.

As for The Del, it's like a living, breathing thing. And I'm not talking about the creaking wood floors. When you enter the lobby, it's like The Del warmly embraces you…offering a welcoming hug. It invites you to get comfortable, like it does to its lingering spirits who are shrouded in mystery. I've never felt unsafe there, and I've never felt alone there either. Cool, huh?

Here are some interesting things about the hotel that aren't mentioned in the book:

- When it opened on February 19, 1888, nearly every room had a fireplace and a wall safe
- It was the largest structure outside of New York City to be electrically lighted
- Two million shingles were used for roofs and siding
- Fourteen-thousand barrels of cement were used to create the hotel's foundation

You wrote about a flat tire caused by a fork in the road...a literal fork. Where did that come from?

It wasn't imaginary. It happened to me in high school, on the way home from the beach one summer afternoon on California Interstate 5 in Santa Ana.

The last thing you *ever* want to hear when you're speeding down the highway (which is a rare thing to be able to do in Southern California) is a disturbing thwack-a-thwack-a-thwack sound coming from your car. But, sure enough, there was a fork stuck right into the rubber of the tire. It smacked the wheel well and fender with each revolution.

I didn't keep the fork, like Penny does in the story, which is odd because I'm a near hoarder-status "keeper" of things.

On some websites, this book is categorized as "historical fiction with romantic elements." Does that mean you made things up?

Yes, it does. I took some plausible liberties to suit this story. And, I did a little time-bending too. I had to for storytelling purposes. Two iconic toys are referenced right off the bat in the first chapter. But they hadn't reached phenomenon status yet in September of 1958 when this book takes place.

For you toy fanatics out there, the Etch A Sketch wasn't mass marketed until Christmas of 1960. It was invented in France and called The Magic Screen. It's the result of the clinging properties of an electrostatic charge that holds a mixture of aluminum powder and tiny plastic beads to the inside of the clear plastic screen. When turned over and shaken, the screen is erased.

Barbie wasn't introduced until March of 1959. Here are few fun facts about her that I discovered during a dive in "History's

Dumpster:"

- Mattel has sold more than one billion Barbie dolls
- She was inspired by a German doll called "Lilli" that was produced beginning in 1955
- Ruth Handler, wife of Mattel's co-founder, bought several Lilli dolls in 1956 while in Europe
- It was Ruth who suggested to her husband, Elliot, that there was a marketplace need for dolls that weren't infants; her idea of an adult-bodied doll was a winner
- Barbie got her name from the daughter of Ruth Handler: Barbara
- Barbie's full name is Barbara Millicent Roberts
- Barbie was first sold for $3 in a black-and-white striped one-piece swimsuit, with her signature topknot ponytail in either blonde or brunette versions
- Her doll clothes were hand-stitched by Japanese workers
- It didn't take long for complaints to be registered about her unattainable body proportions and the unrealistic body image she created in the minds of children
- In human terms, Barbie stands five feet and nine inches tall and weighs 110 pounds (about 30 pounds too light), with measurements 36-18-33 inches
- She's not from Malibu; the fictional town of Willows, Wisconsin, is where she's from
- Barbie was originally a seventeen-year-old "teenage fashion model," but she's had more than 130 careers including nurse, teacher, astronaut, rapper, McDonald's cashier and president of the United States
- She has seven siblings in all: Skipper, Stacie, Chelsea, Krissy, Kelly, Tutti and Todd
- Her boyfriend, Ken, was introduced in 1961; his full name is Kenneth Carson, son of Dr. Carl and Edna Carson
- Ken has never officially married Barbie, though plenty of wedding dresses and miniature wedding cakes have been produced and played with over the years
- Barbie has never been pregnant, only her best friend Midge has
- Barbie's first African-American girlfriend, Christie, came on the scene in 1967, followed by her African-American

boyfriend, Brad, in 1968

Some Like It Hot *went on to become a fan favorite. Did it win any awards?*
It received six Academy Award nominations in 1960, winning one for best costume design. It also got three Golden Globe nominations and won all three categories, including Marilyn Monroe for Best Actress in a Motion Picture—Comedy or Musical.

The romantic romp was voted the number-one comedy of all time by the American Film Institute and named number fourteen on its list of the 100 Greatest Movies.

Marilyn was widely known for being difficult to work with. But reports show she was at the top of her game while shooting at The Del. Is that true?
In his book *Conversations with Wilder* (1999), writer/director Cameron Crowe addressed this aspect of the film with the director, saying: "I grew up in San Diego [and] the legend is that the hotel was the most magical part of the filming...that Marilyn felt relaxed there." To which, Billy Wilder replied, "...that was fun. We had a good time there. Marilyn remembered her lines...everything was going according to schedule."

As another source noted, Wilder speculated that Monroe was inspired at The Del—where adoring spectators were plentiful—because she preferred a live audience.

Is there any truth to the gossip about how Marilyn used to think "Marilyn Monroe" was a character or another person?
When I was doing research, I came across a story told by Truman Capote. He recalled a lunch at which Marilyn disappeared to the bathroom and was gone so long he went looking for her. He found her staring at the mirror. When he asked her what she was doing, she responded, "Looking at her."

Also, Susan Strasberg recalled a moment while she and Marilyn were walking through New York City. They'd been relatively unbothered most of the day. Amazingly, no one seemed to notice the blonde bombshell in public, which Susan found odd.

At one point, Marilyn turned to Susan and said, "Do you want to see me be her?" Susan recalled, "She seemed to make some inner adjustment, something 'turned on' inside her, and suddenly—there she was—not the simple girl I'd been strolling with, but 'Marilyn Monroe.' Now heads turned. People crowded around us."

Is the movie's filming a celebrated milestone in The Del's history?

Hotel del Coronado has hosted *Some Like It Hot* events, including the film's 25th anniversary in 1984 (with Billy Wilder, Tony Curtis and Jack Lemmon in attendance); the Marilyn Monroe U.S. postal stamp dedication in 1995; and the film's 50th anniversary in 2009, when Tony Curtis, the last-surviving star of the film, was joined by some of the original "girls in the band."

I heard there's a Lucy connection with The Del. Is that true?

The hotel was instrumental in helping launch the careers of some television giants. Lucille Ball and Desi Arnaz retreated to The Del in 1950 to polish their comedy routine under the direction of "Pepito the Spanish Clown," a renowned vaudeville performer. They stayed at the hotel for a couple of weeks, where they also developed their "Ricky and Lucy" personas: the serious Cuban bandleader to her zany star-struck wife. They then took their show on the road, eventually landing their own television program, *I Love Lucy*. In one episode, the couple stay at The Del with Fred and Ethel Mertz.

The hotel's ghost stories are real, right?

I kept the stories about Kate Morgan as close to how they've been reported as possible. There are entire books written just about her. Here's a quick version of her story.

Kate Morgan, age 24, arrived on Thanksgiving Day of 1892, alone and unhappy. She registered as Lottie A. Bernard from Detroit. According to hotel employees, she said she was waiting for a gentleman to join her. After five lonely days, Kate was found dead. Police could find nothing to positively identify her, so a description of Kate was telegraphed to police agencies around the country. As a result, newspapers began to refer to Kate as the "beautiful stranger." After her identity was confirmed—she was married, but estranged from her husband—it was concluded she'd arrived at The Del hoping to rendezvous with a lover.

Kate had been employed as a domestic in a wealthy Los Angeles household. From there, she traveled by train to the hotel, where fellow passengers reported that a woman matching Kate's description had argued with a male companion, who then deserted her en route. During her stay, Kate was described as sickly and sorrowful, venturing into San Diego to buy a handgun. The San Diego coroner later confirmed that Kate had died from a self-inflicted gunshot wound.

The story of Kate Morgan continues to intrigue hotel visitors, and the third-floor room in which she stayed is the most requested guestroom at the hotel. Independent paranormal researchers have documented supernatural activity in Kate's room using high-tech gadgetry, including infrared cameras, night-vision goggles, radiation sensors, toxic-chemical indicators, microwave-imaging systems and high-frequency sound detectors.

There have been Kate sightings in hotel hallways and along the seashore.

Another very "active" area is the resort's gift shop, called Est. 1888, where visitors and employees routinely witness giftware mysteriously flying off shelves, oftentimes falling upright and always unbroken.

You have Hotel del Coronado artifacts in your home, don't you?
As I mentioned earlier, The Del has been part of some great highpoints in my life. Naturally, being an antique collector, I have some old stuff from the hotel including: a set of dishes and flatware (all bearing the hotel's signature crown hallmark); postcards, booklets and brochures; and a white-wicker chair from a guest room in the 1920s. I referenced it in this book!

ACKNOWLEDGEMENTS

Here are some of the resources, in book form, that I enjoyed and hope you may too:

- *Beautiful Stranger, The Ghost of Kate Morgan and the Hotel del Coronado* by Hotel del Coronado Heritage Department; *2002*
- *Billy Wilder's Some Like It Hot* by Alison Castle, Taschen; 2010
- *Hotel del Coronado History* by Hotel del Coronado Heritage Department; *2013*
- *Marilyn: Norma Jeane* by Gloria Steinem and George Barris; Henry Hold and Company; 1986
- *Marilyn on Location* by Bart Mills; Pan Books; 1989
- *Some Like It Hot, The Official 50ᵗʰ Anniversary Companion* by Laurence Malson; HarperCollins; 2009
- *The Making of Some Like It Hot, My Memories of Marilyn Monroe and the Classic America Movie* by Tony Curtis with Mark A. Vieira; John Wiley & Sons, Inc.; 2009

CHERISHED RECIPES FROM THE KITCHEN OF TRUDY VANDERHOOVEN

At the request of readers, a selection of Midwestern recipes appears below. They were used by Penny Parker's landlady, Trudy Vanderhooven. While Trudy is a work of fiction, these recipes are time-tested treasures from St. Olaf's Church Ladies Association's cookbook. Enjoy!

Bologna Toasties (from Mrs. Lars Petrovich, Lydia)
- ¾ pound bologna
- 1/3 cup sweet pickle relish
- 1/3 cup mayonnaise
- 1 tablespoon mustard
- 8 slices white bread, buttered
- 8 slices pineapple (canned/drained)

Cut and shred meat. Mix with relish, mayo and mustard in a bowl. Spread ¼ cup on each buttered slice of bread. Add slice of pineapple. Heat slowly on electric grill/griddle or frying pan.

Heavenly Hash (by Mrs. Sven Swenson, Ida)
- 1 large package chocolate chips, melted
- 1 10-ounce package miniature marshmallows
- 1 package Chinese noodles
- 1 4-ounce bag sunflower nutmeats
- 1 cup raisins (optional)

Mix together and drop by tablespoon onto wax paper. Let cool and put into tightly covered container.

Wild Rice Hot Dish (by Mrs. Eugene Lundquist, Doris)
- 2 cups wild rice

- ½ pound bacon, cut in pieces
- ½ cup butter
- 1 cup celery, chopped
- 1 cup onion, chopped
- 1 can cream of mushroom soup

Soak wild rice in warm water overnight. Wash several times. Drain. Boils 3 quarts of water, add rice and bring to boil. Turn off and let stand covered for 10 minutes. Drain. Fry bacon, butter, celery and onions. Combine rice, bacon mixture and soup. Bake 40 minutes at 350 degrees uncovered.

Baked Tuna Fish and Noodles (by Mrs. Alfred Kollmorgen, Esther)

- 1 4-ounce package egg noodles (cooked in salted water)
- 1 can cream of mushroom soup (diluted with an equal quantity of diluted canned milk)
- ½ teaspoon celery salt
- 1 pimiento (chopped, optional)
- 2 teaspoons onion, grated
- 1 7-ounce can tuna fish
- 1 can peas

In a buttered casserole, alternate layers of drained noodles, tuna fish and peas with a layer of noodles on top. Pour cream of mushroom soup to which celery salt, pimiento and onion have been added, over all. Cover top with fine buttered bread crumbs or crushed potato chips. Bake in oven at 350 degrees for 30-40 minutes until bubbly.

Ginger Ale Jello Salad (by Mrs. Bud Olsen, Molly)

- 1 package lemon Jello
- 1 cup boiling water
- 1 cup ginger ale
- 1 ½ cup mixture of cucumbers, peaches, apricots, marshmallows, pineapple and walnuts

Dissolve Jello in boiling water. Cool. Add ginger ale before it starts to gel. When partly gelled, add mixture of vegetables, fruit and nuts. Stir and pour into aluminum or copper mold of your choice. Refrigerate. Before serving, place leafy lettuce and upside-down plate on top of mold. Flip and serve.

Pineapple Icebox Surprise (by Mrs. Ernie Engebretseon, Lydia)

- 40 vanilla wafers
- ½ cup butter
- 1 cup powdered sugar
- 2 eggs
- 1 cup cream (whipped)
- 1 cup crushed pineapple (may substitute with thawed frozen strawberries)

Crush wafers. Spread 1/3 in bottom of buttered 8-inch square pan. Cream butter and sugar. Add eggs, 1 at a time, and continue creaming. Spread this carefully over the crumbs. Cover with second 1/3 of crumbs. Cover this with the pineapple, then the whipped cream. Cover with remaining crumbs. Refrigerate overnight. Cut into squares.

Trudy's Tasty Tapioca Pudding (by Mrs. Vernon Vanderhooven, Trudy)

- 3 cups whole milk
- 1/3 cup small-pearl tapioca (not instant)
- 1/2 cup granulated sugar
- 2 large egg yolks, lightly beaten
- 1 vanilla bean, split lengthwise, seeds scraped and reserved
- 1/8 teaspoon fine salt

Place 1 cup of the milk and the tapioca pearls in a medium saucepan and stir to combine. Let the pearls soak uncovered at room temperature for 1 hour. Add the remaining 2 cups of milk, sugar, egg yolks, vanilla seeds and salt. Stir to combine. Place the pan over medium heat and cook. Whisk frequently, until the mixture just comes to a simmer, about 10 minutes (do not let the mixture boil). Reduce the heat to low and cook. Whisk frequently, until the mixture thickens and the tapioca pearls are softened and translucent, about 15 minutes. Serve warm (the pudding will thicken as it cools) or chill in the refrigerator.

Desperation Hot Dish (Mrs. Edwin Kolstad, Selma)
- 2 cups cooked macaroni
- 1 pound hamburger (ground)
- 1 can whole kernel corn
- 1 can kidney beans
- 1 can tomato soup
- Spices (to taste)

Mix all together, heat thoroughly. Any vegetable may be added in addition to above or in place of. Can be ready to eat in 15 minutes.

Grandma Engebretson's Fattigmand (by Mrs. Fred Engebretson, Myrtle)
- 5 medium eggs
- 3 cups flour
- 6 tablespoons sugar
- 5 tablespoons cream
- Pinch of salt
- 1 tablespoon vanilla
- 2 tablespoons brandy

Beat eggs well (as you would for a sponge cake). Add sugar, beat again. Add cream and brandy, add vanilla and salt. Add flour a little at a time. Roll very thin, use floured pastry cloth for best results. Cut in diamond shapes and cut slits near one point and draw point through. Fry in deep fat using half lard and half Crisco. While frying, keep poking fattigmand with 2 forks, 1 in each hand. Let drain on brown paper. Sprinkle with sugar.

Lefse (by Mrs. Fred Dahl, Klara) (pronounced "lef-sah")
- 2 cups flour
- 2 cups mashed potatoes
- ½ cup teaspoon salt
- 4 tablespoons butter, melted

Mix together to form dough and roll out on a floured board to circles, very thin. Bake on top of a hot stove or put in a heavy skillet, griddle or lefse pan. When bubbles begin to form and brown lightly, turn and bake on the other side. Serve with butter and cinnamon sugar.

ABOUT CHRISTOPHER LENTZ

Christopher Lentz is a matchmaker, midwife and murderer…when he's writing historical and contemporary love stories. His books are about hope, second chances, and outcasts overcoming obstacles. At their core, Christopher's stories are about how love changes everything.

His latest release, *My Friend Marilyn*, is a tale about the unexpected results of Marilyn Monroe transforming a reluctant, curvy Cinderella. It's the first novel in his new Great American Destination Series that offers books about hope, history, romance and self-discovery set at locations readers can visit.

Christopher made his mark as a corporate-marketing executive before penning the Blossom Trilogy, a series that embraces three vibrant generations of Americans who call California home in the early 20th century. *Blossom*, the epic's first installment, cracked Amazon's Top Ten "Hot New Releases" list.

He didn't always love words (in fact, he still has scars from those stand-up-in-front-of-class spelling bees that he was a failure at), but he did learn to master words out of necessity. Christopher was convinced there was a novel hiding somewhere inside him.

With the help of some imaginary friends, he found it.

His first literary crush was Scarlett O'Hara. Then came Dorothy Gale, Jo March, Lizzie Bennet and Blanche DuBois. And truth be told, an infatuation with Mary Poppins transpired. Yes, Mary Poppins.

Christopher loves—and devours—anything related to Disney like a ravenous kid inhales a bowl of Cap'n Crunch. It was a dream come true when he spent his college years immersed in Disneyland's turn-of-the-century Main Street USA selling everything from sticky lollipops to iconic Mickey Mouse ear hats. That experience resulted in a fascination with all things Victorian/Edwardian, not to mention a hoarder-status collection of antiques.

A teenage transplant from Detroit, he married his high-school sweetheart and raised three remarkable daughters and two adorable Yorkshire terriers.

As an active member of Romance Writers of America, he looks forward to writing a bookshelf full of novels about misfits who find ways to fit in.

He's certain he'll never run out of dreams or stories, though he'll undoubtedly run out of time.

To learn more, please visit www.christopherlentz.org or www.blossomtrilogy.com.

Thank you for reading this book. Please take a moment to leave a rating and review at your favorite retailer.

Made in the USA
Coppell, TX
11 September 2022

82917327R00225